Angel of the Lost Treasure

Marie Laval

Choc Lit

Where heroes are like chocolate – irresistible!

Published 2021 by Choc Lit Limited
First published as *Angel Heart* by Accent Press in 2015.
Edited and revised in 2021 by Choc Lit.
Penrose House, Crawley Drive, Camberley, Surrey GU15 2AB, UK
www.choc-lit.com

EPUB ISBN: 978-1-78189-476-7
PRINT ISBN: 978-1-78189-400-2

Acknowledgements

I dedicate *Angel of The Lost Treasure* to my family, and particularly my three children Thomas, Nicolas and Clémence. They are truly 'Mes Soleils', which in English means 'My Sunshines'. Over the years they have been so patient with me and don't find it odd when I suddenly come up with random ideas or bits of dialogue at the dining table and rush to write something down. They are truly wonderful and I would like to thank them for their support and encouragements during the writing and the editing of *Angel of The Lost Treasure*. I love you very, very much.

Thank you too to my sisters Myette and Sabine who are always available for a WhatsApp chat or – and it's more likely – a good moan! Thank you too to my darling mother who left us far too early and who from a young age gave me a love of reading and writing. I am sure you are watching from wherever you are, and you will always be one of the brightest sunshines in my heart.

I would also like to thank the Choc Lit team for their support, and to my brilliant editor for her excellent advice and suggestions to make the story stronger – and shorter! The designers have come up with yet another beautiful cover.

Of course, thanks as always to the Choc Lit Tasting Panel. I am so happy that you enjoyed the story even though it was very different from what I have written for Choc Lit up until now: Gill Leivers, Honor Gilbert, Isabelle D, Melanie Russell, Sharon Walsh, Alma Hough, Jenny Mitchell, Hilary Brown, Fran Stevens, Shona Nicolson and Jo Osborne.

Merci beaucoup!

Chapter One

The cutter was sailing too close to the cliffs, heading straight for the Devil's Tooth.

Marie-Ange's cloak billowed in the blustery wind, the hood blew back and her hair swirled like a golden veil around her. From the cliff top, she watched the small French ship dancing wildly on the waves, its tricolour and white ensign flapping at the top of the mast. If it carried on its course, the ship would be ripped open by the reef. A man stood alone at the prow, oblivious to the danger ahead. He was too far away and the roaring of the waves crashing onto the cliffs was so loud that shouting a warning to him would be useless. She unfastened her cloak, pulled her black shawl from her shoulders, and waved it above her head in the direction of the Devil's Tooth.

A ray of sunshine tearing through the clouds bathed her black-clad silhouette in a bright golden light. For a few seconds the sun was in her eyes, blinding her, before the wind pushed the dark clouds across the sky and the sun disappeared once more. When she looked towards the bay again, the ship was steering east, back to the high sea. She heaved a sigh of relief. The crew must have seen her signals and spotted the reef in time. They were safe.

She resumed her walk on the cliff path to St Nectan's Chapel, a small granite building sailors' wives visited to pray for the safe return of their men. Or rather, they came to the ancient wishing well at the back of the chapel. Today, like so many times before, Marie-Ange wanted to pray for Christopher.

'Six years already, my love,' she whispered, blinking away the tears.

Six years since her husband had been lost at sea when his ship was sunk by French artillery off Coruña. She searched in her pocket for the piece of wedding ribbon she had cut earlier that morning.

'Please, come back to me.' She repeated the words like an incantation and kissed the white satin bow before leaning forward to throw it into the ancient well. It whirled as it flew down, becoming smaller as it was swallowed by the shadows.

Her dream last night still felt so real. Christopher held her in his arms while she touched his face and gazed into his grey eyes … then he melted into the mist, leaving her cold and alone.

Damn this ship. Damn this weather. And damn Malleval. Hugo Saintclair clapped his hands together a few times and blew on them to keep them warm. Around him, the crew shouted orders and heaved on ropes in order to switch sails and change course before they hit the rocks. The Angel warned them, the sailors said, Heaven was on their side. Shaking his head with impatience, he listened to their nonsensical chatter. Angels didn't exist, but the woman who waved at them from the cliff top had saved them from a certain death. The black, fierce-looking rock in the middle of the bay would no doubt have torn the ship open.

It was sobering to think that having survived so many bloody battles in Europe he might have drowned in the grey, stormy waters of the English Channel while carrying out an assignment which had nothing to do with the army, and everything to do with his own foolishness.

He pulled a flask from his coat pocket and drank a swallow of rum to fight the queasy feeling in the pit of his stomach. A grimace twisted his lips as the cheap liquor burned his throat. The sooner they reached the shore, the better. He was a cuirassier officer, damn it, not a sailor. He tightened his lips, squared his jaw. Some cuirassier officer he was! Not only was he stuck on a ship in the middle of a storm, but he was about to play bodyguard to a rich noblewoman who would no doubt turn out to be every bit as spoilt, haughty, and demanding as the other aristocrats he'd had the misfortune to encounter so far.

Gripping the side of the boat, he took a gulp of air. He had nobody to blame but himself. He should have held his liquor better and stopped gambling before it was too late.

It was raining when Marie-Ange finally set off on the path inland. Soon the outline of Norton Place appeared in the distance – the grey, forbidding manor house crouched in a clump of trees. She walked through the gate and sighed as she stepped over several broken slate roof tiles dislodged by the storm. There would be more holes in the roof, as if the old manor house wasn't plagued by enough leaks and draughts already …

She entered the hall, gave her wet cloak to Rosie. Shivering and eager to stand near the fire, she opened the door to the austere oak panelled drawing room. Her fingers were raw and stiff after her long walk and she rubbed them hard over the flames.

'There you are! Any sign of our French guest?'

She turned at the sound of her brother-in-law's voice and smiled. With his tall stature, unruly ash-blond hair and grey eyes, Robert was more like Christopher with every passing day. She shook her head.

'Not yet. Monsieur Malleval wrote that Capitaine Saintclair would be with us mid-January. I wonder if …'

She recalled the cutter that sailed dangerously close to the reef earlier in the day. It flew a French flag – two French flags, in fact – the revolutionary tricolour and the white flag of the newly restored Bourbon monarchy. Maybe Capitaine Saintclair was on board.

'You don't have to travel to France alone with him, you know.' Robert looked at her hopefully. 'I'd be more than willing to come with you. Indeed, I believe that, as the man of the family, I should come with you.'

Marie-Ange smiled. She had trouble considering Robert anything other than a younger brother. Yet, at eighteen, he was almost a man, and she would do well to remember it.

'No, Robert. We talked about it before. Monsieur Malleval is unable to come for me because of his old battle wound but he wrote in his letter that Capitaine Saintclair would be a most reliable escort.'

'Still, we don't know anything about him,' Robert protested.

'We know he is a distinguished officer from the Second Cuirassier Regiment,' Marie-Ange said, patting Robert's forearm. 'And as much as I would like you to come with me, you must stay here and look after the estate. I won't need more than a few weeks to settle my inheritance at Beauregard.'

Robert looked at his boots and frowned. 'But …'

'You know what this bequest means for Norton Place and for you. I will be able to get the roof fixed at last and you will join the Naval Academy.'

Robert pulled a face. His dream was to follow in his brother's footsteps and buy a commission in the Royal Navy but there had been no money for him to do so. Until now.

Two cocker spaniel puppies burst into the drawing room and jumped at her skirt.

'Rusty! Splinter! Calm down!' She laughed and knelt down to stroke the dogs' shiny coats. 'Besides, who would look after my two darlings here?'

Robert still looked disgruntled.

'Cheer up.' She grinned. 'I heard there was jelly for pudding tonight.'

This time there was something akin to anger in his eyes.

'I wish you would stop treating me like a child,' he growled before storming out.

Her breath caught in her throat. What was wrong with him? Robert was the only family she had left. They had never argued before today.

'Come on, boys, let's go out,' she called to the puppies, hoping that taking them out would cheer her up.

She headed towards the cliffs once again. Her boots were soon covered with mud, the hem of her dress drenched, but she didn't notice the rain, the puddles, or the coarse tufts of grass. This time she followed the steep path down onto the pebbly beach, where the sea spray on her face and the roar of waves crashing onto the reef made her heart beat faster. She licked the salt from her lips and took a deep breath. How she would miss these walks along the coast during her time in France … still, it would be worth it. Even though he didn't quote an exact figure in his letter, Uxeloup Malleval had promised a substantial legacy from her mother's family estate in the Beaujolais.

The sky was darkening by the time she made her way back. Her heart skipped a beat when she came in view of Norton Place and she quickened her pace. A carriage was stationed by the front steps. They had a visitor. Perhaps it was Saintclair?

She let herself in, slipped the cloak off her shoulders, and checked her reflection in the hall mirror. Lord, she looked wild. The wind had made her pale blue eyes sparkle and given her complexion a deep rosy blush. She combed her curly blonde hair with her fingers, twisting it into a rough plait. It was far from perfect but it would have to do. She couldn't keep her visitor waiting any longer.

She pushed open the door to the drawing room and hurried inside. Splinter and Rusty ran under her feet, tripping her. Her cry of alarm died on her lips as two strong arms caught her. Surprised, she tilted her head up to look at the tall, dark-haired man holding her against him. His intense blue eyes held her gaze and sent a shiver down her spine. One side of his weather-beaten face was marred by a long, ragged scar. The thin line of the mouth and the tightness in his jaw gave an impression of controlled anger. For a moment fear gathered in her chest. Then he smiled, a slow, confident smile, and he was transformed into the most handsome man she had ever laid eyes on.

The dogs barked at them furiously. Marie-Ange parted her lips to order them to stop but before she could speak Robert took a few steps forward, an angry scowl twisting his face, his fists clenched by his sides.

'Let her go at once, sir,' he warned, 'or …'

'Or what?' The man arched his eyebrows, a mocking smile at the corner of his mouth, as if he dared Robert to come any closer. He shook his head and released her.

'I will ask you to restrain your puppies, Madame. The three of them,' he said as he looked down at her.

'How dare you call me a puppy?' Robert's face flushed a deep red, and he took another step forward.

Marie-Ange found her voice at last.

'Rusty. Splinter. Lie down at once.' She pointed to the rug in front of the fireplace. The dogs whimpered but obeyed. 'Robert.

That's enough. Monsieur was just helping me.'

Robert muttered an apology and crouched beside the dogs to stroke their wet, muddy coats.

'You must be Capitaine Saintclair,' she said, tilting her chin up to look at him again.

The papers had been full of sketches and reports about the famous French cuirassiers and she had no difficulty imagining Saintclair in a dark blue uniform, his chest covered with shiny metal plates and his helmet topped by a black horse mane, charging onto the battlefield. His current attire of black breeches and tall leather riding boots topped by a short brown coat did nothing to dispel the heroic image conjured in her mind.

He clicked his heels together and bowed his head.

'At your service, Madame.'

'Please take a seat.' She pointed to an armchair near the fireplace and sat opposite him.

'I have a letter from Malleval for you.' He pulled a thick envelope out of the leather bag that was strapped to his belt, leant closer and handed it over.

She glanced at the red wax seal bearing the letters *A M* in the centre. She was eager to read Malleval's letter, but not wanting to appear ill-mannered, she dropped the papers in her lap.

'Did you have a pleasant journey, Capitaine?'

'Not really.' He pulled a face. 'The captain is unfamiliar with the waters in these parts. He didn't know about the currents and the reefs and our ship almost tore open on some rocks at the entrance of the bay. It was only by a stroke of luck we avoided disaster. A woman warned us from the cliff.' His lips stretched in a condescending smile. 'The crew said she was an angel descended on a ray of sunshine.'

Marie-Ange cleared her throat, embarrassed. 'It was no angel, I'm afraid, only me. The cutter was heading straight for the Devil's Tooth and I …'

Capitaine Saintclair narrowed his eyes to look at her. Her heartbeat quickened under his scrutiny and an awkward blush heated her face.

A smile stretched his lips. 'Well, thank you, Madame. I owe you my life.'

She nodded but made no answer.

'When can you be ready to leave for France? The cutter is moored in Wellcombe Harbour for now, but I want to sail back as soon as possible.'

Robert raised his head. Marie-Ange was aware of him staring at her with pleading eyes and her heart twisted a bit at the pain her leaving would cause him.

'I have been expecting you for some weeks,' she said. 'My things are ready. We can leave tomorrow if you like.'

'Not tomorrow! Not so soon!' Robert jumped to his feet, stormed out of the drawing room, and slammed the door behind him.

'A hot-blooded young male,' Capitaine Saintclair remarked, arching his eyebrows.

Embarrassed by Robert's outburst, Marie-Ange looked down. The sight of her dirty boots met her appalled gaze. Whatever must the captain think of her? She shuffled her feet under her dark grey skirt, itself damp and splattered with mud, and sat upright. At least Saintclair wouldn't find fault with her demeanour and clothing. She still wore half-mourning clothes – her dresses mostly dark greys, browns and greens, with high collars and long sleeves.

'I apologise for Robert,' she said stiffly. 'He is very protective of me. He is also young and has lacked the presence of a man here. His brother – my husband – was a Royal Navy Commander and was reported missing after the battle of Coruña.' She could never say Christopher was dead. She never truly believed it was so.

'I am sorry.' Saintclair sounded sincere.

She let out a sigh and stared into the fire, her fingers playing with her wedding band. A tingling sensation on her skin soon made her glance up. The capitaine was looking at her, his blue eyes serious and intense once again. Heat spread over her cheeks and throat.

'Please come with me,' she said, standing up. 'It is time you were shown to your room.'

She rang the service bell and led him into the hallway where an elderly servant soon joined them.

'Make a fire in the green room, Francis, and have some hot water and tea brought up straight away for our guest,' she told him. The green room was Norton Place's best bedroom – at least, it was the one with the least damp patches on the ceilings, mould stains on the wallpaper and draughty windows.

As soon as the French officer disappeared up the stairs, Marie-Ange went back into the drawing room to read Uxeloup Malleval's letter.

After enquiring about her health, Malleval explained that the documents concerning her inheritance were ready at Beauregard. He was researching the history of the chateau and asked her to bring along any old family papers she might have, especially regarding her mother's godfather, Count Saint-Germain. Having heard of her mother's talent as a painter, he also wished to see her sketchbook.

Marie-Ange sighed. She didn't have any family papers. In fact, she knew next to nothing about her mother's childhood at Beauregard and the traumatic events she escaped from in 1791. She died when Marie-Ange was five years old, and her father only told her the bare minimum about the French side of her family. 'What is past is past,' William Jones would always say when she asked him about the Beauregards. Since his death, there was nobody who could answer her questions. Would Uxeloup Malleval know anything about her family? The man himself was a bit of a mystery, and so was this bequest he promised her. Maybe Capitaine Saintclair would be able to tell her more.

She went up to her room to finish packing. Opening the drawer of her writing desk, she pulled out a hard leather pouch. Inside was a dagger with a finely carved bone handle Christopher brought back from his first voyage to the West Indies as a good luck charm. He had forgotten to take it on his last mission to Spain … from which he never returned. Thoughtful, she pressed it against her heart for a moment before slipping it into her bag.

Her mother's sketchbook was, as always, on her bedside table. Over the years, she had flipped so often through the pages covered with sketches and watercolours of Beauregard it seemed she already knew the place. It had all the charm of an enchanted castle with its round towers and walled rose garden, its circular dovecote and the park surrounded by a dark forest. She traced with a finger the gold crest embossed on the book's cover – a unicorn surmounted by two *Fleurs de Lys*, Count Saint-Germain's coat of arms.

'An extraordinary man,' her father once said with unusual enthusiasm. 'He was a philosopher, a scientist, and an outstanding statesman. Your mother was very fond of him.'

She slipped the sketchbook into her bag too.

The mantel clock struck seven. She changed quickly into a dove-grey gown and went to the drawing room. Capitaine Saintclair sat in front of the fireplace, holding a glass of whisky in one hand and stroking Splinter with the other. He rose when she came in, but she gestured for him to sit down.

She enquired after his needs and he assured her he was happy with his room. She cleared her throat and hesitated, suddenly shy.

'I hope you will forgive my curiosity, Capitaine,' she started, 'but Monsieur Malleval's letter inviting me to Beauregard to collect a bequest from his father came as a great surprise. May I ask you how long you have been acquainted with him?'

He nodded. 'About fifteen years. We met at the regimental barracks back in 1800 when we were both very young men. I joined the Cuirassiers and Malleval, the Hussars. Since then our regiments have fought all over Europe together.' He drank a sip of whisky.

'So he was a Hussar ...' She knew of the Hussars' reputation, both on, and off the battlefield. 'I hope he is not too seriously injured.'

Saintclair looked up, puzzled. 'Injured?'

'In his letter, he mentioned a battle wound which troubles him greatly. That's why he could not come here himself.'

'Ah. Yes. His battle wound ... well, it depends on ... the weather.'

The French officer's answer lacked conviction. Maybe Malleval was more seriously hurt than he let on.

‘In any case,’ she resumed, ‘it is very chivalrous of you to volunteer to escort me to Beauregard, and I much appreciate it.’

‘It is my pleasure, Madame,’ he answered. ‘I was at a loose end anyway since our new king put most officers on leave. I believe you and Malleval are related, is that right?’

She nodded. ‘In a way. My grandmother, Aline, married his father in 1791 after my grandfather, Philippe, was executed. She was Edmond Malleval’s second wife.’

‘He probably had your grandfather killed to make way for him.’

She gasped. ‘Why did you say that?’

Captaine Saintclair shrugged. ‘As a public prosecutor in Beaujeu, then as a representative of the Public Safety Committee in Lyon during the Revolution, the man sent hundreds of people to their death – not just aristocrats but commoners, too. Anyone he suspected of plotting against the Republic.’ He paused. ‘Or, some have said, of being in the way of his ambition.’

Marie-Ange’s nervous fingers played with her wedding band again.

‘I had no idea he was one of the revolutionaries who terrorised France and turned the country into a giant charnel house. Thank goodness those awful times are over and France is at peace. Now Napoleon has been exiled and the king is back, everything will be all right, won’t it?’

His jaw tightened and his eyes flashed with anger.

‘Spoken like a true royalist, Madame. You will get on well with the captain of our ship. He’s a staunch Bourbon supporter. I think I should warn you however that there isn’t much sympathy among ordinary French people for *émigrés* now flocking back to claim their estates and their fortunes. Neither is there much love for the British nation as a whole. Napoleon is still very much alive in French hearts.’

She raised her chin, stung by his tone.

‘I don’t care what people think. I am a Beauregard and I have every right to visit the chateau of my ancestors.’ She stood up. ‘It’s getting late. Shall we make our way to the dining room?’

Like the rest of the manor house, the dining room was austere, with a damp, frigid feel even with a roaring fire in the fireplace. Robert was there already, a glass of red wine in his hand, which, judging by his flushed cheeks, wasn't his first. She gave him a stern look which he answered with a shrug, and took her place at the head of the table with Robert sitting to her left and Capitaine Saintclair to her right.

Francis served a plain but hearty chicken and vegetable stew. Ignoring her disapproving frowns, Robert poured himself yet more wine. She let out a sigh and turned to Saintclair.

'Are you from the Beaujolais region, Capitaine?'

'No, I'm from Lyon,' he answered curtly.

'That's a very large town, isn't it? Where is your estate?' Robert enquired.

'I don't have one,' Saintclair answered. 'My family isn't from the landed gentry, or any kind of gentry for that matter. My father owns a small silk workshop. He has worked all his life. He still does.' He finished his plate and took hold of his glass.

'Then how did you get to be a senior officer? I thought those positions were reserved for noblemen,' Robert insisted.

The captain's eyes glinted with heat, yet his voice was calm when he spoke.

'Napoleon allowed all men, irrespective of their social standing, access to the highest levels of command. The only things that mattered were ability and bravery. Isn't that the way it should always be?'

Robert shrugged. 'I suppose so,' he muttered before drinking another gulp of wine.

'Unfortunately, our new king is reverting back to the old ways and promoting men according to lineage rather than merit,' Saintclair carried on in sombre tones.

'You must tell us all about the battles you fought,' Robert urged, and he went on to question the French officer about his military career, exclaiming in wonder when Saintclair said he had fought at Jena, Wagram and Austerlitz, to name but a few.

'Did you ever meet Napoleon?'

'The Emperor reviewed our regiment regularly. I often saw him during campaigns but I never personally talked to him.' Saintclair's eyes clouded over and Marie-Ange wondered if the emperor was still very much alive in *his* heart.

Francis brought in a final dish of rhubarb jelly and Robert reached out for the bowl. His face was flushed, his blond hair tousled.

'Look at you, always the first one for pudding.' Marie-Ange laughed as she proceeded to comb his curls away from his forehead with her fingers, the way she had done since he was a young boy.

Saintclair leant back against his seat and looked at her, his eyebrows arched. Suddenly flustered by the intensity of his gaze, she withdrew her hand, pushed her chair back, and stood up.

'I hope you do not mind if I bid you goodnight, Capitaine, I still have a few things to attend to before our journey.' Then turning to Robert, she said, 'Don't be too long.'

Robert shook his head. 'Don't worry. I'll come up to your room shortly.'

A crashing noise startled them both. Marie-Ange whirled about to see Saintclair had dropped his glass of wine, which shattered on the floor.

'Sorry,' he mumbled. Bending down, he started picking up the pieces of glass.

'Leave it, Capitaine. Francis will tidy up.'

Once in her room, she undressed and wrapped herself in Christopher's large, faded blue dressing gown. Although it no longer bore his scent, she still wore it most nights to imagine his arms around her. While waiting for Robert, she set the draught board and pieces on her desk for their nightly game as well as sheets of paper and an inkwell for the French lesson she insisted on giving him while they played.

'I don't know why you still waste your time trying to teach me French,' he said when he joined her shortly after. 'You know how hopeless I am.'

‘You will find it very useful in the Royal Navy,’ she answered with a smile. ‘Not to mention at balls and parties when you want to impress young ladies.’

But he was indeed so hopeless their lessons usually ended up in fits of giggles, and tonight was no exception.

‘I shall miss our evenings,’ he said as he lingered in the corridor, long after midnight.

‘I will soon be back. Hush now, we don’t want to wake Capitaine Saintclair.’

She gave him a kiss on the forehead and watched him climb the stairs to his room on the second floor. A noise at the far end of the corridor startled her. She froze and peered into the darkness, holding her breath, her heart beating uncomfortably hard. Was Capitaine Saintclair awake?

She shook her head. She was being fanciful. It was only the old manor house creaking and groaning in the blustering gale. She should be used to it by now.

Chapter Two

She didn't enjoy the Channel crossing. The rough seas forced her to stay in her tiny cabin, suffering from violent bouts of seasickness. Fortunately, after reaching Le Havre, the cutter sailed down the calmer waters of the River Seine. Despite the cold, she was able to stand on deck much of the time, watching the flat, wintry landscape unfold. For their last evening on the river, they moored at Asnière.

'We'll be in Paris tomorrow morning. Let's hope the river doesn't freeze,' Saintclair said as they walked on deck after the evening meal they shared with the taciturn captain of the ship. He lifted the collar of his coat. 'You'd better go in.'

'Not just yet. I don't like being cooped up in my cabin.' She sighed at the prospect of yet another uncomfortable night. 'Do you know why the captain is so unpleasant?' The man barely acknowledged their presence on board and answered Marie-Ange's questions with a grunt.

Saintclair shrugged. 'It's my fault. I demanded he fly the tricolour as well as the white flag. He doesn't like it. I told you before, he's a monarchist.'

'I see …' So she had been right about Saintclair's loyalties. He didn't support King Louis' new regime.

One of the sailors approached them and asked Saintclair if he fancied a game of cards.

His face lit up. 'Definitely!' I hope you have some of your fine rum left.' He might not get on with the captain, but the man seemed to have no problems with the rest of the crew. They played cards, smoked and drank liquor until late every night.

Marie-Ange was left with no other choice than to retire to her cabin. She lay down in the narrow bunk for a while, tossing and turning. With a sigh of impatience, she sat up and propped a pillow behind her back. The men were laughing and talking in Saintclair's cabin on the other side of the thin partition. She thought she heard her name. They were talking about her! Curious and holding her breath, she got up and placed her ear against the wooden panel.

She heard Saintclair ask for a tumbler of rum, and the game began with the clinking sounds of coins being thrown on a table and the cards being dealt out.

'Is *mademoiselle* your fiancée?' someone asked.

Saintclair let out a good-hearted laugh. 'Fiancée? Hell no! I'm escorting her to the Beaujolais where a fellow officer has some business to conclude with her. I don't believe in love, marriage, and all that nonsense. What's the point of getting chained up to one woman when you can enjoy them all?'

The men laughed and made a few coarse comments about feminine charms. Marie-Ange gasped.

'Anyway, you wouldn't stand a chance with her,' one man said. 'She looks like a true lady.'

'And she's a widow,' another exclaimed.

'So what?' Saintclair laughed again. 'Whether they're tavern girls or ladies, they're all the same. They might put on a good show but there isn't one who can stay true to one man. Women are just like kittens, my friends. A few caresses and they purr in your arms, they just can't help it, especially where I'm concerned. So let's enjoy them while we can.' His words were drowned in laughter.

Marie-Ange put her hands to her burning cheeks. So that was what the capitaine thought of women, and of her – false, easy to seduce, and unable to be faithful. Well, what did he know. She would remain true to Christopher for the rest of her life. As for Saintclair, the man was boorish and arrogant, and she pitied the women who found him attractive. She *certainly* didn't. She stomped back to her bunk, punched the pillow a few times to soften it and lay down. Closing her eyes, she tried to ignore the rowdy laughter coming from the cabin next door and conjured up Christopher's image before drifting into a fitful sleep.

The cutter left Asnière at daybreak. Marie-Ange went up on the bridge as the anchor was raised and the sails hoisted. She smiled with satisfaction when she saw Saintclair, pale and unshaven with dark shadows under his eyes, standing alone at the rail. He held a tin cup of steaming coffee and occasionally rubbed his temple with his fingers. Too much rum and not enough sleep, probably. Dismissing him, she turned her gaze to the French countryside slipping past as they made their way towards Paris.

The ship arrived in the capital mid-morning, sailing past tall, elegant buildings, townhouses, and churches. The quays were alive with the hustle and bustle of mariners, fishermen, and traders. As if he couldn't wait to be on solid ground, Saintclair jumped onto the quay as soon as the cutter moored near the Pont Neuf.

While she waited, he took care of the customs formalities, arranged for their luggage to be loaded into a cart, and hailed a calash to take them to the inn where he had booked two rooms.

'When we're settled at the Le Faisan Doré, I will hire a carriage and a driver for our journey to Beauregard,' he informed her. 'Then I'll show you around the city, if you like.'

'Oh yes, please,' Marie-Ange exclaimed, almost forgetting she was annoyed at him.

There was so much to see. The cobbled-streets heaved with carriages, soldiers, peddlers, carts, and horses. On the pavements, stalls sold everything from flowers to live poultry, fish and wheels of yellow cheese.

Le Faisan Doré was a small, respectable establishment in the Rue Notre-Dame des Champs, close to the Luxembourg Gardens. Saintclair checked them in, promised to return very shortly and left.

There was still no sign of him when night fell. By then Marie-Ange was bored and very cross. He had promised to take her out, and she had waited all afternoon. Where was he?

After a supper of beef stew and apple tart, she went to the landlady, a plump, dark-haired matron.

'Has Capitaine Saintclair not returned yet?'

The woman gave her a knowing grin. 'I wouldn't expect him back anytime soon, dear. He must be at his club or at a lady's house. These cavalry officers can never stay away from women, cards, and drink.'

Marie-Ange pursed her lips in distaste. The landlady was probably right.

'When he comes back, please tell him that I wish to speak with him at once.'

The rest of the evening passed with excruciating slowness. How infuriating to be in Paris and confined to a room. When the mantelpiece clock struck eleven, she decided that Saintclair wasn't coming back so she stripped down to her chemise and removed her stockings before wrapping herself in Christopher's blue dressing gown. She shook her hair loose on her shoulders and was about to snuggle into bed when there was a sharp knock on the door.

Who did the woman think he was to summon him to her room like that? A lackey, probably. His lips twisted in an angry snarl as he climbed the stairs two by two. Madame Norton might live in a ramshackle manor house on the bleak, windswept Devonshire moorland, but she was still a Beauregard on her mother's side and a member of the English gentry by marriage. He should have followed Martin's advice and stayed at the club a while longer.

He walked down the draughty corridor and drummed impatient fingers on her door.

'Who's there?' A timid voice answered.

'Saintclair. Did you want to talk to me?' His tone was short.

The door opened just enough for Madame Norton to peer through.

He exhaled sharply to control his rising temper. 'Are you going to let me in or shall we talk in the corridor?'

She opened the door wider and he strode in.

'Is there a problem?' He looked down at her. Barefoot and swamped in an old dressing gown, the woman hardly reached his shoulder. He wondered what she wore underneath, if anything. His pulse quickened and a sudden rush of heat coursed through his veins as she stepped back and folded her arms on her chest.

'You said you would be back early. I have been waiting here all day for you,' she said, her voice cold and haughty.

Her icy tone did nothing to cool his desire, in fact it had just the opposite effect. He took a deep breath and walked to the fireplace to put some distance between them.

'Sorry. I got … distracted.' He shrugged. 'I did arrange a carriage and a driver for us. We're leaving for Lyon on Saturday.'

She looked at him again in the way a queen might look at a mangy dog.

'Why wait until Saturday? Your instructions are to take me straight to Beauregard.'

If she meant to intimidate him, she had failed. She was starting to amuse him greatly – in more ways than one.

'I have things to do. Anyway, what's the rush? I thought you might like to come to town with me tomorrow and see a play in the evening.'

Her eyes flashed with anger.

'I do not go to the theatre, Capitaine. I am in mourning.'

He arched his eyebrows. 'After six years?'

'My husband was a wonderful man. I will mourn him all my life.' Her eyes filled with tears, she bit her lip.

He didn't answer. There was one thing to be said for her. She was convincing – a first-class actress. He had almost been taken in by her wistful sighs and tearful eyes, by her drab mourning dresses and the almost virginal blushing on her cheeks every time he looked her way. He had almost believed her grief-stricken widow act … until he saw young Norton leave her room in the middle of the night with a wide grin on his face. He knew better than to be fooled by a woman, especially a pretty one.

Still, the way her voice quivered with emotion, her pale blue eyes shone with tears, and her lips trembled did have a strange effect on him. His throat went dry and he swallowed hard, so strong was the urge to crush her mouth under his, rake his fingers in her soft blonde curls, and pull her close. As if she could sense the heat of his desire, a very becoming pink blush covered her cheeks and throat.

Why did he stare at her in this way? His eyes had gone dark. The red glow from the fire cast a sinister, almost evil light across his face. He walked towards her, looking like a wolf about to pounce on its prey. Uneasy, and very conscious of her state of déshabillé, Marie-Ange stepped backward until her back touched the dressing table.

'I bid you goodnight, Capitaine,' she said, striving to keep her voice calm despite the thumping of her heart.

He seemed to snap back to reality and took a deep breath. 'Of course … I have a few errands to run tomorrow morning,' he said, walking to the door and opening it. 'Be ready for ten o'clock if you want to come with me.'

Once alone, she breathed a sigh of relief. For a moment, something in his expression had made her very uncomfortable. He had come so close; the stubble on his cheeks, the outline of his mouth, and the rugged line of the scar had been clearly evident. Shivers rippled on her skin and she wrapped herself more tightly in Christopher's dressing gown. She would have to be very careful where the capitaine was concerned. Despite what Uxeloup Malleval had written, she wasn't sure she could trust him. But who was there to trust here? She was on her own, in a foreign land. France might have been her mother's country, but it wasn't hers.

She pushed the empty plate away and glanced at the clock with dismay. It was only eight o'clock. What would she do for the next two hours? Outside the window, the little bit she could see of Paris was shrouded in a grey, overcast sky. Surely there could be no harm in venturing outside for a short while? Maybe she could take a stroll in the Luxembourg Gardens and return in good time to meet Saintclair. He would never know she had gone out.

Marie-Ange rushed back to her room to collect her cloak, grey bonnet, and gloves. Returning to the lobby wrapped up against the cold, she stepped into the narrow, winding street. She closed her eyes, and took a long breath of fresh air. It was so good to be out at last. The city was busy already despite the early hour and the bitter cold. Shutters were being taken down from shop windows, people queued for bread and pies outside bakeries. In the street, elegant *cabriolets* sped past without a care for pedestrians, and tall, sturdy horses pulled carts laden with wood, casks of ale or fresh produce.

Unfortunately the Luxembourg gates were shut. Disappointed, she stood a while on the pavement, reading public notices about forthcoming fairs and auctions that were pinned on the boards outside the gardens. By the time she finished, the gardens were still closed and a flurry of snowflakes drifted from the low clouds. It soon changed into heavy snow. Maybe she should go back … she stepped onto the carriageway without looking.

'*Attention*,' the driver of a passing coach shouted as his horses almost knocked her over. She retreated onto the pavement and stared as the carriage stopped a few metres away. A tall, blond man in a grey coat jumped down. She narrowed her eyes.

The man's face was partly hidden by the high collar of his coat, but there was something disturbingly familiar about him. Was it his tall figure or the ash-blond hair? She remained frozen on the spot, her mouth dry, her heart beating wildly. The man pushed open a wooden door and disappeared inside a building as the carriage drove away.

A few seconds only must have passed, but time seemed to have stopped. That man … she had to catch up with him, see his face. Marie-Ange ran across the street and pushed the door, only to find herself in an empty courtyard. Pausing to catch her breath, she inspected her surroundings and heaved a sigh of disappointment. There was no trace of the man. The concierge lodge was to her right. She knocked on the door.

'*Qu'est-ce que c'est?*' A grey-haired woman asked as she came out.

Marie-Ange swallowed hard. 'Good morning, *Madame*,' she said in French. 'A tall, blond gentleman wearing a grey coat came in a few minutes ago. Only, he lost his wallet in the street.'

She waved her father's old wallet in front of the concierge, the one she had used ever since he died.

'Tall and blond you said?'

'Yes, he had very light blond hair.' She held her breath.

'That would be Monsieur Joseph Nallay. He comes to see Monsieur Fouché almost every day. On the third floor.' The woman gestured towards the staircase. 'Turn left on the landing.'

'Monsieur Nallay?' Marie-Ange repeated, disappointed by the concierge's response. Against all logic, she had hoped for another name. 'Whom did you say he comes to visit?'

The concierge narrowed her eyes in a suspicious manner. 'Monsieur Fouché, the former Minister of Police. Surely, you know of him?'

'Of course I know of Monsieur Fouché. Who doesn't?' Marie-Ange forced a smile and bade the woman goodbye.

She climbed the stairs. Fouché, described in turn as a master of intrigue, a turncoat, or a brilliant statesman, was one of France's most infamous politicians. How could she have forgotten his name? She was uncertain how to proceed; should she knock on the minister's door and invent a story to get in, or wait for the blond man to come down? She heard footsteps ahead and caught a glimpse of elegant black boots and a grey coat. It was him. He glanced at her, nodded, and carried on.

'*Monsieur, s'il vous plaît!*'

He stopped and turned.

Her pulse quickened as she stared into his face, into her beloved Christopher's face. She staggered against the stairwell banister. Her fingers gripped the handrail.

'Madame? Are you not well?' he asked in French as he leant towards her. She put her hand on his forearm.

'Christopher, my God, it's really you,' she answered in English, gazing into his eyes, her voice filled with wonder. 'I wasn't sure when I saw you in the street …' She let out a choked cry. 'They said you died at Coruña, but I never could believe it. What happened to you? Why didn't you come home?' The words tumbled out of her mouth. She wanted to smile but tears started falling down her cheeks instead.

'I found you at last.' She raised her hand to touch his face.

He frowned and pulled back. '*Désolé, Madame, vous faites erreur,*' he replied, staring at her, his eyes steely and cold, almost angry. '*Excusez-moi.*' He started down the stairs.

'No, Christopher, wait! Don't you remember me?' She ran after him. 'It's been six years, but surely you cannot have forgotten me … please, wait!' Her voice rose to a high pitch.

He turned around and gave her another hostile stare. 'I really don't know what or who you are talking about. I'm afraid you have the wrong man. Now leave me alone. You are making a scene.' This time he spoke in English, perfect English without the trace of an accent.

There was no warmth, no flicker of recognition in his eyes. When he started down the stairs, she didn't follow him but sat on the stone steps, too shaky to stand. How could she have been mistaken? Her chest was so tight it felt like her heart was breaking. She buried her face in her hands. Maybe it was time she accepted her husband was dead and stopped chasing ghosts.

And yet … it was his face, his eyes, his voice. Heavens, she dreamt about him often enough! He was thinner, his face harder, but six years had passed. When she touched his arm a jolt of recognition raced through her, as if her body remembered him. What if he had been injured at Coruña and lost his memory? Those things must happen during battles. She must see him one more time and make sure of his identity one way or another.

She wiped her eyes; it was time to return to the inn or she would be late to meet Saintclair. It was snowing harder when she stepped outside. She walked to the end of the street, and then stared at the crossroads. Where now? *Left, it was left*, she decided, starting down the street. Surely the Le Faisan Doré wasn't that far. She must have missed the turn. Had she passed that bakery, that cobblers' shop on her way to the Luxembourg Gardens?

She heaved a ragged sigh. She couldn't remember anything! Men and women brushed past her, grey shadows in the snow. The blond man's face – *Christopher's face* – danced in front of her. Her eyes filled with tears again, everything around her blurred. She walked faster, her boots slipped on the snow and she fell on the pavement.

'*Attention, ma p'tite dame!*' a passer-by said, holding his hand out to help her back to her feet. She thanked him and asked for directions. She had taken a wrong turn, he said. Shivering in her wet coat, she pulled her collar up against the cold, and retraced her steps.

Church bells chimed eleven when she finally pushed open the door of the Le Faisan Doré, limping in her wet boots.

'Where the hell have you been?' Capitaine Saintclair's thunderous voice greeted her.

'S-sorry,' she stammered.

His angry expression softened immediately. He took her elbow and led her to the drawing room. 'Here, sit close to the fire. You are chilled to the bone.'

He helped her out of her cloak, then called the landlady and ordered some mulled wine. Marie-Ange's hands were shaking as she brought the cup of hot, spicy wine to her lips.

'What happened?' he asked at last.

'I got lost.' She would not share anything of her encounter with the blond man. After all, she didn't know for sure he was Christopher.

Saintclair frowned. 'Don't disappear like that again. The streets of Paris are never safe for a woman on her own, whatever the time of day.' He paused a moment. 'I think you had better stay here and keep warm.'

'No, I wish to come with you. I just need to change my shoes.' She jumped to her feet. The thought of being confined to her room for the rest of the day was unbearable.

A carriage took them to the Faubourg Saint-Honoré. Saintclair offered her his arm to walk along the avenue and pointed out elegant shops and brasseries. She couldn't help but stare at passers-by, hoping against all reason she would see the tall, blond man again.

Street stalls sold roasted chestnuts and fried dough sprinkled with sugar. Marie-Ange breathed in their warm, sweet smell, and realised she was hungry. As if reading her thoughts, Saintclair turned to her.

'We will get something to eat soon.' He hesitated and cleared his throat, looking a little embarrassed. 'First, I promised my sister, Lucie, new handkerchiefs from the most fashionable establishment in Paris. Would you be kind enough to help me choose? I do not know the first thing about ladies' fashion.'

So the tough, cynical capitaine cared enough about his sister to venture into a haberdasher and buy handkerchiefs … she repressed a smile.

'It will be my pleasure. How old is she?'

'Seventeen.'

'Tell me about her.'

Saintclair pushed open the door of a large shop and let her go through first. As they walked around well-appointed shelves and displays of ribbons, shawls, fabric, buttons, and handkerchiefs, he explained that his sister was of delicate health, with dark hair and blue eyes.

Then he shook his head. 'She spends far too long sitting in the drawing room and reading silly stories.'

'Silly stories?' Marie-Ange raised her eyebrows.

'You know, stories about fair ladies and knights who play the harp with a flower between their teeth.'

She laughed. 'You mean love stories. You do not seem to rate romance very high, Capitaine. Yet it is essential for a successful marriage, as I well know.'

He looked down at her, suddenly serious. 'You talk like a middle-aged matron, yet you cannot have been married very long.'

'Only four months, but they were the most blissful months of my life,' she replied as a dreamy smile stretched her lips. She married Christopher a few weeks before her seventeenth birthday, on an unseasonably warm October day. Her wedding dress was silk. She had tied a long satin ribbon in her braids, which Christopher had loosened patiently that night, before laying her in their bed for the first time. She shivered and let out a sigh. Hope blossomed in her chest as she remembered today's encounter and her persistent belief that he was alive.

'Yes, a man must be sensitive to be a good husband,' she whispered, stopping in front of a pile of delicate linens embroidered with lace and tiny rosebuds. 'My husband used to write poems and pick wild flowers for me.'

'Isn't romance for little girls? I thought women wanted men with courage and strength, not milksops.' Saintclair arched his eyebrows.

She looked up at him, her cheeks suddenly very hot. 'A man can be sensitive without being a milksop, Capitaine. Ask anyone who knew my husband and they will tell you how brave, how heroic he was in battle.'

How dare the man make fun of Christopher in this way? Her husband had been worth ten of the capitaine, at least. She pointed to the embroidered handkerchiefs. 'I think Lucie will like those. I should know, since we share the same taste in romance – or "silly stories", as you put it,' she said.

He didn't answer but picked up the fancy linens and took them to the counter.

'Come,' he said when they walked out of the haberdasher. 'I will treat you to a hot chocolate and a cake at Café Benoit.'

Saintclair pushed the door to the café open and found a small table in a corner.

'Saintclair, you devil! Where did you disappear to last night?' A voice boomed from the other side of the crowded room.

Saintclair turned. His face relaxed into a smile. 'What are you doing here, Martin? You said you were going back to Lyon this morning.'

A giant of a man approached their table and bowed in front of Marie-Ange.

'Madame, let me introduce Capitaine Martin, a fellow officer from the Second Cuirassier Regiment.' Saintclair announced. 'Martin, this is Madame Norton. I am escorting her to Lyon to meet her relative, Malleval.'

Martin kissed Marie-Ange's hand, his eyes lingering on her. 'Now I understand why Saintclair was in such a hurry to leave last night. So, you are English?'

She freed her hand and smiled. 'Only partly. My father was English, my mother was French.'

'You know Malleval, do you not?' Saintclair asked his friend.

'Yes, I do,' Martin replied. 'He fleeced me at cards more than once. I always thought he was a prize cheat, but could never prove it. I heard he got you in trouble, too.'

Martin glanced at Saintclair quizzically, but the capitaine grunted rather than answered. A waiter came over and they ordered hot chocolate and cakes.

'Do you mind if I join you?' Martin sat down without waiting for an answer.

The waiter came back with a tray laden with cups, brioches, and pastries. As soon as he left, Martin leant over the table. 'Things are moving, my friend. Everybody's talking about it this morning. Fouché is sending his spies down south. So, of course, is his old enemy, Talleyrand. Lyon will soon be crawling with agents, all waiting for the same thing.'

He lowered his voice. 'According to my contact at the Ministry of War, many in government are preparing to jump ship. It's a wonder the army has not rebelled yet. The king angered everybody by putting officers on half-pay and denying commoners any chance of promotion.'

'I am well aware of the king's actions in that regard,' Saintclair growled.

Martin nodded in sympathy. 'I still cannot believe you were passed over for promotion in favour of that weasel, Comte de Mitre. Anyway, *he* will not be facing much resistance in the army. Like I said, everyone is talking about it. *He* is coming back.'

'Of course, *he* is coming back!' Saintclair put his cup down. Some chocolate spilled onto the saucer. He took a deep breath. 'They gave *him* a small island and a toy garrison to play with, cut *him* off from his wife and son. And now they're talking about sending *him* to an island in the Atlantic, hundreds of miles from anywhere! *He* has nothing to lose.'

Marie-Ange listened with interest. Whoever were they talking about? She bit into a brioche and drank her hot chocolate while the conversation continued as if she were not present. Suddenly her eyes widened in shock and she sat back on her chair. She knew who Capitaine Saintclair and his friend were referring to. Napoleon, of course! Since his abdication in April of the previous year, he had been in exile on Elba, a tiny island off the coast of Tuscany.

'I thought Fouché was no longer the Minister for Police,' she interrupted.

Saintclair and his friend turned to her, surprised, as if they'd both forgotten her presence.

'Joseph Fouché will never give up scheming,' Saintclair said. 'I believe his apartment on Rue de Condé is a hotbed of intrigue. He controls a vast network of spies. Murderers. Traitors. Deserters. You name it.'

She straightened in her chair, stung by his remark. If the man she saw that morning was indeed Christopher, he might be an agent. The concierge said he was a frequent visitor. However, he was bound to have a good reason for working for Fouché. Christopher was nothing like the men described by Saintclair.

'Some people may be forced to become spies, Capitaine. I believe they play a crucial role in politics.'

Saintclair reclined on his seat and studied her for a few moments. 'Do you have any particular knowledge of the affairs of state, Madame Norton?'

She didn't care much for the patronising tone of voice. 'No, but perhaps you should give spies more credit. They must lead a very awkward existence.'

'I would not waste my pity on Fouché's spies,' Saintclair retorted. 'As I said, they're all rogues and scoundrels.'

'My friends, enough of this depressing talk.' Martin held out his hands. 'Let's go to the opera at the Théâtre Italien this evening.'

'I cannot possibly attend the theatre,' Marie-Ange objected.

'Don't worry, I am sure one single outing won't tarnish your impeccable reputation as a war widow,' Saintclair retorted coldly. He turned to his friend. 'Yes, we will come. Could you procure us some tickets, please?'

How dare he talk to her like that? She was too stunned to find a suitable reply.

'So it's settled.' Martin stood up and clicked his heels together.

‘Madame, I shall look forward to seeing you later.’

He turned to Saintclair and winked. ‘Do not dare keep this charming creature to yourself. I know what you’re like with the ladies. After all, your record for the cuirassiers’ aptitude test remains unequalled to this day.’

‘Shut up, Martin.’ Saintclair sounded annoyed.

Martin only laughed. ‘See you tonight,’ he said as he left.

‘What aptitude test?’ Marie-Ange asked.

‘It’s an old story.’ Saintclair stood up and pulled on his coat. ‘Shall we go?’

Chapter Three

With dozens of torches burning high on the six columns of its classical façade, the Théâtre Italien lit up the night sky. *Fiacres*, *cabriolets* and private carriages lined the street. Men in dinner jackets and women wearing sparkling jewellery and rustling evening dresses climbed up the stone steps and made their way through the double doors. The air was full of talk about the evening's performance, *L'Amour Fugitif*, with Angelica Catalani, one of Paris' most acclaimed sopranos.

Marie-Ange held on to Capitaine Saintclair's arm as they entered the lobby. She blinked, intimidated by the scintillating lights and the even more scintillating crowd as Saintclair looked around for his friend.

'He's over there,' he said, gesturing towards the back of the hall.

Capitaine Martin was talking to a tall, dark-haired woman. The light from the chandeliers shone on her raven black hair, which was pinned in an elaborate chignon, with tight ringlets framing her face. A low-cut crimson silk gown emphasized her statuesque figure and a mink stole wrapped loosely around her creamy white shoulders. She was so beautiful, so elegant that Marie-Ange felt an unusual twinge of envy as she approached her. For a few seconds, she wished she had worn a fashionable gown too, instead of her plain grey dress. Her fingers smoothed her hair which she wore in the simple style favoured by her mother – two tight braids twisted together and secured with embossed gold combs – the only style her mother claimed could tame their unruly, curly blonde hair.

'Here you are at last,' Martin said with a happy smile as they approached. 'I managed to get us seats behind the orchestra.'

He turned to his female companion. 'I bumped into Caroline this afternoon and persuaded her to come tonight. Isn't that grand?'

Marie-Ange felt Saintclair's arm stiffen under her hand.

'This is a surprise,' he told the woman coldly. 'I wasn't expecting to see you so soon after you left with de Mitre for Auxerre.'

‘I’ve just come back. Auxerre was boring and de Mitre is so dull. How that man made major instead of you, I really do not understand.’ The woman’s voice was seductively husky and her smouldering gaze darted to Saintclair.

‘So this means I’m all yours. Again.’ She flicked open a large black and red silk fan decorated with ostrich feathers.

Saintclair didn’t reply but turned to Marie-Ange. ‘Madame Norton, this is Caroline Dupin, a friend. Caroline, I am escorting Marie-Ange Norton to Lyon.’

The two women nodded politely to each other.

‘Shall we go in?’ Saintclair asked, taking her arm again to lead the way into the hall.

The opera was a new experience for Marie-Ange. Her only outings these past few years had been the Christmas dance at Wellcombe Village Hall, the spring fair on the green, and an occasional ball marking a betrothal or a wedding at a neighbouring manor house she was required to attend as the representative of the Norton family. The magnificent Théâtre Italien concert hall made her catch her breath with its rows of seats covered with plush red velvet and the private boxes which were already filled with spectators. The stage was hidden behind a thick red curtain, but musicians were tuning their instruments in the orchestra pit and the buzz of conversations, laughter and music was exciting.

‘This is wonderful,’ she exclaimed, feeling a little guilty for enjoying the experience so much.

Saintclair smiled but Caroline Dupin waved her fan. ‘Waiting for the performance is always *so* tedious,’ she said in a bored voice. She leant closer to him. ‘By the way, Hugo, I’m going back to Lyon next week. I hope you’ll come and visit.’

‘Maybe …’ he answered, his eyes still scanning the spectators.

There were loud taps near the stage area. The audience hushed, the gas lights dimmed and the orchestra played the opening notes of the overture. When it was over, the heavy curtain slid open to reveal an elaborate set of painted Italian gardens with a castle in the background.

‘It’s like a fairy tale,’ Marie-Ange whispered.

As soon as the performance started, she lost herself in the music. When Angelica Catalani lamented the loss of her lover, her beautiful voice stirred well-known emotions and tears streamed down her cheeks.

'Are you not feeling well?' Saintclair asked as she pulled a handkerchief from her reticule to dab her eyes.

'I am fine,' she muttered, embarrassed. 'It's the music. I have never heard such beautiful music.'

He arched his eyebrows but thankfully turned his attention back to the stage. At the *entr'acte*, people made their way to the refreshment halls. Saintclair announced he was going for a cigar at the bar with Martin and asked Caroline to take Marie-Ange upstairs to the ladies' parlour. The woman shrugged and complained that she'd much rather have a cigar, too, but she led the way to a gallery on the first floor where waiters rushed around offering drinks to ladies dressed in a rainbow of colours. Marie-Ange chose a glass of lemonade, Caroline a flute of champagne. Looking over Marie-Ange's shoulder, she then waved at someone and walked away, saying she would be back shortly.

As she waited for Caroline to return, Marie-Ange soon became aware of a woman staring at her from the other side of the room. Perplexed, because she was sure she had never seen her before, Marie-Ange nodded and smiled, but instead of smiling back, the woman lifted her white-gloved hand to her throat as if she had seen a ghost and rushed across the room towards her.

'I apologise for my bluntness, *Madame*,' the woman said when she stood in front of her. 'You bear an extraordinary resemblance to someone I used to know, a long time ago, at the Salles Priory. May I ask if you are related to Catherine Beauregard?'

It was Marie-Ange's turn to gasp in surprise. 'She was my mother.'

'*Mon Dieu!* I had no idea Catherine married and had a daughter. She disappeared from Salles in the most distressing circumstances and we were told she died …' She shook her head and smiled. 'But I am forgetting my manners. My name is Louison George.'

Slightly overwhelmed, Marie-Ange introduced herself just as a bell rang the end of the interval. The woman took hold of her hand.

'I'm afraid I cannot let you go already. There are so many things I want to ask you. Would you mind very much if we stayed here and talked?'

'Not at all,' Marie-Ange agreed readily. As much as she was enjoying the performance, talking to a friend of her late mother's was an opportunity she could not pass on. 'I would be delighted to talk to you, Madame George. I don't know much about my mother's life as a girl in France. I was born in England. It is where I have lived all my life and I have never met any of my mother's French friends or relatives.'

They made their way to the sitting area, quiet now that everybody had returned to the concert hall.

'You said Catherine *was* your mother – am I to understand she passed away?' Louison asked after they sat down.

'Yes, she died of pneumonia when I was five. I was brought up by my father.'

'Poor Catherine, she led such a tragic life.' Louison sighed. 'But tell me, how did she manage to escape to England?'

Marie-Ange shook her head. 'I'm not sure. I was far too young for her to confide in me. I only know she came to Plymouth where she married my father. I was born there in December 1791.'

'December?' Louison George frowned and toyed with her pearl necklace.

'Please tell me how you met my mother,' Marie-Ange urged, wondering why the woman looked uneasy.

'Of course. As I said, I met her at Salles where I was a boarder. When Catherine arrived in October 1790, she was very sad, very lonely. Her father was jailed in Beaujeu, and her mother appeared to have abandoned her. I was missing my family too, so we became friends. We used to walk in the cloister gardens after our lessons or sew in the evening.' Her eyes clouded over. 'Sometimes, Catherine sang for me. She had such a lovely voice. I remember a particularly poignant song her godfather had taught her – a song about a dovecote and a girl weeping for her dead lover.'

Marie-Ange looked up sharply. She was certain this was the very song her mother sang to send her to sleep when she was little. What a shame she couldn't remember the words…

'We also enjoyed painting,' Louison resumed. 'Catherine was a good artist, much better than I was. She spent hours drawing in her sketchbook. It was a present for her father. Unfortunately she never had the chance to give it to him, since the poor man was executed. Catherine was inconsolable when she heard the news.' She sighed. 'Then a couple of weeks later, her aunt, the Abbess, informed Catherine her mother had married Edmond Malleval.' She shuddered. 'She was so angry. She could not understand how her mother could marry that man, that monster who had caused the death of so many, especially so soon after her father was killed.' The woman frowned. 'At the time, I too thought the wedding shocking, but as I grew older I understood these were desperate times. Catherine's mother may not have been free in her choices, especially where Edmond Malleval was concerned.'

Marie-Ange's eyes welled up with tears as she listened. How her mother had suffered! It was no wonder she never talked about Beauregard and the people she had left behind.

'One day at the end of March, Malleval's soldiers came to Salles and took Catherine away,' Louison carried on. 'The poor girl hardly had time to gather some of her belongings and bid farewell to her aunt before she was bundled into a carriage. That was the last time I saw her. A couple of weeks later we were told she was dead.'

'But that wasn't true! Who told you that?'

'Edmond Malleval himself. He came back to the Priory with his men to search through the things Catherine had left behind. He ransacked her room, and the whole Priory, too. I do not know what he was after but he did not find it. He was so angry he had the Abbess arrested and the Priory closed.'

'And that was in April?' Marie-Ange asked.

Louison George nodded briefly before looking away.

The blood drained from Marie-Ange's face, the room blurred in front of her eyes. She understood why Louison George looked uneasy. The dates were wrong.

‘You look so much like her,’ Louison resumed. ‘You have the same smile. And your hair, exactly the same colour and curls, the same hairstyle even. I did not hesitate when I saw you earlier. I knew you had to be related. So tell me, why are you in France? Are you married? Is your father here with you?’

‘Sadly my … father died several years ago.’ It was hard to keep her voice calm as she answered. ‘I did marry but …’

‘I have been looking all over for you,’ Capitaine Saintclair’s booming voice interrupted her.

He stood in front of her, arms crossed on his chest, an angry scowl on his face.

‘Why did you not go back to the hall?’

‘Is this gentleman your husband?’ Louison George gave Saintclair an appraising glance.

‘No, Capitaine Saintclair is my escort to Beauregard,’ Marie-Ange corrected. ‘My husband, Commander Christopher Norton, is … was lost at sea.’

‘Pleased to meet you, Capitaine.’ Louison extended her hand for Saintclair to kiss. ‘I am sorry to have kept Marie-Ange from the opera, and from you, but we were busy talking about the past. You see, we have just established that I was a friend of her mother’s.’

The French officer looked stunned. ‘Really?’

‘Is that not extraordinary? Catherine Beauregard and I attended the Priory school at Salles together.’ Louison turned to Marie-Ange in earnest. ‘You said you were on your way to Beauregard. There is someone you must see when you get there. Your great-aunt, Hermine Marzac, your grandfather’s sister. She came back from exile in Switzerland a few years ago.’ She lowered her voice. ‘She might be able to tell you more about your mother.’

The two women looked at each other, a current of understanding passing between them. Marie-Ange nodded. Louison was right. Her aunt might shed some light on the events of that year.

‘There is something else,’ Louison added in a hushed voice, pressing Marie-Ange’s hand with hers. ‘Beware of Uxeloup Malleval. He has a fearsome reputation.’

After taking leave of Louison, Capitaine Saintclair led the way back to the main hall for the end of the performance, but this time Marie-Ange was far too preoccupied to enjoy the music. There were things she needed to think about, alone. After the play, Martin and Caroline asked if she and the capitaine wished to join them for a late supper in a *brasserie* nearby, but Saintclair declined. He said they would be leaving at dawn the following morning.

Saintclair hailed a black cab to return to Le Faisan Doré.

'Have you heard of the Salles Priory?' Marie-Ange asked. 'Apparently the Abbess there was a member of my family.'

Saintclair nodded. 'It was an exclusive boarding school for girls from the aristocracy. You may not realise this, Madame, but before the revolution your mother's family – the Beauregards – were the wealthiest landowners in the whole of the Beaujolais.' He let out a derisive laugh before carrying on. 'In those days, I would not have been allowed to ride in the same carriage as you. I would have been thrown out, beaten like a dog, and left for dead in the gutter just for having the audacity to look at you.' There was bitterness in his tone.

'Things are different now, are they not?' she remarked.

'Not for much longer, if our new king has his way,' he replied, sombrely.

They didn't talk again until they arrived back at Le Faisan Doré. He held her hand to assist her from the carriage and they faced each other for a few seconds.

'Thank you for tonight,' she said at last. 'I didn't think I would, but I enjoyed the opera.' More importantly, she had found out things about her mother's past she never suspected.

He nodded and held the door open for her. 'It was my pleasure.'

'Well, goodnight.' Marie-Ange brushed past him as they walked into the inn.

Once in her room, Marie-Ange lit the fire and sat down. Her thoughts were pensive as her gaze followed the flames rising in the fireplace. The dates were wrong, she thought once again. She had always assumed her mother had gone to England immediately after Aline's marriage to Edmond Malleval in mid-January of 1791, met her father and married more or less straight away. Louison George revealed tonight that Catherine escaped Edmond Malleval in April. It would have taken her several weeks to travel to England. Whoever helped her would have chosen roundabout routes to avoid being caught by Malleval's men or other police and army personnel looking to apprehend fleeing aristocrats.

Marie-Ange was born on the first of December. So unless William Jones met her mother in France, he couldn't be her father. He had said many times he had never set foot in France, which meant Catherine was already pregnant when she arrived in England. Who then was Marie-Ange's father?

Chapter Four

They left Paris at daybreak. As soon as he climbed into the carriage, Saintclair stretched his legs, pulled his collar up, crossed his arms and fell asleep. The snow was now almost completely melted. The streets were covered with brown slush and muddy puddles into which the horses' hooves and the carriage wheels splashed.

Marie-Ange stared out of the window. The grey suburbs of Paris gave way to villages, and then to a very dull, flat and colourless countryside – or perhaps it just looked like that because she was tired. She had spent half the night agonising about Louison George's revelations and playing in her mind images of her childhood and of her father – the man she still thought of as her father, William Jones. Quiet and kind, if a little distant, he was a lawyer and always seemed busy at his Plymouth practice, in his study, or again in the garden where he lovingly tended his roses. The few memories she had left of her parents together were of walks on the seafront, with them linking arms and smiling as she ran ahead; or of quiet Sunday afternoons when he read to her in the drawing room while her mother worked at her embroidery. After her mother's death, William Jones became even more quiet, even more distant. He had, however, never given her any cause to suspect that she wasn't his daughter. Yet he must have known. It might be why he was always so reluctant to talk about her mother's past and her family.

Her thoughts turned to Christopher. Would she see him – or the man called Nallay – again soon? The more she thought about it, the more she recalled his face, the grey eyes and the unusual colour of his hair, the less doubts there were in her heart. Nallay *was* her husband. Something terrible must have happened to him, for it seemed he had lost his memory. But how would she manage to find him? How did one trace a spy?

With a sigh, she leant against the padded seat and closed her eyes. The next thing she knew, her cheek rested against something warm and strong, an arm wrapped around her waist giving a rare sense of security. Mixed scents of sandalwood shaving soap and tobacco tickled her nose. Still half asleep, she patted tentatively at the coarse fabric of a jacket. Her fingers touched a metal button, then another. Goodness! That thumping sound wasn't the horses' galloping hooves, but a heartbeat! She opened her eyes. And pulled out of Saintclair's arms.

'Capitaine, how could you?' she gasped. Her cheeks burning, she slid to the far end of the seat.

He shrugged. 'Next time, I'll let you fall off the seat if you prefer.'

She picked her grey bonnet from the floor and put it back on her dishevelled hair.

'No, Capitaine, next time you will wake me up,' she corrected haughtily, gripping the side of the seat as the carriage turned yet another bend on the bumpy road.

Hugo had rather enjoyed holding her against him while she slept, her fingers lying flat on his chest, her head resting snugly in the hollow of his shoulder, and her curly hair caressing his face. He had never seen a woman's hair so golden, so thick. He longed to unpin it, watch it fall on her shoulders and comb it with his fingers. His throat tightened and he swallowed hard. There were other things he longed to do too … the woman was a mass of contradictions, a fascinating, tempting puzzle. *Too* tempting.

He shook his head. From now on, he would keep away from her. It was his responsibility to deliver her safe and sound to Malleval. It was in his interest too, and he'd better not forget it or the consequences for his family would be dire.

He would pick up a horse at the regimental barracks at Fontainebleau, and ride to Beauregard. They would both breathe more easily if they weren't closeted together in that carriage.

They stopped at a roadside inn to have lunch and rest the horses. He discussed details of the itinerary with the driver, leaving Marie-Ange alone to eat a bowl of soup and drink coffee in the dining room. Back on the bumpy road, he spread the map on his knees and tried to plan the route to Beauregard but the young woman was in a talkative mood. Her incessant chatter made it impossible for him to keep to his resolution and ignore her.

‘Where are we stopping for the night?’

‘Sens.’

‘Is it a large town?’

‘Not really,’ he replied, not even bothering to lift his eyes from the map. Surely she would take the hint and stop talking.

She looked through the window. ‘This looks like wine-growing country. Look. Another beautiful chateau! Do they produce champagne around here?’

He nodded. ‘Some chateaux do.’

‘I have only had champagne twice before,’ she remarked, pulling a face. ‘And I did not like it at all.’

This time he smiled. ‘Then it was not real champagne. Malleval has a well-appointed cellar at Beauregard. I am sure he shall be pleased to do the honours.’ Hugo knew all about the wine in that cellar. It was what got him in trouble in the first place.

She was looking out of the window again. He glanced at her and held his breath, struck by the wonder and innocence in her eyes.

‘Now, that is the most magnificent chateau I have ever seen,’ she whispered.

‘Fontainebleau,’ he announced as the carriage drove into the courtyard of the army barracks. ‘That is where we are stopping.’

‘Why?’

He let out a sigh. ‘I’m picking up a horse. I will ride for the rest of the journey.’

‘Oh …’ She turned away but not before he saw the look of relief on her face.

The carriage stopped and he jumped down.

Marie-Ange watched him talk and joke with his fellow cuirassier officers and the stable lads who pulled several horses from their box to parade in front of him. Saintclair patted the animals’ sides, looked at their hooves, commented on their shiny coats and well-brushed manes. Fifteen minutes later he pointed to a huge charger, black like a moonless night, and highly spirited judging by the way it bucked and stomped on the cobbles. Unconcerned, Saintclair patted its neck and kept on talking as he saddled it. Then he swung up on it in a swift, fluid movement and they set off on the road to Sens.

It was night when they reached the large, comfortable inn on the main square where they would spend the night.

'Tomorrow we will travel through the forest,' Saintclair said when they parted for the night. He warned her of the dangers ahead. Wolves, boars, and robbers. She wasn't overly anxious though. He would protect them. He was a cuirassier, a trained killer, and he carried a pistol tucked in his belt, under his riding coat, she had seen it.

They entered the deep, dark Burgundy forest the following afternoon. The ground was frozen, the trees fluffy with silver frost. Despite the extra blanket the coach driver provided, which she had wrapped around her shoulders, Marie-Ange could not stop shivering. Her feet were like blocks of ice and she had to keep rubbing her gloved hands together to warm them. The horses slowed to a walking pace as the road became a bumpy track and the forest closed in on them.

Daylight was fading when they arrived in a hamlet and stopped in front of a small tavern with a half-timbered black and white façade. The driver opened the door, helped Marie-Ange climb out, and carried her bag inside where they found Saintclair leaning over the counter, arguing with the innkeeper.

'My apologies, Capitaine, I only have the one room,' the innkeeper said, a contrite expression on his face. 'And it won't be available for long. A company of dragoons is heading this way. There must be trouble brewing down south, we already had two infantry battalions stopping by this week. Do you wish to have this room or not?'

'I suppose so,' Saintclair grumbled. He took his purse out and gave the man a few silver coins. 'We require supper too, for the lady, the coach driver, and myself. And mulled wine in the room straight away.'

Marie-Ange stood in the middle of the small room Saintclair escorted her to. Surely she had misunderstood. He wasn't planning to share a bedroom with her, was he? While he busied himself lighting a fire, she looked around with dismay, pulling a face at the two battered armchairs, the bed piled high with quilts and blankets and the rickety washstand with its chipped bowl.

'Don't look so disgusted, it's not that bad,' Saintclair remarked, a wide grin on his face. 'At least we have a room. The coachman has to sleep in the stables with the horses.'

'What about you?' she blurted out. 'Could you not …?'

'What? Sleep in the stables, too? I suppose I could but I do not wish to.' He narrowed his eyes and paused. 'I will manage very well with these two armchairs, unless you would rather share the bed. It would be warmer and certainly a lot more pleasant for both of us.'

His audacity left her speechless. His words about women purring like kittens in his arms echoed in her mind, and she didn't need to look at her reflection in the mirror to guess that her face and throat had turned crimson. She took a deep breath.

'A gentleman would never place a woman in this situation, much less make such salacious comments, Capitaine,' she said when she trusted her voice not to shake.

He stepped forward, forcing her to tilt her head all the way up to look at him. She didn't step back. He wasn't going to intimidate her so easily. When he was only a few paces away, he stared into her eyes.

'I never said I was a gentleman, Madame,' he said, his voice almost too calm.

'Very well, you can have the room to yourself. I will sleep quite comfortably in the lounge downstairs.' She crossed her arms on her chest.

He took another step towards her. 'I don't think so. Did you not hear what the innkeeper said? He is expecting a company of dragoons tonight. You will stay where I can keep an eye on you, is that clear?' His voice had a steely edge to it that brooked no disagreement.

He seemed about to add something when there was a knock on the door and a servant boy entered carrying a tray with pitchers of mulled wine.

'Good lad. I'll take that.' Saintclair placed the tray on the dressing table and gave the boy a coin.

'You should drink while it's hot,' he said, handing a pitcher to Marie-Ange.

Their fingers brushed when she took hold of it. She jerked back and tightened her lips. Saintclair shrugged, turned to the fireplace and downed his steaming hot drink in a few gulps. He then declared he had to see to his horse.

'I will meet you in the dining room in an hour,' he said before walking out.

Heaving a sigh of relief now she was alone, she sat down near the fireplace and sipped the mulled wine. How was she going to bear the next few days travelling with such a brute? And how was she going to survive a night in the same room? She finished her drink and got up to unpack some of her clothes before going downstairs to ask the innkeeper for some hot water to be brought up to the room. After a quick toilette, she changed into a dark green dress and made her way down to the dining room, her freshly brushed hair tied loosely at the nape of her neck.

The company of dragoons had arrived. The dining room was packed with soldiers in grey and blue uniforms, eating, drinking, and getting more rowdy by the second. A few were in shirtsleeves, having thrown their coats on the floor. Others were already slumped in a drunken stupor against the walls. Saintclair waved at her from a table at the back. The dragoons stared as Marie-Ange walked across. Whistles and crude comments filled the air.

Saintclair stood up at once, his eyes cold and his face set in stone as he surveyed the room. 'Behave, dragoons, and do your regiment proud,' he said in a strong voice. Although he wasn't wearing his uniform, his air of command quelled the situation. The men muttered apologies and went back to their pitchers of wine and ale. Saintclair pulled out a chair for Marie-Ange.

'Let's get this meal over with quickly,' he said as a servant brought bowls of soup, ham, and thick slices of bread.

He glanced around the room with a preoccupied air. 'They are from the Fourth Regiment of Dragoons. Their major and half the company are stopping at a village nearby, leaving only a handful of low-ranking officers in charge here, and I'll be damned if I know where they are right now, probably dealing with supplies.' He shook his head, disgusted. 'Look at them! They are a disgrace. I would not tolerate such behaviour from my men.'

Night had fallen and campfires could be seen through the inn's dirty windows. There were tents, horses, men all over the courtyard, and probably all over the village, too.

'Do you understand now why you won't be sleeping in the lounge tonight, Madame?' he asked.

'Yes.' She sighed.

They finished their meal in silence and Saintclair escorted her to the bottom of the stairs.

'I will come up shortly. In the meantime, bar the door.'

Back upstairs, she stood in the room, wondering whether to undress or sleep fully clothed. Having decided that the thick quilts and blankets piled on top of the bed would offer enough privacy, she stripped out of her dress, stockings and underwear, and slipped her white nightdress on. She was tightening the belt of Christopher's faded blue dressing gown around her waist when Saintclair called from behind the door. There was a flicker of surprise in his eyes when he saw her nightclothes and she wondered if she had done the right thing. Saintclair was carrying a pillow and a couple of blankets, which he dropped on the floor.

Unsure what to do next, she sat in the armchair and tucked her feet under her. Saintclair sat in the chair opposite. They stared into the fire without talking for a while. The noise of the soldiers' raucous laughter downstairs and in the camp outside echoed into the night.

'I fear it's going to be a long night …' he said at last, breaking the silence.

She bit her lower lip. There was much she wanted to ask him about Uxeloup Malleval and his father, but she wasn't quite sure how to start, especially after their unpleasant altercation earlier on. She cleared her throat.

'It was a stroke of luck to meet Madame George the other night at the opera and to hear her stories about Edmond Malleval,' she said at last. 'He really sounds like a frightful man.'

Saintclair nodded without looking her way.

'You are correct. He wasn't mourned by many when he passed away a few months ago. In fact, he was known as "The Butcher of Lyon" and was, together with his two associates, Fouché and Collot d'Herbois, one of the most bloodthirsty and fanatical men the Revolution ever produced. Not surprising really, considering where he was from.'

'Where was that?'

'A village in the Pilat, a godforsaken place to the south-west of Lyon, with mountains and gorges, deep forests and torrents gushing down rocky slopes. The people who live there are as harsh and unforgiving as their land. The village he came from is actually called Malleval.'

'It is a rather sinister name, is it not?'

He nodded again. 'It means "Bad Valley". It was for centuries the lair of brigands who rampaged through the whole region.'

He hesitated. 'Actually, I might as well tell you since you will only hear it from somebody else. These brigands were led by the Malleval family. That's how they made their fortune, from robbing and killing.'

'Really? Then how did Edmond become such a prominent statesman during the Revolution?' Her voice was barely a whisper, her fingers tightly crossed in her lap.

'The Revolution gave opportunities to all kinds of fanatics, rogues, and gold-diggers to rise to the top. Edmond Malleval was one of them.'

'Madame George said he took my mother away by force from the Priory, and later he claimed she was dead.'

And yet her grandmother married him ... why?

'What is his son Uxeloup like?' she asked.

Saintclair sighed, and raked his dark hair with his fingers.

'He is not in the least like his father, if that's what you're worried about. He is far too self-absorbed and too concerned with having a good time. But for all his faults, he is a good fighter, a great Hussar.' He smiled encouragingly.

'What can you tell me about Fouché?'

He sat back in the armchair and studied her with half-closed eyes.

'I am starting to wonder why you are taking such an interest in our former Minister of Police, Madame. Are you thinking of becoming one of his spies?'

She let out an impatient sigh.

'Of course not. You said he had been an associate of Edmond Malleval. Does Uxeloup Malleval know him well, too?'

He nodded. 'I believe they are close, although I really cannot understand why any man would wish to call that snake his friend. You'll be able to make up your own mind about Fouché very soon. He is attending a ball on Saturday night in Lyon where Malleval is invited, so if we make it to Beauregard by Thursday as planned, you will meet him there.'

Her heart made a leap. 'I will? That would be wonderful. We simply must be there on time.'

'Why do you want to meet Fouché so badly?' he asked, frowning with suspicion.

She ignored his question and jumped to her feet. 'I wish you goodnight, Capitaine.'

He stood up too and pointed to the dressing gown. 'Is not that a little big for you?'

She tilted her chin. 'It was my husband's. I always wear it in the evenings. It reminds me of him.'

'Ah. I see.'

He turned away, grabbed the pillow and the blankets and made a makeshift bed on the two armchairs. She slid into the cold, stiff, scratchy bedcovers, pulled the quilted counterpanes up to her neck and curled into a ball to keep warm. She couldn't stop thinking about what Saintclair had said. She would meet Fouché soon, and perhaps have the chance to ask him about Joseph Nallay. Even better, if the former minister of police travelled with his agents, she might even see him. This time she would establish the man's identity for sure. And if, as she suspected, he was indeed Christopher, she would take him back to Norton Place, where he belonged. She fell asleep, a smile on her lips and her heart filled with hope.

It was only dawn, but already raucous voices shouted orders outside, dogs barked, horses stomped and neighed in the courtyard. The dragoons were getting ready to leave. Marie-Ange sat up and yawned. Capitaine Saintclair was fast asleep, stripped down to his shirt and sitting at an awkward angle in the armchair. The blankets had fallen off in a heap on the floor.

Reluctantly Marie-Ange had to admit she was glad he hadn't left her alone in the room. It had been a noisy and troubled night, especially when a whole gang of dragoons, fired up by too much liquor, had come pounding on the door in the early hours. They hadn't known Saintclair was in the room. It had only taken him a couple of minutes to send them all back downstairs but she dreaded to think what might have happened had she been on her own.

Barefoot, and in her white nightdress, she walked to the fireplace. Saintclair had kept the fire smouldering all night, so all she had to do to get it going again was to place a handful of twigs and a few logs onto the grate and poke at them a few times.

Saintclair's coat had fallen on the floor, and as she bent down to pick it up, she noticed a piece of paper next to it. It looked like a letter and must have dropped out of the pocket. The first lines caught her eye. She recognised Uxeloup Malleval's handwriting. Curious, she raised the paper to the window to read.

"This is to certify that your debt of honour will be cancelled as soon as you have delivered Madame Norton at Beauregard. Should you fail to do so, I will call for the immediate transfer of the deeds

of your St Genis house in repayment of your gambling debt, unless, that is, you can repay the five thousand francs you owe me. UM."

Thoughtful, she folded the note and placed it back inside Saintclair's pocket.

So that was the real reason behind his trip to escort her from Devon to Beauregard. He had claimed he was bored and had taken the assignment as a favour to a friend. The truth was he was indebted to Malleval. She stood a while in front of the fire, rubbing her hands together to warm them and pondering the new information.

Uxeloup Malleval was prepared to give up a lot of money or the deeds of a house he had won at cards, in exchange for her presence at Beauregard, ostensibly to make sure she received her inheritance. It appeared most generous of him. However, it didn't really tally with what she knew of him and of his father. A noise made her spin round. Saintclair was looking at her.

'Good morning, Madame,' he said, his eyes skimming over her body. A slow, seductive smile appeared on his lips. 'There is nothing like a beautiful woman in her nightshirt before breakfast to put me in a good mood.'

He stood up and towered over her. The room was suddenly very small.

'G-g-good morning,' she stammered, crossing her arms over her chest. She couldn't get Christopher's dressing gown to cover herself with because Saintclair stood between her and the bed. The fireplace behind her didn't allow the possibility of stepping back either.

Saintclair lifted a hand and gently brushed a curl off her forehead. Her breath caught in her throat. His touch burned her skin and sent shivers through her at the same time.

'Whatever are you doing, Capitaine? You forget your place,' she snapped, shocked by his gesture but more so by the way her body had responded.

'And where would that be, Madame Norton? Of course, I forgot. The stables,' he said, shooting an amused glance at her before turning away. 'Don't worry, I'm going,' he added before she could answer. He rubbed his chin. 'I need a wash and a shave. I'll ask the landlord to have a pail of hot water brought up to you at once.'

Grabbing his boots in one hand, he unbarred the door and went out.

She stood for a moment in the middle of the room, annoyed with the man and at her reaction to him. Around him she sounded snooty and disagreeable, when she had never paid much attention to the issues of class or status. Heavens, how could she ever think she was superior to him, or to anyone else, just because her mother was a Beauregard and her husband a member of the English gentry? She lived in a run-down manor house and the only reason she was travelling across France was to collect an inheritance to enable her to fix a leaky roof.

She didn't feel superior to Saintclair at all, but it was true she didn't like him and despised his manners. However she would have to put up with him until they reached Beauregard. After that, she did not plan to ever lay eyes on the man again.

A servant girl brought the promised bucket of warm water and Marie-Ange had a wash and got dressed. As an afterthought she pulled Christopher's dagger out of her travelling bag and slid it inside one of her boots.

When Saintclair came back, he was clean-shaven, his dark hair damp and combed back. He turned away and proceeded to peel off his shirt. Although she carried on with her packing, she couldn't help stealing a glance towards him. Her heart skipped a beat, and she stifled a gasp with her hand. His broad back and powerful shoulders were criss-crossed with scars. A lifetime on the battlefields had certainly left marks on his body – on his heart and soul too, she would wager.

He pulled a fresh shirt out of his travel bag and put it on.

'I hope you're ready to face a few excitable dragoons downstairs,' he remarked as he turned to her after tucking his shirt into his breeches. 'They're so loud I think some have already supped a cask of ale for breakfast.'

She sat on the bed and let out a sigh, realising she had been holding her breath while staring at him.

'It was fortunate you were here last night,' she said, aware of sounding a little breathless. 'I … I am grateful.'

'That's part of my job,' he replied matter-of-factly.

Her cheeks felt too warm and her hand shook when she picked up her hairbrush and brushed her curls in fast, vigorous strokes. Watching him get dressed had given her a tight, uncomfortable feeling in the pit of her stomach. She plaited her hair and tied a green ribbon at the tip.

'I had a word with the dragoons' officers in charge,' he said. 'They are en route to Lyon. There'll be no room left in the barracks by the time I get there.'

She looked at him. 'You live in barracks in Lyon? What about your family?'

'They live in my house in St Genis, a small village a few leagues to the south.'

The house he had lost at cards to Malleval.

'Lucie's physician recommended a change of air for her health, so I … ahem … acquired the house for her and my parents.' He put his jacket on. 'Ready?'

They went down to the dining room, which by then was almost empty. After a quick breakfast of hot porridge and coffee, it was time to set off in the cold, grey morning on the road to Dijon.

They made good time, blessed with a mostly empty road all day, stopping only a couple of times to rest the horses and eat. When daylight started to fade, Marie-Ange reclined on the seat of the carriage and listened to the sounds of owls hooting in the forest. Suddenly, the sound of horses galloping and men shouting close by brought her upright. The coach stopped abruptly and she was thrown onto the floor.

Chapter Five

'Nobody moves or I shoot!'

Angry shouts were followed by gunshots and sounds of a struggle.

'Damn the bastard! Hold him down and knock him out. I don't want him shooting any more of us. And get that bloody coach driver on the ground right now,' someone yelled.

They were being attacked. Marie-Ange felt for the knife she had slipped inside her boot earlier but the door of the carriage flew open before she could take it out.

'What have we got here?'

A man wearing a dirty brown overcoat, his face partly obscured by a black large-rimmed hat leant forward, grabbed her arm, pulled her from the carriage and threw her onto the frozen ground. She cried out in pain, panic taking her breath away. Her stunned gaze took in the scene around her. Three men lay dead on the ground, probably shot by Saintclair before he was disarmed, a couple of highwaymen stood near the coach driver who lay in a puddle of partly frozen mud, another two held Saintclair down. The cuirassier struggled but the two men kicked him until he slumped on the ground with a groan of pain.

What could she do? Her dagger was in her boot, out of reach for now. Her heart beat so hard it hurt and she didn't think she was breathing any more. The man with the black hat pulled her to her feet, put his finger under her chin, and raised her head sharply.

'Pretty … but she sure don't look rich.' He opened up her cloak to reveal her plain green dress, and clucked his tongue. She wore no jewellery, only her wedding band. He turned to his acolytes and laughed. 'Too bad! I'll have to take payment in kind.'

Saintclair fought to break free again. This time the men kicked him so hard he stopped moving altogether.

'Don't damage her too much,' one of them called. 'Save some for the rest of us.'

The highwayman grinned, uncovering yellow stumps of teeth. He pushed Marie-Ange inside the coach, scrambled in beside her, and slammed the door shut behind him. She quailed away from him against the squabs of the carriage.

'Just you and me, *ma belle*,' he grunted, his eyes glinting with lust. He unbuckled his pistol belt and threw it down before giving her a hard shove.

She tried to kick him and push him away, but he ripped the cloak off her shoulders, pinned her to the seat and placed his forearm across her throat. She could hardly breathe, let alone fight him off. She stopped struggling as he proceeded to lift the hem of her skirts and petticoats, then fumbled with the laces on his breeches before climbing on top of her. Her only hope was to get the dagger out before he could molest her but she must be quick.

Gasping for breath she slid her hand down his body, then moved her fingers towards her boot.

The man's breathing turned short and raspy and he groaned when he finally managed to undo the last of his ties. It was now or never.

She pulled the dagger from her boot and held it against his throat, but her hand shook so badly she feared she would drop it

'Move off me,' she said, her voice barely a whisper.

He became very still.

'What the hell?' he growled, his eyes focused on her face.

She tightened her grip on the handle. 'I mean it. Get up, slowly.'

She would get hold of the guns he had discarded in his haste. And after that … she didn't know, she hadn't thought that far ahead.

His lips twisted into a grimace. 'Oh no, *ma belle*, I don't think so,' he sniggered.

Everything then happened too fast. He grabbed hold of her wrist, tried to prise the dagger from her fingers. The blade sliced through the palm of his hand. He cried out, pushed her off the seat. Her back slammed against the floor and he fell on top of her.

The dagger made a slurping sound as it went deep into the man's chest. His eyes opened wide in shock, blood squirted out of the wound, and he shuddered violently. With a cry she pushed him off her, pulled her skirts down and sat up. Shaking, she wiped the blood off her hand on her dress, again and again. A sickening, metallic smell filled her nostrils and bile rose in her throat.

But now wasn't the time to faint or to be sick. She had to help Saintclair. She glanced around to locate the highwayman's weapon belt, pulled his two pistols out of the holsters and extracted a couple of cartridges from his leather pouch before proceeding to arm the pistols.

She worked fast, like Robert had shown her. When the pistols were loaded, she said a silent 'thank you' for the shooting lessons he had given her the previous summer, took a deep breath, and kicked the door open.

As she jumped down, a pistol in each hand, the highwaymen spun towards her, wide-eyed and open-mouthed. She aimed at the two holding Saintclair and shot them straight through the chest. Immediately, Saintclair scrambled to his feet and retrieved a pistol from the ground. He checked the priming and aimed at the remaining two highwaymen.

'Come here, you two, slowly,' he ordered coldly. 'Throw your weapons on the ground and kneel down.'

The men looked at each other and shrugged before stepping forward. They placed their firearms on the ground and complied.

'Now, put your hands behind your head.'

They did as they were told.

'What now, Capitaine?' the coach driver enquired.

'Get something to bind them with,' Saintclair instructed. The driver searched the box next to the driver's seat, produced some rope, and proceeded to tie the brigands' hands and feet.

'Make sure it's tight. We're not taking them with us to Dijon, they'd only slow us down. We shall leave them here for the gendarmes to find tomorrow.'

He walked past Marie-Ange, who hadn't moved since she had shot the highwaymen, and peered inside the carriage and cursed.

'Shame, I wanted to kill the bastard myself,' he said. He pulled the brigand's lifeless body out. It fell on the ground with a heavy thud, the carved bone hilt of Christopher's dagger sticking out of his chest.

'How the hell did you manage that?' he asked, turning to her. 'You saved us all.'

She still didn't speak but stood shivering and staring at the dead man, the pistols gripped tightly in her hands.

'If I am not mistaken, this is the second time I owe you my life,' he added. 'I am beginning to think the sailors were right when they said you were an angel.'

'How can you call me an angel?' she whispered at last. 'I have just killed three men.' Tears now ran down her face.

Saintclair frowned. He retrieved her cloak from the carriage and placed it onto her shoulders before gently easing her grip around the pistols and taking them from her. He slid them into his belt and started to turn away to deal with the dead bodies when a whimper escaped from her lips, then another, and another.

She was in his arms before she realised it, her trembling body pressed close to his own.

'It made such a horrible noise. I didn't want to kill him, but he wouldn't do as I said. He wanted to … he was going to …' She hiccuped as tears streamed down her face.

'And the other two, I had no choice, you know that, do you not?' she stammered before hiding her face against his chest.

'You were very brave. You did what you must, they would have killed us all,' he said, holding her more tightly and resting his chin on the top of her head.

His arms were around her, warm and strong. She buried her head against his chest and for a few moments all she heard were his heartbeat and his breathing. He rubbed her back slowly, his touch leaving a burning trail along her spine, before pulling away and meeting her gaze. His blue eyes seemed overly bright as they searched her face.

'We need to set off now. Dijon is still a good distance away. Will you be all right?'

She sniffed, wiped her wet cheeks with her hands. 'Where is my dagger?'

'Here.' He stepped aside, pulled the knife from the dead highwayman's chest and wiped it on the man's coat before handing it to her.

She slid the knife into her boot without a word.

'Well done, Madame,' the coach driver called to her, a beaming smile on his face as she climbed into the carriage. Turning to Saintclair he added, 'Such a small woman, who would have thought she had it in her to dispatch three men to the Devil?'

Saintclair didn't reply. He jumped on his horse and set off at the front.

'You can't leave us here all night,' the brigands protested. 'There are wolves in the forest. And bears.'

'Do not fear. They won't come near you. You stink too much.' The coach driver laughed and whipped the horses into a trot.

They reached Dijon two hours later. Immediately after checking in at an inn on the market square, Saintclair ordered a stable lad to fetch the gendarmes.

'We might as well get comfortable and order some food while we're waiting.' He took her arm to lead her to the lounge.

'You're hurt,' Marie-Ange said when she noticed the nasty bruise on his cheekbone. His posture was a little stiff too, which wasn't surprising considering the beating he had endured at the hands of the brigands.

'It's nothing.' He shrugged and pulled a chair out for her to sit on.

It wasn't long before a duty officer reported to the inn. Saintclair gave him a succinct account of the attack in the forest. The gendarme then turned to Marie-Ange for her version of events.

'The capitaine said you killed one man with a knife and two others with a pistol, is this correct?' He sounded sceptical.

Silently she nodded and closed her eyes. The sound the knife had made when she pushed it into the highwayman's flesh, the warm, viscous feel of his blood on her hand and the startled expression in the eyes of his accomplices as she shot them would never leave her.

'Can I see your knife?' the gendarme enquired.

She bent down, lifted her skirt above the ankle and removed the dagger from her boot. She handed it to the policeman without a word. Saintclair stood behind the gendarme in order to view the dagger, too.

'That is a rather strange-looking knife,' the gendarme said a moment later, returning the dagger to her.

'It was my husband's,' she whispered. 'He brought it back from the West Indies.'

'The West Indies? That explains it ... you were very brave, Madame.' He smiled and added before taking his leave, 'I'll dispatch a patrol to the forest at first light but with luck, the brigands will have frozen to death. Thanks to you, they won't terrorise innocent travellers any longer.'

A servant girl appeared with some ale and two plates piled high with beef stew and vegetables. Marie-Ange protested that she wasn't hungry.

'You must eat,' Saintclair objected.

'I cannot.' She pushed her plate away.

He pushed the plate back to her. 'We have a long journey ahead of us tomorrow. I want to reach Beauregard by nightfall. The last thing I need is for you to be ill or too exhausted to travel. I promised Malleval I would look after you and I mean to do so, even if I did not exactly cover myself with glory back there in the forest,' he added with a grimace. 'Saved by a woman! I will be the regiment's laughing stock if the story gets out.'

Marie-Ange remained silent and toyed with the dagger on the table.

'Where did you learn to shoot?' he asked, before tucking into his meal with relish. 'You didn't hesitate when you aimed at the men and both your shots hit their mark.'

It was obvious he wouldn't let a few dead bodies spoil his

appetite, she thought, watching him eat. He must have seen hundreds on battlefields all over Europe. It was different for her. She probably wouldn't be able to sleep for a long time.

'Robert taught me last summer,' she explained. 'He did not want to at first but I insisted. We made a bargain. He taught me to shoot and in return, I taught him … other things.'

She promised Robert she would never tell anyone about their French lessons. He was embarrassed at being so bad at languages. She drank a sip of ale, toyed with her food.

Saintclair stopped eating and looked at her. His blue eyes shone with curiosity.

'What kind of things?'

'Things that can help a young man both in a career and in polite society,' she replied, deliberately vague. 'We have had lessons every evening since he left boarding school.'

'Is that what you were doing the other night?'

She felt she was blushing. So he had heard them giggling. 'I am sorry if we kept you awake.'

Saintclair leant forward, his eyes intense now. 'He must have enjoyed that particular lesson. He had a very happy grin on his face when he left your bedroom.' He added in a low, slightly hoarse voice. 'In fact, I wouldn't mind a few lessons myself.'

She shrugged.

'Oh no, he doesn't like it, and he isn't particularly talented but I do insist he stick at it. He will thank me in the long run.' She looked up and added. 'As for you, why would you need any lessons? You *are* French. You know all about …'

Saintclair was still staring at her. The silence between them sizzled with tension. Why was he looking at her like that, so close she could see the golden specks in the iris of his blue eyes and feel his warm breath on her face? And what exactly did he believe she had been doing in her room with Robert? Her face and throat started to burn, her fingers gripped the side of the table so hard her knuckles went white as realisation dawned on her.

'You cannot actually believe that Robert and I were …' She

couldn't bring herself to say the word.

He didn't answer.

'Do you really think so little of me?' She almost stammered with outrage. 'Well, if you must know, I teach him French every evening while we play draughts in my room. Robert is hopeless at languages, whereas Christopher was fluent in French, German, and Spanish. He wants to be a naval officer like his brother and knows he will need to speak French to improve his prospects.'

Saintclair threw his head back and burst out laughing.

'You teach him French? Well, I never ... I do apologise.' He drank a few sips of beer to calm himself down, then he drank some more, but his lips were still twitching when he put the empty pitcher of ale on the table.

She threw him a furious glance and hardly realised she was gripping Christopher's dagger tightly to stop her hand shaking. Now she understood the comments he had made over the past few days. All this time he thought she was having a liaison with her brother-in-law while pretending to be a grieving widow.

'Please don't wave that thing about, you might hurt yourself.' Saintclair gestured towards the dagger.

She hissed an angry breath between her teeth and put the dagger down, but she didn't let go of it. It had saved her life today – Saintclair's and the coachman's, too. It felt like a good omen. She tilted her chin up.

'Christopher was everything to me, Capitaine. He still is. He used to say this dagger was his lucky charm, I never knew why he left it behind when he left for Coruña.' She paused. 'Did you fight in the Spanish wars?'

Saintclair looked taken aback by her sudden question. 'Some of them. Why?'

'Were you at Coruña in January, 1809?'

He shook his head. 'No, I was in Madrid at the time. Was your husband killed at Coruña?'

'He served on board the HMS *Amazon* which was sunk by French artillery as it moored in the harbour. No member of the crew, and none of the British soldiers they rescued, made it alive. Or so they said.'

'It was a bad business, from what I heard,' he replied.

'In your experience, is it possible for a soldier or a sailor to be declared dead when in fact he is still alive?' She looked at him in earnest.

He shrugged, raked his fingers in his dark hair. 'It could happen, I suppose. People get lost, or disappear in the heat of battle.'

'I never believed Christopher died. I never felt it, here.' She put her hand on her heart. 'And now I know he is alive.' She leant across the table. 'I saw him in Paris, two days ago.' Ignoring the look of disbelief on his face, she carried on. 'It was in a building on Rue de Condé. I am almost certain it was him. Christopher had the most unusual blond hair, pale, almost like white gold.' Her eyes became dreamy and her fingers caressed the blade of the dagger, not stopping to think that a few hours before it had killed a man.

'I went after him. The concierge told me this was where Fouché lived.'

'So that was why you were so interested in Fouché and his spies,' Saintclair exclaimed. 'I will be blunt, Madame Norton. I do not think that the man you saw could be—'

She interrupted again. 'Will you help me find him? You must know lots of people in the army and the government. You have contacts at the ministry of war and in many regiments. The man I saw is named Joseph Nallay.'

This time, Saintclair looked stunned. 'You actually found out this man's name?'

There was something akin to admiration in his eyes. He finished his ale and asked the servant for another pint. Then he raised his hand to stop Marie-Ange from talking.

'Hear me out, please. I think you must take time to consider the facts. The crew of the other English ships at Coruña looked for any missing sailors and officers. They would never have left without making sure there were no survivors.' He sighed. 'I don't quite know how to say this but don't you think you wanted this man to be your husband so much that you have convinced yourself it was him?

It *has* been six years after all. You were tired, confused.'

'No, Capitaine, I am almost sure it was him; this Nallay has his face, his eyes, his voice … he even spoke English without the trace of an accent! Something terrible must have happened to him, though. He doesn't remember me. He doesn't even remember his own name.'

Saintclair didn't answer as the servant placed a pint of ale in front of him.

'It is obvious you have turned your husband into some kind of heroic figure,' he said before lifting his pitcher to his lips. 'According to you, he was the bravest, the kindest.'

'It's because he was – he is,' she said softly.

'Why then would he work as a spy for Fouché? Assuming that he did get injured in Spain, why did he not return to England when he was fit enough to do so… unless, of course, he was a spy all along, a traitor to his country.'

'No,' Marie-Ange cried. 'Christopher would never betray his country! Very well, I will find him myself since I see you have no intention of helping me.'

'I apologise, Madame,' Saintclair mumbled, looking a little contrite. 'I should not have spoken so.'

She picked the knife up from the table and put it in her reticule before standing up.

'No, you should not have. Goodnight, Capitaine.'

Saintclair stood up, bowed his head slightly then took his pint and went to sit near the fire. She turned round from the doorway and saw him gazing into the flames, his legs stretched in front of him and crossed at the ankles.

Once upstairs, she locked the bedroom door behind her and leant against it. She was still reeling from what Saintclair had said. Yet, when her anger subsided and she could think more clearly, she had to admit the French cuirassier had a point. It didn't make sense that Christopher hadn't made his way back home. Even if it had taken months for him to recover after Coruña, he should still have come back to England. And to her.

Chapter Six

'The chateau is at the end of the track. I'll ride ahead and announce our arrival.'

Saintclair touched his heels to the horse's side and disappeared down the lane winding its way through the forest. Despite the cold, Marie-Ange pulled the carriage window all the way down and leant out, eager for her first glimpse of Beauregard. As the road forked to the left, the chateau appeared through the trees. It seemed to glow in the fading light, ghostly white and luminous like the snow that covered the ground. On an impulse, she shouted to the driver to stop.

'I'll walk from here,' she declared, jumping down.

Gathering the folds of her cloak, she started down the snowy track towards the iron gates marking the entrance of the estate. The forest gave way to a rolling park with a large pond in the middle, its waters still, dark, and slimy, with dead lily pads and broken reeds covering its surface.

She faced the chateau. Her breath caught in her throat, her eyes welled up with tears. This was where generations of her family had been born and brought up. This was the place her mother left when she was sixteen, never to return. The home she had painted, over and over again, like a haunting dream.

Capitaine Saintclair was waiting at the front porch and turned an impatient face towards her. Of course, he must be in a hurry to deliver her to Malleval and return to Lyon, his regiment and his family. And to make sure he had repaid his gambling debt.

They were shown inside by an elderly servant. As she walked into the hall, it was like stepping into her mother's sketchbook. Nothing appeared to have changed since Catherine had painted the chateau twenty-five years before. She almost expected her mother, as a young girl, to appear from behind a door and skip alongside her in the corridor.

'Monsieur is in the library,' the servant explained before knocking on a door hidden behind a black velvet curtain.

'*Oui. Entrez*,' a voice responded.

Saintclair opened the door onto a room full of shadows that was lit only by the fire in the hearth. A man reclined on a couch. Propped on his elbow, he sucked on the tube of a strange smoking implement that made a gurgling sound as if it was filled with water. Marie-Ange stopped in the doorway and wriggled her nose at the sweet, sickening smoke floating in the room.

'What are you doing hiding in the dark, Malleval?' Saintclair said as he walked in.

The other man looked up.

'Saintclair. At last! I was expecting you yesterday.' He turned his head towards the door and gestured for Marie-Ange to enter without getting up from the sofa. '*Approchez donc, ma chère*.'

She obeyed, frowning at the unconventional and rather discourteous welcome by the relative she had travelled hundreds of miles to meet. Maybe Malleval was too injured to stand.

'Good evening, Monsieur. I am delighted to meet you.' By the light of the fire, she saw that Malleval was a very handsome man, despite being thin and pale. He had the most peculiar eyes, dark brown with a yellow centre and pupils no bigger than a pin. His lips stretched into a lazy smile.

'So am I, my dear Marie-Ange. I trust Saintclair took good care of you?' His speech was slurred.

'Yes, he did,' she answered. Somehow she didn't think he would be interested in hearing about their encounter with bandits in the forest right now.

'*Bon*. Sophie, my housekeeper, will show you to your room.' Malleval turned to Saintclair. 'You are staying the night, of course. Sophie has your usual room prepared.'

'I was hoping to get back to my regiment tonight,' Saintclair objected, although not very strongly.

Malleval waved his hand in a dismissive gesture. 'You'll go back tomorrow. I'm sure they are not expecting you in Lyon just yet.'

'Very well,' Saintclair acquiesced. 'I will stay the night.'

‘You should go out, Malleval, get some fresh air,’ he added, gesturing to the shuttered windows. ‘It cannot be good for you to stay in here and smoke this thing all the time.’

‘You are right, my friend,’ Malleval answered, ‘but it’s been a rotten few months for me, as you well know, and this is one of the few things which brings me a little peace.’ He pointed at the pipe.

‘I will see you both at eight, then.’

He reclined against the back of the sofa, took a long pull on his pipe and closed his eyes. So that was it. She had crossed the English Channel and most of France at his request, braved highwaymen and rowdy soldiers, suffered discomfort and Capitaine Saintclair’s short temper and arrogant manners, and she was being dismissed after a five-minute interview!

Saintclair sighed and took hold of Marie-Ange’s elbow to lead her out of the library.

‘I’m sure he will be in a more amenable disposition later,’ he remarked as they walked back to the hall.

‘This wasn’t the welcome I was expecting,’ she said. ‘What is he smoking? It has a very unpleasant smell.’

‘Opium.’

‘Is that not a dangerous substance? Does he take it because of his battle wound?’

Saintclair tightened his mouth. ‘Ah … yes, I believe it helps with … the pain.’

A young woman was waiting for them in the hall.

‘*Bonsoir*, Sophie. You are looking beautiful as usual.’ Saintclair kissed the back of the woman’s hand.

‘Good evening, Capitaine,’ she replied, a smile lighting her pretty face and warm, brown eyes. ‘It’s nice to see you again. You can go straight to your room, I am sure you remember the way.’ Saintclair nodded and started climbing the stairs. The young woman turned to Marie-Ange and curtsied.

‘I am Sophie, Monsieur Malleval’s housekeeper. Please follow me.’

The green silk of her fashionable gown whispered as she led the way across the hall.

'You must be exhausted after your journey,' she remarked, pausing at the foot of the stairs to tuck a loose strand of long brown hair into the bun at the nape of her neck. The light from the chandelier flashed on the large cabochon ruby set in the gold ring on her finger. Marie-Ange frowned, surprised. Not only was Sophie very young, but her dress and jewellery seemed out of keeping with her position at Beauregard.

They went up to the first floor, and then along a wide corridor.

'I hope you like your room,' Sophie said, opening a door. 'I believe it was your grandmother's.'

Marie-Ange stepped into the spacious bedroom where a welcoming fire burned in a white marble fireplace. The walls were painted white and blue and the ceiling reminded her of a summer sky scattered with wispy white clouds. Her mother had sketched the room and it, too, hadn't changed. Sophie ordered her trunk to be unpacked and a bath to be prepared in the adjoining dressing room, asked her if she needed anything else and left when Marie-Ange said she was fine.

Once alone Marie-Ange ran her fingers along the smooth marble mantelpiece, touched the perfume bottles, the cloisonné jewellery boxes, and the delicate porcelain figurines of shepherds and shepherdesses adorning the writing desk near the window. Maybe these had belonged to her grandmother, Aline. Maybe her mother had admired them too, even played with them. She lay on the blue counterpane and gazed at the intricate patterns on the ceiling. She could almost hear a long-lost voice – her mother's, laughing, talking, and singing to her. Tonight she felt her presence more strongly than she had in years. The mantel clock striking seven brought her back to reality.

After a quick bath in the now lukewarm rose-scented water, she wrapped herself in a soft towel and sat down in front of the fireplace to rub her hair dry. What she wanted more than anything else was to explore the chateau, open all the doors, look through cupboards and wardrobes for trinkets, clothes or books her mother or grandmother might have left behind. But that would have to wait.

She made her way downstairs. Saintclair and Malleval were talking in the drawing room. She heard her name mentioned and paused outside the door.

'When do you want me to take Madame Norton back to England?'

'I have no intention of letting her out of my sight just now. I have plans for her.' Malleval chuckled.

'What do you mean you have plans? I thought she was here to sign some papers regarding a bequest from your father.'

'That's what she believes, too.'

'What are you playing at, Malleval?' Saintclair sounded wary.

What did he mean indeed? She wanted to know more but she heard footsteps behind her. Someone was coming. She took a deep breath and entered the room.

Malleval was a different man this evening. Clad in a smart black suit with a crisp white shirt and an elaborate *cravate,* he walked towards her, a wide smile on his face.

'Here she is! *Chère* Marie-Ange!' He took her hand affectionately, his peculiar brown eyes searching her face.

'I trust you find your room agreeable.'

'Yes, it's beautiful,' she answered truthfully.

Malleval let go of Marie-Ange's hand to walk towards a console and pour three glasses of sherry, which he handed to his guests.

'I suspect you have many questions for me,' he said after inviting her to sit down.

She nodded. 'I do, indeed, but first I would like to know how you managed to trace me to Norton Place. I was very surprised to receive your letter at the end of November.'

In business, there was nothing better than a direct approach. That was what William Jones used to say. Malleval cocked his head to one side and sighed.

'It was not an easy task, believe me. My father started looking for your mother a long, long time ago. His agents searched all over

Germany, Belgium, Switzerland, and England without success, but he was determined not to give up. Before he passed away last summer I promised him I would keep on searching. At last, a few months ago, our men stumbled upon records of your parents' wedding – July 1791, I believe – of your christening and regrettably, of your mother's death in a church register in Plymouth … after that it was only matter of days for them to pick up your trail.'

Marie-Ange closed her eyes briefly. She had not known the date of her parents' wedding. Her suspicions regarding her birth were now confirmed. William Jones married her mother in July. She was born five months later. Would she ever find out who her real father was?

She drank a sip of sherry and carried on. 'I apologise if I sound blunt, but I am surprised at your father's generosity. After all, nothing obliged him to leave my mother a share of the Beauregard fortune. From what I heard, he was far from being caring and sentimental.'

Malleval pulled a face. '*Touché*! You are correct. My father was a harsh man indeed, but he deeply regretted some of his actions and would not rest easy until he put them to rights. He had a certain … ahem … attachment to your mother and wanted to do the right thing by her.'

He smiled and took her hand. 'There. Have I satisfied your curiosity?'

Although she wasn't convinced by his explanations, she nodded slowly.

'When can I sign the papers to release your father's bequest?' she asked, pulling her hand out of his.

Malleval chuckled again. 'You certainly do not beat about the bush, dear Marie-Ange! I have always admired the no-nonsense Anglo-Saxon approach. We will visit my notary in Lyon very soon, together with Saintclair. My notary, Maitre Bernard, needs to finalise our … how shall we call it?' He turned to Saintclair. 'Our *arrangement*.'

Saintclair looked distinctly uneasy as he glanced at Marie-Ange.

She suspected he would be even more embarrassed if he knew she was fully aware of his *arrangement* with Malleval and of his gambling debt.

'But you wrote that the papers were ready for me to sign, here at Beauregard!' She remembered Malleval's most recent letter.

He arched his eyebrows. 'Did I? I do not recall. Anyway, you will enjoy Lyon. Even though it's dull and provincial compared to Paris, it is still more exciting than the Beaujolais. Apart from hunting, there is really nothing to do here. And the neighbours are all frightful old bores.'

'Actually, there is someone I would like to meet – Hermine Marzac, my great-aunt. I believe she lives around here.'

Malleval snorted.

'The old battleaxe? Don't count on me to take you to Marzac! Hermine is a fossil from the *Ancien Régime*. She believes in the God-given superiority of the aristocracy, whereas Saintclair and I, together with the best part of the population, are nothing but dirty peasants unworthy of cleaning her boots. And, of course, she particularly hates me, seeing that my father married into her family under rather difficult circumstances.' He let out a sigh, shook his head. 'However, I can understand why you wish to meet her. After all, you and she are, I believe, the only living Beauregards left in the country.'

He stood up, impatient all of a sudden. 'I will see what is keeping Sophie. I won't be long,' he muttered before walking out.

'So what do you think of the chateau? Is it as you had imagined?' Saintclair asked when they were alone.

'It is … I feel like I've come home,' she mused wistfully. 'Or rather I feel like I have been here in dreams and I remember …'

Malleval came back to say that supper was ready, and they followed him into the dining room.

He sat at the head of the table, with Marie-Ange and Saintclair on either side and Sophie opposite him. The young woman had lost her kind smile tonight. She sniffled, held a handkerchief to her red, swollen eyes all through the meal and hardly said a word, even when Malleval praised her for the sumptuous food.

'If you are going to be miserable all evening, you might as well stay in your room,' he snapped at last. 'You know I cannot stand weeping females.'

A strangled cry escaped her and she ran out, holding the handkerchief to her mouth.

'There was no need for that,' Saintclair remarked. 'She doesn't look well.'

Malleval laughed. 'Sophie's just being unreasonable. What is it with women? Whatever you do, you can never please them.' He cut a large piece of cake and poured cream all over it before stabbing his fork into it.

He seemed a volatile character. He drank large quantities of red wine and alternated between indolence, anger, and good humour. When a maid brought a basket of fruit and a platter of cheese at the end of the meal, he leant over and wrapped his arm around her waist before whispering something in her ear. The girl giggled and swayed her hips as she walked out, casting him a provocative glance over her shoulder.

'You will have to come hunting here again when I am better,' he told Saintclair. 'Remember the great times we used to have? What fun! What was the name of the dark beauty who accompanied you sometimes?'

Saintclair opened his mouth to reply but Malleval raised his hand.

'Wait, I remember. Her name was Caroline, was it not? You too seemed to get along very well … '

Marie-Ange looked down at her plate and tightened her lips. So Caroline Dupin and Capitaine Saintclair were lovers, and had been for some time. For some unknown reason, it annoyed her.

'Have you done much hunting this winter?' Saintclair asked.

'No. I haven't been up to much,' Malleval replied. 'But it's all about to change, thanks to Marie-Ange here.'

She looked up, surprised.

'Yes, my dear,' Malleval said cheerfully. 'You are going to make everything wonderful again.'

'I don't understand.'

Malleval drained his glass of wine and threw his napkin onto the table.

'Come with me, I want to show you something.'

He took them to the library, a lot more welcoming tonight thanks to numerous candelabras giving off a warm, bright light and a fire burning high in the hearth. Malleval's opium-smoking contraption had been removed, but the sickening smell lingered.

'Take a look at this.' Malleval gestured for Marie-Ange to join him in front of a painting, the portrait of a man.

'Count Saint-Germain,' he announced. 'The mysterious, legendary, elusive, Count Saint-Germain.'

'My mother's godfather?' She stepped closer to the painting, curious.

The painting depicted a man of average height wearing a plain dark grey suit. He had intelligent brown eyes and a kind smile, and he held a roll of parchment and a gold cross encrusted with precious gems which seemed clipped onto some kind of glass phial. Marie-Ange stepped closer and repressed a cry of surprise. Saint-Germain wore a golden locket that looked identical to one of her mother's – the only piece of jewellery she had inherited from her.

'I can't read the date,' she remarked, pointing to the bottom of the painting.

'This was painted in 1783,' Malleval replied. 'One year later Saint-Germain supposedly died at the court of the Grand Duke of Holstein in Denmark.'

She turned to him. 'Supposedly?'

He fixed his intense brown eyes on her. 'Saint-Germain did not die.'

'Come on, Malleval!' Saintclair interrupted. 'You cannot believe the tales about the man being immortal! I always thought it was a shame that legends surrounding Saint-Germain overshadowed his achievements as a statesman and diplomat, not to mention a painter and musician. All people ever remember are these silly stories about him being a Rosicrucian, an alchemist able to turn copper coins into gold, melt small diamonds to produce larger ones and, of course, being immortal.'

Marie-Ange gazed at the portrait again. Her father had never mentioned alchemy, let alone immortality.

'Saint-Germain was – and still is – a mystery,' Malleval carried on. 'He held everyone under his spell. King Louis XV was so taken by him he sent him on missions all over Europe. He valued his advice on all matters, especially occult sciences. Even a hardened sceptic like Voltaire famously said of him, and I quote, "Count Saint-German is a man who was never born, who will never die, and who knows everything."'

Saintclair burst out laughing. 'Well, if you believe that, you'll believe anything. The man had great talents – I grant you that – especially for pulling the wool over people's eyes when it suited him.'

'What is he holding?' Marie-Ange pointed to the cross.

'It is called *La Croix de Vie*,' Malleval answered slowly. 'Like the *Crux Vaticana* which holds pieces of the True Cross, it contains a relic. A most wonderful relic.'

'That piece of white cloth here in the phial?' She pointed to the base of the Cross.

Malleval nodded. 'A long time ago, documents came into my family's possession relating to the Cross.'

He walked to a glass cabinet displaying ancient manuscripts and gestured for Marie-Ange to join him.

'Have you ever heard of Polycarpe de la Rivière?' he asked. 'He was a prior and a famous scholar back in the seventeenth century. He discovered these documents relating to the Cross.' He pointed to the manuscripts in the cabinet. 'They are coded documents written by the Knights Templar themselves, as far back as the 1100s, when they were keepers of the Cross.'

Marie-Ange leant forward to examine the thick, yellow parchments and frowned. She had seen such symbols before, on papers her father had left on his desk, but why would William Jones have documents written in the Templar code in his possession? He was a lawyer, not a historian.

‘As you can see, the scroll Saint-Germain holds is written in the same code.’ Malleval pointed to the portrait. ‘These parchments relate the story of the Cross of Life and its extraordinary power.’

Saintclair raked his hair with his fingers and sighed. ‘What power are we talking about now?’ he asked, faintly amused. ‘The faculty to change metal into gold or make a man invisible?’

Malleval’s eyes shone with excitement. ‘The power to give eternal life.’

‘You need to ask your physician for a draught to clear your head. You’re not making any sense!’ Saintclair paused. ‘Anyway, you said the Cross belonged to the Knights Templar … how then did it come to France and into the possession of Saint-Germain?’

‘After the fall of St Jean d’Acre in 1291, the body of Guillaume de Beaujeu, the Grand Master Templar, was taken to Paris and buried in the Temple’s chapel along with the Order’s most precious objects and documents,’ Malleval explained. ‘Among these was the Cross of Life. When the Order was disbanded by Philippe le Bel in 1307, Jacques Molay – the last Grand Master – asked Guichard de Beaujeu to rescue the treasure hidden in his ancestor’s tomb. Guillaume’s body, along with the treasure, was reburied in the family chateau in Arginy, not far from here.’

‘So the Cross of Life was hidden in Arginy when the Templar Order was dissolved?’

Malleval nodded. ‘Yes, until Anne de Beaujeu searched the crypt of the chateau and discovered it in the fifteenth century. I don’t know how Saint-Germain came to have it in his possession, but it was the Cross and its relic which made him immortal.’

‘This relic … could it be the bones of a saint?’ Marie-Ange asked.

Malleval smiled. ‘Oh no, my dear, it’s much better than that.’

‘In Saint-Germain’s portrait, it looks like a piece of white cloth in the glass phial,’ she remarked.

‘Never mind that for now … Saint-Germain hid the Cross before he faked his death.’ Malleval grabbed Marie-Ange’s wrists and pulled her towards him. ‘Your mother knew where it was and she told you before she died, didn’t she? You must tell me where it is.

You must!' He gripped more tightly and shook her. The candlelight cast strange shadows on his face, the yellowy centre of his irises glowed and made him look deranged.

'Malleval! What on earth are you doing?' Saintclair roared as he moved forward with his fists clenched.

'Calm down, Saintclair.' Malleval let go of Marie-Ange, who stumbled backwards. 'I have no intention of hurting my guest. She is far too precious to me.'

Marie-Ange quickly stepped towards the door.

'I will go up to my room now, Monsieur.' she said. 'I don't have the faintest idea what you're talking about, and I really can't help you.' Her head high, she turned and walked out.

'Oh, but you can, my dear, and you will,' she heard Malleval say.

The man was a lunatic – a dangerous lunatic! As she walked out of the library she heard Saintclair call after her. She ignored him. She wanted to be alone. He caught up with her on the stairs.

'Did he hurt you?' he asked.

'A little.' She rubbed her wrist where a red mark had appeared. 'Why didn't you warn me that he was crazy?'

He shook his head. 'I've never heard him talk about all this nonsense before. Do you still want to stay until you have signed the papers? If you don't, I suppose I will have to take you back to England, but I will require a couple of days to make arrangements.'

For a moment, she thought he looked genuinely concerned. Then she shook her head. Who was she kidding? He was only worried because if she left Beauregard now, Malleval would demand the repayment of his gambling debt and get his hands on his family house.

She tilted her chin to look at him. 'Don't worry about me, Capitaine. I can take care of myself.'

She left him on the staircase and went back to her room, but once alone the reality of her predicament hit her. She was on her own, at the mercy of a madman. The Cross of Life, the Knights Templar, a crypt in a nearby castle, her mother's godfather being immortal ... how could anyone in their right mind believe in immortality?

She remembered her mother's locket. Pulling it out of her velvet jewellery pouch, she held it in the candlelight. It was solid gold, its cover embossed with the design of a five-petal rose and with a heart at its centre it looked identical to the one Saint-Germain wore in the painting. Thoughtful, she slipped it back inside the pouch.

What was she going to do? Was it safer to play along with Malleval and pretend she knew about this Cross, at least until he gave her the money he had promised? Or should she tell him the truth, namely that she had no idea what he was talking about?

A couple of hours later, she still hadn't reached a decision. By then, the fire had died down, and the chateau sounded quiet, as if it were asleep. She disrobed, put her nightdress on, and unpinned her hair, which tumbled down her shoulders. She took her time brushing it, feeling the knot of anxiety at the pit of her stomach slowly loosen with each long, soothing stroke.

The scream came from the rooms above and echoed in the chateau. She dropped the brush onto the floor.

Chapter Seven

Marie-Ange held her breath but there was only silence. She tiptoed to the door and opened it just as Saintclair was walking down the dark corridor, a candle in his hand. His shirt hung open at the chest, as if he too had been ready to go to bed. She stepped out of her room to meet him, far too alarmed to notice the cold or the fact she was only wearing her nightdress.

'What was that, Capitaine?' she whispered.

He gave her a quick glance then gestured to the staircase.

'It came from upstairs. Malleval must be up to his old tricks.'

'What old tricks?'

He tightened his mouth. 'Stay here. I will go up and take a look. I'm sure there's nothing to worry about.'

'How can you say that? Whoever screamed sounded in terrible pain.'

'I said, stay here,' he instructed once again.

Just as he started going up the staircase, another high-pitched cry resounded in the chateau. Marie-Ange gasped and put her hand to her heart. There was no way she was staying down here on her own. She raced up the stairs after Saintclair.

He turned to look at her, a deep frown creasing his forehead.

'What do you think you're doing? This is no place for you. Go back down.'

'Why? What is he doing in there?'

He let out an impatient sigh.

'If you cannot do as you're told, stay behind me. But I'm warning you, you won't like it,' he grunted before knocking on a double door at the end of the second floor corridor.

'Malleval! It's Saintclair. Is everything all right?'

There were a few seconds of silence, followed by sounds of a man and woman laughing inside the room. Then the door opened.

'Saintclair. Have you come to join us?' Malleval exclaimed.

Marie-Ange peeped from behind Saintclair but recoiled at the man's flushed face and feverish eyes. He was stripped to the waist and held a short leather whip. A strange tattoo of a snake biting its tail adorned his chest.

'You're here too, *chérie*,' he added when he saw her. 'Do come in.' He opened the door wider.

'Who is it?' a woman called.

She was lying naked on black silk sheets on the massive bed at the centre of the room. Rolling over, she stood up and walked unsteadily towards them, kicking several empty bottles of wine out of the way with her bare foot. Marie-Ange recognised the maid who had served them at supper. She gripped Saintclair's arm and opened her mouth in shock. Red marks marred the maid's milky white thighs and buttocks. 'I'm sorry if I woke you, but Monsieur likes it when I scream.' The girl threw her head back and let out a drunken laugh.

Saintclair sighed. 'Come on, Madame Norton, everything's fine. Let's go back down.'

Marie-Ange glared at him. 'But … are you not going to do anything?'

The officer glared back. 'Do what exactly?'

Malleval placed a hand on the woman's waist, another on her shoulder. The girl laughed again and snuggled close to him, seemingly oblivious to the fact she was naked in front of strangers. 'See?' he told Marie-Ange. 'There's nothing to worry about.'

Disgusted, Marie-Ange turned away. She walked as fast as her shaky legs allowed but the girl's loud, cajoling voice pursued her down the corridor.

'Your friend here is a true Hussar, Capitaine,' she was saying. 'But I'm ready to wager you're not bad in bed yourself. Maybe you could let me find out?'

Saintclair muttered something and Malleval's bedroom door slammed shut. He caught up with her in a few long strides and glanced her way.

'Sorry about that,' he said, his tone casual. 'I did tell you to stay in your room.'

'So you knew what was going on up there?' She breathed out, incensed.

She didn't give him time to reply. Her cheeks burned with anger, her heart beat fast, too fast. 'Of course you knew! You must have had your fair share of that kind of … entertainment! After all, Malleval did talk at supper about the wild nights you two used to have during the hunting season.'

She ran down the stairs but wasn't fast enough. He caught up with her outside her door, put his hand on her arm, and spun her round to face him.

'For the record,' he said, his eyes narrowed in anger, his grip a tight vice on her arm, 'I have never treated, and will never treat, a woman like that. I can assure you that I know of more pleasurable ways to make a woman scream.'

She let out a gasp. How conceited of him! But why was she surprised? He was the man who claimed all women were helpless in his arms. He was the man who believed women were too shallow, too inconsistent to experience honest, true and long-lasting feelings.

They faced each other in the dark corridor, the candle throwing gigantic shadows onto the walls. He looked down at her, his eyes skimming her body from her tousled hair, which covered her shoulders and breasts, down to her bare feet, then back up again. Her lips parted and she breathed faster, acutely aware of the heat from his body, of the burning touch of his fingers on her arm. Her whole body tingled, tightened. She should avert her eyes, turn away. Yet, like a mouse mesmerised by a feline, she stood petrified and unable to move.

He spoke in a very low voice, breaking the spell. 'Get back in your room and lock your door. I will take you to your aunt Marzac in the morning.' Without another word, he opened her door and left her there.

Snapping out of her trance, she did as he ordered. She wrapped herself in Christopher's dressing gown and sat in front of the dying fire. Never could she have imagined her journey to Beauregard would turn out this way.

If only she didn't need that bequest so badly, she could leave the following morning. If only Norton Place and Robert weren't relying on her. If only she wasn't so desperate to meet Fouché and ask him about Joseph Nallay …

It was very late when she finally slid Christopher's dagger under her pillow and got into bed.

The cooing of doves on her windowsill woke her the following morning. She turned in the soft feather bed, opened her eyes and yawned. Her few hours of fitful sleep had left her with a headache and a heavy, anxious feeling in the pit of her stomach, made worse at the thought of having to face Saintclair and Malleval.

A maid came in to pull the curtains open onto a grey morning and help her get ready. Marie-Ange chose her best dress – a dark blue silk gown with white lace at the collar and at the wrists. She wanted to make a good impression on her great-aunt Hermine today.

She ventured downstairs, hoping Malleval was still in his room sleeping off the excesses of the night and found Saintclair in the dining room, eating eggs and ham and drinking black coffee. Without a word, he stood and pulled a chair out for her. A servant girl brought her plate and some coffee.

'I have arranged to borrow Malleval's carriage and a driver to go to Marzac this morning,' Saintclair said when the girl had left. 'Then I am going back to Lyon.'

She felt a sudden, incomprehensible stab of sadness at the news. She might not like his arrogance and resent what he implied about Christopher, but he was the only man she trusted in this place. When he left, she would be alone with Uxeloup Malleval …

'Will you be at the ball tomorrow night in Lyon?' she enquired.

'I suppose so,' he answered with a shrug. 'I don't care much for these events. Too much prancing around for my taste, but my superiors expect me to put in an appearance. Thankfully the Palace Saint-Pierre is across the square from the barracks, so I can leave when I have had enough.' He hesitated, cleared his throat. 'Madame Norton, about last night …'

'I do not wish to be reminded of last night and the awful things which went on upstairs,' she retorted primly, shuddering at the memories of Malleval's crazed eyes, his fingers gripping the handle of the whip and the servant's white body covered with bloody marks. She was annoyed to see Saintclair smile.

'I'm not talking about Malleval's bedroom antics but about the story he told us in the library about the Cross of Life. What do you intend to do about it?'

Should she tell him of her plan? Somehow she didn't think he would betray her to Malleval. She leant over the table and answered in a hushed voice.

'I never heard about it before yesterday. I don't know much about Saint-Germain either. My mother died when I was little and my … father …' She swallowed hard. William Jones would always be her father since he was the man who had brought her up. 'He never talked much about Beauregard. I can't give Malleval what he wants. However, he strikes me as dangerously obsessed. It is in my best interest to pretend I can help him find this Cross. Until he has released my inheritance, that is. Then I shall return to England and never see him again.'

He raised his eyebrows and laughed. 'I admire your bluff, Madame. You would make an ideal partner at cards.' Serious again, he considered her for a few seconds. 'You're doing the right thing, of course. Go along with him for as long as you can.'

They left for Marzac after breakfast.

Located in a wine-growing valley north of Beaujeu, Marzac was an impressive medieval castle with round turrets, high walls, and a deep moat complete with drawbridge. As the carriage drove through the gates, Marie-Ange's nervous fingers fiddled with the ties of her cloak, adjusted the ribbon of her bonnet under her chin. Hermine was the first member of her mother's family she would meet. Malleval called her a 'battleaxe', a woman stuck in the *old regime*. Would she be happy, tearful or indifferent to see her? Maybe she wouldn't care at all for her long-lost great-niece.

The carriage stopped in front of the main entrance and Saintclair jumped down from his horse to open the door. He held her hand tightly as she stepped down, glanced around, and whistled between his teeth. 'It's quite a place.'

They climbed the imposing stone porch and found an elderly servant waiting at the top of the steps. As she came nearer, the man let out a loud gasp, and his face drained of all colour, and when she told him her name, she was sure she saw tears shine in his eyes. He coughed to clear his throat and asked them to follow him into a parlour. Soon after, a small woman with light grey hair walked in, leaning heavily on a walking stick with a carved silver pommel.

'So you are Catherine's daughter,' she declared without preamble.

Marie-Ange curtsied. 'Yes, Madame.'

The woman turned to Saintclair. 'And you are?'

Saintclair bowed. 'Capitaine Saintclair, of the Second Regiment of Cuirassiers. I escorted Madame Norton from England.'

'A cavalry officer?' Her tone was disapproving. 'Well, I suppose she needed a man for the journey.' She turned to Marie-Ange again. 'Where is your mother?'

Her cold, abrupt voice made Marie-Ange wince. 'She died a long time ago, Madame.'

'Oh …' The old woman's face seemed to crumple. She closed her pale grey eyes a few seconds. 'I am sorry, child. I must have sounded cold-hearted just then. The thing is, your arrival took me by surprise. I had no idea you existed. Last time I heard about Catherine was when she sent me a note to let me know she had reached England safely. That was in July of 1791.'

'I wasn't aware of your existence either, Madame, until a chance encounter in Paris with a former friend of my mother's a few days ago.'

Hermine Marzac's face softened, and she raised a hand to touch Marie-Ange's cheek.

'You have her hair and her smile, definitely. You must tell me all about her and yourself. But before …'

She turned to Saintclair. 'You may wait in the kitchen. I am sure my servants will put up with you for a little while. They might even give you a bowl of soup if you ask nicely. But beware! I do not tolerate gambling or funny goings-on with my girls.'

Saintclair's face grew pale under the insult.

'Capitaine Saintclair has been a most valued travel companion,' Marie-Ange said quickly, embarrassed by the way her aunt had dismissed him. 'I would never have reached Beauregard safely without him.'

Saintclair walked to her. 'It was my pleasure, Madame, but now is the time for me to take my leave. As I said before, I must return to Lyon.'

She gave him her hand and he brushed it lightly with his lips. She was surprised once again at the sadness the thought of his leaving awoke in her.

He bowed stiffly to Hermine Marzac. 'Madame.' And he left.

The old lady tapped her stick onto the floor.

'These cavalry officers, so many of them are lowly born ruffians. Napoleon has a lot to answer for by allowing thugs and rabble to the highest ranks of our once great army. Fortunately, our royal family is back in charge. Even if they cannot undo all the harm that was inflicted on our poor country, they will rid us of the riff-raff.'

She sighed. 'Now, I want to know everything about you and your poor mother.' She slid her arm under Marie-Ange's and the two women walked to a small, cosy drawing room.

Marie-Ange spent the next hour answering her great-aunt's questions about her parents, about Christopher, and her life at Norton Place. She said nothing however about her suspicions that William Jones wasn't her real father or about her brief encounter with the man she believed to be Christopher.

After lunch, it was her turn to question Hermine about her family's past.

'Would you mind telling me about the winter of 1791, when my grandfather Philippe was arrested?'

Hermine heaved a shaky breath.

'Even after all this time, I cannot forgive or forget what happened. My brother didn't deserve to be executed. He was a good man who always tried to improve the estate and the life of his people.'

The elderly woman stood up and pulled a cord next to the fireplace. 'I will let you read Aline's letters. I still have most of them, and they will answer your questions better than I.'

A short while later Hermine's servant walked in and gave her a bundle of papers.

'Thank you, Pierre.'

She handed the letters to Marie-Ange before walking to the door. 'Take your time, child.'

Marie-Ange untied the blue ribbon that kept the letters together and looked through the papers. The letters spanned several years and started with the announcement of her mother's birth.

Paris, 28th July 1775

Dear Hermine,

Philippe and I are delighted to let you know of the birth of our daughter, Catherine Marie-Ange, who was born ten days ago. She was christened at the Saint-Louis Church yesterday. Our friend, Saint-Germain, kindly agreed to be her godfather and my aunt, Abbess Antoinette Fleury, is Catherine's godmother.

I hope you and dear Armand are keeping well and I am looking forward to seeing you again. Philippe sends his regards.

With love,

Aline R. Beauregard

The next letter had been written some years later.

Beauregard, 4th January 1783

Dear Hermine,

I hope that my letter finds you in good health and that you are enjoying your stay at Versailles. I am missing you dearly.

Count Saint-Germain paid us a long visit at Christmas. He seems rather taken by his god-daughter. He gave Catherine a wonderful gift: a gold locket, which had belonged to our cousins, the Beaujeus. He also gave her an art book as he said she had a talent for drawing and painting.

Saint-Germain said Beauregard wouldn't be complete without a dovecote and promised to send a team of craftsmen – from Malta of all places! – to build one in the rose garden. Doves at Beauregard! How wonderful!

Yours respectfully,

Aline R. Beauregard

So her locket had indeed belonged to Saint-Germain, and to the wealthy and powerful Beaujeus before him, the family who according to Malleval had hidden the mysterious Cross of Life at Arginy.

Aline's next letter was dated a few months later.

Beauregard, 10th May 1783

Dear Sister,

The dovecote is finished at last. Philippe had two dozen pairs of doves sent from a breeder in Belleville. Our rose garden now echoes with the birds' cooing and I do not tire of listening to them and watching them fly around the park.

Saint-Germain's Maltese builders were most intriguing. There were five of them, including an interpreter, a charming young man who introduced himself as Baldassare dei Conti. The servants were rather terrified of them, but Catherine wasn't in the slightest impressed. In fact, she befriended the interpreter and they spent many hours together, although I am not sure what they found to talk about!

The men set up camp in the park. It was most peculiar; a fire burnt at the entrance of their tent and a guard kept watch at all times. But they worked wonders and I never saw a more beautiful dovecote.

I remain as always,

Yours,

Aline R. Beauregard

The following letter reminded her of Malleval.

Beauregard, 30thMarch 1784

Dearest Hermine,

We were all deeply aggrieved to learn that our dear friend, Saint-Germain, died of pneumonia at the court of the Grand Duke of Holstein in Denmark last month. I cannot bring myself to believe this is real. He always had such a strong constitution, I never saw him ill or even unwell once in all the years I have known him. Poor Saint-Germain ... he died abroad, without his closest friends and family. The shocking news was that there was no funeral mass held for him and he now rests in an unmarked grave somewhere in a far off Danish cemetery.

Yours,

Aline R. Beauregard

Thoughtful, Marie-Ange put the letter down. No wonder Malleval, and others, believed Saint-Germain hadn't really died. She read through several more letters spanning the next few years. Catherine, her mother, was growing into a vivacious young girl. With the passing of time, Aline seemed even more proud of her husband as Philippe became involved in social reforms on the Beauregard estate. He represented the local gentry during the *États-Généraux*, which opened in Versailles in May 1789, charged with reforming the country's finances and introducing social reforms, but he returned home in July, only days before the turmoil of the revolution. Aline and Philippe spent the following year at Beauregard. The relative tranquillity of their lives came to an end in October 1790. By then, Hermine and her husband, Armand Marzac, had fled to Neuchatel in Switzerland, and this was where Aline now wrote to them.

Beauregard, 20th October 1790

My dear Hermine,

I am concerned for our safety. Despite the terrible unrest that has engulfed the whole country this last year, we were fortunate to live a relatively sheltered existence here. The reforms Philippe started years ago won him the trust and respect of the municipal committee.

However things have changed. Moderate members of the committee were replaced recently by hateful and vindictive men. The new public prosecutor, Edmond Malleval, visited Beauregard last week, demanding a tour of the chateau and the estate.

I was not present that day but Philippe reported that Malleval was particularly critical of his reforms. There was a strange incident, too. Malleval was so taken by the portrait of our dear Saint-Germain in the library he made an offer to buy it there and then. He was furious when Philippe refused.

He has now summoned Philippe to appear in front of the Tribunal at Beaujeu for treason. Philippe assures me his allies will vouch for him, but I fear I cannot share his optimism. I heard that Malleval is a close associate of Joseph Fouché and Jean-Marie Collot d'Herbois, and that, like them, he is an ambitious, bloodthirsty brute. I sent Catherine to her godmother at Salles for her safety. I will write to you as soon as I can.

Yours,

Aline R. Beauregard

Marie-Ange stared into the flames. She knew what happened next.

Beaujeu, 26th October 1790

Dear Sister,

I have terrible news. Philippe's trial took place yesterday. He was found guilty of being an enemy of the National Assembly and sent to jail, awaiting execution. He was not even allowed to speak in his own defence. I am staying at the Jument Blanche Inn for now. I fear I will be here for some time as I cannot bear to go back to Beauregard without my husband.

Yours,

Aline R. Beauregard

Beaujeu, 28th October 1790

Dear Hermine,

I met with the Devil today. Edmond Malleval summoned me this morning and made me the most objectionable proposition.

He promised to spare Philippe if I became his mistress. He has given me until tomorrow night to make my decision. Should I refuse him, he will have Philippe executed at the end of the week. However, I have no guarantee he will spare my husband if I give in. When this letter reaches you, I will have made my decision. Whatever it is, I will have lost my heart or my soul, or both.

Please pray for me.

Yours,

Aline R. Beauregard

Marie-Ange dropped the letter onto her lap. So that was how Edmond formed his relationship with Aline. He blackmailed her.

Beaujeu, 30th October 1790

Dear Hermine,

I am lost and broken and have no honour left. Even if Philippe is indeed spared, I will never be able to look into his eyes again. Citizen Malleval is a brutal and lecherous man. Everything in him repulses me. He has forbidden me to leave Beaujeu and has taken away my certificate of citizenship and my travel permit.

Yours,

Aline

Marie-Ange noticed her grandmother had dropped her husband's name. Did she feel she no longer deserved to be called a Beauregard? Yet, what had she done wrong? She had sacrificed her honour in exchange for her husband's life.

Beaujeu, 17th December 1790

Dear Hermine,

Your kind words cannot soothe my broken heart, but I thank you for not giving up on me. Citizen Malleval has decided I shall reside at his Beaujeu townhouse as his official concubine. My shame is therefore public. I pray that Philippe never hears of this, or indeed my sweet Catherine at Salles.

Malleval keeps asking about Count Saint-Germain. He is fascinated by our friend and wants to know everything about him. He is particularly interested in a sacred object Saint-Germain had in his possession – the Cross depicted in his portrait – which Malleval says used to belong to the Knights Templar. He got very angry when I assured him I knew nothing about it.

Pray for me and for Philippe.

Yours,

Aline

So Edmond Malleval coveted the Cross of Life too!

Beaujeu, 20th January 1791

Dear Sister,

It was all in vain. Philippe was executed on the Place des Terreaux in Lyon. Malleval now insists that we wed as soon as possible and threatens to harm Catherine if I refuse. I fear Catherine will hate me when she learns of my union with the very man who sent her father to his death. Yet, what can I do? I must spare my daughter from the same fate as mine.

I do not care about myself any longer. I am following my own path to Hell.

Citizen Malleval has been enquiring about Saint-Germain again. For some strange reason he does not believe our friend died in Denmark ... I fear the man is mad as well as evil.

Pray for me and for the soul of my Philippe.

Yours,

Aline

When she finished reading the letter, Marie-Ange had to force herself to breathe in slowly.

Beaujeu, 31st January 1791

Dear Hermine,

The deed is done. I was married to Malleval this morning by a municipal officer. Malleval now owns the estate of Beauregard and all of Philippe's assets. He owns me and my daughter and has threatened to take Catherine away from Salles and hold her captive in a secret location until I tell him where the Cross is. He has brought a strange man to Beauregard – a physician named Karloff – to 'treat me' for memory loss. I told him it was useless since I did not forget about the Cross, I just never knew where it was in the first place.

Yours,

Aline

There were only two letters left.

Beauregard, 25th March 1791

Dear Hermine,

Malleval told me today he is keeping Catherine in his family's stronghold in the Pilat. He now believes that she is the one who holds the secret he so desperately wants. I am beyond myself with worry about my daughter. His physician, Karloff, left Beauregard after confirming that I had indeed no knowledge of the Cross of Life. He was a strange, frightening man who could control my very thoughts and my very being by staring into my eyes and talking to me with his deep, soothing voice.

I live in the hope of holding my daughter in my arms again – that is, if she ever forgives me for marrying her father's murderer. My health has been poor since I came back to Beauregard. Being here, surrounded by the memories of happier times, is breaking my heart.

Yours,

Aline

Marie-Ange read Aline's last letter with tears streaming down her face.

Beauregard, 15th April 1791

Dearest Hermine,

My life is finished. Malleval told me Catherine died of illness some days ago, although he would not tell me what ailed her. The thought of my sweet daughter alone and frightened as she lay dying is more than I can bear. I have no intention of remaining Malleval's wife a day longer. Take great care, dearest Hermine, and pray for my soul.

Yours forever,

Aline

Chapter Eight

Hermine walked back into the drawing room, leaning heavily on her walking stick.

'How did my grandmother die?' Marie-Ange asked.

'She drowned in the pond at Beauregard.' The old lady's voice quivered.

The pond with the dead lily pads floating over the dark, slimy waters. Marie-Ange shivered. Believing Catherine to be dead, her grandmother had chosen to end her life. She had nothing and no one to live for and it was all because of one man. Edmond Malleval. She clenched her fists in anger. She now understood why she was here.

'Edmond Malleval didn't search for my mother all over Europe to bestow some money from Beauregard on her,' she stated. 'No! He believed she could give him what he so desperately wanted. The Cross of Life. And now his son is asking the same thing of me.'

Her great-aunt frowned. 'He asked you about the Cross?'

'Last night. He claimed the Cross made people immortal. He even insisted Saint-Germain had lived for centuries and was still alive! It sounds as if his father passed his obsession on to him.'

She glanced at the window. The sky was darkening. 'I must get back to Beauregard.'

Her heart felt heavy at the prospect of a night in the chateau now that Saintclair had left. With him around, she didn't fear Malleval. She didn't fear anything. She shook her head. Enough of these silly thoughts! Why should she miss the presence of the arrogant, short-tempered cuirassier? She was more than capable of dealing with Malleval on her own.

The two women hugged and promised to meet again soon.

'You don't have to go back to Uxeloup Malleval,' Hermine said. 'You could stay here for a while. We could get to know each other.'

'I must go back.' She didn't want to tell her aunt about the ball in Lyon where she was hoping to meet Fouché and ask him about

Nallay. 'But I will visit you again very soon.'

Hermine nodded. 'Please do, and next time, I will tell you what I know about the Cross of Life.'

It was pitch-black when Marie-Ange arrived back at a very quiet Beauregard. She found Sophie sitting in the drawing room with some embroidery on her lap. The young housekeeper didn't look much happier than the previous evening, but at least she wasn't crying.

'Did you enjoy your visit to Marzac?' Sophie asked. 'Is your great-aunt well?'

Marie-Ange nodded. 'She is, thank you … Why is the chateau so quiet tonight and where is Monsieur Malleval?'

'He left for Lyon with some of the staff this afternoon. There were final preparations for the ball to be made. His man, Rochefort, will take you to his townhouse in the morning.'

Marie-Ange couldn't hide her relief to learn that Malleval was absent. 'Are you not coming to Lyon too?'

Sophie shook her head. 'Oh no, I never go anywhere with Uxeloup … with *Monsieur*, I mean,' she corrected hastily. She bent her head and toyed with the linen on her lap, looking forlorn. A servant girl announced supper was served and the two women made their way to the dining room. During the meal, Marie-Ange asked Sophie about herself.

'There's not much to tell.' The young woman put her hand on her throat. The large ruby she wore on her wedding finger glittered in the light of the candles. Surely no ordinary housekeeper wore such a beautiful jewel. Tonight again, Sophie wore an exquisite gown, this time of cream and pink silk. Perhaps the relationship between Sophie and Malleval was more complex than the one between a master and his housekeeper? Perhaps she was *more* than an employee …

Sophie confided she had started as a housemaid seven years before, as a girl of sixteen. 'I became Beauregard's housekeeper a few months ago, after Monsieur Edmond passed away. Monsieur Uxeloup was always very good to me.' She smiled and looked at her ring.

'Tell me, what was Monsieur Edmond like?'

Sophie's face contracted in a grimace. 'He was a hard master. Nothing ever pleased him.' She lowered her voice. 'He was frightening too, especially when he became obsessed with the dark arts.'

'The dark arts?'

Sophie looked around her uneasily. 'Wizardry and witchcraft … all kinds of strange men and women visited here, but out of them all, Karloff was always the worst.' She raised the glass to her pale lips and drank the red wine in one gulp.

Marie-Ange stared at her. He was the man her grandmother mentioned in her letter. 'Who is he?'

'Monsieur Karloff is a physician,' Sophie answered. 'If you ask me, he's really a wizard. He can make you do things just by looking into your eyes. He can put thoughts in your mind or make you fall asleep.' She shivered.

'Is Monsieur Uxeloup involved with him too?'

Sophie nodded. 'Oh yes, Karloff is his physician, just like he was Monsieur Edmond's and he visits quite often. Actually, I heard him talk to Monsieur about you.'

'Really?' Marie-Ange put her knife and fork down, dread creeping through her.

'It was after Monsieur Edmond's death.' Sophie lowered her voice. 'When the village priest came to talk about arrangements for the funeral, Karloff shooed him away and ordered that Monsieur's body be put in an iron cask and taken away to his village in the mountains. I heard him tell Monsieur Uxeloup that they would keep him there, in the vaults of their fortress, until the "Beauregard girl" was found.' She looked at Marie-Ange nervously. 'That's you, isn't it?'

Marie-Ange pushed her plate away, her appetite fleeing as fear formed a hard ball in her stomach.

'You mean to say Edmond Malleval was not buried and his body is still …'

Sophie nodded and bit her lip. 'I'm sorry, I shouldn't have said anything. I didn't mean to frighten you, just to warn you about Monsieur Karloff. He may be at the ball in Lyon tomorrow.'

'The ball … Fouché will be there too, will he not? Does he ever come to Beauregard?'

Sophie nodded. 'Sometimes, for hunting, although he hasn't been here since Monsieur Edmond died. I don't like him much.'

Her face brightened up. 'Anyway, you'll have nothing to worry about. Capitaine Saintclair will look after you. He may be a little wild but he's a man of honour.'

Marie-Ange tightened her lips. Capitaine Saintclair's notion of honour was probably very different from hers.

'About tomorrow night,' Sophie said, 'would you like me to ask the chambermaid to press your ball gown?'

'I have no ball gown.' Marie-Ange pointed to her dark blue silk dress. 'This is my best dress and it will have to do.'

'Why don't you wear one of your grandmother's gowns? They are still in a closet in the dressing room. I am sure we could find one to fit you.'

Curious, Marie-Ange followed Sophie up the stairs.

There were rows and rows of dresses wrapped in silk covers. Sophie pulled several out and shook her head.

'What a shame, this one was eaten by moths. The light green one wouldn't suit your colouring at all. And that white gown has yellowed … ah, this is more like it!' She held out a silk and gauze azure-blue gown. Its bodice was covered with embroidered rosebuds, and a white lace border ran along the low-cut *décolleté* and cap sleeves.

Marie-Ange touched the delicate fabric. 'It is ravishing but look, there's a tear in the skirt.'

'That's not a problem,' Sophie declared. 'A cousin of mine is a seamstress in Macon. I shall have her fetched this instant.'

'Oh no, do not drag a poor woman out of her home in the middle of the night on my account,' Marie-Ange protested.

'I will make sure she gets adequately rewarded. Monsieur

Uxeloup leaves me in charge of the household expenses.' She gave Marie-Ange a knowing smile and leant towards her to confide excitedly. 'I know I shouldn't speak about it just yet but …'

She showed Marie-Ange her ruby ring. 'Uxeloup gave it to me last month. He said we would get married soon, when his health improves.'

Without giving Marie-Ange time to absorb her news, she pointed to the dress. 'You should try it on, to see if anything else needs altering.'

The dress fitted perfectly. Its delicate fabric hugged Marie-Ange's body, emphasizing her high, slim waist and round shoulders. The colour was almost identical to the aquamarine shade of her eyes.

'Isn't it a little too revealing?' Marie-Ange frowned and tried to pull the dress up to cover the top of her breasts.

'Not at all. It looks as if it was made for you,' Sophie said, dreamily.

Was she thinking of a day when she too would wear a ball gown, maybe even a wedding gown? Marie-Ange doubted the event would ever take place. Malleval didn't strike her as the type of man who had any scruples discarding girls after bedding them. Having said that, he might have feelings for the girl, otherwise why would he bother giving Sophie an engagement ring?

In any case, it was obvious Sophie loved him, although Marie-Ange couldn't understand what she saw in him.

Sophie's cousin, a plump, middle-aged woman with a ready smile, arrived within the hour, and when she handed the dress back to Marie-Ange, it looked as good as new.

Eager to set off for Lyon, Marie-Ange went out early the following morning to find Malleval's carriage already stationed in front of the chateau. She paused a moment at the top of the front porch steps. The morning was still and silent. Ribbons of mist curled around the treetops and hovered above the lawn in the park, lending Beauregard a dreamy, almost ghostly appearance.

A huge man dressed in a long furry brown coat appeared from behind Malleval's carriage and charged like a bear towards her. Marie-Ange recoiled, a cry of alarm escaping from her lips. The man's face was covered with a bushy beard, his small, beady black eyes shone under thick eyebrows. It was hard to see where his brown fur hat and shag pile coat started and his long, grizzly hair and beard stopped.

'Are these yours?' he grunted, pointing to her bags.

He must be Rochefort, Malleval's coachman. She nodded and he lifted her travel bags and threw them onto the rack on top of the carriage as if they were no heavier than feather pillows.

'Get in, M'ame,' he said then, flinging the door open for her. 'If we set off now, we'll be in Lyon before dinner.'

And with another grunt he climbed onto the driver's box.

The roads were busy. From time to time Rochefort let out a raucous shout, and even though Marie-Ange didn't always understand what he was saying, it seemed to have some effect in persuading people to move aside and let them through.

Malleval's townhouse was on Isle Barbe, an island on the River Saône, one of Lyon's two rivers. The coach proceeded onto a narrow wooden bridge, and then drove through a village square lined with lime trees, their branches now winter-bare. At the end of the lane, Rochefort waited for a pair of imposing cast iron gates to be opened. They were adorned with an intricate medallion bearing Malleval's coat of arms – the letters *A* and *M* intertwined. The carriage rumbled into a cobblestone courtyard and Marie-Ange's heart sank when the tall gates closed behind them, like prison doors.

Malleval's house occupied the tip of the island in the middle of the Saône, and as she stood on the balcony Marie-Ange couldn't help but feel it was like standing on the deck of a ship, cut off from the world.

Shivering with cold, she walked back into her room, sank onto the chaise longue near the fireplace, and glanced nervously at the mantel clock. Time had dragged since she arrived, or was it because she felt anxious about the ball, about seeing Malleval again and meeting Fouché?

At last a maid arrived to help her dress for the evening.

'What a beautiful shade of blue,' the girl marvelled once she'd slipped the gown over Marie-Ange's head and settled it around her hips. The maid brushed her hair until it shone like gold, parted it in the middle and twisted each side into a coil secured with pins, leaving strands of golden curls to fall around her face. Marie-Ange clasped her mother's gold locket around her neck. She didn't often wear it but tonight the feel of it against her skin was reassuring. To finish, she slid her arms into long white gloves the maid held for her.

When she stood in front of the full-length mirror, Marie-Ange couldn't repress a gasp of astonishment. It was the first time in six years that she'd worn anything other than a plain, long-sleeved, dark coloured gown and she could hardly recognise herself. Tentatively, her hands skimmed over the bodice of the dress, smoothed over the folds of the skirt before touching the curls framing her face.

'You look beautiful, Madame,' the girl exclaimed with a beaming smile on her face, before leading her down the stairs into the lobby where Rochefort was waiting to take her to the ball.

Capitaine Saintclair had explained that Palais Saint Pierre stood in the heart of the city. A former Benedictine convent, it had been closed down at the Revolution and was now the seat of the newly established chamber of commerce.

The Palais did look like a monastery with its austere, grey stone walls and large gates opening onto a cloister garden. Rochefort stopped the carriage outside the gates, helped her step down and said he would be waiting for her. Alone and slightly intimidated, Marie-Ange followed the crowd of gentlemen in black evening suits, ladies in ball gowns, and officers in various regimental uniforms, up to the first floor.

The ballroom was ablaze with light. Crystal chandeliers glittered and were reflected in massive gilded mirrors on the walls. Couples danced to the music of a small string orchestra while onlookers chattered and enjoyed a glass of champagne. She stepped into the room and glanced around, unsure of what to do next.

'Madame Norton!'

Her heart skipped a beat and she could only stare as Saintclair strode through the crowd towards her, magnificent in his parade uniform. The imperial blue jacket ornamented with bright red épaulettes and his crisp white shirt underneath made a stark contrast with his dark hair and tanned complexion. White breeches tucked into Hessian boots fitted his muscular legs snugly and a sword hanging on his side glinted under the lights.

He took his hat off and bowed in front of her.

'Capitaine. I am glad to see you … were you released from your duties for the ball?' She was annoyed to hear that she sounded a little breathless as she extended her hand and he lifted it to his lips, his eyes never leaving hers.

The warmth of his mouth through her glove sent shivers down her spine.

'I was indeed.' He cocked his head to one side to gaze at her. 'You look … different tonight,' he remarked, an intense look in his blue eyes, before taking her elbow and guiding her through the crowd.

He pointed to a closed door. 'Malleval disappeared with Fouché in the billiard room a while ago. Private meeting, I believe.'

A couple of men in cuirassier uniforms approached them.

'Saintclair! Are you keeping this lovely lady to yourself?' one of them asked, detailing Marie-Ange.

'What are you doing here, de Mitre?' Saintclair's voice was cold. 'I thought Colonel Mougeon asked you to supervise the barracks tonight.'

She remembered that name. Capitaine Martin said that de Mitre was given Saintclair's promotion because he was a member of an old, aristocratic family, and Caroline Dupin had also mentioned him.

De Mitre laughed. 'I delegated. One of the things I do well, I believe. I'd rather be here than in our stinky barracks with all those new recruits. Have you seen the state of them? Peasants, the lot of them! They couldn't tell a horse's mouth from its arse, never mind fight on one.'

'What a pity our old cuirassiers' test was abolished last year,' the other man said. 'Not a single one of these new recruits would pass.'

'Capitaine Martin mentioned that test before, did he not?' Marie-Ange enquired of Saintclair. 'What exactly did it consist of?'

Saintclair stared at her blankly while the other two laughed.

'Shall you tell her or shall I?' de Mitre asked Saintclair.

'I don't think it's necessary to tell Madame anything,' Saintclair replied. He turned away. 'Come, I will show you the gardens,' he said, putting his hand on Marie-Ange's forearm to lead her away.

'Not so fast,' de Mitre protested. 'Don't be so modest, Saintclair. After all, Madame has the right to know what to expect from you.' He turned to her. 'You see, dear Madame, in the good old days, aspiring cuirassiers would be given three horses, three bottles of champagne, and three willing women. The test was to cover twenty miles, drink the champagne and … well … see to the ladies in three hours, and in any order they saw fit. Saintclair here still holds the regiment's record. Two hours and … forty minutes. Was it? The ladies demanded an encore. The horses collapsed, exhausted. Saintclair asked for more champagne, and gallant as ever, he granted the three ladies their request.'

The men laughed coarsely. Marie-Ange felt her cheeks grow hot. Saintclair glanced at her, sighed impatiently and pointed to the other side of the ballroom.

'Here are Malleval and Fouché. I will take you to them now.' He sounded relieved to walk away.

Marie-Ange's first impression of Joseph Fouché was that of a snake. He surveyed the ballroom crowd with cold, unflinching heavy-lidded eyes, barely acknowledging the men who nodded a deferential salute to him. His thin lips didn't smile, his long face remained impassive. In fact, Marie-Ange thought, as she approached, he stood very much in the superior manner of a Roman emperor – or maybe it was the image he tried to convey with the way he wore his steel-grey hair, short all over with a few flicks on his high forehead.

Next to him, Malleval stood, very handsome in his black suit and white necktie. It was hard to reconcile the image of elegance he now presented with the memory of the half-naked madman of a couple of nights before at Beauregard.

'Dear Marie-Ange, here you are at last!' He took her hand and lifted it to his lips. 'You look ravishing.'

He leant forward and stared at her jewellery.

'This locket,' he whispered, 'it's the same as Saint-Germain's.'

'It was my mother's,' Marie-Ange answered, uneasy, and covering the locket with her hand. Maybe it had been a mistake wearing it that evening.

'Aren't you going to introduce us?' Fouché interrupted.

Malleval took a deep breath and turned. 'I am sorry, Fouché. Please allow me to introduce a long-lost relative, Marie-Ange Norton, who just arrived from Devonshire.'

Fouché bowed, his lips stretched into a thin smile that didn't reach his eyes. A shiver of repulsion skittered along her spine as his mouth brushed her gloved hand. She would be wasting her time trying to extract information from him about Nallay. This man would give nothing away. He had, after all, survived four successive regimes, turning from one master to another, betraying former associates – and even his emperor. He would keep his secrets close to his heart – if he had one – which, looking into his emotionless face, she very much doubted.

The orchestra was playing a quadrille and Malleval offered Marie-Ange his arm.

'Will you do me the honour, dear Marie-Ange?'

There was no way she could refuse without being rude, so she walked with him to the centre of the parquet floor where they took their place with a dozen other couples. Throughout the dance she was aware of Saintclair's intense blue gaze on her, and even though she tried to ignore him she missed her steps a few times.

After the quadrille, the orchestra started the first notes of a waltz. The dance had caused scandal in England a few years before. Attempts had even been made to have it banned. It was now fashionable in London but still very much frowned upon in the rest of the country and had never been played at the Wellcombe Village ball. Having never danced a waltz, she asked Malleval to excuse her.

'You have never danced a waltz? What kind of barbarians do you mix with back in Devonshire?' Malleval laughed as they walked back to Fouché and Saintclair.

'Saintclair, you must show Marie-Ange how it is done.'

'How what is done?' Saintclair raised his eyebrows.

'Dancing the waltz, of course. Our dear girl has never waltzed before,' Malleval explained.

'In that case, I will be happy to oblige. Shall we?' Saintclair offered his arm and led her to the dance floor.

Her heart beat faster as he placed one hand on her waist and started turning slowly, guiding her through the steps. Although their bodies never actually touched, she could feel the heat from his arm around her, the strength of his hand holding hers. Her cheeks burning, she concentrated on the steps, too embarrassed to look up at him. After a while however, her body responded to the music and she started enjoying swirling among other couples. She looked up and smiled.

Then she saw him. Christopher. Nallay. Or rather, she caught a glimpse of his reflection in a mirror. She stiffened in Saintclair's arms.

'What's wrong?' he asked, alarm deepening his voice.

'He's here!' She lifted her chin and pointed towards the entrance. Freeing herself from Saintclair's arms, she ran out of the ballroom, bumping into people who stood in her way. Nallay was descending the staircase. Once on the ground floor, he walked towards the cloister gardens and vanished.

The gardens gleamed under the moonlight. Breathless, Marie-Ange looked around. Where could he have gone? She ventured into the shadows. Suddenly her arm was wrenched behind her, and a hand covered her mouth. She wriggled to free herself but the man holding her was too strong. He pulled her further into the darkness.

'*Je vous connais, je vous ai déjà vue* … I've seen you before.

Who are you? Why are you following me?' He spoke French, his voice a harsh whisper. He opened his hand slightly to enable Marie-Ange to answer but applied more pressure to her arm as a warning not to scream.

'Of course you have seen me before. I am …' she answered in English.

'I remember. It was in Paris, Rue de Condé,' he interrupted impatiently, switching to English too. 'So you're English. Who are you working for? Talleyrand?'

There was no doubt in her mind. This man was her beloved Christopher. When he leant over her shoulder, she breathed in his familiar scent.

'Christopher, it is me, Marie-Ange.' She turned her body towards him so he could see her face in the moonlight. 'Don't you recognise your wife?'

His hold slackened for a few seconds, but then he tightened his grip again.

'You're hurting me,' she protested.

'Tell me who you're working for, or I shall hurt you even more.'

There were footsteps in the garden and a man's voice called her name.

'Madame Norton. Are you here?' It was Saintclair's voice. He had come after her.

Christopher pressed his hand hard on her mouth and whispered in her ear.

'This is not over. I will find you and you will tell me the truth,' he warned. He twisted her arm so tightly she gasped with pain before he released her and melted into the night.

Marie-Ange collapsed on the ground with a small cry of pain and dismay. Saintclair rushed to her side.

'Are you hurt? What did the bastard do to you?' he asked, lifting her to her feet.

The pain subsided, but the shock of her discovery overwhelmed her. Christopher was alive! Her darling husband was not dead, but he didn't know her.

Sobs shook her as she stood in Saintclair's grasp. How could Christopher have forgotten her? The capitaine touched her hair with an awkward hand. Her cheeks wet with tears, she tilted her face towards his, and Saintclair enfolded her into his arms, pressing her breasts against his chest.

'He has f-forgotten me,' she stammered.

Abruptly, he put her away from him but still held her in the circle of his arms.

'Who has forgotten you?' His voice was a hoarse whisper. He didn't give her time to answer but added, 'How could any man ever forget you?'

He lifted his hand to her cheek to wipe her tears in a soft caress that sent shivers all over her body. She didn't react when he slid a finger under her chin to tilt her face up and bent down to kiss her. For a few seconds, all she could do was stare into his eyes as the world around vanished, and time stopped.

A woman's laughter and the crunching of footsteps on the gravel path nearby brought her back to reality. What was she doing in Saintclair's arms? Had she completely lost her mind?

She lowered her hands onto his chest, and pushed him away with all her strength. He breathed in sharply and let his hands fall to his sides.

Without a word, and thankful for the darkness hiding her burning cheeks, she gathered her skirts and fled on the path towards the stairway.

'Where do you think you're going?' Saintclair grabbed her arm and spun her round.

'I'm going to confront Fouché and ask him about my husband. Please let me go!'

'What husband?' He looked down and frowned. 'You mean that man who was there with you just then was …'

She nodded.

He cursed under his breath.

‘And what exactly are you planning to ask Fouché? Do you really think he will acknowledge your husband – if it’s indeed him – is his spy and give you an address where you can find him?’

‘I don’t know what he’ll say, but I have to try something – anything – to find Christopher. Now let me go!’ Her voice rose to a high pitch. She tried to shake free but his hand was a grip of steel on her arm.

‘Think about it,’ Saintclair carried on, calmly. ‘If this man is your husband and works for Fouché, then he belongs to the underworld. He is a master at hiding, concealing his identity. Fouché will never admit to employing any agents, especially when he is no longer Minister of Police. And if you think for one minute he’ll take pity on you, you are sorely mistaken.’

He released her at last.

Her shoulders slumped, and she heaved a ragged sigh. He was right. Fouché was hardly likely to be swayed by her tears.

‘What shall I do, then? I have been waiting for him all these years. I always knew he wasn’t dead, but tonight, I actually talked to him, touched him …’ She looked up. ‘Please, Capitaine, help me.’

‘Help you do what?’ His voice was harsh.

‘Find him, of course. I would do anything to see him again. I want my Christopher back.’

A sardonic grin appeared on his mouth. ‘Are you sure? He did not appear to be in a flower picking or ballad singing mood tonight. He wanted to hurt you.’

‘It’s not his fault. He’s lost his memory, but I shall find him and make him remember me.’

Saintclair didn’t reply. Why did he stand there, impassive, when he was her only hope? Christopher was so close, yet still out of reach. She collapsed to her knees, buried her face in her hands. She could hardly breathe as deep, raking sobs shook her body. Saintclair lifted her up and held her against him for what felt like a long time.

‘You’re in no fit state to be seen like this,’ he said at last. ‘We will go to my rooms across the square.’

Chapter Nine

Hugo nodded at the sentinel guarding the entrance to the cuirassiers barracks and led Marie-Ange across a courtyard and along the stable blocks before climbing up to the first floor of the officers' wing. He wasn't expecting to be stopped. Nobody cared these days if officers brought women in.

The barracks were almost as busy as the Palais Saint Pierre across the square, albeit the men looked coarser, the women more dishevelled, and the conversation was much cruder. The place was like a tavern. It made his blood boil to see what had become of the strict and well-disciplined regiment under its new leadership.

He unlocked his door.

'Wait here while I get some light,' he said as he walked in and closed the door behind them. She leant against the wooden pane while he lit an oil lamp and placed it on the table. He then took her hand, pulled a chair out, and helped her sit down. She immediately started crying again.

'I don't know what to do. I just feel so helpless.' She was crying so hard she could hardly talk.

He frowned. The woman needed to calm down. She was making herself ill. He opened a cupboard, pulled out a bottle of cognac.

'Drink this.' He gave her a glass full of liquor.

Her hand shook as she lifted the glass to her lips but she managed to drink a few sips.

'Drink it all,' he insisted. She emptied the glass.

'Better?'

She nodded and lifted her gaze to him. Her eyes were a little heavier now, but at least they were dry.

'Thank you, Capitaine. You are the only person I can turn to.' Her voice broke into a sob.

He sighed with impatience.

'*Ah non!* You're not going to start crying again! Here, let me make you more comfortable.'

He pulled her to her feet and did what he had been dreaming of for days. Slowly, almost tenderly, he took the pins out of her hair. It cascaded down onto her shoulders and into the middle of her back. He slid his fingers in the thick mass of curls. His throat was tight, his breathing fast, his body ached with the need to touch and kiss her.

She stiffened and raised her face towards his.

'Capitaine, I don't think …' she protested weakly, closing her eyes as she swayed against him.

'I have wanted to do this ever since I first saw you,' he said. He bent down and kissed her lips until they opened under the gentle pressure.

Damn, she tasted good, a mixture of brandy and tears and her own sweet taste. His kiss deepened, became forceful. She gasped and melted against him, as if he was taking her breath, her strength away.

She made no move to resist him as his mouth trailed along her neck to her bare shoulder, and then slowly back up again. With one hand, he undid the buttons of his jacket, which he discarded impatiently on the floor. He rolled Marie-Ange's white gloves down along her forearms and took them off with a sharp pull. He looked at her. Her slightly bewildered gaze met his.

'Tell me now if you want me to stop.'

She opened her mouth to speak but didn't say a word.

So he pulled her close and kissed her again. Tentatively, she put her arms around his shoulders, slid her hands behind his neck, and tangled her fingers in his hair. His heart about to burst, his body throbbing with need, he proceeded to unfasten the hooks at the back of her dress before pulling down the delicate muslin gown from her shoulders. His fingers stroked the swelling of her breasts above her corset, ventured lower. She shuddered and threw her head back, offering more of her to his caresses. He groaned as he pulled her chemise lower and touched the tight, pink tips of her breasts. He traced light patterns with his thumbs, teasing and caressing until she let out a moan he stifled with a long, hard kiss.

She heaved out a shaky breath.

'Christopher.'

It was like a direct hit to the chest. He pulled away, staggered back, and held her at arm's length.

Her eyes opened, dreamy, unfocused. Her lips were still parted, rosy and swollen from his kisses.

'I'll be dammed if you call another man's name while you're in my arms,' he growled.

He turned away and raked his dark hair with his fingers. How he wanted to punch something, or someone – preferably the man she believed was her husband. He swallowed hard, took a deep breath and sat at the table, grabbed the bottle of cognac, and poured a generous measure, which he drank in one gulp. Hell, he needed more than that to quell the fire in his body.

He glanced up at the woman standing, silent, in the middle of the room. Her eyes were lowered to the ground, her cheeks and throat flushed, her blonde hair tousled. With her arms folded across her chest, she looked lost and vulnerable. His anger subsided at once.

'My apologies,' he muttered. 'I shouldn't have taken advantage of your distress. It won't happen again.'

He poured himself another drink.

She neither answered nor looked at him but put her dress in order with trembling hands. Desire, anger, regret stabbed at his chest – and then a flash of desire again as she pulled her dress to cover the swell of her breasts. He took a deep, ragged, breath. Sensations burned through him like a firebrand – the feel of her against him, the silk of her skin under his fingertips, her feverish abandon as he trailed kisses along her throat to the tip of her breasts. *And all along, it was her husband she pined for*. He could almost laugh. Almost.

He clenched his jaw and gestured for the woman to sit at the table opposite him.

'Tell me about Coruña.'

Her face flushed, she sat opposite him, folded her hands in her lap and closed her eyes, perhaps to collect her thoughts.

'The HMS *Amazon* moored in the bay of Coruña between January sixteenth and eighteenth of 1809. Christopher was supervising the repatriation of the sick and the wounded soldiers ordered by General Moore. The *Amazon* was hit by French fire at nightfall on the eighteenth. It sank rapidly and rescue attempts were hindered by the French artillery, which continued firing throughout the night. Not a single member of the crew was found alive.'

'Yes. That is pretty much what I heard too,' Hugo said, thoughtful. He poured a glass of cognac, which he handed to her but this time she left it untouched in front of her.

'I have been thinking a lot these past few days about what might have happened,' she said. 'What if Christopher was able to grab a piece of wood, a barrel, anything, and the current carried him away from the rest of the fleet further down the coast? He might have been wounded or in shock, his uniform torn, with nothing to identify him as British.'

Hugo crossed his arms on his chest. 'Go on.'

'Later he might have been sent to a French field hospital, seriously wounded and unable to remember who he was. And when he recovered, he could have been transferred to a French regiment and finished the war on the French side. He spoke perfect French.'

'You are positive that the man you saw, tonight and in Paris, is *your husband*?'

Marie-Ange nodded. 'I know it is him. But he does not,' she replied quietly.

The conviction in her voice was unmistakable. 'Yes, I suppose it's possible,' he said. 'Stranger things have happened. You said he now went under the name of …?'

'Nallay,' she replied. 'Joseph Nallay.'

His mind was made up. One way or another he would get hold of this Nallay. If nothing else, he'd give the man a good beating for manhandling Marie-Ange in the Palais Saint-Pierre's gardens and would get rid of one of Fouché's spies at the same time. And if the man turned out to be her husband, well, things would get complicated.

'You do realise that you may not like what we find,' he said, glancing at her.

She nodded. 'I must know, Capitaine,' was all she answered.

'Well then …'

He stood up, retrieved his jacket from the floor, and put it back on. 'Come, I'll escort you back to the ball and start looking for Nallay. I have a few contacts here in Lyon I can put on the man's trail.' He buttoned his jacket.

Marie-Ange stood and asked timidly, 'Please, Capitaine? I cannot manage these.' She pointed to her dress.

He gave an impatient grunt before standing behind her to fasten the tiny hooks, all the time striving to resist the urge to draw her into his arms again. When he finished, he couldn't resist stroking the silky, creamy skin across her shoulders. She shivered violently under his touch, hissed a sharp breath, and pulled away as if she'd been burnt. She probably didn't trust him not to touch her again because she walked to the other side of the room to twist her hair in a plait and put her white gloves back on.

At last she said she was ready and they made their way out.

'Do you think you can find Rochefort, Capitaine? I want to go back to Uxeloup's house,' she said as they crossed the square towards the Palais Saint Pierre. Hugo looked for Malleval's carriage among the barouches, cabriolets, and Berlins lining the square.

At last he spied the man's bulky figure. 'Rochefort is over there.'

The big man was smoking a clay pipe and talking with other drivers.

'Madame Norton is tired,' Hugo told him, opening the carriage door and helping her inside.

'Very well,' Rochefort tapped his pipe against the sole of his boot, put it back into his coat pocket, and jumped up onto the driver's box.

Hugo leant inside to speak quietly with Marie-Ange. 'I'll let Malleval know you weren't feeling well … and I'll be in touch when I have news.' He closed the door and stepped aside.

As soon as the carriage pulled away, he strode off towards the Saint Paul district. With its seedy taverns frequented by men from all walks of life, from army personnel, municipal officers, and professionals in search of illicit thrills, to larceners, pickpockets, and hardened criminals, it was the place to fish for information about Joseph Nallay.

Chapter Ten

Marie-Ange reclined on the seat and attempted to marshal her whirling thoughts and emotions to bring the night's events into some semblance of order. Christopher was alive, but he was amnesic and so changed it was hard to reconcile the man who handled her so roughly this evening with the gentle husband who treasured her. Her throat tightened with pity and sadness. Heaven knew what life he had led, what terrible sufferings he had endured since Coruña. She pressed her hand against her heart and took a deep breath. Well, she would find him and do everything in her power to help him remember his past.

And then what? Would they go back to Wellcombe as man and wife? The prospect of resuming her married life, which would have filled her with joy a few weeks ago, now made her uneasy. The man she had encountered tonight was cold and cruel, with an almost inhuman harshness in his eyes. What if he did not change once he got back to Norton Place? Or worse, what if he never regained his memory? She shook her head. She was being silly. Of course, he would remember, and then everything would be fine.

There was, however, the burning issue of Capitaine Saintclair. She closed her eyes and swallowed hard. She couldn't deny any longer that she was attracted to him. Shame heated her cheeks as she recalled how quickly she had forgotten her husband tonight in the arms of the French officer. How she yearned for him to touch and kiss her and make her body alive. She let out a sob, clenched her fist, and brought it to her mouth.

She was weak and pathetic. She had to get a grip on herself and fight the attraction. Saintclair might have set her senses on fire but he did not have her heart. Her heart would always belong to Christopher.

There were still lights inside Malleval's mansion. The young maid who had helped her get ready before opened the front door.

'A visitor is waiting for you in the study, Madame,' she announced.

'Who is that?'

'Monsieur Karloff.'

Karloff! The physician employed by Edmond Malleval to induce her grandmother to talk about the Cross of Life and Saint-Germain. The man who had denied Malleval a Christian burial and who eagerly waited for her arrival from England …

Entirely clad in black, in the manner of a priest, Karloff sat in an armchair near the fire, holding a book. He appeared so absorbed in his reading he didn't raise his head when she walked in and all she could see of his face was his sharp, beaky nose and the grey hair he wore loose and so long it brushed the pages of the book.

She approached cautiously. 'Monsieur?'

He looked up. She hardly took in his features – the lean face, hollow cheeks and thin lips – so intense were the dark brown eyes fixed upon her.

'Madame Norton, it is a pleasure to meet you at last. I am Gustave Karloff, an old friend of Monsieur Malleval.' He stood up and bowed in front of her before gesturing to one of the armchairs positioned near the fireplace. 'Will you sit down?'

She couldn't think of an excuse to refuse, so she took a seat in the armchair opposite his.

'There is no point wasting time in formalities.' He smiled. 'I believe Uxeloup already told you we are interested in an object which used to be in your family's possession. The Cross of Life.'

'He has indeed.' So there it was again. The mysterious Cross of Life and its links to her family.

Karloff suddenly frowned. He bent forward and pointed to her throat, a covetous gleam in his eyes just like Uxeloup had earlier at the ball.

'*Tudieu*! Your locket! It looks remarkably similar to the one Saint-Germain is wearing in his portrait at Beauregard. Could I take a look at it, please?'

Marie-Ange's response was instinctive. Her hand flew to her throat, her fingers closed protectively over the case, and she shook her head.

‘Very well,’ he muttered, tightening his thin lips.

He reclined in his chair, crossed his long legs, and entwined his fingers. ‘I know your mother had a rare talent as a painter and kept her watercolours and drawings of Beauregard in a sketchbook she took with her when she left for England.’

‘You mean when she escaped from Edmond Malleval’s fortress where he kept her a prisoner?’ Marie-Ange snapped. Even though she didn’t want to openly confront the physician, she was unable to hide her hostility. Together with Edmond Malleval, the man facing her had instigated her grandmother’s death and caused great harm to her mother, too. ‘Yes, she did have a sketchbook. Why should you be interested?’

‘I would like very much to see it. I believe the drawings hold clues as to the location of the Cross.’

‘Why would they?’ she asked. ‘And more to the point, why should I help you and Uxeloup Malleval get hold of this Cross? If it is as precious as you suggest, it should belong to the Church.’

She stood up. ‘Now if you will excuse me, I wish to retire to my room.’

She moved to the door but Karloff was faster and blocked her way out.

‘You don’t understand how important the Cross is for me, for Malleval. For all of us,’ he said, staring into her eyes. ‘You must help me. You must hand over your mother’s sketchbook and the locket.’

Marie-Ange parted her lips to breathe but there was no air in the room. Karloff’s eyes became darker and so large it felt as if she was being sucked into two bottomless pits with everything around her blurred like in a dream – or a nightmare. Tingling sensations, like pins and needles, crept onto her face and neck, and her body felt suddenly heavy and limp.

Fear made Marie-Ange’s heart pound so hard it hurt. It took all her willpower to tear herself away from his deep gaze. Immediately her heartbeat returned to normal and the room came back into focus. She swallowed hard.

‘I regret I cannot help you, Monsieur Karloff, and I can assure you there is nothing in my mother's paintings that can be of interest to you.'

She tilted her head up and added. 'Now please let me through or I shall call for help.'

Karloff reluctantly stepped away from the door. 'Very well, but you know something, and I will find out what it is,' he warned before opening the door.

She made her way to her bedroom through dark and quiet corridors. Dealing with Karloff after her encounter with Christopher and her sensual duel with Saintclair left her drained and nauseous. The physician was odd and intense, and just as obsessed as Malleval. Once in her room, she stripped off, bathed her face with cold water and slipped into her nightdress. She opened her travel bag to pull out her mother's art book and settled into bed. Why were both men so certain her mother knew about the Cross of Life and had passed on her knowledge to her? And why did Karloff believe there were clues in the drawings?

Even though she had no idea what she was looking for, she studied every one of the sketches and watercolours until late into the night. She didn't discern anything new. What was she missing?

Sighing, she closed the book shut. On an impulse, she wrapped it in one of her chemises, and together with the locket, hid it at the bottom of the bag under a pile of undergarments and clothing. She slid into bed and blew out the candle. Through the open curtains the city lights flickered in the distance on either sides of the river. She closed her eyes and drifted to sleep.

She had no idea how long she had been dozing when she became aware of a presence in the room.

'Do you remember the words, Marie-Ange?' a man's voice said close to her. She cried out. Her heart hammering against her ribs, she sat up to glance around the room. It was empty.

She heaved a sigh of relief. So it was just a dream.

She lay down and fell asleep again.

'Tell me the words of the song your mother taught you, and then give me the sketchbook and the locket.' The voice intruded on her dreams, this time with more insistence.

Startled, she opened her eyes to find she wasn't lying in bed any longer but sitting against one of the bed posts. A tall, lean man stood facing her. Karloff! Why was he there? How did he get in? She tried to move but her body did not respond, and when she opened her mouth to protest, no sound came out.

Karloff bent down. His dark brown eyes shone like diamonds and locked on hers like a serpent's compelling gaze. This time, Marie-Ange couldn't look away.

'You want to remember, don't you? You want to tell me the words.' His voice was smooth and persuasive.

Strangely, Marie-Ange knew exactly what he meant.

'Yes,' she said. 'I do.'

A tiny, childlike voice rose from deep within her and she started singing, using old French words.

Ma mie, ma rose de mai

Ma rose aux cinq pétales,

Qui dans la tour aux colombes

Pleure ton amant dans sa tombe.

'This is lovely. This is what I want. Carry on, Marie-Ange.'

At that moment, the wind rattling tree branches against the window broke the spell. She looked away from him for the briefest moment and the words of the song vanished from her memory like clouds of mist evaporating under the sun.

Karloff got up from the bed and cursed under his breath.

'*Tudieu!* I almost had it.' He stalked across the room, opened the door, and sneaked out like a shadow.

Marie-Ange collapsed on the bed. Her eyes closed and she slid into a deep sleep.

She woke to the sounds of water washing against the rocks under her window, river fowl splashing in the rushes, and birds calling in the evergreens. The room was bathed in a grey and pink light. She stretched, enjoying the sensual feeling of the fine linen sheets against her skin, but immediately images from her dream came flooding back – Karloff, in her room, asking her about a song while she sat on the bed, unable to move.

She frowned. What a disturbing, unpleasant dream it had been, and yet it seemed so real.

A winter sun rose over the city, staining the sky with a bloody, fiery glow. She got out of bed, opened the window, and breathed in the cool morning air that carried the silt scent of the river. The morning might look tranquil, yet she felt anything but peaceful. She dressed and went downstairs to the dining room where two maids were setting the breakfast table. They placed a basket of bread rolls and brioches, a plate of eggs and ham, and a cup of coffee in front of her.

'Did Madame sleep well?' one of the girls enquired.

'Yes, thank you,' Marie-Ange lied. 'The house is very quiet this morning.'

'Monsieur Uxeloup didn't return until dawn. He'll sleep until lunchtime now. Monsieur likes his sleep, especially when he's been smoking his pipe.'

'Justine! Shh … don't be so indiscreet,' the other maid scolded.

'What about Monsieur Karloff?' Marie-Ange hoped she wouldn't see him this morning.

The girl called Justine shrugged. 'He already left. He said he had patients waiting for him. He's a well-known physician, you know. People come from all over France, Europe even, for his treatments and potions.' She shuddered. 'My grandma says he's one of those hypnotists who can make you do things just by looking into your eyes.' She lowered her voice. 'She also says he belongs to some secret society …'

'Justine!' the other maid remonstrated forcefully. 'You'll never keep your place if you gossip about Monsieur and his guests.'

'I'm only speaking the truth,' Justine grumbled before going out.

Over breakfast, Marie-Ange pondered what the girl had said. So

Karloff knew how to hypnotise people, like Anton Mesmer, a doctor who had caused a scandal some years ago for claiming he could treat his patients with the power of suggestion alone. Wasn't that exactly what her grandmother had written about in her letter and what Sophie had mentioned at Beauregard?

She sat back in her chair. How had she failed to understand before? She hadn't dreamt the incident with Karloff last night. The man had actually come into her bedroom and tried to hypnotise her. A sudden, fierce anxiety constricted her throat and her hand shook so much she had to put her cup of coffee down. What intrigue had she got herself mixed up with? By coming here, she had fallen into a trap set by Malleval and his physician. Last night Karloff wanted the words of a song, the very same song her mother used to sing to send her to sleep. A song Marie-Ange had all but forgotten. Until now.

My sweet rose of May

My rose with the five petals,

You cry in the dovecote

For your lover, cold in his tomb.

What about the rest? She frowned with concentration, but it was no good, she couldn't remember any more.

She had been so young when her mother died. Sometimes she wasn't sure if her memories were real or mixed with dreams and stories she had made up later. One thing however was certain. The song had been important. Her mother had sung it to her in the evening, over and over again.

She pushed her chair back and sprang to her feet. She needed some air, and a place to figure out what to do next. A walk on the island or into the city would clear her head. She rushed up to her room to fetch her cloak, bonnet and gloves, and ran back down again.

'I'm going out,' she informed Justine as they passed in the hall.

The young maid looked panic-stricken. 'You can't! I mean Monsieur said you weren't to leave the house. Let me call

Rochefort.'

Marie-Ange shook her head. 'No, I want to be by myself.'

She opened the front door and walked to the gates. They were locked, a thick metal bar across them. Disappointed, she turned round. There must be another way out of the estate.

'Wait!' Rochefort hailed her. He strode her way with a determined look on his thick, brutish features. 'You're not to go anywhere without me.'

Marie-Ange leant against the gates and pressed her hands against her throat to fight a wave of nausea. She wasn't Malleval's guest any longer. She was his prisoner.

Chapter Eleven

Glancing around uneasily for fear of being discovered eavesdropping on Malleval's and Capitaine Saintclair's conversation, Marie-Ange tiptoed outside the study's closed door.

'I hope you're not going back on your word. You can't do that to her, not after she came all this way.' Saintclair sounded angry but Malleval only laughed.

'What I do with Marie-Ange Norton is none of your business, so keep well out of it. Don't force me to review our arrangement, Saintclair. You owe me five thousand francs, remember? You don't want to cross me and have the bailiffs knocking at your door in St Genis and dragging your family out into the street at dawn. Think about poor Lucie's health, your mother's tears and your father's shame if they found out their son lost their lovely house in a game of cards. Actually I find the whole thing is rather ironic, since that's how you got the damned house in the first place.'

'Don't you dare threaten my family with eviction,' Saintclair replied in a low, growling voice. 'I will pay you back every *sou* I owe you, but you will have to give me a little time.'

Malleval laughed. 'And where the devil will you find five thousand francs?'

Saintclair muttered something Marie-Ange didn't hear. She stepped closer to the door but voices nearby announced people were coming this way. Her heart fluttering, she pulled away from the door and walked to the drawing room.

Standing near the fireplace she waited for Capitaine Saintclair, anxious for news about his search for Christopher. Three days had passed since the ball. Three days, during which she had been in virtual house arrest, allowed only to take short walks in the park, always with Rochefort at her heels. Malleval had kept to his room, claiming the old battle wound was causing him too much pain to visit his notary and formalise her inheritance. Marie-Ange now doubted the existence of this mysterious injury – he had, after all, been well enough to dance at the ball.

She stifled a yawn. She hadn't slept much the night before, haunted once again by strange and terrifying images and voices. The dreams always started in the same way. Karloff's deep, soothing voice intruded into her sleep and asked her to remember the words of her mother's song, which she never could. She saw a tall, round tower with strange symbols carved on its walls. One side of the wall opened onto a staircase descending into the bowels of the earth, to a place filled with obscurity, horrid whistling, thudding noises, and distant screams. There were shadows down there, entities that sought to snatch something from her.

Every time, she woke shaking with fear and drenched in sweat.

She shivered and wrapped her shawl more closely around her shoulders. Footsteps in the corridor made her turn and look expectantly towards the door. She hadn't seen Saintclair since the evening of the ball. The memories of his caresses and her own unbridled desire still made her blush with shame. Even now as she put her hands to her cheeks she could feel they were burning.

Saintclair entered. His expression was sombre and tired. He bowed silently, his blue glare filtered through his black eyelashes.

'Malleval was always a wastrel but at least he used to keep his word,' he declared without preamble, anger bubbling in his voice. 'I fear he has now lost the last threads of decency he possessed.' He took a deep breath. 'I don't think he has any intention of giving you what he promised – what you came all this way for.'

'I see …' She twisted her wedding ring around her finger.

'He said he was in no hurry to settle your bequest, that he had plans for you, whatever that means.' He sighed. 'I am sorry I ever agreed to escort you to France. I never thought …'

She had herself reached the same conclusion – Malleval had lured her to France under a false pretence when all he wanted was the Cross of Life. Hearing Saintclair voice his opinion was the catalyst she needed and in a flash her resolve to flee solidified.

'Will you help me get away from here?' she asked, her voice barely a whisper. 'If you take me to a coach terminal in Lyon, I will buy a passage to Beaujeu. I have enough money left. After that, I shall ask my great-aunt for help.'

‘Are you sure that’s wise?’ Saintclair’s face was impassive. ‘If you leave now, there’ll be no chance at all of any money coming to you.’

‘There was never an inheritance,’ she retorted. ‘Malleval fooled me. I need to get away from this house but Rochefort follows me everywhere.’ She moved closer and put her hand on his forearm. ‘Please, Capitaine. I know you have an agreement with Malleval about a gambling debt but …’

He glanced at her, startled. ‘Did he tell you that?’

‘No. Never mind how I found out,’ she replied, unwilling to reveal she had read his correspondence while he slept, as well as eavesdropped on his private conversations.

She bit her bottom lip as she waited anxiously for his response. She was asking him to betray a fellow cavalry officer – a man he had known and fought beside for years – and to jeopardise any chance of wiping his gambling debt off. Yet it only took Saintclair a few seconds to make his decision.

‘Get a few things together, only the essentials, and not your travel bag. We don’t want to arouse anyone’s suspicions,’ he instructed.

Marie-Ange nodded and went to her room. She put her mother’s sketchbook, a couple of undergarments, and what was left of her travel money into a small bag before clasping the gold locket around her neck and grabbing her cloak, hat, and gloves. She glanced at Christopher’s dressing gown with a twinge of regret, started towards it, hesitated, but she had to leave it behind. There was no room for it in her bag.

She returned to the drawing room quietly, anxious to avoid any member of Malleval’s household staff, especially Rochefort.

‘Ready?’ Saintclair took her arm and they made their way from the house.

Marie-Ange’s heart sank when she saw Rochefort grooming a horse in the courtyard. The big man stared at them suspiciously and dropped his bristle brush in a bucket of water.

‘Where are you going, Capitaine?’ he asked.

‘I’m taking Madame Norton to a seamstress in town for a dress fitting. Malleval’s orders. I’ll bring her back later,’ Saintclair replied with a tone that suffered no questioning. ‘Bring my horse now.’

Rochefort frowned but fetched Saintclair’s horse from the stable block. The capitaine lifted Marie-Ange up and helped her sit side-saddle. He mounted behind her, loosened the reins, and touched the horse with his legs to send it forward and out of the courtyard.

‘We’d better hurry,’ he said, spurring the horse on as soon as they were on the lane. ‘Malleval will probably send his men after us as soon as he finds out we’re gone. He knows the only place you can go is your aunt’s castle in Marzac, so his men will check the inns where coaches depart for Belleville and Beaujeu first.’ He paused. ‘Which is why we’re not going there.’

‘Where are we going, then?’ Marie-Ange’s face brushed against his shoulder as she turned to speak to him. She sat uneasy, her back stiff against his chest. The warmth of his body brought back sensations she had tried to forget since the night of the ball. She wriggled and attempted to shift forward, away from him.

‘I’m taking you to my family in St Genis.’ His arms closed in tightly around her.

‘Will I be welcome? They do not know me.’ She stuttered and shuffled uncomfortably on the saddle again.

‘My family may be of humble origin, Madame, but they know how to welcome guests,’ he retorted, tightening his grip around her. ‘Now, will you sit still? You’re going to get us both thrown.’

‘Sorry,’ she muttered.

They rode in silence until they crossed the bridge over the River Saône. Soon they were on the main road leading to the town centre.

‘I met Malleval’s doctor, Gustave Karloff, the other night after the ball,’ Marie-Ange said. ‘He asked me about the Cross of Life. He too seems to believe I can find it.’

‘I wish I understood what this business of the Cross was all about. Karloff is a strange man who fancies himself as some sort of wise man or mage. I know Malleval trusts him with his … ahem … condition. I don’t. I am always suspicious of fanatics.'

'Yes, he is very peculiar,' she agreed, 'and just as obsessed as Malleval.' She wondered whether to tell him the old man had intruded into her bedroom and tried to hypnotise her, and that she heard his voice in her sleep every night, but decided against it. Better wait until she understood what it all meant.

'Have you heard anything about my husband?' she asked.

Saintclair tensed against her.

'Not yet. I sent word that I'm looking for a man who calls himself Nallay. I wrote to my friend, Martin, requesting he do the same in Paris. We have to wait for his move now. If Nallay is indeed one of Fouché's men, he will get in touch, one way or another.'

When they reached the Place Louis le Grand Saintclair halted and dismounted in front of La Gargote, a large inn at the corner of the square. In one swift movement he swung Marie-Ange to the ground and set her gently on her feet. She grasped his arm for a moment until her legs were steady.

'I will procure a place on the coach to St Genis for you and follow on horseback,' he said before handing his mount to a stable boy. He held the door open and followed her into the inn. They were in luck. A coach was ready to leave for Vienne, stopping at various towns and villages on the way, including St Genis.

The coach pulled onto St Genis' market square just over an hour later. They walked through the village's narrow cobbled streets, with Saintclair leading his horse by the reins. It was after lunch and the village was quiet, apart from the immediate surroundings of a small tavern where several drunkards were causing a disturbance. One of them shouted as they walked past. He was short and stocky, with matted straw blond hair and bloodshot blue eyes. His clothes were filthy rags and his bare feet were stuck in clogs far too large for him.

'*Oye*, Saintclair! Remember me?' he called. 'You threw me out of your regiment six months ago. You said I wasn't good enough, not even to scrub horse dung from your boots!' He spat on the floor.

Saintclair ignored him and walked on, which served to make the man even more belligerent.

'You think you're so high and mighty, don't you? But you'd better beware. I'll show you and your family what I can do.'

'Wait here,' Saintclair told Marie-Ange.

He didn't seem in any hurry as he tied the reins of his horse to a post and walked towards the drunk who suddenly appeared to lose all his bravado and cowered against the wall. Saintclair grabbed the collar of his dirty shirt, lifted him up effortlessly, and pinned him against the wall. The man's feet wriggled above the ground, he waved his arms about but couldn't break free from the cuirassier's iron grip.

'Don't you ever threaten my family again,' Saintclair said in a low, growling voice. 'Or I'll slice you open and leave your carcass to rot in the gutter. Understood?'

The drunk nodded, his bloodshot blue eyes bulging, his face turning beetroot red. Saintclair released him and he fell in a heap onto the cobbles. Saintclair wiped his hands on his breeches and turned round. The man picked himself up and scampered away after shooting him a look so filled with hatred it sent a shiver of fear down Marie-Ange's back.

'That man wishes you harm,' she remarked.

The officer shrugged. 'He's a drunk. He'll be dead in a matter of months, in a brawl if not from the bottle.' His tone was dismissive, but she couldn't help looking over her shoulder.

'Here we are.' He stopped outside a garden wall and pushed a freshly painted green gate open. A gravel path led to an elegant, two-storey house covered with ivy. The door opened to reveal a middle-aged woman dressed in a simple grey dress and white pinafore. Her dark hair was neatly tucked under a white bonnet and she had the same piercing blue eyes as Saintclair.

'Hugo! You never sent word that you were coming. Two visits in less than a week. We *are* lucky,' she exclaimed, her face radiant.

She turned towards Marie-Ange. 'And you brought a guest, too. Good afternoon, Madame. I am Hugo's mother, Emilie Saintclair.'

She curtsied briefly. Saintclair introduced Marie-Ange, said something about going to the stables, and disappeared with his horse towards the back of the house.

'Please come in.' Madame Saintclair gestured to the open door.

Marie-Ange entered the black and white tiled hall. Rust-coloured paper adorned the walls, houseplants on a sideboard and a couple of landscape paintings near an oak staircase gave the hallway a welcoming, if unpretentious, appearance. Emilie Saintclair took Marie-Ange's coat and gloves and hung them on the tall hallstand. There were cleaning cloths and some polishing balm on a console.

'Hugo decided I should have a maid and a cook but I just can't get used to it,' she explained, her voice apologetic and her cheeks a little flushed as she folded the cloths and screwed the top back on the pot of polish. 'It is so tedious to sit in the parlour, being waited upon all day. I much prefer to do my own chores.'

Saintclair came back, shook his boots on the mat and took his riding jacket off. He bent towards his mother and kissed her cheek.

'How are you, Mother? And how is Lucie today?'

'I am fine, my love, but your sister hasn't been very well. Her cough has been troubling her again and her eyes …' She didn't finish but a heavy sigh escaped her lips. She led the way to a room at the back of the house.

Marie-Ange's first impression of Lucie was of a fragile lily. The pale and slender girl was lying on a chaise longue near the window overlooking a large garden.

'Hugo. What a lovely surprise.' She tried to get up but was overcome by a fit of coughing and reclined onto the cushions, a handkerchief pressed to her pale lips. Saintclair rushed to her side and took her hands.

'Don't get up, darling.' He kissed her forehead and arranged a few cushions around her. He turned towards Marie-Ange. 'Lucie, this is Madame Norton. She is going to stay here a few days.'

Lucie's face lit up. 'You're the lady who helped Hugo choose these lovely kerchiefs in Paris for me!' She showed Marie-Ange the delicately embroidered white and pink linen square she was clutching in her slim hand. 'Come closer so I can see you.' Lucie blinked a few times. Her eyes were inflamed and swollen.

'You are as beautiful as Hugo said.'

Marie-Ange felt she was blushing.

'Please come and sit near me. Hugo said you lived in England near the sea. I wish to know all about your house, and all about you.'

'Of course.' Marie-Ange sat next to the girl and took her hand, feeling an instinctive sympathy for Saintclair's sister.

'Can I leave you two ladies to chat while I ask *Maman* to get us something to eat? I'm famished.' Saintclair walked towards the door, but lingered just inside the room for a moment.

'So do you really live in an old castle?' Lucie asked.

Marie-Ange shook her head. 'It isn't a real castle but it is indeed old – so old tiles fall off the roof almost every day, the chimneys don't work properly, and the doors don't shut right. It's always cold and draughty too, as we are on the moors. Having said that, the coast is beautiful.' Marie-Ange smiled wistfully as she spoke of Norton Place.

She turned to Saintclair. His expression was so tender and loving as he looked at his sister her throat tightened and tears pricked her eyes. He wasn't the cynical cuirassier officer any longer but a deeply caring man, a loving brother.

'I won't be long,' he promised before walking out.

Later in the afternoon, after a collation of hot chocolate and cakes for the ladies and thick slabs of bread, roast meat, and a pitcher of ale for Saintclair, Madame Saintclair showed Marie-Ange to her room. It was small but comfortable, with dark green curtains framing two windows overlooking the garden, and a large double bed covered with a thick pink and white counterpane.

'Please make yourself at home, dear. I know this isn't what you're used to.'

'This is perfect. You have such a lovely house, Madame Saintclair.'

'Hugo works very hard for us all. Quite how he has managed to buy this property on an officer's pay, I'll never know.'

She gave a resigned smile. 'Or maybe I'd rather not know. He was adamant that Lucie should move from our house in the old weavers' district of Lyon. He was right, of course. It was far too damp for the girl, being so close to the river.'

The woman walked to the window and added quietly, 'He is a good son, and a devoted brother.' She turned to Marie-Ange, a little hesitant. 'He told me you were in a spot of trouble. I want you to know that you are welcome to stay here for as long as you need.' She curtsied again.

'I am grateful for your hospitality, Madame Saintclair,' Marie-Ange replied, her chest tight with guilt. Because of her, the Saintclairs risked losing the house, which meant so much to them.

She put her bag on the bed and proceeded to take out the few items she managed to cram in before fleeing Isle Barbe. She could do with more clothes and toiletries. All her things were either at Malleval's mansion on the island or at Beauregard and who knew if she would be able to go back there anytime soon? She asked Madame Saintclair to recommend a laundry woman to help with her washing and a seamstress who could turn out a dress or two quickly.

'Not to worry, dear. Give me your things and I will see that they are laundered. As for a seamstress, look no further. It was my occupation before we came to live here. My husband, Horace, has a small silk workshop in Lyon.' She let out a sigh. 'He always entertained the hope that Hugo would resign from the army and learn the trade, but I don't think my son will ever consider becoming a *soyeux*. He is far too keen on travel and adventure.' She sighed. 'At any rate, I used to make dresses and ladies accessories and it would please me very much to make a dress for you.'

'Oh, no, I really couldn't let you,' Marie-Ange protested.

'I would be delighted. We will ask my husband to bring some samples from the workshop. For now, I will leave you to rest. You must be tired.'

Madame Saintclair closed the door softly behind her and Marie-Ange lay down on the bed. For the first time in days, she felt safe – safe enough to close her eyes and fall asleep in a matter of seconds.

She dreamt of her mother and it was her voice she heard, not Karloff's. It was her beautiful face she saw instead of frightening shadows, and the warmth of her arms she felt around her instead of the cold, damp darkness.

Ma mie, ma rose de mai

Ma rose aux cinq pétales,

Qui dans la tour aux colombes,

Pleure l'amant dans la tombe ...

Écoute moi, ne pleure pas,

Ton bel amour tu reverras,

La rose sur le coeur, tourne cinq fois,

Lève les yeux et l'aile tu trouveras.

Mais choisis bien, prudente et sage,

Si l'aile de la colombe

Est blanche comme celle de l'ange,

Elle n'ouvre pas les tombes.

The voice faded away and her mother's face became fainter.

Marie-Ange opened her eyes. That was the song. She remembered it now, all of it! She sang the words aloud a couple of times to make sure she memorised them. What a strange song it was, about a girl called Rose who cried for her dead lover. The girl went into a dovecote to retrieve an angel wing that would make her lover come back to life. This was the song Karloff so desperately wanted her to remember – a song about eternal life.

A rush of excitement surged through her. Perhaps the song referred to the Cross of Life and its relic? If so, they were hidden in a dovecote. She put her hand on her pounding heart. Could it be the dovecote at Beauregard, the one Count Saint-Germain ordered a team of craftsmen to build? Feverishly, she took the sketchbook and turned the pages. There it was! She had always been fascinated by the drawings of the dovecote and the intricate carvings of roses inside it. Dozens and dozens of roses. Now that she looked more closely, she noticed that they were all very similar to her locket. She unclasped the locket from her neck and held it in front of her.

'*Ma rose aux cinq pétales,*' she whispered. The rose embossed on the locket had five petals, too.

She knew a little about roses, as they had been her father's passion. William Jones had grown them and tended to them lovingly in the garden of their Plymouth townhouse. He had collected paintings, etchings, and writings about them and, naturally, Marie-Ange had taken an interest in the flowers, too. Roses were powerful, conflicting, symbols of life and death, desire, passion, and virginity; and because their heart was hidden in their fragrant folds, of esoteric knowledge and secrecy.

She recalled a medieval pamphlet she had read about the depiction of roses. A five-petaled rose symbolised life, a six-petaled rose represented love. The rarest was a flower with eight petals and it represented mystery. The roses on the locket, in the dovecote, and in the song all had five petals. They stood for the Fifth Element. Life force. Immortality.

Marie-Ange sang the song to herself again. How did the girl in the song get hold of the relic? She placed a rose on a heart and gave five turns. Were these supposed to be a real flower, a real heart? She looked down at the locket which Saint-Germain had given her mother during his last visit at Beauregard, shortly before the dovecote was built and a few months before his death. It was important. She could sense it, but why?

She pressed it against her own heart and sighed. She was missing something. She leant over the drawing of the dovecote again. After several minutes of intense scrutiny she finally saw it. In the middle of the central beam, hidden among carvings of roses, was a heart shape.

The locket, the rose and the heart … she thought about it for a while. There was only one way to find out if she was right. She had to go back to Beauregard.

A knock on the door startled her.

'Supper is ready, dear,' Madame Saintclair informed her.

Saintclair and Lucie were playing a game of piquet at the dining room table.

'Hugo! You should be ashamed of yourself. Put those cards away. You are not in your officers' canteen,' Madame Saintclair reprimanded, a smile belying the severe tone of her voice.

Lucie laughed when she saw her brother put on a contrite expression.

'Yes, Mother.' He gathered the cards and slipped them in his pocket.

A tall and strongly built man with steel grey hair entered and took his place at the head of the table. He bowed to Marie-Ange.

'Madame, we are honoured to have you as our guest.' His voice was deep and pleasant. He bowed his head and joined his hands to say grace. They were rough and calloused, probably because of his work with silk weaving looms.

During dinner, they talked about Lyon and the silk industry, which was experiencing a revival in peacetime.

'My son and I disagreed about Napoleon for a long time,' Monsieur Saintclair said. 'Hugo was enthralled by him but I always had my doubts. He did our country a great deal of harm. All these wars almost ruined me and my fellow guild members, not to mention the hundreds of thousands of dead on the battlefields.'

Hugo nodded. 'I have come to agree with you, Father. I'll never be a royalist but now recognise that Napoleon's wars cost far too many lives, caused too much destruction.' He looked down and added in a low voice. 'I shall never forget the horrors I saw during the Russian campaign. My men forced to slaughter and eat their horses; then force-marched in ragged uniforms on frozen roads for days, suffering from frostbite, crying with hunger and pain, hallucinating in the white hell.' His voice was flat and distant, as if he was reliving terrible nightmares.

'Hugo, my love,' Madame Saintclair said quietly. 'Not now.'

'Sorry, Mother.' He shook his head, let out a long sigh, and looked up.

Marie-Ange tightened her grip on her knife and fork to fight the overwhelming urge to touch the side of his face and soothe away the pain in his eyes.

'Why don't you leave the army and join Father at the workshop?' Lucie asked brightly. 'You know how much it would mean to us all, we wouldn't have to worry about you getting killed or wounded anymore. And you could live nearby all the time. Maybe even marry.'

'Lucie, please. The army is my life, you know that,' Hugo said, his voice stern.

'But I miss you so much when you are away.'

Hugo leant towards her and kissed her cheek. 'I miss you too, sweetheart. Well, maybe one day …'

But Marie-Ange could see he didn't mean it.

To lighten the mood, Madame Saintclair asked Marie-Ange about the latest fashion in England.

'I am definitely not the right person to ask about fashion,' Marie-Ange replied, pulling a face. 'Most of my dresses are very dull. I never go to any elegant gatherings. I did not even know how to dance the waltz before your son showed me at Fouché's ball the other night!'

She looked at him and the words died on her lips. Her cheeks became painfully hot as she remembered what had happened after the dance at the cuirassiers' barracks.

Saintclair held her gaze. A mischievous smile appeared on his lips. 'I thought you managed very well, for someone so inexperienced,' he said.

She looked down and fussed with her napkin.

'You saw Fouché, then?' Hugo's father asked.

'Yes, he was there.'

'At least we have always agreed on that man. He is despicable, without honour or loyalty. How Napoleon tolerated him for so long is beyond me.'

'He is a snake, I'll grant you that,' Hugo agreed. 'His strength lies in the fact that he has no loyalty except to himself, and in the network of spies he has built over the years. Ministers, generals, members of the royal family and the emperor's former entourage, everybody is afraid of him and of the information he holds on them.'

He didn't look her way, but Marie-Ange knew it was for her benefit he spoke. She heaved a sigh. She didn't like being reminded that Christopher was probably one of Fouché's spies, even though he must have his reasons.

After supper, Lucie announced that she was weary and wished to retire and her parents went upstairs with her, leaving Saintclair and Marie-Ange to sit alone in the drawing room.

'You are lucky to have your family. They are kind and loving people.'

She spared a thought for Robert who must be waiting anxiously for news at Norton Place. She should write to him but was reluctant to mention her meeting with Christopher. She didn't want to raise his hopes about his brother being alive just yet.

She leant towards Saintclair and whispered.

'I think I know where to find the Cross of Life.'

Saintclair arched his eyebrows. 'Go on.'

She explained about the song, the drawings of the dovecote, and about Aline's letter. 'My grandmother wrote that Saint-Germain sent a team of craftsmen to build the dovecote. That was back in 1783, a few months before his death. Maybe he sensed it was time he hid the Cross.' She paused and looked into the flames. 'Perhaps he knew he would soon die.'

She closed her eyes, trying to remember more details of the letters. 'Aline wrote that the men worked relentlessly day and night. They camped in the grounds of Beauregard. One man guarded the entrance to the tent at all times. My grandmother wondered what they had in there that was so valuable. What if it was the Cross?'

'Among the hiding places he had access to all over Europe, why would Saint-Germain choose to build a dovecote at Beauregard to hide it?' He sounded sceptical.

'I'm not sure but it fits with the words of the song. Doves, a rose garden, the wing of an angel.'

Saintclair stared at her. 'Your name, Marie-Ange, is rather unusual,' he remarked.

'My mother was called Catherine Marie-Ange, too. It was Saint-Germain, her godfather, who named her.'

'So Malleval may not be that mad after all. You do know how to retrieve that mysterious Cross and its relic, whatever that is.'

'The song says it's an angel wing.' She smiled. 'Well, obviously, it can't be – angels don't exist.'

Saintclair poked the fire and turned to gaze at her, his eyes smouldering and so caressing she felt her body respond.

'Don't they?' he said, with a low voice.

Her lips parted, her breath quickened, her skin prickled all over. He stepped closer, took her hand and turned it over to caress her palm and then her wrist with his lips. It was so soft, so light and yet so powerful her breath left her in a gentle sigh. Desire shot through her veins. She threw her head back and closed her eyes.

He cleared his throat, let go of her hand, and she was jerked back to reality.

'I am returning to Lyon tonight,' he said. 'I won't be able to visit for a few days but when I come back, I will take you to Beauregard. We will go into the dovecote and resolve once and for all the mystery of the Cross of Life.'

He bowed in front of her. 'Goodnight, Marie-Ange,' he said. It was the first time he had called her by her first name. His voice and the way he looked at her made her shiver all over again.

'Thank you for your help,' she said with a tight smile. 'And thank you for letting me stay with your family.'

He nodded and left. She sat in the drawing room a long time. Would he find news of Christopher waiting for him when he got back tonight? As she stared into the dying flames of the fire, she realised with a twinge of shame that the feelings Christopher's name aroused in her heart tonight had faded and were no longer those of an all-consuming love.

Chapter Twelve

The following days were happy and peaceful. Capitaine Saintclair's family seemed to have adopted her unreservedly, and she found herself growing attached to them, particularly Lucie. The night terrors had stopped, and she was even considering the future with more optimism. She didn't need Malleval's money at all. Her great-aunt would probably help with her expenses while she waited for news of Christopher. And when she was reunited with him, he would sort out all her worries, and she would forget about the Cross of Life.

She spent her time with Lucie and Madame Saintclair, mostly in the cosy drawing room overlooking the garden. In the mornings she helped with Lucie's medication. She brewed her ginseng tea, prepared eyebright poultices that the young girl had to keep on at least an hour every day to help reduce the inflammation of her eyes.

One day, Marie-Ange was sitting at the kitchen table, grinding the white medicinal flowers on a wooden board when she heard a man shout outside the garden door.

'Give me more money, Martine. This is no way near enough for a crust of bread and a pitcher of wine.'

The voice sounded familiar. She stopped what she was doing to listen.

'I need at least two francs. I know the Saintclairs pay you well, the least you can do is help me out since it's their son who threw me out of the army.'

It was the drunken soldier who had threatened Saintclair outside the tavern.

'Stop this racket or someone will hear you,' the woman answered back. 'There, I'll give you one franc. Try not to waste it all at the inn. Hurry now!'

The door opened and the scullery maid entered, dishevelled and her cheeks bright red. She looked surprised to see Marie-Ange in the kitchen and mumbled a greeting.

‘Why is that man coming here, Martine?’ Marie-Ange asked. She hadn’t forgotten the soldier’s threats against Saintclair and his family.

The woman put her fists on her hips and retorted defiantly, ‘Antoine is my cousin. I help him out sometimes, I give him scraps of food, and a bit of money.’

‘I don’t think Capitaine Saintclair would approve of him coming into the garden or the house,’ Marie-Ange remonstrated. In fact, she was sure he would be irate if he ever found out. He would probably send the maid away too.

Martine approached and tugged at her arm. ‘Please, Madame, don’t tell him. I promise I won’t let Antoine in again.’

Marie-Ange hesitated, bit her lower lip. ‘I don’t know … all right then, but you must give your word.’

Martine swore Antoine wouldn’t come in. ‘Not even in the garden,’ she added.

Still uneasy, Marie-Ange resumed preparing Lucie’s poultices. It didn’t feel right to hide the drunken soldier’s visits from the Saintclairs. They were such kind people. Madame Saintclair was even making dresses for her, having ordered silks in soft shades of periwinkle and coral from her husband’s workshop. Marie-Ange had suggested more muted colours, but Madame Saintclair had shaken her head.

‘These shades of blue and pink suit you. Surely, you can now put an end to your mourning. In France, nobody would have any objections to a widow wearing bright colours after six years.’

So Marie-Ange had relented. After all, she wasn’t a widow any longer.

In the afternoon, when a pale sunshine pierced the clouds, she usually took Lucie for a stroll in the garden. They would link arms and walk along the gravel lanes. The girl had submitted her to a thorough interrogation and now knew all about Wellcombe, about Norton Place and its occupants, including Robert, the servants and the two spaniels, Rusty and Splinter. Marie-Ange hadn’t said much about Christopher, only that he had been lost at sea. Lucie, however, wasn’t in the least interested in Christopher. She much preferred talking about Hugo, her hero.

'It has been wonderful to have him at home these past few months,' Lucie said during one of their walks. 'I, for one, am glad peace has been restored and Napoleon sent into exile. Before, we would spend months without any news and Maman was worried sick about him. Hugo has been on so many campaigns, so many battlefields, all over Europe. I know that the worst was Russia. He was much changed when he came back.'

One afternoon, they ventured outside the walled garden into the village. Lucie had talked about getting a dog and Martine mentioned a lady who lived near the church who had puppies for sale.

'We will go today,' Lucie had decreed. It was cold, grey, and misty, but she was determined to take a look at the puppies.

As they walked through the winding village streets, she spoke about the ambush in the forest. 'Hugo said you were the bravest woman he ever met.'

Marie-Ange tutted. 'He shouldn't have told you about the highwaymen. I am not proud of what I did.' In fact, she was positively angry at Saintclair for telling his young sister she had killed three men.

'Why not?' Lucie leant towards her and squeezed her arm. 'He thinks very highly of you, you know. I do hope you will live close by when you get married. You could even live in St Genis. Wouldn't that be wonderful?' Lucie clapped her hands together and laughed.

Marie-Ange gasped. What was the girl talking about? What had given her the idea that she would marry her brother?

'Lucie, your brother and I are not getting married.'

'Of course you are,' the girl retorted. 'I see the way you two look at each other. It's just like in my romance novels. I am sure he is waiting for his promotion to major before he proposes. Hugo was always so determined to make it to the top but I sometimes fear his ambition will get the better of him. It is as if he wants to constantly prove his worth to the world … or to himself.'

Marie-Ange thought Lucie's remarks about her brother's character very insightful for a young girl. Saintclair did indeed burn with ambition to pursue his military career to the very top. However, she couldn't be more wrong about him wanting to marry her or being in love with her. The man had made it clear he didn't believe in romance or marriage. As for her, she would never marry him, even if she wasn't already married. The capitaine possessed too many undesirable traits. And, of course, she did not love him.

She looked around uneasily. A thick fog had descended and covered the village roofs. The church spire had already disappeared.

'We should go back, Lucie.'

The girl ignored her.

'I wonder what your brother-in-law will say when he reads your letter. I hope you told him that Hugo was the bravest, the most honourable of men.'

Marie-Ange had at last written to Robert about the developments of her travel to France – or at least about some of them. It was only fair he should know there would be no inheritance, and therefore no prospect of him going to the Naval Academy just yet. She had not, however, mentioned Christopher.

'Lucie, I don't know why you think …'

The streets were very quiet now that the fog had thickened further, turning houses and trees into ghostly shapes. There was nobody else but them in the street. Suddenly the eerie silence was broken by the thunderous sounds of a horse-drawn carriage behind them. Marie-Ange put her arm around Lucie's shoulders to push her against the wall, out of harm's way. Instead of overtaking them, the carriage stopped and blocked the street. A man sprang up in front of them, reeking of cheap wine and unwashed rags. It was the ex-soldier.

'Here they are! The capitaine's strumpet and his little sister.'

He walked up to Marie-Ange, so close she saw the burst veins in his eyes and winced at the smell of his foul breath. He raised a grimy hand towards her face and she stepped back in disgust.

'You sure are pretty, miss! Pretty enough to kiss.'

'Enough! Shut up and scarper!' A booming voice called from behind.

Marie-Ange turned round, her heart sinking as she recognised Rochefort. He climbed from the driver's seat. He was holding a black hood and a length of rope in his hands.

'You promised me three francs. I told you they'd be here, and here they are,' the drunkard protested.

So it was a trap. Martine had lured them to this deserted alleyway at the back of the church on behalf of her cousin. There were no puppies for sale.

Rochefort threw a few coins on the ground, which the man picked up before running off, swallowed by the fog. Lucie held onto Marie-Ange's arm, terrified. Her breathing had become laboured and wheezy.

Marie-Ange decided to gain time.

'Good afternoon, Monsieur Rochefort,' she said with assurance. 'Do you just happen to be visiting St Genis or did you come especially for me?'

'If you come with me without making any fuss, the girl won't be harmed and I won't need to use these on you.' He showed the black hood and the rope.

'Where exactly are we going?'

'You'll find out soon enough, M'ame. Hurry now, get in.' Rochefort stepped forward.

'Marie-Ange, who is this man?' Lucie asked, her voice quivering with fear. She was deadly pale now. Her lips had taken a blue tinge. With her hand pressed against her chest as if trying to slow her heartbeats, she looked about to faint. Marie-Ange took one look at her and decided she could not put the girl in any more danger.

'It's all right, Lucie. You can go home.'

Lucie shook her head. 'No, I won't leave you alone with him.'

'Don't argue with me. Go now!' Marie-Ange almost shouted, pushing Lucie forward into the street.

She walked towards Rochefort. 'I am coming.'

He grunted and gestured for her to get into the carriage. She opened the door. The thick black curtains were pulled across the windows but she glimpsed the black-clad figure of a man sitting in a corner. He leapt forward, grabbed her wrists to pull her to him and before she could scream, pressed a cloth on her face, forcing her to breathe in a strong, acrid substance. As she lost consciousness, Marie-Ange recognised the gleaming, dark brown eyes of Gustave Karloff.

She coughed, shivered violently, and opened her eyes. Her fingers scraped the hard, wet floor on which she was lying before she managed to sit up against the cold stone wall. Her head throbbed. She licked her dry lips and took several deep breaths to control the nausea that threatened to overtake her. When she felt a little steadier and the world had stopped spinning, she looked around. She was in a cell. There were iron rings and chains fastened to the bare stone walls and a couple of old straw beds on the floor. Where had Rochefort and Karloff taken her?

She put her hands in front of her. At least her wrists weren't bound. She patted her dress. It was wet through – no wonder she was frozen to the core. She tried to get up but her legs wouldn't obey and she slumped back against the wall.

Heavy footsteps outside and the noise of keys rattling against the door sent her heart pounding and she pressed herself against the damp, cold wall. The door creaked open and Rochefort came in.

'Can you walk?' he asked, gruff and with a scowl on his face. 'I'll carry you if you can't.'

'Where am I?' She didn't move.

'Malleval,' he replied. 'I asked you if you could walk.'

'Why am I here?'

'Not my place to tell.' He marched towards her, grabbed her arm and pulled her up roughly. His fingers formed an iron ring around her arm. It was pointless to resist as he dragged her along a dark corridor and up two dozen roughly carved stone steps. He opened a thick wooden door and pushed her through it. She stumbled into a brightly lit hall, with a chequered black and white tiled floor and dark wood-panelled walls covered with hunting trophies – stuffed heads of deer, complete with huge antlers, snarling silver wolves and brown bears.

Rochefort gestured her to a staircase.

'Up there.'

They climbed to the first floor. Rochefort opened a door and Marie-Ange stepped into a large, almost entirely black bedroom lit by thick, tall candles. The walls and the ceiling were painted black, too. The chimney breast was carved black granite. In a corner of the room was a four-poster bed covered with black silk blankets and with black veils hanging down. It was the most sinister place she'd ever seen.

'Sit down over there,' Rochefort ordered.

Marie-Ange crossed her arms on her chest. 'First I want to know why I'm here. And then I want you to take me back to St Genis,' she said haughtily. Her voice faltered when she saw the mocking grin on Rochefort's face.

'Do as you're told or I'll give you another dose of medicine.' He pointed to a basin of water near the fireplace. 'There's hot water and a change of clothes, if you want.'

He left, a key grated in the lock.

As soon as Rochefort was gone, she walked to the windows and lifted the black curtains. The windows were encased in thick iron bars. She pressed her face to the pane but it was too dark outside to see anything. Saintclair had said the village of Malleval was located in a small mountain range, with nothing but precipices and forests for miles around. She might as well be alone in the world.

She prayed Lucie had arrived home safely and raised the alarm, and that Monsieur and Madame Saintclair had alerted their son of her abduction by now. Capitaine Saintclair was her only hope.

Shivering, she turned back into the bedroom. Heavens, this place was ghastly! She walked to the washstand and dipped her fingers into the warm, fragranced water. She washed her face and her hands, but refrained from undressing and slipping into the black robe that was draped on the back of the armchair.

She stood in front of the fire in an attempt to dry her dress. The spicy scent of the water in the washstand was overpowering, the heat of the fire made her lethargic and sleepy. She sat down, closed her eyes and rested her head against the soft cushions of the armchair.

She had no idea how long she slept. When she woke up, Karloff and Malleval were sitting opposite her, conversing in very low voices. She straightened up. The room seemed to move in front of her as if she was at sea.

Karloff bent over, frowning with concern. He put his hand on her forehead and turned to Malleval. 'She's burning with a fever. I think we should let her rest now. I'll give her something.'

'No, we will proceed as planned,' Malleval retorted sharply.

Marie-Ange tried to focus her eyes on his face. He looked paler, thinner tonight.

'How dare you keep me against my will? I want you to take me back to St Genis,' she said, but her voice sounded weak, barely more than a whisper.

'What happens next depends on you, dear Marie-Ange,' Malleval replied. 'And what you'll tell us. Hopefully our conversation will be fruitful, and painless.'

He nodded to Karloff, who produced a gold pocket watch from his waistcoat pocket. Leaning towards her the physician dangled the chain in a slow, regular movement in front of her face.

'Last time, we were interrupted by the noise of branches rattling on the window,' he explained. 'I hope we reach the desired conclusion tonight.'

He gazed deep into Marie-Ange's eyes and started talking with the soothing, monotonous voice she remembered only too well from her nightmares.

'Have you been hearing my voice in your dreams? I have been calling to you every night. I hope it helped you remember the words.'

The gold pocket watch glistened in the light of the fire, the flames reflecting on its smooth, shiny cover.

'You are tired, Marie-Ange. You are so tired. Your limbs are heavy. You are unable to move. You desperately want to close your eyes and sleep. But you can't. Not yet. First you must tell us what we want to know, and then you will be able to sleep for as long as you wish.' Karloff's voice became soft and caressing. 'Your reward is to sleep, in a nice, warm bed, safe and secure.'

His pocket watch rocked with a regular pendulum motion from left to right, catching the light of the flames as it moved. Marie-Ange was fascinated by the glittering metal and its regular, rhythmical motion. She yearned for sleep, Karloff was right about that. More than anything else she wanted to lie down, to be safe and warm.

'Remember the words, Marie-Ange. The words of the song your mother taught you. The words her godfather Saint-Germain taught her. The secret words.'

Karloff repeated his instructions several times, until Marie-Ange's lips opened as if of their own accord and she sang the first verse. There was only one thought in her mind. All she had to do was tell them the words, and then she would be able to rest.

Ma mie, ma rose de mai

Ma rose aux cinq pétales,

Qui dans la tour aux colombes,

Pleure l'amant dans la tombe ...

'This is all very well, but we already know the first verse,' Malleval cut in, impatient.

'Shh!' Karloff turned towards him. 'Don't interrupt again or she might wake up.'

He kept his voice even and soothing but it was too late. The spell was broken. Just like in her bedroom on Isle Barbe, Marie-Ange managed to snap out of her trance. She had been about to reveal the secret. With the song, Malleval and Karloff would find the Cross of Life in the dovecote. Her mind was racing now. Maybe she could change a few of the words whilst pretending to be still under Karloff's spell.

She sang the last verses very slowly.

Listen to me, don't despair,

Your lover you'll see again,

Place your hand *on the rose, give* one *turn,*

Lower *your eyes, and the wing you will find.*

But you must choose wisely,

For if the wing of the dove

Is as white as the angel's

It will not open your lover's tomb.

Exhausted, Marie-Ange reclined against the back of the armchair. She had managed to change what she considered to be the most important words. She had turned the instruction‘ put the rose on the heart and turn five times’ into ‘put your hand on the rose and turn once’. Then, she had said that they had to look ‘down’ instead of ‘up’ to find the wing.

Would the two men notice her subterfuge? And would these little changes make any difference and prevent them from finding the Cross?

Malleval finished scribbling the words on a thick piece of paper, put his quill down, and blew on the sheet to dry the ink.

‘There, that wasn't so hard, was it?’ Karloff whispered, putting his watch back in his pocket. ‘Now you can rest, as promised.’

He turned towards Malleval, a little anxious.

‘Will that be all for now? The girl needs to sleep or she will be useless to us for the rest.’

Malleval didn't answer but came to stand behind her armchair. He leant slightly forward. His fingers touched her hair and played with her golden curls. Suddenly they slid down to her throat and pressed hard. Unable to breathe she tried to wriggle out of his grip as he pinned her against the back of the armchair.

‘Do not move,’ he instructed coldly. ‘A word of warning, my dear. Never, ever, make a fool of me again. I really didn't appreciate your escaping from Isle Barbe with Saintclair.'

He pressed his fingers harder against her neck until her vision dimmed and blurred. 'As for my good friend, he is as good as dead,' he finished.

He released her suddenly. She gasped and panted, in a desperate attempt to catch her breath.

'You are mad! Mad and dangerous,' she managed to say.

Malleval chuckled. He walked across the room and opened the door.

'Give her something for the fever and let her sleep, Karloff. We don't want her to be ill for Beauregard. We will leave as soon as the snow stops.'

A look of triumph lit up his face. 'Soon, my father will be proud of me.' And he went out.

Karloff got up and pulled Marie-Ange from the chair. She was too weak to walk so he carried her to the bed and laid her down. With one hand he swept her hair away from her face in a gentle gesture.

'I have been trying to get into your mind for days, or rather nights, but you are very strong. Much stronger than I thought. Anyway, I was right, you are the one. You are of the true blood of the Keepers. It was written in your stars and in your mother's stars that you would find the Cross for us.'

'Did you send me the shadows?' she whispered.

'Which shadows?'

'The shadows in my dreams. They want to take something from me. They are angry.' Her head was burning. She closed her eyes.

'There are no shadows. You are delirious. I will ask a chambermaid to get you out of these wet clothes, and shall come back with a draught. You have caught a nasty chill.'

His footsteps receded and then a key turned in the lock.

Chapter Thirteen

Huge ravens shrieked as they circled the grey skies outside the grilled window. The mountains and pine forests clinging to their steep slopes were covered in a thick carpet of snow. All morning Marie-Ange had hoped to see a tall figure riding through the village, but Saintclair hadn't come. Did he know she had been taken? Did he even care? Maybe he had second thoughts about helping her out of Malleval's clutches and decided to put his family's interests before her.

Another thought troubled her. What if Malleval had already carried out his threat and Saintclair was dead? She closed her eyes and conjured up an image of the cuirassier officer, with his bright blue eyes, in turn frosty or smouldering, and the quick smile that so often appeared on the corner of his mouth. Catching her breath, she recalled for the hundredth time the sensual caress of his lips over her mouth, of his hands over her skin, the way she felt the night of the ball, out of control and wanting more. She hated herself for it. What kind of woman longed for a man she had only just met, and who had ideas and values so different from her own? The only man she should be thinking of was her husband.

She turned towards the bedroom that had become her prison. Three times a day a servant woman brought her food and a tonic Karloff prepared to help her recover from her fever. Now she was better they would probably set off for Beauregard. When Malleval realised she had lied about the song, he would be angry. He might even hurt her again. She touched her throat where his tight grip had left painful bruises.

Karloff came in, silent as always. The man slipped in and out of the room like a ghost. He was dressed for an outing, in a black cloak lined with brown fur and a hat.

'Would you like to join me for a short walk in the village, my dear? Now that you're no longer ill, I think fresh air would do you good.' He closed the door behind him. 'Actually we should go now, while Monsieur Uxeloup is busy in his study.'

It sounded as if he was anxious to get out without Malleval

knowing. Marie-Ange acquiesced, only too glad of the chance to escape the sinister black room. Rochefort waited for them in the hall. They stepped out into the courtyard and Marie-Ange pointed to Malleval's coat of arms carved above the door – *A* and *M* intertwined – and asked Karloff what the letters stood for.

'*Ante Mortem*. Before Death. It's the old Malleval motto. Enjoy life before it's too late,' Karloff added, muttering to himself. 'Of course, the motto will take an entirely different meaning soon.'

Before she could ask him what he meant, he led the way down the narrow street that zigzagged through the village. She was struck once again by the wilderness of the setting. Stone houses were built directly into the rock, their grated windows commanding a view of steep precipices below and dense woods covering the mountains. From the street, Malleval's manor house looked as impregnable as the mountain itself.

'Impressive, is it not?' Karloff asked. 'The Mallevals built their castle like a fortress back in the 1640s.'

'They must have been very successful highwaymen,' Marie-Ange remarked.

He shot her an amused glance. 'I see you know about the family's infamous past. Well, I suppose it's no secret, they were indeed a gang of highwaymen who pillaged neighbouring towns, ransomed travellers, and robbed boats and barges as far as the river Rhône.'

'Did they ever get caught?'

He shrugged. 'Nobody dared challenge them.' He stepped closer to Marie-Ange and added in a low voice. 'You can trust me with your secret. Sometimes men have to choose the wrong allies in order to win a just cause. I may have joined forces with the Mallevals to find the Cross but my motives are pure.'

Her heart beat faster. Had he guessed she had misled them about the song?

'Follow me. I want to explain something to you.'

Karloff set off and stopped a little further along in front of a house with a six-branched star carved above its door.

‘This was the family house of Polycarpe de la Rivière, a most saintly man, and an outstanding but misunderstood scholar.’ Karloff kept his voice low as if he didn’t want Rochefort to overhear.

Marie-Ange frowned. ‘I remember that name.’ On her first evening at Beauregard, Malleval had shown her a manuscript written in the Templar code. He said it had been in Polycarpe’s possession before his family got hold of it.

Karloff took a deep breath. ‘Let me tell you about myself and about Polycarpe, then maybe you’ll agree to help me. I belong to an organisation called the *Société Angélique*,’ he started. ‘It was founded in Venice during the Renaissance, disbanded after accusations of heresy by the Vatican but later re-formed in Lyon. Over the centuries, our members have been among the most talented writers and artists in France. Men such as Rabelais or Nicolas Poussin, the painter. And, of course, Polycarpe de la Rivière.’

‘What exactly is this *Société Angélique*?’

‘Our sole purpose is to communicate with angels. Thanks to the Cross of Life, this will soon be possible.’

‘Really? How?’

Karloff smiled. ‘The angel will come to us when we find the Cross.’

She wanted to retort that angels didn’t exist, but asked instead, ‘What about Poylcarpe? Why is he important?’

‘He was the prior at Sainte-Croix-en-Jarez, a nearby charterhouse, in the 1620s, where he discovered a casket of precious artefacts and scrolls in a cache behind the walls of the cloister. Although he never disclosed the exact content of the papers, he confided to a friend, Sebastien de Grief, from the *Société Angélique* that they were coded documents written by the Knights Templar. He managed to decipher them and found they spoke of the Templars’ most treasured relic – the Cross of Life.’

Karloff breathed in and carried on. ‘On de Grief’s advice, Polycarpe used the decoded parchments as the basis for his most famous work, *Angels and Immortality of the Soul*. However, as soon as it was published the treatise was placed on the list of forbidden books and every copy seized by the Church. Polycarpe himself was demoted and sent to a remote abbey in Provence.'

'What was the book about?' Marie-Ange was intrigued. Despite shivering with cold in the freezing wind, which was now blowing across the village, she had no intention of going back to Malleval's fortress just yet and wanted to keep Karloff talking.

'It related the story of the Cross of Life the Knights Templar brought back from Palestine after their ultimate defeat at St Jean d'Acre, and its extraordinary powers to confer eternal life and enable contact with celestial beings.' He sighed. 'As I said, every single copy of Polycarpe's book was destroyed, but his correspondence with de Grief, as well as many details about the decoded parchments and the cipher used by the Knight Templars, remained in the *Société Angélique's* archives.'

'So what happened to Polycarpe?'

'In 1639, he left his abbey with several faithful servants to take up a new post in Burgundy. He visited his family here in Malleval on the way, but he never arrived in Burgundy. He and his men disappeared in the mountains, together with the casket of precious objects he was taking to his new abbey and the scrolls he carried with him at all times.' Karloff paused and stared into her eyes. 'The Malleval clan killed him and stole his gold and his parchments.'

Marie-Ange gasped. 'What makes you think that?'

'Firstly, the family became very wealthy around that time. They built their fortress and gave up some of their criminal activities, no doubt thanks to Polycarpe's gold and precious artefacts. Secondly, it would explain how they acquired the coded Templar scroll. When Edmond Malleval contacted me at the *Société Angélique* in the autumn of 1790 he said his family had had it for well over a century.'

'Is that the parchment which is now in the library at Beauregard?'

Karloff nodded. 'The very one. Edmond said he had forgotten all about it until he saw Count Saint-Germain's portrait at Beauregard, holding a similar parchment and a beautiful bejewelled Cross. It so intrigued him he tried to acquire the painting straight away.'

'My grandmother wrote that he was very angry when her

husband Philippe refused to sell him the painting,' Marie-Ange remarked. 'So, you were the one who decoded the parchment?'

Karloff nodded. 'I found the key to the Knights Templar's code in the *Société Angélique*'s archives – each letter of the alphabet is replaced with a section of the Templar Cross. The parchment was the transcription of messages from past Templar Masters about the Cross of Life and its powers. From the moment I handed Edmond the translated document, he became obsessed with obtaining the Cross and cheating death.'

He paused again. 'As for me, I knew that at last the relic was within my grasp. Ever since Polycarpe wrote his forbidden book, members of our society have searched for it. I advised Edmond to keep a close watch on Aline Beauregard because I believed she knew where the Cross was hidden. He decided that marrying her was the best way to gain control over her and Beauregard. When we realised she didn't know anything about the Cross, we turned to Catherine, your mother, with whom Saint-Germain had formed a special bond.'

Marie-Ange stared at the physician coldly. '*You* are responsible for my grandfather's execution and my grandmother's suicide, and for my mother's imprisonment in this godforsaken place.' She gestured towards Malleval's fortress. 'And now I'm here too, at Malleval's mercy, and all that for an old cross and a far-fetched legend.'

Karloff shook his head. 'Oh, but it isn't any old cross. It was the most treasured possession of the Knights Templar. The relic hidden inside the Cross confers eternal life, but under one condition only.'

His dark eyes were feverish. 'According to the scroll I deciphered, it can only unleash its powers if handled by the chosen one – a pure heart, someone of the same bloodline as a Grand Master of the Templar Order. Edmond Malleval wasn't a pure heart, not by a long shot. Nor was he related to any former Knight Templar. So even if he had found the Cross he wouldn't have become immortal. He needed the chosen one to help him.'

He paused. 'Your mother was the one. She was a Beauregard, a cousin of the Beaujeus who counted Guillaume as a Grand Master. She was also Saint-Germain's precious god-daughter. He must have told her where the Cross was hidden. Edmond went mad when she escaped. He looked for her for years and years.'

His eyes clouded over. 'When he became ill, he made Uxeloup swear he would carry on with the search. And finally we found you.'

He stepped towards Marie-Ange and took her hand. 'Your mother told you the secret, didn't she? She told you and now you must find the Cross for me.'

'What makes you so different from Uxeloup and his father? You and your fanciful stories are responsible for destroying my family,' she said, pulling her hand from his.

'Uxeloup, like his father before him, only wants the Cross for himself. I, on the other hand, want to make contact with the angel who, the parchment claims, will appear when the Cross is returned to its rightful place by the chosen one – the pure heart. In other words, you, now your mother is dead.'

Marie-Ange shook her head with dismay. The man was just as crazy as the Mallevals.

'You are strong-willed, like your mother. I never could exercise enough control on her mind to make her reveal the secret … you were very clever about it but I know you changed the words of the song. If you help me, I promise you will return to England safe and sound.'

It was snowing. Thick, fluffy flakes swirled all around them. In the corner of her eye, Marie-Ange saw two grey shadows advance silently towards them. She caught her breath. In a few seconds, they were upon Rochefort. The big man, taken by surprise, crumpled, unconscious, onto the ground without offering any resistance. Karloff turned round but one of the attackers grabbed him by the throat and he too collapsed without a sound.

'Come with me,' one of the men told her, extending his gloved hand.

'Who are you?' she asked, her heart beating wildly, but not from fear.

He loosened his scarf to uncover his face. He had a handsome, lean and weather-beaten face. The lines around his mouth, on his forehead and at the corner of his eyes indicated he wasn't a young man, but it was his eyes that held her attention. They were a pale aquamarine, the exact same colour as her own. She knew who he was before he answered.

'My name is Baldassare dei Conti. I am your father.'

Now wasn't the time for questions so she took his hand and ran with him down the street, their footsteps muffled by the snow.

Another man was waiting with the horses behind a wall at the entrance of the village. The man who called himself Baldassare lifted Marie-Ange up onto his horse and mounted behind her. Within a few seconds, they were galloping on the narrow road, which wound its way up the mountain towards the pass. She should have been terrified. There were deep ravines on both sides and the road was covered with snow. Yet she felt elated. She was escaping Uxeloup Malleval and his prison. First and foremost, she had found her father.

They rode until dusk. They had to walk after reaching the pass because of the deep snow. Then they rode again until the track dipped into a gorge where they dismounted and walked through the dark night. After a time, the outline of a partly ruined barn stood out amongst the trees. The men opened its rickety wooden doors. One of them led the horses to a corner and took their tack off while another fetched wood from the forest to make a fire. Baldassare cleared a space in a corner of the barn to make their camp.

His companion brought several leather bags over and proceeded to pull out packets of food, utensils, and colourful woven blankets. The other man came back, his arms full of more twigs and branches, and built up the fire.

'Sit down,' Baldassare told Marie-Ange, arranging blankets on the ground.

Soon, flames rose towards the high-beamed ceiling, the smoke escaping through the many holes pitting the roof. One man filled a tin pot with snow and placed it on the fire. When the snow had melted and the water was hot, he threw a handful of herbs into it to make tea. Then he cut slices of bread and strips of meat, and the men took their hooded capes off to sit down for supper.

'I expect you have questions for me,' Baldassare said, as he poured steaming hot tea into a cup and handed it to her.

She nodded. She did have questions, so many of them, but where to start?

'You are one of the men who came to Beauregard to build the dovecote, aren't you? Did you hide the Cross of Life in there?'

He smiled and nodded.

'Did you rescue my mother from Malleval's fortress after he took her away from Salles?'

'If you know about that, then you know everything, daughter.' He paused, poking the fire with a long stick to keep it burning high.

'No, I don't know everything. I just guessed. I don't know who you really are or where you are from. I don't know why you abandoned my mother when she was pregnant, or why you waited until now to meet me. And I don't know anything about the Cross of Life apart from a lot of ridiculous stories.'

She was so angry suddenly that the words tumbled out of her mouth. 'Why did your men hide the Cross at Beauregard? Is the relic really the wing of an angel, can it really make people immortal?' She glared at the man with the pale blue eyes who sat near the fire.

'I understand your dismay, daughter, but I cannot answer all your questions tonight. The object we are seeking is one of the most precious and powerful ever held by men. It has now exceeded its time on this earth. You were chosen to return it to its rightful place.'

'But what …?'

Baldassare raised his hand to silence her. He poked the fire again, gestured towards the other two men.

'Let me tell you about us first. My companions and I are Turcopilars, members of a secret armed force serving the Order of the Knights Hospitaller, also known as the Knights of St John. We were banished from our base at Fort Saint Angel in Malta when Napoleon invaded the island in 1798. When they took over, the British refused to allow us back on the island, so we now wander between the Order's priories across Europe, from Paris to Sicily, from Cyprus to Russia.'

'I don't understand. Aren't the Knights Hospitaller the same as the Knights Templar?'

'No, the Hospitaller knights were always a distinct entity. They never provoked the ire of Philippe Le Bel or Pope Clement V and therefore were allowed to take over much of the Knights Templar wealth when they were disbanded.' Baldassare paused. 'They also inherited their secrets, and us – the Turcopilars. Our mission is to help our brothers wherever they need us. We are an army of shadows. Nobody sees us. Nobody knows we exist.'

Baldassare looked at Marie-Ange and smiled softly. 'I first met your mother as a young man when I was entrusted with the very special mission by our Great Bailiff of building a secure hiding place for the Cross of Life. Our brother Saint-Germain feared he could no longer guarantee its safety.'

'Why Beauregard?'

Baldassare smiled again. 'It was Saint-Germain's idea. Beauregard was close to Arginy Castle where the Cross must be returned. He also knew it would be safe there with his god-daughter – your mother.'

A tender expression appeared on his face. 'She was wise, brave, and talented beyond her years. Saint-Germain taught her the secret words she would need to retrieve the Cross when the time came. She never betrayed his trust.'

The men finished eating and drinking. They exchanged a few words in a language that sounded a little like Italian, and one of them walked out.

'First watch,' Baldassare explained. 'We should rest now. We have a long ride ahead of us tomorrow.' He wrapped a blanket around his shoulders but Marie-Ange would not let him sleep just yet.

'How did you rescue my mother from Malleval's fortress?'

He stared into the fire, a look of sadness on his beautiful, chiselled features.

'Catherine's godmother, the Abbess at Salles Priory, knew about us. She sent her manservant, Pierre, to warn me that your mother had been taken by Edmond Malleval, and to give me Catherine's sketchbook and the locket she had managed to hide – it was lucky because Malleval later searched the Priory and, as you may have gathered, both the locket and the sketchbook hold clues as to the Cross' hiding place.'

Baldassare paused. 'I rode to Malleval and watched the fortress for days but Edmond kept your mother under tight supervision. Finally, I managed to get in and reach Catherine's bedchamber in the tower. Your mother and I escaped and rode day and night for weeks towards the North coast. We became close during our long journey. She was beautiful and kind. She was a treasure.'

'So why did you abandon her? You must have known she was expecting a child.' Marie-Ange wasn't angry anymore. She could see the sadness in her father's eyes and hear the regret in his voice.

'I was a Turcopilar. Having sworn a vow of allegiance to my order, I wasn't a free man. Catherine knew it, she understood. It was arranged she would board a ship for England and that one of our brothers would meet her in Devonshire and look after her.'

'My father? William Jones?' She was confused. 'You mean he was one of yours?'

Baldassare nodded. 'I knew he would take good care of Catherine and of our baby. And he did, didn't he?' He smiled.

Marie-Ange shook her head in disbelief. William Jones, the quiet and taciturn Plymouth lawyer, had been part of a secret brotherhood charged with protecting the Knights Templar secrets all over Europe.

Neither of them spoke for a while. They listened to the crackling of the fire, the hooting of the owls in the woods and the light snoring of the man next to them, who had fallen asleep, wrapped up in his blanket.

'How did you find me today?' she asked, breaking the silence.

'Pierre again. He is an old man now. You met him at Marzac where he has been in your great-aunt's service for some years. He sent a message to our Prior in Paris after your visit to Marzac. He was worried about your safety. He was right. As we arrived in Lyon we heard reports of your escape from Isle Barbe, and then about you being abducted by Rochefort in St Genis. I guessed you were at the fortress in Malleval and we travelled with God's speed to reach you. I am sorry it took us so long.'

There were tears in his eyes when he took hold of her hand and brought it to his lips. Moved with the sudden realisation that this man was her father, she leant closer to him and rested her head against his shoulder. He still had much to explain, particularly about the Cross, but for now she was content just to be close to him.

Baldassare smiled. 'By the way, I must thank the French officer who has been looking after you. Capitaine Saintclair.'

She glanced at him, anxious. 'Malleval wants to kill him.' And she explained how Saintclair assisted her to escape from Isle Barbe.

'I'm sure the man can take care of himself,' Baldassare said reassuringly. 'You must rest now. We will talk some more tomorrow.'

There were still many questions Marie-Ange wanted to ask her father, but her strength seemed to desert her all of a sudden. She wrapped a blanket around her, lay down, and was about to close her eyes when she remembered something.

'The locket. I left it at Saintclair's house in St Genis. I need it to open the secret cache in the dovecote, don't I?'

Baldassare nodded. 'You do indeed. We will get the locket and your mother's sketchbook on our way to Beauregard, don't worry. Go to sleep now.'

Surprisingly, despite the hard cold ground, her aching limbs, and the extraordinary events of the evening, she fell asleep in minutes and slept soundly until dawn.

'Daughter. You must wake up.' Baldassare shook her shoulder gently and handed her a cup of tea.

She smiled and sat up to drink the hot, fragranced drink, which tasted of mint and spices. Then she stood up and stretched her aching limbs as the first glimmers of daylight broke the darkness in the east.

The dawn quiet was suddenly broken by men's voices shouting outside. Baldassare put his hand to his side and pulled a long, curved dagger. He gestured to Marie-Ange to stay inside and sneaked out of the barn. Looking through the barn's broken shutters, she saw three men fighting on the frozen ground, two of them her father's companions. The third man, their assailant, was dark-haired and looked tall and strong. Through his torn coat, the golden buttons of his brown jacket glinted in the first rays of the rising sun.

Her heart jumped in her chest. She rushed out as her father was about to join in the fighting.

'Don't! It's Capitaine Saintclair,' she shouted.

Baldassare froze. Still holding his dagger, he gave a short command for his men to get up.

Saintclair glared at them as they released him, jumped to his feet, and blinked with disbelief when he saw her standing next to the barn door.

'What the hell are you doing here?' he bellowed as he rushed to her side. 'Are you all right?' He held her at arm's length to look at her before wrapping his arm around her waist to pull her against him.

'I'm fine,' she answered.

He turned to glare at her father and his companions. 'If you hurt her, I swear I'll …'

'I said I was fine,' she said, struggling to breathe against his chest and dizzy with relief. He was safe, he had come for her.

She closed her eyes, inhaled his scent of leather, shaving soap and tobacco, and listened to his thundering heartbeat. A warm, heart-clenching feeling flooded her. A thought flashed through her mind. This is where she wanted to be, where she was meant to be – in his arms.

Someone coughed behind them, bringing her back to reality.

'So, this is Capitaine Saintclair,' her father said.

Her cheeks hot, Marie-Ange tried to pull away but Saintclair's arm was like a band of steel around her waist.

'Who are you?' he asked Baldassare, putting his hand on his holster and cursing when he found it empty.

'Is this what you're looking for?' Her father didn't reply but handed him his weapon, a smile on his face.

With a growl, Saintclair took the pistol from him.

'Capitaine, this is my father, Baldassare dei Conti,' Marie-Ange said matter-of-factly, taking advantage of the cuirassier putting his pistol back into his holster to step out of his grasp. 'He and his men rescued me from Malleval yesterday.'

'Your father?' Saintclair puzzled, a deep frown creasing his forehead. 'How is it possible? You said your father was dead, you said he was—'

'English?' she finished. 'I thought so, too, until very recently.'

He scowled at her. 'He could be lying, for all you know.' Turning to her father, he asked, 'Where are you from, and what do you want?'

'This is a story my daughter will tell you later,' her father answered. 'For now you will have to trust me. We have a long way to go to reach Beauregard and it looks as if it's going to snow again.'

'Why Beauregard?'

'We are going to find the Cross,' Marie-Ange replied.

'Very well. I'm coming with you,' Saintclair declared. 'Many of the passes and roads are closed because of the snow. I had to cut through the woods, pulling my horse behind me.' He rubbed his bristly face and let out a deep sigh. 'I was preparing myself for a very unpleasant argument with Malleval, a fight even, to get you out of his fortress.'

'He wishes to do more than argue or fight with you,' she remarked, sombre. 'He said he would kill you.'

He shrugged. 'He's all talk these days.'

'We will get ready to leave now,' Baldassare said. His men went back into the barn, kicked some soil onto the fire, packed up their bags, and they set off. The path was treacherous in places, the snow so deep it reached up to their knees. Marie-Ange's dress was soon soaking wet but she never complained. After a couple of hours, however, her legs were sore and heavy, her feet numb with cold. She stumbled and fell in the snow, exhausted. Saintclair pulled her up. He rubbed her frozen hands in his, looked at her with concern and declared they should rest.

'Not now,' she protested bravely. 'There is no time.'

'She is right,' Baldassare said. 'We will stop later, when we get out of the forest.'

So they carried on and thread their way through the woods until at last they reached open farmland. They sat on tree stumps and shared a quick, tasteless meal of cold meat and hard bread before starting on the road to Vienne. Saintclair said he knew where they could safely spend the night.

'Blanchard, a former lieutenant of mine, bought a tavern in Vienne when he left the cavalry. He won't ask any questions.'

They reached the town as night drew in, rode across the main square which featured the ruins of an impressive Roman temple. They left their horses in a stable block at the back of the temple and carried their bags into a small inn tucked away in a narrow street.

'Capitaine! What brings you here?' a tall, large man exclaimed when Saintclair walked in, followed by Marie-Ange, her father and his two companions.

The two men shook hands and gave each other a few resounding slaps on the back as greeting. Saintclair then imparted some news of his regiment before taking his former lieutenant to one side.

'We need board and lodging for tonight,' he said. 'And we don't want anyone else to know we're here, if you catch my drift.'

'No problem, Capitaine, I'll shut the inn for tonight – you will be my only patrons.'

Baldassare and his two Turcopilars climbed up to their rooms. Marie-Ange was about to follow them when Saintclair put his hand on her arm to stop her.

‘We need to talk,’ he said with a low voice. ‘It’s about your husband.’

Chapter Fourteen

Blanchard showed them into an empty parlour after Saintclair asked for a quiet place. Marie-Ange sat near the fireplace, Saintclair pulled a chair opposite her. Despite shivering in her wet clothes and waterlogged boots, she longed to hear what he had to say.

'This was the note waiting for me when I came back from St Genis the other night.' He produced a crumpled piece of paper from his pocket and handed it to Marie-Ange.

Her fingers shook as she unfolded it.

'The man you want will be at the Mère Vitry Inn on Saturday evening. 21:00.'

That was all.

'Is it your husband's hand?'

She dropped the note in her lap and shook her head. 'I don't recognise it. We must go to Lyon for the meeting, of course.'

She put her hand on her heart. It was beating too fast. Her head was spinning. Tomorrow night, she would see Christopher. She would have the chance to speak to him and help him remember who he was, at last.

'What about this relic?' Saintclair's voice interrupted her thoughts. 'What if Malleval and Karloff are already on their way to Beauregard? Do you want to run the risk of them getting there before you?'

'They can't find the Cross on their own,' she said with confidence. 'What is more important right now is that I meet Christopher tomorrow night.'

'You will do no such thing,' Saintclair cut in. '*I* will go to the rendez-vous and *you* will wait in my quarters. The man is dangerous. He already tried to hurt you once, remember?'

'That was because he didn't know me. When I explain …'

'I will do the explaining and you will wait in a safe place. Is that understood?'

Marie-Ange bowed her head and muttered a vague agreement. It was easier to pretend to go along with his instructions for now.

'Thank you, Capitaine, for all you have done for me. You cannot imagine how grateful I am. You helped me escape from Malleval and welcomed me in your family. You came to my rescue, and now you may have found my husband. I will be forever in your debt.'

He showed no sign that he had heard her but stared hard at the flames, his face set in stone. He turned to her suddenly and asked, 'Who are these men upstairs? How can you be sure their leader is really your father? He could be an impostor.'

'He is my father, there is no doubt about it,' she said softly, recalling the extraordinary feeling she had experienced when she set eyes on Baldassare dei Conti for the first time. Somehow, she had recognised him for who he was.

'Of course, there are still many things I don't know, or don't understand, especially about the Cross of Life and about my father. He says that he is a Turcopilar.'

Saintclair almost jumped out of his seat.

'A Turcopilar? That's impossible!'

'Why is that? Who exactly are these Turcopilars?'

'They were the light cavalry for the Crusader armies, mostly mercenaries recruited among Christian populations rescued from Ottoman provinces. At one time, in the twelfth and thirteenth centuries, they numbered hundreds of thousands. The Crusaders couldn't have fought any battles without them. They were disbanded in the fourteenth century when the Templar Order was broken up, or so I believed.'

He smiled dreamily. 'They are the stuff of legend … But how did he meet your mother?'

'My father came with the men who built the dovecote at Beauregard. Years later, when my mother was abducted by Edmond Malleval's men, he rescued her and helped her reach the north of France where she boarded a ship to England. On the way, they fell in love and …'

'Did your father explain about the relic?'

'Not really.' She sighed. 'It appears it is indeed the wing of an angel …' she hesitated, 'which can make people immortal.'

Saintclair whistled between his teeth, and then let out a short laugh.

'Angels and eternal life! Is that all? I need a stiff drink.'

He got up and came back a few minutes later with two pitchers of mulled wine. He handed one to Marie-Ange.

'Go on. Tell me all about angels.' He directed his bright blue eyes at Marie-Ange, his lips stretched into a smile. Her pulse quickened under his gaze and she drank a sip of mulled wine to hide her confusion.

'Well, let me see … angels do God's work on earth. Some bring messages. For example, Uriel warned Noah about the flood; Gabriel appeared to Mary and told her she was going to have a baby. Others carry out special missions – Raphael, for example, has healing powers and Michael does God's justice on earth.' She shrugged. 'I am afraid that's all I know.'

'Hmm …' Saintclair stretched his legs and sighed contentedly. She couldn't tell if that was because of what she had said or because he was enjoying his spiced wine. She suspected it was probably the latter.

'Oh, yes! I forgot about the seraphim and cherubim who guard the gates of the Garden of Eden.'

'The Garden of Eden? Is that where Adam and Eve cavorted naked, blissfully happy until Eve succumbed to the urge to eat an apple and got poor Adam into trouble?' He looked at her, a grin on his face and her cheeks became hot again.

A voice called from the doorway. 'Angels are sublime beings, and spirits of love. They guide humans through ordeals and take them to Paradise.' Baldassare entered; he was dressed in an austere dark grey jacket and breeches. 'I see you are not a believer.' He regarded Saintclair severely.

Saintclair shrugged. 'I'm afraid not. I have seen too much suffering on the battlefields of Europe to believe in a benevolent God. Anyway, what is it about this relic?'

Baldassare pulled a chair and sat next to Marie-Ange. 'The Cross must be returned to the Keepers as soon as possible. We cannot let Malleval get hold of it.'

'What Keepers?' Sainclair asked.

'Those who brought the Cross over from Palestine.'

'You mean the Knights Templar? Aren't they all dead?'

Baldassare nodded. 'The Keepers are the souls of eleven Knights Templar who guard the vaults at Arginy.'

Turning to Marie-Ange, he added, 'Since your mother is no longer with us, you are the one chosen to find the Cross and put it back where it belongs.'

'No!' She stood up so abruptly her chair fell behind her.

Her father's words had conjured up nightmarish images of a dark chamber filled with distant screams and whimpers of suffering, of ghostly, faceless shadows crowding around her. Of the nightmares she had suffered from whilst at Uxeloup's house on Isle Barbe.

'I don't want to do it. I don't want to go down there.'

Baldassare got up and took his daughter's hands in his. 'You have to, daughter.'

Marie-Ange put her hands to her throat, struggling for breath as panic welled up inside her. Saintclair sprung to his feet and scooped her in his arms. She rested her head against his shoulder, too exhausted to protest.

'I'll take you to your room.' Holding her tight, he looked at Baldassare sternly. 'And let's have no more talk of angels, ghostly Knights Templar, or holy relics for now. She needs to get warm and to rest.'

He carried Marie-Ange to her room and laid her gently onto the bed. 'Your dress is soaking wet. No wonder you're not feeling well,' he remarked, his voice gruff. 'I will ask Blanchard's wife to lend you some clothes.' With a last look at her, he went out.

Baldassare entered as Saintclair left. 'I am sorry if I frightened you, Marie-Ange.'

She closed her eyes and whispered, 'I had nightmares about that place, the vaults at Arginy. I saw the shadows, I heard the screams.' She took a deep breath, opened her eyes, and gestured for her father to come closer. 'Father, there is something you must know, something which will delay my journey to Beauregard.' It was time to tell him about Christopher.

She could sense her father's mounting disbelief as she explained how her English husband, who had been lost at sea off the coast of Spain six years previously, was alive and, she suspected, working as a spy for Fouché.

'I will know for sure tomorrow night when we meet him at the inn in Lyon,' she finished.

'Then I shall come with you. The man sounds dangerous.'

'He is my husband. He will not harm me,' she protested feebly. She wasn't so sure about that any longer.

'Head injuries can change people, turn them into somebody else entirely,' Baldassare said. 'From what you said, that's what seemed to have happened to your husband ... if the man you met *is* your husband.'

A knock on the door announced the entrance of a plump, red-cheeked woman holding a selection of underclothes and dresses.

'Capitaine Saintclair asked me to bring you these, Madame.'

She put the clothes on a chair. 'I'll have a tub and some hot water brought up for you right away,' she added.

Marie-Ange could think of nothing she wanted more than a hot bath and dry, clean garments.

'I shall leave you now. We'll talk during dinner.' Baldassare squeezed her hand and left.

A short while later, Marie-Ange discarded her wet clothes and got into the tin bath Blanchard and two servants had brought up and filled with warm water for her. She didn't want to think any longer, not about the Cross, not about Christopher, and certainly not about Saintclair. Yet, as soon as she closed her eyes and reclined in the tub, her thoughts drifted towards the capitaine again. She had been so happy to see him outside the barn that morning. What she felt for him then had been overwhelming, exhilarating, almost like love … she stopped the silly, unwelcome thought the second it popped into her mind.

No. She was feeling grateful, that was all. Saintclair came to rescue her, braving the snowstorm and the Pilat mountains' inhospitable terrain. He had been prepared to face Malleval and his henchmen alone. And tomorrow, he would take her to Christopher. She owed him a lot, more than she could ever say.

Christopher … would she be able to make him remember her? She heaved a sigh and said a silent prayer, hoping that the kind, gentle man she married was still there, underneath the harsh and ruthless exterior of the agent he had become.

When the water had gone tepid, she stepped out of the bath and scrubbed herself dry until her skin was bright pink and her hair shone and curled on her shoulders. The clothes Madame Blanchard had left for her were all too big, but at least they were dry and clean. She left her damp hair to dry loose on her shoulders. By the time she was dressed, she was ravenous.

Saintclair, her father and his two companions were already sitting at a table in the dining room. Baldassare gestured to Marie-Ange to sit next to him and scooped a generous helping of chicken and root vegetable stew onto her plate. The men resumed their conversation about travel arrangements for the following day. Saintclair persuaded Baldassare that he was more than capable of seeing to his daughter's safety in Lyon and it was decided that the Turcopilars would ride straight to Beauregard, where Saintclair and Marie-Ange would join them after meeting Christopher.

'Malleval may take a few days to get there anyway. He can't travel as fast as he used to. He isn't well,' Saintclair remarked.

'I don't understand. According to his letters, he was wounded, yet he was dancing the other night at the ball,' Marie-Ange said.

Saintclair put his knife and fork down on his plate. 'There was no battle wound, I'm afraid. Malleval caught syphilis two years ago from Spanish brothels,' he declared.

Marie-Ange put her hand to her mouth, shocked. There was no known cure for syphilis. Malleval would die in terrible pain, and he would probably lose his mind, too. What would happen to Sophie, his fiancée, and the servant girl he'd been with the other night?

'So that's why he wants the Cross, he knows he is lost,' Baldassare remarked. 'Who was that old man you were with in the village? I have the feeling I have seen him before.'

'You may have, years ago, when you rescued my mother from Edmond Malleval. He is known as Karloff and belongs to the *Société Angélique*, a secret organisation.' Marie-Ange went on to explain about Polycarpe de la Rivière and the coded parchments stolen by the Malleval clan almost two centuries ago and which Karloff had deciphered for Edmond Malleval. She shook her head. 'The man is completely deluded. He thinks an angel will appear when we get hold of the Cross. Isn't that just crazy?'

She waited for her father to agree but he didn't say anything.

'How did you manage to find out so much?' Saintclair looked at her, a faint smile on his lips.

'Karloff wants the Cross as badly as Malleval. He tried to hypnotise me twice but I managed to hold on and not reveal the words of my mother's song. The first time, he came to my bedroom one night on Isle Barbe and it was …'

Saintclair put his pitcher of wine down on the table with such force that some wine spilt out onto the table. 'He came into your room?'

Marie-Ange blushed and nodded. 'He tried to hypnotise me, but there was some noise and I woke up. It is very odd this ability he has to make you tingle all over and to send you into a trance just by looking into your eyes. His voice is very persuasive.' She shuddered.

'What happened at Malleval?' Saintclair asked with a low voice, leaning towards her. There was concern in his eyes and a deep line at the corner of his mouth.

'Malleval and Karloff wanted the words of my mother's song. I managed to give them the wrong words, but they guessed that the Cross was in the dovecote, even if they have no idea how to get to it.'

Baldassare put his hand on her shoulder. 'You did well. You

were very brave.'

'Oh no, I wasn't brave. I was terrified.'

Saintclair gestured to her neck. 'I couldn't help but notice.'

She put her hands to her throat to hide the ugly bruises Malleval had left, and swallowed hard. 'Malleval was angry we had escaped and made a fool of him.'

Saintclair narrowed his eyes and clenched his fists. 'Wait until I lay my hands on him. Sick or not, he has no right to hurt you.'

When they finished their meal, Saintclair decreed they should retire as he wanted to leave early the following morning.

'We will call at my house in St Genis first. I want Lucie to see that you are safe. She has been sick with worry about you.'

'I was very concerned about her, too. Poor Lucie, she was so scared I thought she was going to faint. I will get my bag and my locket from your house before we go to Lyon.' Marie-Ange put her hand on her heart, and smiled. 'Oh, Capitaine, I cannot believe that thanks to you I will see my husband tomorrow night and have another chance to talk to him.' Hopefully this time she would convince him that she was telling the truth and he would remember who he really was.

Saintclair glared at her.

'I think you should wait before thanking me. You don't know what we'll find in Lyon.' He slammed his empty pitcher down on the table and hailed Blanchard for more wine.

She stared at him, puzzled. Why was he so disgruntled all of a sudden, when all she had done was express her gratitude for his help? She sighed and bade him goodnight. He didn't even reply.

Chapter Fifteen

'Thank God you're safe.' Lucie greeted her with a huge smile.

Marie-Ange rushed across the drawing room to take her in her arms. The girl felt frail. She looked ill too. There were dark circles under her red, swollen eyes, her skin was so pale it was almost transparent, and her breathing was laboured and wheezy.

Emilie Saintclair invited her guest to sit down before leaving the drawing room to organise some refreshments.

'Where were you? Who was that horrible man driving the carriage?' Lucie squeezed Marie-Ange's hand. 'It was awful to watch you disappear into the fog and not being able to help.' She turned to her brother and gave him a tender look. 'Luckily, there is nothing Hugo cannot do. I knew he would bring you back to us.'

'We can't stay long,' Saintclair said. 'We have to be in Lyon tonight.'

Lucie's face crumpled with disappointment. 'Why so soon?' She turned to Marie-Ange. 'You haven't even tried the dresses *Maman* made for you. They are beautiful, I'm sure you'll love them.'

'I promise I'll be back soon.' The moment she spoke, Marie-Ange bit her lips, wishing she could take the words back. It wasn't true. She may never return to St Genis. For a moment she longed to stay here, surrounded by the warmth and affection of Saintclair's family. Her future however depended on the outcome of tonight's meeting with Christopher and her quest for the Cross at Beauregard.

Saintclair glanced at her but said nothing. He was probably thinking the same thing.

His mother returned to the drawing room, followed by a young maid carrying a tray with cups of coffee, hot chocolate, and a two-tiered cream cake. The girl was new. On their way to St Genis, Saintclair explained he had dismissed Martine as soon as he found out she had helped her cousin lure Marie-Ange and Lucie into a trap. 'She tried to deny it at first but she broke down eventually and admitted the man forced her to lie about the puppies for sale in the village. As for him, he won't be hanging around here anymore,' he had said without offering further explanations.

Madame Saintclair poured hot chocolate for the ladies and black coffee for Hugo. 'What an ordeal this has been for you, poor Marie-Ange.' She patted her hand. 'You don't mind if I call you Marie-Ange, do you? You must call me Emilie too. After all, you are practically family now. Lucie told me your wonderful news.'

'What news?' Saintclair and Marie-Ange asked in one voice.

'Your engagement, of course!' Madame Saintclair was beaming. 'I knew there was something Hugo wasn't telling me. You are the first lady he has ever brought home and I can see by the way he looks at you how much he loves you.'

'Mother,' Saintclair interrupted, a little shortly. 'Marie-Ange and I are not engaged. In fact …'

Marie-Ange sat very still, holding her cup of cocoa, hardly daring to breathe.

'It appears that her husband, a Royal Navy Commander who was reported missing in action some years ago, is still alive.' He paused and looked at Marie-Ange, his expression unreadable. 'We are meeting him in Lyon tonight. If everything goes to plan, Marie-Ange will return to England with him.' He drank his coffee and put the cup back onto the table.

The only sound in the drawing room was the tick-tock of the clock on the mantelpiece. Then Lucie started crying, quietly, holding her handkerchief against her mouth.

'My poor Hugo,' she whispered. She turned to Marie-Ange and shot her an angry glance. 'You lied to me, to us,' she hissed before running out. Her mother shook her head in dismay and went after her, leaving Marie-Ange alone with Saintclair.

'I didn't realise Lucie entertained such fanciful ideas about you and I …' He sighed. 'I keep telling her real life is nothing like her silly romantic stories but she won't believe me.' He got up and walked to the door. 'Get what you need from your room. I want to leave as soon as possible.'

She nodded. 'Of course.'

But she didn't move. She needed a few moments alone to think about what Emilie Saintclair had said before Hugo interrupted her. That her son loved her. She put her hand on her heart. She couldn't understand why she suddenly felt like crying and laughing at the same time.

The door opened and Madame Saintclair entered the room. She closed the door and turned towards her hesitantly. 'I am so sorry, my dear, for what just happened. Lucie and I got it all wrong. Of course, had we known about your husband …' She sighed. 'In any case, it was presumptuous of me to think that you would ever contemplate marrying my son. He doesn't deserve a proper lady like you.'

Marie-Ange couldn't stand the apologetic tone of her voice. She owed her the truth.

'I am no lady, Madame Saintclair,' she confessed. 'I made several shocking discoveries these past few weeks, one of them being that I'm the illegitimate daughter of a Maltese soldier who seduced my mother when she was sixteen and abandoned her once she was pregnant. So, please, don't call me a lady.' She took Emilie Saintclair's hands in hers and carried on with a passion she was hardly aware of. 'Your son helped me well beyond the call of duty. He has shown great courage, loyalty, and honour. He is a strong, brave, and wonderful man. Any woman would be proud to be his wife and I …'

The words died on her lips. This time the true nature of her feelings for Hugo Saintclair hit her like a blow to the heart, so hard she gasped and had to close her eyes. She couldn't hide from the truth any longer. What she felt wasn't just physical attraction. She loved him.

Madame Saintclair patted her hand and smiled. There was sympathy in her eyes.

'I see … well, if things don't turn out the way you expect in Lyon tonight, you will always be welcome in our house. But for now, I think you had better get ready. Hugo is waiting outside.'

Marie-Ange nodded, her throat tight, and went up to her room to gather her things. She thrust her mother's sketchbook and the few garments she had left behind in her bag. She slipped Christopher's dagger into her boot before finally clasping her locket around her neck. Grabbing her small bag, she closed the door with a heavy heart. Would she ever come back to Saintclair's house?

There was no coach leaving St Genis for Lyon that afternoon so Saintclair decided they would ride his horse. It was no easy journey. She sat side-saddle in front of him, the warmth of his arms around her, the feel of his broad, hard chest against her cheek a sweet torture. Impatient and bad-tempered, Saintclair didn't speak a word to her. He spurred his horse on to gain speed or pulled at the reins, cursing under his breath, when travellers got in his path.

As they made their way into the city she became increasingly anxious about the forthcoming meeting at the Mère Vitry. She no longer knew what she wanted. Too preoccupied with her quest for Christopher, she had failed to grasp the true nature of her feelings for Saintclair and had ignored all the signs. Now she was about to be reunited with her husband, thoughts whirled in her mind … what if Christopher had lost his memory for good and didn't want to resume his life at Norton Place? Her throat tightened and she closed her eyes in anguish. What if he *wanted* to resume their married life?

As soon as they arrived at the cuirassiers' barracks, Saintclair called for his batman and gave him instructions to bring some wine and a collation.

'Will madame be staying here tonight?' the man eyed Marie-Ange up and down. His impudence brought a flush to her cheeks and made her look away. It was obvious the man assumed she was his capitaine's latest conquest.

Saintclair waved his hand in a dismissive gesture. 'I'm not sure yet, but make the spare bed up, just in case, will you? And not a word about madame to anyone, do you understand?'

The batman winked at her before clicking his heels.

'*Oui, mon Capitaine!*' Later he brought them soup, a loaf of bread, and a pitcher of wine and they sat at the table to eat.

'The Mère Vitry Inn is in the old district on the other side of the Saône,' Saintclair explained, darting his cold blue eyes towards her. 'Once I have spoken with … your husband,' he paused, 'and I'm sure it's safe, I will come back for you.' He finished his meal and looked towards the clock on the mantelpiece. 'It's time.' He got up, put his coat on, and went to the door.

'Capitaine,' Marie-Ange called. She walked up to him, tilted her face. They exchanged a long, intense look. 'Please be careful.'

He nodded. 'Of course. Lock the door behind me.' And he left.

Marie-Ange had no intention of waiting for his return. She wrapped herself in her cloak, covered her head with the hood, and slipped out of the room. As well as wishing to speak to Christopher, she feared for Saintclair's safety. The meeting at the Mère Vitry might be a trap. If Christopher was indeed one of Fouché's men, a ruthless spy and killer, she had to watch Saintclair's back. She couldn't let the officer get hurt because of her. She was armed. She had her dagger.

Marie-Ange hastened towards the inn, keeping her head down so as not to attract the attention of passers-by. Ignoring the beggars who pleaded for a few *sous* at every corner along the way, she kept her eyes on Saintclair's tall silhouette ahead. He walked very fast and she had to run to keep up with him as he crossed the bridge over the River Saône, and then reached the far side of Place Saint Paul.

She caught a glimpse of Hugo as he walked in the Mère Vitry, looked for somewhere to hide and chose an empty doorway from where she could keep watch. She didn't have to wait long before two familiar figures emerged into the street.

Christopher came out first, followed by Saintclair, and together they started down the street, with Marie-Ange close behind. They turned into a narrow alley and disappeared into a doorway. It wasn't the entrance to a dwelling but a long passage dimly lit with torches, which seemed to go on forever. It was probably one of the *traboules* Madame Saintclair told her about. Silk workers used the covered passages to carry their wares across the district without getting them wet with rain.

She couldn't see the men or hear their footsteps any longer. Fearing she had lost them, she started to run. When she reached the end of the *traboule* she was back on Place Saint Paul. She spotted Saintclair and Christopher just as they disappeared around the bend of a steep alley climbing towards Fourvière, one of the hills overlooking the city. Where were they going? Her heart beating fast, she started after them. Halfway up the hill, Saintclair and Christopher took a fork to the right into a small public garden. She slid behind a tree to listen.

'Now tell me why you're looking for me and who you're working for,' Christopher said.

'I'm not working for anyone. I'm helping out a young lady who wants to meet you,' Saintclair answered calmly. 'She believes you are …'

'Wait! Do you mean you're associated with that Englishwoman, the pretty blonde who claims I'm her husband? That woman is mad.'

Marie-Ange's heart was beating so hard it hurt. She resisted the urge to step out and speak with Christopher herself.

'No, she isn't mad,' Saintclair replied, still calm.

'Who is she? And, more importantly, who does she think I am?'

'Her name is Marie-Ange. She says you are Christopher Norton, from Norton Place in Devonshire. Six years ago, you were Commander on HMS *Amazon*, which sank off the coast of Coruña.'

Christopher laughed. 'Me, an English naval officer? Impossible! I don't believe a word of this nonsense.' He cursed loudly. 'You're lying. You both work for Talleyrand or the Police Prefect Bourienne. You seek to sabotage my mission here in Lyon.'

'What mission?' This time Hugo's voice was strained. There was a silence and he resumed. 'At any rate, you are mistaken about Marie-Ange. She wants to talk to you, that's all. What shall I tell her? Will you at least agree to meet her? It's the least you could do.'

Christopher didn't answer straight away. 'Very well,' he replied at last. 'If it will get you off my tail, tell her to be at the Mère Vitry Inn at midnight.'

Saintclair nodded. 'We'll meet you there.'

As he turned and walked away, the moonlight flashed on the knife Christopher pulled from his coat. In a swift movement he caught up with Saintclair and before Marie-Ange could react or call out a warning, he stabbed him in the back. The French officer stumbled to the ground with a grunt of pain. Christopher delivered a hard kick to the fallen man and raised the weapon to strike again.

'Christopher! Stop,' Marie-Ange cried, bolting from the shadow of the tree. She threw herself down next to Saintclair, touched the side of his neck to feel for a pulse. He was unconscious, but alive. Christopher loomed above her.

'You!' He snarled before grabbing her arm. He pulled her up roughly.

'Listen to me,' she implored. 'You have to believe me. I am your wife, Christopher.'

'This was a trap, wasn't it? Where are the others?' He looked around, and then glared at her with a look of pure hatred on his face.

Marie-Ange breathed in deeply. This man was a stranger, a cruel, harsh stranger. Still she went on. 'You are so very wrong. There is no trap. All I want is for you to remember.' She carried on talking. 'You are thirty-three years old. Your parents were Lady Susan and Sir George Norton. Sadly they both passed away. You have a younger brother, Robert, who is now eighteen and dreams of becoming a naval officer like you. You were a Commander on HMS *Amazon*—'

'So your friend said,' he interrupted, pointing to the unconscious body of Saintclair. He pulled Marie-Ange against him and pinned both her arms behind her back. 'So, my darling, tell me, how long were we married?'

She could tell he didn't believe her but carried on regardless. Maybe one tiny detail would jolt his memory. 'We were married on October the twelfth, 1808 in Plymouth. It was beautiful and warm, almost like a summer day. We were so happy together at Norton Place, but we only lived there together for four months. In January you boarded the HMS *Amazon* bound for Coruña. They said your ship sank, that you were dead, but I always knew you were alive.' Marie-Ange tried to find a glint of recognition, of warmth, in his eyes. There was nothing.

'The only problem, my darling, is that I'm not your Christopher.'

'Who are you then? Do you even know?' she cried in desperation. 'What do you remember of your childhood? What is your earliest memory? I bet it's that of a battlefield or a French military hospital in Spain.'

A spasm of surprise crossed his face before he could hide it.

'I knew it! You can't remember anything of your life before Spain, can you? You were found unconscious near Coruña by Spanish fishermen or farmers, or perhaps by the French army. Maybe you were in possession of another man's coat, or carried a French soldier's identification, a man called Nallay. Am I right? Did you ever wonder why you speak such good English? That's because you are …'

Christopher twisted her arms even tighter, and she let out a whimper of pain.

'Stop this, you are driving me insane. I'll tell you what, darling. Since you say we are married, I might as well use you. I could do with a woman tonight.' His voice was hoarse and his eyes burned with an unholy hunger. Panic rose inside her and she tried to wriggle out of his grip.

'No! You cannot mean to …'

'You wouldn't deny me my conjugal rights, would you?' he snarled.

She faced him, defiantly. 'I won't leave Saintclair. He will die if he stays out here in the freezing cold.'

Christopher looked down, a cruel smile on his thin lips. 'You don't have a choice.' He produced his knife and walked next to Saintclair's body. 'Come with me now, or I finish him off.'

He grabbed her arm and led her, shaking with fear, out of the garden. She stole a last glance at Saintclair's inert body before starting on the steep lane down the hill. This was a nightmare, not the loving reunion she'd been dreaming of for the past six years. Christopher didn't remember anything. He didn't *want* to remember anything. He was a dangerous man, a killer, and at this moment, she hated him.

They walked back to Place Saint Paul, then on the embankment along the Saône, across a bridge, and down a series of narrow streets until Christopher stopped in front of a porch. Marie-Ange looked up but couldn't see a plaque with the name of the street.

Christopher pushed open a heavy wooden door and she found herself in a courtyard with a staircase at the far end.

'This way, up to the second floor.'

A short while later he pushed her into a small but comfortably furnished apartment. He closed the front door but left the key in the lock.

'Get in.'

Shivering with fear, she followed him into the drawing room where he proceeded to take his coat and jacket off. He smiled, loosened his black *cravate* and untied the top of his shirt and sat on the sofa.

'Come here, wife, remind me of the old times,' he said, patting his knees. 'That's what you wanted, wasn't it?'

Marie-Ange didn't move. There was no love, no warmth for him in her heart. There was nothing but fear and desolation.

'Come here, I said,' he repeated, louder.

'What happened to change you so much?' she whispered. 'You were the gentlest, the most honourable of men.' At last she found the courage to cross the room and kneel in front of him. 'Christopher. Why do you not remember? We used to walk along the cliffs and on the beach. I collected shells and wild flowers, you recited poetry.'

Christopher grabbed her arms and pulled her into his lap. She struggled but he wrapped his arms around her to keep her still. 'Shut up. I didn't bring you here to talk. If you really want me to remember you, you'll have to show me a bit more.'

He laughed, lifted his fingers to her throat and ripped the collar of her dress. Marie-Ange cried out but he laughed again. Pulling her hair back, he kissed her mouth hungrily, forcing her lips open and biting her. She struggled to get away but his grip was too strong.

'What's the matter? Don't you like your husband anymore?' he uttered harshly. His breath was short, his eyes heavy as he looked down at her chest. The locket glittered in the light.

'I've seen this before.' He frowned. 'Where did you get it?'

He toyed with the chain a few seconds and held the locket closer to his face to examine it.

'It was my mother's,' she answered, hope surging inside her. Maybe he was starting to remember at last.

But he let the locket drop. 'You're beautiful, I'll grant you that.' He groaned with desire as his fingers brushed over her breasts. He bent down to bite at her throat and she winced in pain. She wouldn't let him rape her, at least not without putting up a fight. She bent sideways, just enough to reach into her boot and pull the dagger out. Quick as a flash, she brought the blade up and pressed the tip on his neck.

'Let go of me,' she ordered, panting. Her hand shook as the memory of the highwayman flashed through her mind and she almost dropped the dagger.

He laughed but there was surprise in his eyes. He lifted his hands in the air. 'Careful, woman. I don't want you perforating my neck by accident.'

'If I stab you, it won't be an accident,' she promised. Still holding the blade in front of her, she got up and walked backward across the room, away from him. 'I realise now it was a waste of time. There is nothing left in you of the man I loved.' She lifted her chin, willing her voice to stop trembling. He was Nallay, not Christopher. He was a monster.

She retreated to the front door, grabbing her cloak on the way. He stood up and advanced on her, his face twisted with fury. She had to be fast. The key was still in the lock. She turned it, pulled it out, and opened the door. She slipped through and slammed it shut behind her. As she locked the door from outside, Nallay's fists pounded the wood.

'Let me out, *garce*! I'll find you and teach you a lesson you won't soon forget. That's a promise!'

She threw her cloak onto her shoulders and haphazardly fastened the ties whilst running down the staircase, where in her haste she dropped the key. The crash of Nallay's blows echoed behind her. Thankfully his apartment was on the second floor, too high for him to jump from the window without risking an injury.

Once in the street, she sprinted in the direction of the embankment and crossed the bridge to Place Saint Paul. The streets were quieter now. Her footsteps and the sound of her breathing echoed in the night. She ran across the square and started on the steep alley up to the gardens where Saintclair lay wounded. Would he still be there or had he managed to drag himself back to his barracks? It was so dark she didn't see him and almost stumbled onto his body.

'Capitaine, wake up!'

She touched his face. It was cold. She put her hand onto his chest and felt it move ever so slightly. He was breathing. She slapped his cheek until his eyes opened, focussed onto her face.

'Capitaine, we must leave,' she said. 'Nallay is after us and this time, he will kill us both.'

Saintclair grunted with pain as consciousness returned and he attempted to move. '*Bon sang*! That bastard stabbed me in the shoulder.' He winced and raised his hand to his head. 'He knocked me out, too.' He looked at her. 'What are you doing here?'

'I will explain later. Come on.'

'Help me up,' he ordered.

He stood up and she put her arm around his waist to steady him. Their progress down the hill was slow but eventually they made it back to the barracks.

'Get me the physician,' Saintclair instructed the sentry when they staggered into the courtyard.

Marie-Ange opened his door and helped him out of his coat and jacket. He sat on a chair, holding his right hand to his wounded shoulder.

'Take your shirt off, too,' she said. 'It's soaked with blood.'

He shook his head. 'No, I'll wait for the physician. In the meantime, please get me some brandy.'

She retrieved the bottle of cognac from the sideboard and handed it to him. He took hold of it and drank a long gulp, then another.

When the doctor came, he instructed Marie-Ange to boil some

water over the fire and rip strips of cloth from a sheet she found in a cupboard. He cut Saintclair's shirt off and dabbed on some medicinal alcohol to clean the wound.

'How did you come to be injured?' he asked.

'A brawl in a tavern,' Saintclair replied dismissively.

'You were very lucky,' the doctor concluded after examining his shoulder. 'The blade missed the lung. There should not be any lasting damage but you must rest. No riding, and no drills for two weeks at least.' He finished dressing the wound and checked Saintclair's head. 'Lucky you have a thick skull too,' he remarked.

He turned to Marie-Ange at last. 'Will you see that the capitaine does as I say, Madame? Knowing him, he'll be on horseback before I reach home.' Before he packed his bag, he handed Saintclair a small vial. 'Laudanum, for the pain,' he explained. 'One spoonful now. Then one in the morning and another at night if needed.' Saintclair protested he didn't want any but the physician was adamant. In fact, he refused to leave until Saintclair swallowed the medicine.

'I'll let you get into bed now,' Marie-Ange said once the doctor left. She moved towards the smaller room where his batman had prepared another couch.

'Not so fast,' Saintclair said in a gruff voice, moving to block her retreat. 'There are a few things you need to explain first.'

'I think you should follow the doctor's instructions and get some rest.' She tilted her chin up to look at him.

He stepped closer. 'I want to know how you found me tonight.'

She blinked and took a few deep breaths. 'I followed you.'

'I specifically told you to stay here.'

'It's just as well I did not obey, Capitaine,' she argued, staring him in the eye. 'You would have bled or frozen to death had I not been there.'

He sighed. 'Perhaps. Where is your husband now?'

She bit her lip and bent her head in an attempt to hide the tears gathering in her eyelashes. 'I left him in his apartment,' she whispered. 'He … forced me to go there with him but I managed to lock him in and run back to you.'

He frowned. 'I don't understand. Did you not talk to him?'

She toyed with the fastening of her cloak. With his free hand, he lifted her chin up. Tears welled in her eyes in spite of her best efforts to quell them.

'What happened?' Saintclair asked once more. This time, his voice was softer. 'What did the bastard do to you?'

She pressed her hand to her collar. His fingers slid down her throat and swiftly unfastened her cloak. It dropped on the floor and revealed the ripped dress.

'Damn. Did he …?' His lips tightened.

She shook her head and he breathed a sigh of relief. 'My father was right. You were right. The man I knew as Christopher Norton might as well be dead.' Her voice trembled. She pulled on the fabric to cover her throat.

'He didn't believe you, then?'

'No.'

'None of it? Even when you told him about …' he hesitated '… your married life?'

'He thinks I am some agent out to get him.' She looked down at her hand, at the wedding ring that glittered in the candlelight and with a heart-rending sob pulled it off and put it on the table. 'My marriage is over.'

Hugo's eyes went to the ring and back to her face before lifting his uninjured arm to gently wipe her tears with the pad of his thumb.

Finally he turned away. 'I need some sleep,' he muttered, rubbing his face roughly and walking to his bed. He sat on the mattress and bent to take off his boots.

'Let me do this, please.' She rushed to his side and knelt to help him. After she placed some cushions on the bed, he lay down and closed his eyes.

When his breathing was slow and regular and she was certain he was asleep, she leant over him, stroked the side of his face and whispered, ‘I am so sorry. All this is my fault. I wish I never laid eyes on Christopher in Paris. I wish he were dead.’

Chapter Sixteen

'What happened to *mon Capitaine*?' the batman asked with a low voice so as not to wake up Saintclair. He set a tray with coffee, thick slices of buttered bread, and a pot of jam on the table.

'He got hurt in an altercation between drunks in a tavern,' Marie-Ange lied, reaching out for a cup of coffee.

The batman whistled softly. 'Now I understand why two messieurs from the police were asking for him a few moments ago.'

'The police? Did they say what they wanted?' she asked, alarmed.

He snorted. 'No, and I didn't ask. I told them the capitaine had gone out. They said they'd come back later.' He winked. 'I thought you two were busy.'

Concerned about the news that the police had come looking for Saintclair, she ignored the man's lewd remark. 'Did they leave their name?'

The sergeant shook his head. 'No, but they were from the municipal police. I'd recognise their type anywhere.'

She asked him for a needle and some thread to make repairs to her dress. He came back shortly with a rusty sewing tin and a newspaper.

'I thought it might help you pass the time while the capitaine is out cold.'

Saintclair slept through the morning. It was odd to watch over him as he lay in bed, oblivious to her presence, vulnerable for once. She put her hand on his forehead. Her fingers brushed his dark hair, slid down along the side of his face, and along the rugged line of his scar. She wondered in which battle he got it ... there was so much she didn't know about him. So much she wanted to learn.

He muttered something in his sleep. She gasped and withdrew her hand but didn't move away. The sight of his mouth, his broad chest, and strong shoulders filled her with longing and fear of what the future held. How she wanted to nestle against him and forget about the world, about Malleval, and Christopher – Nallay, as she would call her husband from now on.

When Saintclair woke up he would probably be sick of her and the problems she had caused him. Because of her, he jeopardised his family home in St Genis and risked his life. It wasn't only Malleval and his henchmen who were after him now, but Nallay and Fouché, too.

Glancing at her bare hand, she was reminded of the wedding ring she had taken off the night before and which was still on the table. Such a little thing, but it had meant so much. Although she never wanted to wear it again, she couldn't quite bring herself to throw it away.

After lunch, she pulled a chair next to Saintclair's bed and sat down with the newspaper on her lap, but her eyes soon closed and she fell asleep. It was late afternoon when she woke up. Saintclair was sitting up, looking at her.

'Oh … I am sorry. I wanted to watch over you and I fell asleep.' She rubbed her eyes and combed strands of hair away from her face. 'How are you feeling?'

'Like hell,' he said, wincing when he tried to lean onto his arm to get up.

'Don't try to move just now. Let me get you a hot drink and something to eat first.' She busied herself warming some soup and coffee the batman had left on the stove, and brought a tray over to him.

'I'd rather have some brandy,' he grumbled, but he tucked his spoon into the bowl and finished the hot soup in minutes. 'I won't take any more laudanum. I could never stand the stuff. I lost most of the day thanks to that damned physician and his drug when there were so many things I needed to sort out.' He pushed the tray away and looked at her.

'You can't stay here tonight. I'm in no state for a fight if that husband of yours, or Malleval's henchmen, come after you. As a former Hussar, Malleval can get into the barracks as he pleases, and being Fouché's man, *your husband*,' he stared at Marie-Ange, 'will find a way.'

He was right, of course. She informed Saintclair of the visit by two policemen that morning, and his face became even more sombre.

'They'll be Fouché's men – he may not be the Minister for Police anymore, but he still has many staff in his pocket.'

'I could go to Beauregard by stagecoach and try to find my father,' she suggested.

'Certainly not! It's too risky on your own.' He closed his eyes. 'Last night your husband said he was on some kind of mission. A mission Talleyrand and Police Prefect Bourienne were eager to sabotage. I have to follow this through.'

'Do you have any idea what it could be?'

'No. I am setting off for Paris as soon as I have seen to your safety. I must talk to my superiors at the Ministry of War and to Talleyrand at Palais Vendôme. Something is brewing. And when this something involves Fouché, it's never good news.'

He paused and his lips stretched into one of his sudden smiles. 'You are certainly keeping me busy. Here was I, a few weeks ago, thinking I was doing a straightforward trip to England and back to fetch an heiress for Malleval … I'm sorry it turned out like this. Instead of an inheritance, you found a load of trouble.'

She put her hand on top of his. 'Capitaine, you are the one who got hurt because of me. I shall never forget it.'

The intensity of his gaze burnt through her. He leant forward, and his jaw tightened. For a few seconds, she was sure he was going to kiss her and her whole body tingled with anticipation. Instead, he sighed, withdrew his hand, and reclined against his chair.

'We need to go. I'll arrange for my batman to see you safely to your great-aunt Hermine at Marzac. Once there you can make contact with your father. But you need to change first. Someone might be watching the barracks on behalf of Malleval or your husband. They mustn't recognise you.'

He instructed his batman to get him a set of men's clothes in the smallest size he could find. For the first time in her life, Marie-Ange slipped into a pair of breeches and high boots, a man's white shirt and a short grey jacket. Her disguise was completed by a brown hat.

‘Not bad.’ Saintclair eyed her from top to toe when she walked back into the room, his eyes lingering on her legs clad in the high boots and the curves of her hips. ‘But you need to cover up more. An overcoat should do.’

He got up, said he was going to get ready, and went out. When he came back, he handed her a coat that she slipped on her shoulders. He was freshly shaven and wore his cuirassier uniform. The dark blue coat with white and silver épaulettes and white breeches tucked into black boots complemented his rugged physique and Marie-Ange forced herself to tear her gaze from him.

‘What about the physician’s orders? You need to rest. You’re wounded.’

He let out a short laugh. ‘As if that ever stopped me.’

Chapter Seventeen

'My poor child. What on earth happened to you? You look about to pass out.'

Hermine stood in her nightclothes and frilly lace bonnet in the cold and dark hallway of Marzac Manor. She gave instructions for food and drinks to be brought up immediately and led the way to the drawing room where her old manservant Pierre was busy lighting a fire.

'I was expecting you, but certainly not in this accoutrement,' her great-aunt said as Marie-Ange stumbled into an armchair near the fire.

The stagecoach journey had left her weak, cold and shivery. Saintclair's batman had ridden alongside to make sure she was safe, and left when they had reached Marzac and she'd had to walk the remaining couple of miles.

'That good-for-nothing Uxeloup Malleval paid me a visit two days ago. He said you absconded with this Capitaine Saintclair who came here with you last time, and demanded I let him know immediately if I heard from you.'

She gave Marie-Ange a stern look and crossed her arms on her chest.

'So, what have you got to say and what on earth have you let yourself in for? Has this *cuirassier* dishonoured you?' She almost spat the words, making it very obvious what she thought about Saintclair.

Marie-Ange sighed. She took her hat off, shook her head, and combed her hair roughly with shaky fingers.

'I'm afraid I have not been completely honest with you, Aunt Hermine.'

The old lady narrowed her eyes. 'As I suspected!'

Marie-Ange told her about Christopher losing his memory and working as a spy for Fouché.

‘You are saying your husband survived a shipwreck and has been living for the past six years in France under a false identity while you lamented his death in England? This is extraordinary … but are you sure it’s him? I mean, a person’s appearance can alter a lot in six years.’

Marie-Ange sighed. ‘It is him. He has indeed changed very much, but not in appearance. He has become a cruel, dangerous man. He even stabbed Capitaine Saintclair in the back when he was only trying to help me.’

‘Ah yes, Capitaine Saintclair. You seem to hold him in great esteem,’ Hermine sneered. ‘Yet he’s nothing but one of those ruffian officers promoted by Napoleon.’

‘You’re not being fair, Aunt Hermine. He has been a great help over the past few weeks and has risked much for me,’ she said with passion.

‘I see.’ Hermine pursed her lips, still disapproving. ‘What are your intentions regarding your husband, then? What happens if he doesn’t regain his memory? Will you go back to Devonshire, pretend you never met him and carry on as if he were dead, marry again, maybe?’

‘No, it would be bigamy.’ Marie-Ange bent her head and sighed. ‘Anyway, there is no man I wish to marry.’ But even as she said the words, she knew it was a lie.

‘Tell me, child, why does Malleval want to get hold of you so badly? Is it because of what we discussed last time – the Cross?’ Hermine lowered her voice.

‘Yes, he is obsessed with it. He held me captive twice, once at his house on Isle Barbe and later in his fortress in the mountains. He even had his physician, Karloff, hypnotise me, to reveal the words to a song my mother knew – a song that points to the location of the Cross at Beauregard.’

‘Karloff! He was the physician who dealt with Aline, was he not?’

‘Yes. He is involved in some kind of secret society and just as desperate to lay his hands on the Cross as Malleval.’

‘How did you escape from Malleval?’

She took a deep breath. The moment of revealing the existence of her real father had come.

'A man helped me …' she began. 'His name is Baldassare dei Conti. He is a Turcopilar.'

Hermine opened her eyes wide.

'The name sounds familiar. Where did I hear of him? You said he was a Turk? Why would a Turk help you out?'

'Not a Turk, a Turcopilar.' Marie-Ange quickly explained about Turcopilars, the Order of the Knights Hospitaller, and the Knights Templar and said that Baldassare was the man Aline had written about, the young interpreter sent by Saint-Germain with a team of craftsmen to build the dovecote at Beauregard, and who later rescued her mother from Malleval's claws.

A sleepy-eyed maid walked in with two cups of hot milk and slices of cake. Marie-Ange welcomed the interruption. She needed a little more time for the revelation that was to come. She drank some of her hot milk, but had to force a few bites of cake down.

'Aunt Hermine, Baldassare told me something else …' she put her almost untouched cake on a side table.. 'You see, I am his … well, he is my …'

'What is it? Get on with it, girl.' The elderly lady rapped her cane on the floor.

'He is my father, my real father.' There! She had said it. Hermine would be horrified at the thought her niece Catherine had conceived a child out of wedlock and with a mysterious foreign agent who lived the life of an errand knight.

'Oh! But how …? And what about your father, the English gentleman?' Hermine looked confused. Her hand shook as she lifted her cup of milk to her lips.

'Baldassare said he had to let my mother go to England alone because, as a Turcopilar, he wasn't allowed to have a family life.'

'Pity he didn't think about that before.' Hermine put her cup down.

'Baldassare and his companions are now hiding near Beauregard. I need to find them tomorrow,' Marie-Ange added.

'You need to rest first. Then I shall send my two stable lads with you, although I'm afraid they won't be much help against Malleval's men. I heard he has some brutes from his mountain clan with him at Beauregard. What about your capitaine? Where is *he* now?' Hermine sneered. 'No, don't answer that. He is probably rolling in a warm bed with some dancing girl.'

'No. He had to go to Paris, talk to people, about Christopher.'

'Hmm …'

The two women didn't speak for a while.

'Aunt Hermine,' Marie-Ange resumed, fighting against the urge to curl up in the armchair, close her eyes and fall asleep. 'What can you tell me about the Cross of Life? Baldassare said I had to find it and take it back to Arginy.'

Hermine sat back in her chair and considered her a moment in silence. 'Do you know about Guillaume de Beaujeu, the Great Templar Master?'

'Malleval said his body was first laid in the chapel of the Temple of Paris, but that a member of his family, his nephew I think, later took his remains to Arginy, together with documents and artefacts, among which was the Cross of Life.'

'That's right. Guichard de Beaujeu reburied Guillaume's body and hid part of the Templar treasure in the crypt at Arginy back in 1307.'

'Malleval also said that at the end of the fifteenth century, Anne de Beaujeu searched Arginy and found the Cross.'

Hermine sighed. 'Anne ordered her men to go down into the crypt, despite the traps Guichard had planted to protect the Templar treasure. Many of the men died a horrible death, their limbs crushed by stones, their bodies pierced by lances, their skin burned by fireballs … some claimed the crypt was cursed by the Knights Templar. The poor man who *did* manage to bring the Cross back became a raving lunatic, ranting about shadows wanting to rip his soul out of his body. After the Cross was found, Anne had the entrance to the crypt walled up. There is supposed to be another entrance somewhere, but nobody knows where it is.'

The more Hermine talked about Arginy, the more Marie-Ange

was reminded of her nightmares about a tall, round tower and an opening in the wall leading down to a slippery stone staircase and the vaults, where she heard whimpers of pain and where the shadows waited. Yet, why should she dream of a place she'd never been to?

She whispered. 'Why do I have to take the Cross to Arginy? Why can I not just give it to the bishop, or any other church authorities, once I have found it?'

'Our family stole it from the crypt – well, it was Anne de Beaujeu, but we, as Beauregards, are her nearest blood relatives, so it's our responsibility to put it back. And the legend says that only someone of the same bloodline as a past Grand Master – that is a Beaujeu or a Beauregard – can handle the Cross without any risk to their life, to their sanity and their soul.' She paused. 'It must be done, child, because only when the Cross is back at Arginy will the eleven Templar guardians be able to rest.'

They were the eleven shadows haunting her nightmares, the Keepers her father had told her about.

'What did Anne de Beaujeu do with the Cross?'

'Towards the end of her life, Anne believed she was cursed,' Hermine answered. 'She was plagued by horrifying visions that drove her almost insane. She only found peace after she gave the Cross to a dear friend of hers shortly before her death in the 1520s. The man was a scholar, alchemist, and a member of the Rosicrucian order which had vowed to guard the Templar Knights' secrets. She knew the Cross would be safe with him.'

'Who was he?'

'Count Saint-Germain.'

'But that's impossible! How can Anne de Beaujeu know Saint-Germain? She lived centuries before him.'

Hermine arched her eyebrows but said nothing.

'You cannot seriously believe Saint-Germain was alive in the fifteenth century and lived through to the 1780s,' Marie-Ange protested, incredulous.

'There have been too many reliable witnesses who testified

meeting Saint-Germain across the centuries to doubt that it is true. Some claim to have talked to him only recently.'

Marie-Ange shrugged. 'This is nonsense. Nothing can make a man immortal.'

'Don't forget the Cross' extraordinary powers, child,' Hermine said with quiet assurance.

It was useless to argue, her great-aunt would not see sense, and she was far too tired anyway.

'What do you know about the relic inside the Cross?' she asked. 'Karloff claims it belongs to an angel.'

'That's right, child.'

'I don't believe a word of it.'

'And yet it is true, the story was passed down in our family through generations. The relic is a piece of clothing worn by an angel who appeared to two veterans of the First Crusades, the French knights Hugues de Payens and Godfrey de Saint-Omer. The angel asked them to create a military order to protect pilgrims travelling to the Holy Land. They obeyed and that's how the Order of the Knights Templar was founded in 1119.'

'Angels don't exist,' Marie-Ange objected once again.

'They do, but we just don't realise they wander the earth among us undetected because they can take a human form,' Hermine declared matter-of-factly. 'The angel came to Payens and Saint-Omer as a man, but his appearance changed once he had delivered his message. Witnessing the transformation, Hughes de Payens rushed to ask for his benediction but accidentally tore a piece of his clothing.'

'My mother's song refers to a wing.'

Hermine nodded. 'That's right. I was told the relic was a very fine, translucent, piece of fabric that glowed like the brightest moonlight. I believe the cloth was indeed from the angel's wing as he changed back to his celestial form.'

Marie-Ange pulled a face. 'Why did Saint-Germain choose Beauregard to hide the Cross?'

'Because it was close to Arginy and belonged to our family. He could not foresee that Edmond Malleval would one day own the place. That man was evil. I am glad he is rotting in the ground,' the old lady hissed the words vehemently between her teeth.

'Edmond Malleval wasn't buried, Aunt Hermine.'

Hermine gasped and put her hand in front of her mouth.

'My God. So he is waiting ...'

'What do you mean, waiting? He is dead.'

'He is waiting for his son to get the Cross, and raise him from the dead.'

Marie-Ange shook her head. Clearly her great-aunt was as deluded about the Cross' powers as Malleval and Karloff. She was however far too exhausted to protest.

Marie-Ange slept most of the next day, and the day after that. She had developed a fever and a sore throat and her great-aunt asked for a physician to attend to her. The man diagnosed a chill and prescribed complete bedrest, poultices twice a day and hot tea and honey drinks.

It took over a week to be well enough to get out of bed, and she was enjoying a late supper in the lounge with Hermine when Pierre walked in, looking agitated. 'A gentleman requests an urgent interview with you, Madame. A Capitaine Saintclair. What shall I tell him?'

'Saintclair!' Marie-Ange stood up, her heart leaped with joy. He was back from Paris. He had come for her. She smoothed down the folds of the dress Hermine had lent her and turned a hopeful face towards her aunt.

'Please, Aunt Hermine. Let him in. He must have news.'

Hermine sighed. 'Very well. I suppose we'd better hear what the man has to say.'

Marie-Ange sat down and took a few deep, calming breaths but her heart still beat wildly and her face was hot when Saintclair entered the room. His dark blue coat was dusty, a leather satchel was slung across his chest. She couldn't repress a happy smile when he took his hat off and bowed deeply in front of her. 'How are you, Madame?'

'Monsieur Saintclair, what brings you here?' Hermine asked before Marie-Ange gathered her wits to reply.

'The safety of your niece, Madame,' he replied. 'I do apologise for the lateness of the hour but I had to make sure that all was well with Madame Norton.'

'I am very grateful for your concern for my niece, Capitaine,' Hermine interrupted calmly. 'Let me offer you some refreshments. A little brandy maybe, or a cup of mulled wine? And please sit down and make yourself comfortable.'

Marie-Ange glanced up, surprised by her aunt's uncharacteristic politeness towards the cuirassier she seemed to despise so much. Saintclair asked for mulled wine. Marie-Ange declared she would have some, too.

Hermine turned to him. 'I know you are a brave, honourable man. You have proved it by coming all this way to make sure Marie-Ange was safe. There is one thing I must ask of you. Please go with her to look for the Cross of Life at Beauregard and return it where it belongs, at Arginy.'

Saintclair put his cup down. 'Of course, Madame. That's why I'm here. We will go to Beauregard tomorrow morning at first light.'

'Very well, it is settled then.' Hermine sighed, satisfied. 'Where are you staying tonight, Capitaine?'

He shrugged. 'I don't know yet. I will find a tavern in Beaujeu.'

'It would be more convenient for you to stay here. I will ask Pierre to prepare a room for you. I'm afraid Marie-Ange has been poorly and needs to rest. Come along, child,' she said, sliding her hand under the young woman's arm to lead her out. She obviously wanted to make sure she stayed well away from the officer. They walked up to the first floor and stopped outside Marie-Ange's bedroom.

'Sleep well,' the old lady said. 'You will need all your strength for tomorrow.'

Marie-Ange closed the door behind her and leant against the wooden pane, all her senses alert. She was waiting for Saintclair to come up. When she heard voices in the corridor, she half-opened the door and peered outside to see which room he was going into. As soon as the house was quiet, she tiptoed out of her room and knocked softly onto his door.

'Capitaine.'

Saintclair appeared in the doorway. He had taken his overcoat and blue jacket off. A small bandage around his left shoulder was visible under his white shirt.

He opened his door, and she slipped in. Pierre had lit a fire in the fireplace and brought up a tray with a pitcher of wine and a cup and some food. Now she was on her own with Saintclair, she was nervous. Maybe a glass of wine would soothe her nerves.

'Could you pour a glass out for me?' she asked.

He passed her a cup and she raised it to her lips, but the sharpness of the wine tickled her throat and made her cough. Without a word, Saintclair pulled out a handkerchief from his pocket and handed it to her before leaning back against the wooden bedpost. She wiped her face, cursing herself and feeling like crying for making such a display of herself.

'What did you learn in Paris?' she asked at last.

'That the king is coming to Lyon next week to review the troops and there are rumours of an attempt on his life. Fouché is the one most likely to mastermind such a coup.' He paused. 'I think Nallay's mission in Lyon is to kill the king.'

'Why would anyone want to kill the king?' she said.

'To make way for Napoleon, or replace the king with someone more amenable to certain policies or politicians? Or even to discredit forever Napoleon and his followers, who knows?' He shrugged.

'My Christopher would never have been capable of killing the king, or anyone, in cold blood.'

Saintclair laughed bitterly. 'Well, he was capable of stabbing me in the back. He is certainly no longer the sensitive soul you once married.'

She bowed her head. 'That's because he isn't Christopher anymore … and I am sorry you got hurt.'

'It wasn't your fault. I was careless. I should have been prepared,' he said with a soft voice. 'We are caught in a frightening web of intrigues. Your husband's involvement with Fouché …'

'Stop calling him my husband. I told you before. Christopher Norton is dead. The man who calls himself Nallay is a stranger to me.'

She lifted her head towards him and smiled tentatively. 'But you are right. I am frightened.'

Hugo narrowed his eyes. The way he was looking at her now reminded her of the night of the ball. Her skin tingled all over, her cheeks burned, her breathing became fast, too fast.

'You mean you wouldn't take Norton back even if he begged you to?' he asked after a while.

She shook her head slowly. 'I could never share my life with him ever again.'

He let out a long sigh and stepped forward.

'I must tell you about the Cross of Life and Arginy. I have seen terrible dangers in my dreams,' she said, flustered from his nearness.

'I don't care much about dreams.' His voice was hoarse.

He stood in front of her, so close she could feel the heat from his body. The intensity in his eyes, the tautness of his jaw warned her to keep still.

'In fact, I never dream,' he carried on. 'Dreams are a waste of time. I only care about what's real, about what I can touch, and kiss.' He slid his finger under her chin to tilt her head up, then bent down and kissed her lips.

'I have wanted you since I first laid eyes on you. I think you want me, too. So why don't we just enjoy the moment?'

'I'm not like you,' she said, placing her hand on his to stop him. 'I couldn't just do this, and then forget all about it. I have feelings.'

What she really meant was she loved him. She loved him and she wanted to be his, but she knew what he thought about love and women.

'I have feelings too,' he replied lightly.

She let go of his hand. His fingers stroked her throat again.

'As I said, I want you. All of you.'

'That isn't the kind of feelings I mean.' She was too hot, breathless, blood pulsed in her veins.

He put a finger on her lips. 'Is there any other kind? Now stop talking, you're driving me crazy.'

She knew then she was lost. Unhurriedly, he kissed her mouth. She let out a small gasp as he buried his face in her neck, and kissed her softly. The stubble on his cheeks scraped her skin, his warm breath tickled, and his mouth sent shivers of delight that made her body tighten and melt at the same time.

He pulled her against his chest and whispered, 'All that matters is here and now.'

His warmth, his caresses were so tantalising she gave in with a shaky sigh. Her body moulded itself more tightly against his.

Her hand went down to his wounded shoulder.

'Does it still hurt?'

He shrugged. 'Sometimes. You'll have to take my mind off it.'

She nestled against him while he encircled her waist and held her tight. He kissed her again, a little harder, and waves of pleasure carried her away once more to the marvellous place where only he had the power to take her. She saw the same longing in his eyes, caressed the outline of his face, her fingers lingering on the scar that marked one side of his face. He took her hand and brought it to his lips.

She closed her eyes. The only sounds were their breathing and the crackling of the logs in the fireplace. It was as if they were alone in the world.

She threw her head back to offer her throat to his lips. Her heart beat wildly, out of control, as he undid her dress and dropped it to her feet.

'I want you naked in my arms.'

He took the last of her clothes off and held her against him, and she moaned when his fingers stroked the tender skin on the inside of her thighs. Shaking in his arms, she threw her head back. Her breasts jutted out and this time it was he who moaned as he bent down to kiss and tease.

She arched her hips against him, wanting, needing to get closer still.

'Hugo,' she gasped. There wasn't a clear thought left in her mind. There were only feelings and sensations and overwhelming desire.

'Hmm … I like it when you say my name.'

She grabbed hold of his shoulders as his hands brushed past her hips and her stomach. She was aching for him to touch her again. As if he had understood her most intimate desires, he caressed and explored, gentle and insistent in turn, arousing sensations so wild, so tormenting she cried out loud.

'I must have you now, or I'll go mad,' he said with some urgency as he lifted her up against him. He was about to carry her onto the bed when he pulled away.

'What's that noise?' He froze, and his eyes focused on the window.

Outside in the night, horses neighed, men shouted and banged loudly on the castle door.

He turned to Marie-Ange. 'Put your clothes back on. Quick! Something's happening.' He fastened his belt and checked his sword and his pistol and put his jacket and overcoat on.

Someone rapped on the door.

'Capitaine, there are men outside asking for you,' Pierre called.

Saintclair frowned, but he waited for Marie-Ange to dress before opening the door to let the old servant in.

'Monsieur,' Pierre was breathless. His eyes opened wide with shock when he saw Marie-Ange was there, partly clothed. 'They say they are bailiffs sent by Monsieur Malleval to take you to the debtors' jail in Beaujeu. If you come with me now, I'll show you the old way out of the castle, but please hurry!'

Saintclair nodded. 'Give me a minute.' He looked at Marie-Ange. 'You're coming too.' It was not a question but a command.

Chapter Eighteen

They followed Pierre down the service staircase and along the dark and draughty corridors of the deserted servants' quarters. Pierre's candle flickered and threw huge shadows onto the walls.

'This way, please.'

They were in a small parlour now. Pierre asked Saintclair to hold the candle. He lifted the corner of a large tapestry that covered the better part of the wall and disappeared behind it. There were sounds of a door being unlocked.

'Hurry.'

Saintclair and Marie-Ange ducked under the tapestry and found themselves in another room.

'Where does this lead?' Saintclair looked around, holding the candle high.

'Down to the cellars and the vineyards,' the old man answered as he ushered them down a bare stone wall passage. 'Not many people know about it.'

They reached a basement filled with oak barrels and winemaking apparatus. Pierre pushed open a wooden door and they walked out into the night and across a cobblestone courtyard. At the far end was a small building that looked abandoned. Pierre opened the door and led them in.

'This was the lodge for the vineyard. It's empty now; nobody's been making any wine at Marzac for years.' He stuck the candle on a tall candelabrum on the table and gestured towards a couple of rickety chairs and a straw bed tucked into the corner of the room.

'You can wait in here until dawn. I'll send one of the lads with your horse when it's safe.'

Saintclair nodded to the old man. 'What will you tell the bailiffs?'

'That they've just missed you. I'll say I heard you two planning to ride back to Lyon.' Pierre smiled.

Marie-Ange put her hand on his arm. 'Thank you, Pierre, for all you help. I know you tried to help my mother when Edmond Malleval took her away from the Priory. And you alerted Baldassare dei Conti, my father, a few weeks ago.'

'These Mallevals, father and son, they were always wicked,' the old man said, shaking his head.

'Goodnight for now.'

Once alone, Marie-Ange and Saintclair stood awkwardly in front of each other. Hugo pointed to the bed. 'You'd better get some sleep.'

She sat on the couch. It was rough and stiff with dirt and grime. Straw sprouted from the ripped cover. There was no way she would be able to sleep now; not only was the bed uncomfortable, but too many conflicting emotions raged through her. Fear, love, desire.

She watched Hugo carry out a brief inspection of the lodge and check windows and doors. Her lips were still swollen with his kisses. Her body resonated with the memory of his caresses. She hadn't tried to stop him earlier even if he had made it quite clear he didn't have any feelings for her. Or at least not the kind of feelings she wished for. However, even knowing he didn't love her made no difference to her yearning for him. He, on the other hand, looked calm, almost detached, as if the feverish passion they had just shared was all but a distant memory. They were very different. She would do well to remember it, or she would get hurt.

'Tell me what happened in Paris,' she asked.

He sat down on a chair. It creaked under his weight. 'I spoke to my colonel and he instructed me to ride to Paris immediately and request an interview with Talleyrand in his office at the Hôtel Vendôme.'

He told her that the elderly, but still powerful Talleyrand hadn't looked fazed in the slightest by his news. There were indeed reports of intense activity from Fouché's camp to prepare the ground for Napoleon's return. Fouché himself was under surveillance. However he still controlled a secret army of loyal agents on whom there was very little information and whose movements were almost impossible to trace.

'Men like … Nallay,' Saintclair finished, 'with no past, no identity, and no country.'

'What will you do if – or when – Napoleon comes back?'

Saintclair sighed. 'I served him with undying loyalty for fifteen years. Yet, towards the end, even I had my doubts. There were too many deaths, too much carnage and ruin … no, I don't want him back, not if it means that the country is engulfed in war again. But …' He looked at Marie-Ange. 'I may not have a choice.'

They remained silent for a while.

'What I really want is to be free.' His voice was so low she had to strain to hear him. 'Free from the army, from rigid social conventions, class, and status.'

He leant towards her and searched her face. 'Is there such a place, do you think, where a man can live his life without having to answer to anyone, where he can make his own fortune, be master of his own destiny even if he wasn't born rich and titled?'

It was the first time he had opened his mind, his soul, to her. She took a few moments to answer. 'I don't know … I once read that the greatest obstacles to freedom are the ones we place upon ourselves. You say you long for freedom, but you also yearn for military honours and recognition by your superiors, otherwise you would have left the army long ago to join your father's business.'

She stopped and glanced at him tentatively, unsure how he would respond. He smiled in the dim light.

'Very well spoken, Madame,' he said with a trace of irony. 'You are right. I am my worst enemy. My ambition was always to reach the top. With the Bourbons back at the head of the country it will never happen. Maybe I should do as you suggest and fulfil my father's wishes, but I can't help thinking that there is something else out there for me, somewhere …'

She would have liked to have been brave enough to tell him she was there for him, but she remained silent.

He broke the silence. 'Tell me about the Cross of Life. You said it was in the dovecote at Beauregard. Our biggest challenge tomorrow will be to avoid Malleval and his men.'

'I'm so scared of going down into the crypt at Arginy,' she said weakly, burying her face into her hands.

He was next to her in a couple of seconds. He put his arm around her shoulders, and she snuggled against him.

'I don't understand why you have to take the Cross there. What has it got to do with you? Why can't your father do it? And why does anyone have to do anything at all?'

Marie-Ange told him what her great-aunt had said about family duty and the Beaujeus and Beauregards bloodline. 'My mother was meant to take the Cross back,' she added. 'She passed her duty to me. But I am so afraid of what is down there.'

'Probably rats, a cold draughty room, and the tombs of former lords and ladies of the manor.'

'There are shadows and ghosts, too,' she whispered.

'Ghosts don't exist.' He stared into her eyes with such certainty that she almost believed him. 'You said you knew how to find the Cross at Beauregard?'

'I will follow the clues in the song my mother taught me. I know I need my locket to work the mechanism but I don't understand how to use it.'

'Tell me the words again. I remember you said something about a rose and a heart.'

Marie-Ange recited the words slowly:

'My sweet rose of May

My rose with five petals,

You cry in the dovecote

For your lover, cold in his tomb ...

Listen to me, don't despair,

Your lover you'll see again,

Place the rose on the heart, give five turns,

Raise your eyes, the wing you will find.

But you must choose wisely,

For if the wing of the dove

Is as white as the angel's

It will not open your lover's tomb.'

Hugo listened intently and shook his head. 'Let's hope it makes sense tomorrow when we are in the dovecote.'

He looked through the grimy window partly hidden behind thick cobwebs. It was pitch-black. 'With luck Malleval and his men are spending the night smoking opium and drinking. They will be hung-over in the morning.' It was very cold in the old lodge so he took his overcoat off and wrapped it around her shoulders.

'What's going to happen to you and your family?' she asked, placing her hands on his. 'Malleval seems determined to send you to the debtors' jail.'

'I'll worry about that later.' He gestured dismissively. 'Now, get some sleep. I'll keep watch and wake you up at first light.'

Marie-Ange lay down and curled up on the bed, wrapped in Hugo's coat, while he sat at the table. He blew the candle out and remained immobile in the darkness.

It was barely light when they set off a few hours later. As promised, a stable lad had brought Hugo's horse to the vineyard lodge.

'Ready?' Hugo asked, encircling Marie-Ange's waist with his hands and lifting her onto his horse. He then mounted behind her and spurred the horse into a trot on the road to St Rigaud Hill where he said her father and his men were hiding.

'Let's hope they're still there,' he said, steering the horse onto a lane leading through the forest.

Halfway up, he dismounted to guide the horse through the rocky path. A sharp bird call, like a warning echoed in the eerie silence of the forest. A Turcopilar appeared in front of them, stepping silently from behind a tree, and the horse baulked in surprise, almost throwing Marie-Ange onto the ground. Hugo held firmly to the reins and managed to calm the animal.

'Steady on, man,' he growled. 'It's only us.'

'Pardon, Capitaine. Madame,' the Turcopilar mumbled when he recognised them.

'Is my father here?' she asked. The man nodded and whistled again and soon two familiar figures emerged from the sheepfold.

'Daughter! Here you are at last.'

Hugo helped Marie-Ange get down and she ran to Baldassare. He held her against him and kissed her forehead.

They agreed that they should leave for Beauregard without delay and Baldassare gave instructions to his companions to get the horses ready.

It was decided that Saintclair would go into the dovecote with Marie-Ange, and that Hafiz, one of the Turcopilars, would guard the entrance to the rose garden while Baldassare and his other companion kept watch at the edge of the forest and deal with Malleval's patrols. They were outnumbered but there was no other choice.

'Do you have your locket?' Baldassare asked. Marie-Ange nodded.

'Let's go,' said Saintclair. Nobody talked as they made their way through the woods to Beauregard. When they reached the estate, they tied their horses to tree branches. Baldassare went ahead and came back soon after, gesturing that the grounds were clear.

As Hafiz took his position, Marie-Ange and Hugo hurried towards the dovecote.

Now the moment of truth had come and she put her hand on the door handle, Marie-Ange had a second of awful doubt. What if the whole story was a myth? What if there was no Cross and no relic hidden in there? It was, however, too late to worry about it now. She pushed the door and walked in with Hugo right behind her.

The dovecote looked very different from her mother's paintings. It was dark and filthy. The floor was covered with a thick layer of feathers and bird droppings. The wooden beams that had looked so beautiful on paper were so black and grimy no pattern or engraving could be seen on their surface at all. Marie-Ange walked around the central beam, pulled her knife from her boot and scraped the dirt to reveal the wood below, careful not to erase the original carvings she knew were there. Saintclair pulled his own knife too and they worked in silence for a while.

'It's pointless.' Marie-Ange shook her head after a while. 'It's going to take forever!'

Just then a dove flew in through one of the circular openings in the top half of the tower, and perched on one of the beams that criss-crossed the eaves. It settled and started cooing as a pale sunray filtered inside the dovecote onto the central beam, highlighting the carvings in a play of shadows and light. Marie-Ange held her breath. *There* was what she had been looking for. The pattern of a rose within a heart.

'It's up there!' She pointed to the dove, still perching on the beam, oblivious to their presence.

'I'll go,' Hugo suggested, but she shook her head.

'No. My father said that it had to be me.'

'I really don't see why,' he mumbled, pulling a ladder across the floor. He held it while she climbed up towards the dove. The bird didn't move but observed her movements with great curiosity. She took her knife, and holding onto the ladder with one hand, scratched carefully at the layer of dirt to reveal the heart carving she had spotted from below. Inside the heart was indeed the outline of a rose. She traced the pattern, the five petals, with her finger.

The song said she had to fit the locket into the rose pattern and turn it five times to reveal the relic's hiding place. Would it work?

With a silent prayer, she took off her locket and inserted it into the carving on the beam. It fitted perfectly. She tried turning it to the right, but the locket refused to move.

'I can't do it.' She tried again, with more strength this time.

'Do you want me to try?' Hugo asked, still holding the ladder. 'It may be stuck.'

She was about to get down and let him have a go when she had a thought. What if she turned the locket the other way? She pressed it into the carving again and pushed it to the left. Of course. Towards the heart, on the left-hand side of the body. This time, she heard a clicking sound. The locket penetrated deep into the wood. Holding her breath, she gave five turns and looked up towards the doves' nests.

'Right at the top!' Hugo pointed to the nests closest to the roof line. 'Three boxes have opened.'

The ladder wasn't high enough for Marie-Ange to reach them – she would have to climb onto the beams that crisscrossed the top of the tower.

'It's far too high for you. Get down. I'll do it,' Hugo said once again, but she refused.

'This is something I have to finish, no one else can.'

Hugo sighed with impatience.

'Take my bag then to put the … thing in … whatever it is.' He stepped onto the ladder and handed her the satchel, which she slung across her body, looping the long strap over her shoulder.

She climbed to the top of the ladder and balanced on the top beam. Without looking down, she stepped onto another joist and made her way towards the nests. The beam was wide enough for her to walk on it without too much difficulty. Nevertheless she was relieved to reach the wall. She slid her hand into one of the openings. Carefully, she explored the inside of the nest with her fingers until she touched something hard. She pulled a cylinder out and held it in front of her. She wiped its surface quickly. It was made of thick glass and inside was a beautiful, delicate, white, almost translucent object she couldn't immediately identify. She held it in the sunlight. It looked like it was made of white feathers. Was this the angel wing?

She put it in Hugo's bag and walked to the next nest. This time, she pulled out a heavy, ornate box. There was a long line of symbols across the cover – the Templars' code – and the engraving of a rose and a heart in the left-hand corner. As she brushed the dirt off the cover with her hand, she realised it was solid gold and decorated with dozens of rubies, emeralds, and sapphires. She placed the box in the satchel too. There was one last niche in the beam to explore. Inside was a small cloth bag. She carefully pulled it out and opened it up. It was another phial, this time with a piece of fine, dull, grey fabric inside. Which phial contained the angel wing? There was no time to think about it now.

She was about to step onto the ladder when there were pistol shots outside.

'Hurry!' Hugo urged. He pulled his pistol out and walked to the door.

Her chest tight with fear, she returned to the ladder and made her way down as quickly as she could.

'Stay here.' Hugo opened the door cautiously and stepped outside. Marie-Ange heard Hafiz's breathless voice.

'I shot two men but more are coming from the chateau.'

'Watch out! Behind you!' Hugo yelled.

There were more gunshots, a lot of shouting. Standing behind the door, she held her hand to her heart in agony, desperate to find out what was happening outside.

'Let me go, you bastards,' Hugo roared at last. 'Malleval, tell them to let go of me.'

Malleval's harsh voice sent shivers down Marie-Ange's spine. 'It's too late, Saintclair. You really disappointed me, my friend … I presume the lovely Marie-Ange is inside?' He broke into a raucous cough and took a long time to catch his breath. 'I told you to leave her alone. Look at the mess you're in now. It was clever of you to escape the bailiffs last night but it's only a matter of time before they catch up with you. I hope you warned your parents to pack up.'

'Leave me a few more weeks. I'll get the money to pay you back. You know I will,' Hugo said, a hint of despair in his voice.

Malleval laughed. 'You should have thought about that before helping Marie-Ange escape me. You cost me precious time, which I haven't got, unfortunately. Take him away.'

Marie-Ange couldn't stay in the dovecote any longer. She pushed the door open and stepped out into the pale morning light. Malleval, Karloff, and a dozen men dressed in sheepskins, and holding daggers and pistols, stood in the rose garden.

Malleval's face was so emaciated it looked like a skull with deep, purple bruises underneath his feverish brown eyes. A dry, raspy cough shook his thin frame. Marie-Ange was surprised he could even stand in the cold breeze.

Hugo was slumped on the ground next to Hafiz's lifeless body, his face and jacket smeared with blood. One bandit pointed a pistol to his head. Instinctively, she rushed to his side, but a man grabbed her arm and held her back.

Malleval chuckled weakly. 'How touching. But don't worry, dear Marie-Ange. He'll live … for now.'

He raised his white, bony hand. 'Hand over the bag.'

She tightened her grip on the satchel and desperately looked around. Where was her father? Had he been caught too? One of the men snatched the bag from her and gave it to Malleval. He opened it and thrust his hand inside, gasped, and withdrew it as if he had been burned.

'Bring them both to the chateau.'

Chapter Nineteen

Hugo tried one last desperate move. He lunged forward and tackled the man standing closest to him. He knocked him out but before he could pick up his gun, two of Malleval's thugs jumped on him and kicked him back onto the frozen ground.

Malleval turned round and narrowed his eyes in anger.

'That was a mistake, Saintclair – your last mistake, I daresay. Make sure he doesn't interfere with my business again,' he told his men. 'I've had enough of my troublesome friend. He's of no use to me anymore.'

He hurried towards the chateau, clutching the satchel against his frail body. One of the men clubbed Hugo in the face with the grip of his pistol until he stopped struggling.

'Hugo,' Marie-Ange cried out in anguish as his body was dragged away. Malleval had just signed his death warrant.

'Take her to the library,' Karloff ordered.

Marie-Ange was frogmarched through the garden, into Beauregard's hall and along the corridor. A man kicked the library door open and pushed her inside.

There was no fire in the hearth today. The pale morning sun had already disappeared behind snow clouds and a grey light now filtered through the partly drawn green velvet curtains. Marie-Ange breathed in the sickly scent of cold opium smoke that lingered in the room. She rubbed her arms with the palm of her hands to warm herself up. Her teeth chattered, and she shivered with cold as she stood in front of Saint-Germain's portrait.

'What do I do now?' she asked aloud.

She looked at Saint-Germain's gentle smile, his warm, intelligent brown eyes. Even if she didn't believe he was immortal or had lived for over two hundred years, that he was a Rosicrucian who held the key to the mysteries of life and death, he was still an enigma. He had been in touch with the Knights Hospitaller and the Turcopilars. He believed in the relic, had kept hold of the Cross of Life for years before deciding it was time to hide it. He had given her mother his locket and patiently instructed her with the secret song to enable her to find the Cross when the time came.

She stared at the painting. If only he could answer …

What she dreaded most had happened. Malleval was in possession of the Cross and the relic. Rather, she corrected, he had two relics and, according to her mother's song, only one of them had any power.

Hugo was in mortal danger, prisoner somewhere in the chateau. Hafiz had been killed. She felt a lump in her throat at the thought of the man lying dead in the rose garden. At least it seemed her father and the other Turcopilar had managed to avoid detection. She hoped they wouldn't be caught. They were her last chance. As for her, she was at the mercy of her sick, demented relative and his obsession.

A noise by the door made her jump. Karloff entered; the physician was pale. His grey hair fell in long, unkempt strands around his face and his hands shook as he unbuttoned his coat.

He turned towards Marie-Ange in earnest. 'There are two phials but only one is the angel's wing. Which one is it? You must tell me. Malleval is very agitated. I had to wrestle the phials from him. He is so desperate he was about to break them open regardless of the danger.'

He looked deep into Marie-Ange's eyes but this time his intense gaze had no effect on her. 'According to Polycarpe's parchment, only the pure heart can release the relic's powers. Only the pure heart knows which phial is the angel's wing. You must tell me!'

She didn't reply. If she was the pure heart the Templar Knights had written about, why didn't she know which phial contained the true relic? There was only one thing she knew for sure.

'We must go to Arginy,' she said.

Karloff looked up, surprised. 'Arginy? What for?'

She would tell him part of the truth. 'The Cross must be in the vault to release its true magic.'

She wouldn't explain about the Keepers, the eleven Templar entities, as Baldassare and her great-aunt had called them, who waited for the relic to be returned.

Karloff remained silent a few moments. 'Yes. I suppose that makes sense. It's where Guichard de Beaujeu hid it when he retrieved it from the Temple of Paris, where most of the Templar treasure was hidden.' He turned to her. 'I don't have the faintest idea how to get into the crypt. The entrance to the underground passages was walled up by Anne de Beaujeu before she died. Do you know how to get in?'

Marie-Ange didn't want to admit she didn't know either. In her dreams, she always stood in a tall, round tower before descending underground.

'Yes, of course,' she lied, crossing her arms on her chest. 'But I will only go if Capitaine Saintclair comes too.'

She would make the most of her position. If Malleval and Karloff needed her so badly, they would have to keep Hugo alive.

Karloff sighed before walking to the door. 'I'll see what I can do.'

A few moments later, Sophie came in with some food and drinks. Her eyes were red, her face tear-stricken.

'I will light a fire for you. It's too cold in here,' she said with a broken voice before burying her face in her hand and sobbing loudly. Marie-Ange went over to her and put her arm around her shoulders.

'I don't understand what is happening,' Sophie said, wiping her eyes with the back of her hand. 'I don't recognise Uxeloup anymore, he frightens me. The things he talks about, the men he brought back from Malleval, the way he's treating you and Capitaine Saintclair who has always been his friend, all that is so unlike him.' She lowered her voice. 'He is obsessed with ancient papers and legends, he even had this horrid snake – an Uroboros, he calls it – tattooed on his chest. He says it's a symbol of eternal life. He claims he is going to be cured and everything will be back to normal, but …'

Marie-Ange sighed. Malleval's health had deteriorated so much these past few weeks there could be no doubt about his prospects. The disease caused terrible ravages, not only to patient's bodies but to their minds, too. 'What about you? Are you ill too?' she asked with hesitation.

'No, he never …' Sophie looked up, her eyes shiny with tears. 'He said he loved me too much to take me to his bed, and that he would wait until he was cured. He bedded other women, though, even maids here at Beauregard. It used to make me miserable and jealous, even if I knew he was only sparing me.' She joined her hands. 'I want him back. I want the carefree and wild Hussar he used to be. What he has become now, it's not him anymore. He says he needs you to make him get better, but I fear he has gone … mad.' Sophie twisted the ruby ring around her finger nervously.

She got up and lit the fire. Marie-Ange was strangely touched by the young woman's admission that Malleval had abstained from making love to her for fear of passing on his deadly disease. He must truly love her. However there was no hope he would ever recover. Nobody recovered from syphilis. She didn't believe for a second that the Cross would make him immortal. These things weren't possible, whatever Karloff, Malleval, or her great-aunt Hermine claimed.

She poured a cup of coffee, nibbled at a slice of bread covered with jam. She had to eat in order to keep her strength for the day to come. She thought about Hugo, injured, cold and alone in the cellars and put the bread back on the plate, her throat tight.

'Malleval is angry with Hugo,' she said. 'He helped me and now he will lose his family house … and probably his life.'

Sophie shrugged. 'He tricked him during the card game, you know.'

Marie-Ange looked at her sharply. 'Tricked him?'

Sophie nodded. 'He desperately needed a strong, reliable man to escort you back from England to Beauregard so he invited Saintclair over for a game of cards, knowing how much the capitaine likes to gamble. And …' Sophie bent her head, embarrassed.

'And?'

'He asked me to drug his wine during the game. I gave him some draught Karloff made to cloud his mind. I couldn't refuse,' Sophie said, on the defensive.

Marie-Ange frowned. 'If Saintclair's debt towards Malleval was fraudulently obtained, it could be cancelled.'

'I won't say anything to the gendarmes. I will not betray Uxeloup,' she added, very agitated. Claiming she had things to take care of, she left.

The day passed with excruciating slowness. By the afternoon a strong wind started blowing which dispersed the clouds. Malleval came into the library. Once again she was struck by the ghastly paleness of his face, the fever burning in his yellowish-brown eyes.

'We're leaving. Saintclair is coming with us, as you wished.' He coughed and wiped his mouth with a handkerchief. 'Karloff said you were the only one who could do it … open the phial and take the true relic out. Why can't I open the bloody bottle myself, right now, I wonder? It's not as if I care about eternal damnation!'

He took a few steps towards her and dug his bony claw-like fingers into her shoulders. 'You will hand the relic over to me as soon as we reach the crypt, is that clear?'

She nodded. At this point, she would agree to anything. He released her. She put her coat on and followed him out. Two black carriages waited in front of the chateau and half a dozen armed riders stood guard.

Malleval opened the door of the first coach. Marie-Ange glanced at the heavy carriage stationed behind. It looked like a hearse.

'Climb in.' He pushed her inside.

She sat next to Karloff, who was holding the two phials and the box on his lap, while Malleval took a place next to Hugo on the seat opposite.

'He doesn't look so clever now, does he?' He sneered, gesturing towards Hugo who was unconscious. The bruises and cuts on his face testified to the treatment he had received, his hands were bound in front of him. Marie-Ange ached to sit next to him, touch him, and wake him up, but she knew better than provoke Malleval.

The strange convoy started down the road to the castle of Arginy.

'It's only half a dozen miles from here,' Karloff remarked.

The outline of the castle soon rose on the horizon, dark and sinister against the fierce, red winter sunset and the snowy ground. Arginy had four mismatched towers, with three medium-sized ones and a very tall one. Marie-Ange's heartbeat quickened.

'This is the place, the entrance to the crypt,' she told Karloff.

'The Tower of Eight Beatitudes, I thought as much,' he whispered.

'What a strange name.' Beatitude, peacefulness and contentment, were the last things she expected to find at Arginy.

Karloff smiled tightly. 'It's the oldest tower, the only one left from the original medieval building. People round here claim it is haunted. They talk of shadows seeping out, whimpers of pain and growling noises, stinking balls of fire, and blue lights hovering near the entrance.'

The carriages and the men went over the drawbridge. A nauseating stench rose from the slimy green waters and permeated the close confines of the coach.

'The current owners, the Rosemonts, live in Paris most of the time. Taking care of their house staff won't be a problem,' Karloff explained.

'At last … This is the moment I and my father have been waiting for,' Malleval whispered as the carriage stopped.

He stepped out of the carriage, followed by Karloff who held the boxes. Marie-Ange came last. She cast a look towards the unconscious Hugo and prayed he would soon recover. Outside, two men opened the back of the hearse. They pulled a grey coffin shaped box out and she was reminded of what Sophie had said about Edmond Malleval's body being removed from Beauregard in an iron cask. Karloff had later told her Edmond wasn't buried. Dear God, it must be his body in the coffin.

'This way.' One of Malleval's men pushed her in front.

They walked across the courtyard towards the tower. Malleval ordered two men to stand guard at the drawbridge, instructed two others to take care of the household staff. Only Rochefort and the two pallbearers would go down the crypt with Malleval, Marie-Ange and Karloff.

She climbed up the uneven steps leading into the Tower of Eight Beatitudes, her chest tight with apprehension. What if she couldn't find the way to the crypt?

Rochefort gave her a lantern, which she held high in front of her as she walked around the empty tower to study the myriads of drawings and carvings on the walls.

'This is amazing,' she whispered.

'One of the Beaujeus was a keen alchemist, hence the symbols,' Karloff explained.

She held the lantern close to the walls to examine every one of the patterns. It was lucky she knew what she was looking for, and after a few minutes she found it. It was the carving of a rose with five petals inside a heart, the same one as in the dovecote. Without hesitation she pulled her locket out of her pocket and placed it at the centre of the carving. She turned five times to the left and sure enough, there was a loud clicking noise and the bottom half of the wall descended slowly into the ground, revealing a large black hole. She removed the locket and put it back into her pocket.

Malleval turned to his men. 'Get Father's coffin now.' He gestured to the entrance of the crypt and shouted to Rochefort. 'You get down there first.'

So Hermine had been right. It wasn't only himself Malleval was hoping to save with the Cross of Life. She fought a wave of nausea as she stared at the casket with his father's body inside, but Rochefort was already leading the way into the dank depths, followed by Malleval, and then Karloff holding the box and the phials. His torch threw some light onto slimy stone walls and slippery steps. Marie-Ange reluctantly began the descent. Behind her came the pallbearers with Edmond Malleval's coffin.

As they went deeper and deeper into the subterranean passage, the odour of putrefaction emanating from the moat waters just beyond the walls became so pungent it made her heave. Rivulets of slime ran down the stonework, giving out a constant dripping sound that echoed in the enclosed space.

At last, they reached the end of the staircase and walked on a long, straight corridor.

‘What’s that noise?’ Rochefort stopped and held his hand up.

A hissing, grinding, creaking sound was getting louder and nearer.

‘It’s coming from over there.’ Rochefort pointed to the darkness in front of him. A large stone appeared before them, swinging from the ceiling and travelling swiftly in an arc that was sure to crush any intruders.

‘Get down,’ he yelled, dropping his torch and crouching low against the floor

Malleval pulled Marie-Ange down too. The millstone passed just centimetres above their heads, carried on down the corridor and hit the stairs with a loud crashing noise. The pallbearers were still on the steps, which was the only thing that saved their lives.

‘It’s coming back.’

They remained in their crouching positions while the stone rolled back along the ceiling and disappeared into the darkness.

‘Anybody hurt?’ Malleval called to the men behind. They assured him they were unharmed.

‘That was the first trap,’ Karloff said as he stood up again. ‘So the rumours are true. The place is booby-trapped.’

‘It’s a wonder the devices still work,’ Malleval remarked. ‘It’s been centuries since they were installed down here to protect the Templar treasure.’

They resumed their walk, scouring the darkness around them anxiously for any sign of danger.

‘Stay back while I have a look further ahead,’ Rochefort said before walking away, his torchlight disappearing in the darkness.

His voice called from the darkness a few seconds later. ‘I think I found the crypt. There’s a tomb in the middle. I’m taking a closer look.’

Just then there was a loud creaking noise, a blood-curdling scream. And silence.

‘What on earth …?’ Malleval sputtered. ‘Rochefort, what’s going on?’

No one answered. Marie-Ange's heart pounded in her chest. Staring towards the end of the corridor, she blinked a few times. Were her eyes playing tricks on her? She could see shadows moving.

'Damn it! He must have got caught in some trap. Let's go,' Malleval ordered. 'We've come this far. We'll carry on.'

They moved forward cautiously into the murk. A cold wind howled around them, threatening to blow out the torches.

'Where's that draft coming from? It's freezing,' one of the pallbearers complained.

When they reached the crypt, Malleval raised his torch. There were vaulted alcoves all around and a large stone tomb decorated with the Templar Cross at the centre. Rochefort was nowhere to be seen. He had vanished without a trace.

'Is this Guillaume de Beaujeu's tomb?' Marie-Ange enquired.

'Yes, this must be where Guichard placed his remains after removing them from the Temple of Paris,' Karloff affirmed. 'The treasure must be inside.'

So this was where she was expected to return the Cross. She walked to the tomb and inspected the lid. There was a carving at the centre. A five-petal rose inside the heart shape. Discreetly, she took her locket out of her pocket and inserted it into the hole. It clicked.

The pallbearers placed Edmond Malleval's coffin in front of the tomb and Uxeloup gestured impatiently to Karloff.

'Put the box and the phials on the coffin.'

The physician obeyed reluctantly.

'Let's not waste any more time. Go on, open the phials now,' Malleval instructed Marie-Ange.

A gust of wind extinguished the two torchlights, plunging the crypt into darkness.

'Light the torches again,' Malleval ordered his men, but nobody answered.

'What are you waiting for, you fools?'

As her eyes grew accustomed to the darkness, Marie-Ange could make out two bodies on the ground. Malleval took a few steps forward, tripping over one of them. He bent down and touched the man.

'He's dead.' His voice was shaky.

'What do you mean, dead?' Karloff demanded, approaching the other pallbearer. Then he added. 'They're both dead. How is that possible?'

Karloff and Malleval looked around the crypt and froze in front of her, an expression of utter disbelief on their faces. Slowly, she turned to her left, and then to her right. Were her eyes deceiving her again? She was surrounded by shadowy figures, darker than the darkness itself. So, the Keepers were gathering. The time had come. Unlike in her dreams, she wasn't afraid. A diffuse bluish light shone through an opening in the vaulted ceiling, bathing the crypt.

'What is that light?' Malleval asked.

'It's the blue light people have talked about,' Karloff whispered. 'The blue light that shines through the tower sometimes, coming from the inside of the earth.'

'I must place the Cross and the relic on the tomb,' Marie-Ange interrupted. She opened the box and carefully lifted the Cross of Life out. It was heavy but smaller than she'd expected. She put it in the hole at the centre of the tomb.

'I will open Father's coffin now.' Malleval pulled a long knife from his belt, and with growing urgency, popped the nails of the lid. Then he lifted the cover and discarded it to the side. An abominable stench filled the room. Marie-Ange put her hand in front of her mouth and nose, trying not to gag. She had to concentrate on her next task.

Malleval walked towards her. 'Take the relic out of the phial and give it to me. Let me touch the angel and be saved.' He pointed to the phial with the white wing inside.

Karloff stepped forward, too. The two men stood side by side in front of the tomb. Marie-Ange could feel their tension, their eagerness. They were seconds away from the realisation of their dream, immortality for Malleval and proof of the existence of angels for Karloff.

Marie-Ange's fingers traced the outline of the phial with her finger. Sure enough, there was a pure white wing inside, but a voice inside her murmured this wasn't the angel's wing. She turned to the other, plainer phial containing the dull piece of fabric and clipped the Cross on top of it.

'What are you doing?' Malleval shouted. 'That's not right!'

Suddenly, the content of the phial started glowing and changing shape.

'Look!' Karloff pointed to the piece of cloth that seemed to float inside the glass.

'Give it to me.' Malleval seized the Cross before Marie-Ange could step away.

'You're not worthy of the angel,' Karloff protested. 'He won't come to you. Remember the parchment. Only a pure heart from the Keepers' bloodline can touch it.' He tried to wrestle the cross out of Malleval's hands.

It fell onto the ground, and the two men bent down to get at it.

'That's enough. Get up, both of you.' Hugo's voice echoed from a corner of the crypt.

Marie-Ange's heart leaped with relief as Hugo and her father walked towards her. Hugo had a dagger in one hand, and a pistol in the other. He gestured to Malleval and Karloff to step aside. Baldassare picked up the Cross and placed it on the tomb.

'Where were you? I was so worried about you,' Marie-Ange squeezed her father's hand.

'I was waiting here,' he replied quietly.

'How did you get in?'

'I found the other entrance to the crypt. The one Anne de Beaujeu had walled in. The mortar had become brittle; it didn't take long to break a passage into it.'

He gestured to the Cross. 'You must hurry now.'

'I don't know what to do,' she objected.

‘Who are you?’ Malleval interrupted.

‘I am here to put things right,’ Baldassare answered calmly.

‘You’re the envoy, aren’t you?’ Karloff asked. ‘The man from the Templar Order.’

‘Don’t be stupid, Karloff. There are no longer any Knights Templar. Did you kill Rochefort, and my men here?’ Malleval’s voice was raspy and breathless.

‘I don’t know what happened to Rochefort,’ Hugo replied. He sounded puzzled. ‘We were coming towards the crypt from the other side of the corridor when we heard him scream. But yes, we took care of these men when the torches blew out.’ He shoved the bodies on the ground with his boot. ‘And we will kill you both too if you move.’

Karloff stepped towards Marie-Ange, a pleading look on his face. ‘Madame, please remember that my intentions are pure. I have nothing to do with Malleval.’

Malleval laughed bitterly. ‘What are you talking about? We’re in this together, old fool.’

‘No we’re not,’ Karloff retorted with passion. ‘I’m here to talk with my angels, whereas you want the relic for yourself and for your father, this abomination over there.’

He pointed to the open coffin.

‘Shut up, both of you,’ Hugo ordered.

He raised his hand, trying to touch the shadows that still hovered around. A strange smell lingered around the crypt.

‘This smell, it reminds me of some place I’ve been,’ he remarked. ‘And the shadows, what are they? They move then disappear …’

‘They’re the Keepers’ souls,’ Baldassare said. ‘The eleven Great Templar Masters.’

‘Nonsense.’ Hugo walked around, a thoughtful expression on his face. ‘I remember. I have seen similar shadows before, in a mine in Poland where we hid during the Russian retreat. There were pockets of gas in there. We only just made it out before the place blew up. I wonder if …'

'Saintclair, I'm begging you, let me have the angel,' Malleval pleaded. 'Without it, I'm a dead man. I will give you anything you want. I will give you your house back, of course, and half my fortune. Beauregard … anything! Please.'

For a second Marie-Ange feared he was tempted to let the sick man get his hands on the relic, but he shook his head.

'Malleval, this isn't going to work, you should know that.'

'Look,' Karloff exclaimed, pointing to the tombstone. A strong light was now coming out of the phial. The shape of the piece of cloth had changed. It was as bright as moonlight and lit up the whole crypt.

'The angel wing.' Karloff looked around expectantly. 'But where is he? According to the parchments the angel should appear now.'

Next to him, Marie-Ange placed the Cross inside the hole at the centre of the tomb and turned her locket to the left. Immediately, with a loud creaking and grinding noise, the tomb descended into the ground, faster and faster, leaving a great black gap in the ground.

'No,' Malleval yelled and he threw himself onto the tombstone as it disappeared into the chasm.

'Watch out!' Hugo grabbed hold of Marie-Ange and held her tight to keep her from falling in. She buried her face in his shoulder as the tomb disappeared with Malleval still clinging to it leaving only a gaping hole inside the crypt.

Hugo leant forward and peered into the pit.

'Where has Malleval gone? I can't see anything.'

He took a deep breath. 'This smell again …' He turned back to Baldassare. 'We have to get out of here, fast.'

He pulled Marie-Ange's hand and Baldassare pushed Karloff forward. The physician didn't offer any resistance.

'Hugo, look!' Marie-Ange turned round and pointed to the shadows. They had changed shape yet again to become tall and lean, like men. They hovered in a circle in the middle of the crypt where the tomb had been.

'Hurry!' he urged. He towed her in his wake as he ran from the crypt.

'Can't you hear? The walls are giving way,' Baldassare cried. 'The moat waters are coming through.'

They finally reached the stairs. As they started climbing, there was a blinding flash of light, followed by a sucking noise. It was as if the darkness was breathing in.

'Get up the stairs,' Hugo shouted, pulling Marie-Ange behind him. 'The place is about to blow up!'

The explosion was deafening and rocked the very foundations of the tower. Blocks of stone fell around them and the walls caved in under the pressure of the moat waters. Hugo was the first one to reach the entrance. He lifted Marie-Ange out, half-carrying her into the courtyard and then helped Baldassare and Karloff to safety. Seconds later, the ground shook underneath them. The Tower of Eight Beatitudes swayed in the fading evening light, but didn't fall.

'It's over,' Baldassare said. 'Nobody will find the crypt ever again.'

Chapter Twenty

'It may be over,' Marie-Ange remarked, 'but I can't help feeling I failed.' She stood next to her father. The horizon was bleeding to the west as a bright red sun set behind the castle towers where stars already glittered in a sapphire-coloured sky to the east.

'What makes you say that, daughter? The Cross is back where it should be.'

'Perhaps, but the Templar tomb is destroyed along with the treasure and the crypt.' And I lost the locket, she added to herself. The loss stung, it was one of the few things she possessed of her mother's.

Baldassare shrugged. 'You returned the Cross and the relic where they belonged. You fulfilled your duty.' He sighed. 'Men died tonight because of their arrogance and stupidity. Malleval thought he and his father could join the immortal beings. Become angels. He angered the Keepers and fell into the pit of Hell.'

Hugo looked at the Tower of Eight Beatitudes.

'I don't believe in the mysteries, Templar ghosts, or eternal damnation,' he said. His face was stern, he looked angry. 'The explosion was caused by a trap laid by Guichard de Beaujeu centuries ago and a build up of gas. As for Malleval,' his voice became thoughtful, 'he was killed by his own madness. I shall never forget how he threw himself into that hole in the ground. I'll check the grounds while there's still light. Who knows? Maybe there's a chance Malleval and Rochefort survived after all.'

His tall figure disappeared into the thickening shadows.

'He will need time to accept what happened here. Malleval used to be his friend, after all.' Baldassare pointed to Karloff. 'The physician is alone now. We will have to take him to Marzac with us tonight.'

Karloff sat, immobile, on the front steps of the castle. He looked stunned, exhausted, lost in a trance.

'Have you been at Arginy since this morning?' Marie-Ange

asked her father.

Baldassare nodded. He explained he rode to Arginy with Marco, the only remaining Turcopilar, after fleeing Beauregard. They persuaded the Rosemonts' household staff to hide in the attic and laid in wait for Malleval and his thugs.

'We dealt with them,' he said. 'Then went after you.'

'How did you manage to wake up Capitaine Saintclair? He was unconscious when we got here. I think Karloff drugged him.'

Baldassare smiled and pointed to a small leather pouch hanging from his belt.

'I gave him some of my very special snuff. It can raise a dead camel.'

'It stinks like one, too,' Hugo called out, a brief smile on his lips, as he came back. His face became serious again and he shook his head. 'There's no sign of them. They must be dead, swallowed by the ground.'

Marie-Ange's father had taken Hugo's horse when he and his companion fled Beauregard that morning and hidden it in the stables at Arginy as they lay in wait for Malleval. He now retrieved it and tied it at the back of the carriage.

It was pitch-black when they finally set off for Marzac. Hugo drove the carriage with Marie-Ange and Karloff inside. Baldassare and Marco rode in front.

When they reached Marzac, Karloff leant forward and took hold of her hand. 'It wasn't supposed to be like that, you know. I was going to meet one of the celestial beings at last …'

He bent his head. 'I don't understand. I need to examine Polycarpe's documents again. Maybe I missed something.'

Marie-Ange had no comforting words for him. She shivered as she relived Malleval's last moments. She could still hear his cry of terror as he was plunged into the dark hole, holding onto the Templar's tomb and the Cross of Life. She hoped he died quickly.

'Here we are.' Hugo opened the door and helped Marie-Ange out. He held her close to him a few seconds and she sighed with contentment as his arms closed around her.

‘Are you coming in?’ she asked, tilting her chin up to look at him.

‘Somehow, I don’t think I would be welcome tonight.’ He gestured towards the castle. ‘Now I’ve served my purpose.’

‘What do you mean?’

‘I know what your great-aunt thinks of me. She only tolerated my presence last night because she wanted me to help you.’

‘That’s not true!’

He smiled. ‘You know it is. Anyway, I must go back to Lyon and alert Colonel Dery about Nort … about Nallay,’ he corrected. ‘We can’t leave him on the loose with the king’s visit looming. And there’s the matter of my debt to see to. As far as I know, I am still wanted by the gendarmes and the bailiffs. I must tell them Malleval is dead, it’ll give me time to sort things out.’

‘Sophie told me she drugged your wine during the card game,’ Marie-Ange said.

He took a deep breath. ‘That explains a lot … although drugged or not, I should have known when to stop that game. Well, I’ll be on my way.’

‘Can you not wait until morning?’

He interrupted her protest with a kiss. His lips caressed hers lightly. She felt the rough stubble on his cheeks against her skin, and remembered with a shiver of delight their embrace, interrupted far too abruptly by the gendarmes the previous night. Her hands clung to his shoulders.

‘You’re safe, now.’ He pulled away.

‘Capitaine,’ Baldassare called. ‘I can never thank you enough for your help. We may not agree on everything but it was an honour to meet you.’

The two men shook hands. Baldassare untied Hugo’s black horse from the back of the carriage and handed him the reins. After a last look at Marie-Ange, Saintclair climbed onto his horse and set off into the night on the road to Lyon. He was right, of course. Nallay was still out there, waiting to kill the king. He had to be stopped.

Baldassare took her arm. 'Let's go in, daughter.'

They found Hermine in the drawing room. She hugged Marie-Ange and turned to Baldassare, her eyes shining with curiosity. It was true he looked unusual, wrapped in a dark grey cloak, his short, black hair streaked with grey and his clear blue eyes contrasting vividly with his suntanned skin. After a moment of hesitation, she held out her hand to him.

'I am delighted to meet you. Marie-Ange told me everything. I hope that you two will have time to talk.'

Baldassare sighed. 'Sadly, I must leave in the morning. I must report the outcome of my mission to my superiors in Catania.'

'So soon!' Marie-Ange cried out. 'There are so many things I want to ask you, about yourself, your family, and my mother.' Her voice quivered and she bent her head, overwhelmed at the thought of losing the father she had only just found.

'I am not free of my duties, daughter,' he said gently. 'However, I will try to tell you as much as I can about my family – our family – tonight.'

'What you need for now is a rest and a warm meal,' Hermine decreed. 'I will have rooms prepared straight away.'

She turned to Marie-Ange. 'Where is Capitaine Saintclair? I heard the commotion last night. Oh … the shame of it, having bailiffs knocking at my door to take him to debtors' jail.' She tapped her cane on the floor. 'Although I don't know why I was surprised. I shouldn't have expected any less from that man.'

'Capitaine Saintclair did nothing wrong, Aunt Hermine.' Marie-Ange's cheeks burnt with anger. 'He was tricked by Malleval during a game of cards.'

Hermine gave a short, derisive laugh and crossed her arms on her chest.

'A game of cards, of course! I am disappointed in you, girl. You seem to harbour certain feelings for the capitaine. You should remember that not only are you still married, but you are also the last of the Beauregards. You owe it to yourself and your family not to be compromised by a man such as Saintclair. He is a commoner, a vulgar soldier.'

So Hugo had been right. Hermine had been cordial to him last night only because she wanted his help. Now he had served his purpose, she could cast him aside. No wonder he was bitter about the arrogance of aristocrats.

'Dear Madame,' her father started, 'since when has a man's worth got anything to do with his lineage? You know as well as I do that a man needs to prove himself before he can earn respect, whatever his status in society. Saintclair has a distinguished military record. He came to Marie-Ange's rescue several times, causing himself great danger in the process. That is a good enough indication of his valour to me, and it should be the same for you.'

He turned to Marie-Ange with a smile. 'My daughter thinks very highly of him, and I trust her judgement. Now, shall we go upstairs and have a rest before the feast your great-aunt promised us?' He linked arms with her and they left the drawing room under Hermine's chastened gaze.

'Thank you,' Marie-Ange said as they climbed up the imposing staircase behind Pierre.

'Saintclair is a solid, honest man. I like him.' Baldassare smiled. 'And more to the point, *you* like him. You are a grown woman and free to make your own choices.'

After bathing and changing into one of her aunt's gowns, Marie-Ange made her way to the dining room where Hermine did the honours over a sumptuous meal. Karloff had declined to join them and remained prostrate, closeted in his room. He didn't even seem to care that the gendarmes would call for him in the morning to take him into custody.

At the dinner table, nobody spoke about Arginy and the abyss that had engulfed Malleval and the Cross of Life. And even though her mind often wandered to Saintclair, Marie-Ange was happy to listen to her father telling her about Malta and the dei Conti family, and his sister Agata who he promised she would meet one day.

'How did you become a Turcopilar?'

'I was chosen by the Bailiff of the Knights Hospitaller who requested my presence at the *Commanderie* in Valetta … but I'm not at liberty to speak about it. Much of what we do is secret,' he apologised. 'I think Capitaine Saintclair explained, didn't he? We Turcopilars aren't even supposed to exist anymore, so you are going to have to keep my presence here a secret.'

Marie-Ange didn't dare broach the subject of the short-lived romance between Baldassare and her mother. It was Hermine, with her usual bluntness, who asked him about it.

'What happened between Catherine and you? Well, I mean, apart from the obvious. How did you help her escape to England?'

He took time to drink a sip of wine before answering.

'Catherine was a beautiful young woman. She had such spirit! She was brave and resilient even after her father's execution, her abduction by Edmond Malleval, and her captivity in his fortress.'

He talked about their journey to the north coast of France. 'We forgot that we would have to part. I certainly forgot I wasn't a free man, but I have no regrets.'

Once again, Marie-Ange saw the sadness in his eyes. He turned to her and smiled. 'She would be very proud of you,' he said.

It was late when Baldassare stood up and declared he needed to get some rest. He planned to set off for Sicily early the following morning.

Marie-Ange got up in the early hours to wave farewell to her father and his companion, and remained in the courtyard, wrapped up against the cold long after they had disappeared in the grey dawn mists. The two men she loved and trusted more than any others in the world had now left her.

'Beauregard is back in our family, at last,' Hermine exclaimed at the breakfast table, spreading butter and jam on her brioche. 'As Malleval didn't have any siblings or children, you are now the sole heiress.'

Marie-Ange wanted to go there straight away and tell Sophie about Malleval's death, but Hermine said she must wait for the gendarmes.

'What shall I say about the Cross of Life, and about Malleval's death?'

'Tell them the truth – or rather part of the truth. The Cross belonged to our family, the Beauregards. You found it in the dovecote, but Malleval abducted you because he wanted to steal it from you. He took you to Arginy to perform some kind of ceremony – don't say anything more than that – the man fell into a trap and disappeared.'

Hermine finished her cup of tea. 'It's well known around here that Arginy is full of dangerous traps. As for Karloff, he was Malleval's accomplice. He will be taken to Beaujeu for interrogation.'

They didn't have to wait long before Commandant Picard and a small detachment of gendarmes were announced. Picard took off his hat and bowed deeply before Hermine and Marie-Ange.

'*Mesdames, c'est un honneur,*' he said.

Marie-Ange told him, almost word for word, what her great-aunt had advised. It was a shortened, sanitised version of the truth. She didn't mention any angels or relics. She did however tell Commandant Picard about Edmond Malleval's coffin being taken into the vault by Uxeloup and later lost in the explosion.

'You mean Monsieur Malleval Père wasn't buried?' Picard exclaimed, shocked. '*Mon Dieu, mais pourquoi*?'

Marie-Ange raised her hands in dismay, as if she didn't have any idea. There was no point mentioning the Cross of Life's alleged powers in bestowing immortality.

'We shall send a search party to Arginy straight away,' Picard decided. 'We need to look for the bodies of Monsieur Uxeloup and his guard, Monsieur Rochefort. Do not worry, Mesdames, I will solve this riddle.'

He then asked to interview Karloff and retired to Hermine's study with the physician. The two men spent almost an hour in conversation, after which Commandant Picard said he wanted to speak to Marie-Ange again.

'Monsieur Karloff mentioned the presence yesterday at Arginy of several gentlemen you failed to tell me about. A Capitaine Saintclair, who, if I recall correctly, is wanted by the king's bailiffs, and two other men who he says were foreign agents – some kind of

Turks, I believe. Would you care to explain who these men are?'

Fortunately, Marie-Ange had prepared her answer.

'I didn't want to implicate Capitaine Saintclair because he did me a great favour in helping me yesterday when he was supposed to be on duty at the barracks in Lyon. He could get into serious trouble for defaulting from his post. As for his debt, I learned it was fraudulently obtained by Monsieur Malleval when he cheated during a game of cards.'

'I see,' Picard remarked, nodding his head.

'The other gentlemen were scouts from a foreign battalion who came with Capitaine Saintclair. I do not recall their names.'

Picard seemed satisfied, and said he needed to take Karloff to Beaujeu for further questioning.

He came back for Marie-Ange in the afternoon and said she could now travel to Beauregard. The chateau and the grounds had been searched and not a single one of Malleval's mountain thugs remained. 'They ran away like rabbits when they saw my gendarmes,' he laughed.

So Marie-Ange bade her great-aunt farewell. Today, she was going home.

Chapter Twenty-One

Beauregard, 20 March 1815 (three weeks later)

Jerusalem, 1230 Anno Domini

Note to our Brothers –

Our much revered Brother Bernard de Clairvaux wrote that a Templar Knight feared neither demons nor men because his soul was protected by an armour of Faith, just as his body was protected by an armour of steel. He will not fear death either if he kneels in front of the Cross of Life in our chapel at Temple Mount for he will live forever.

May I remind you, Brothers, how this most sacred relic came to be in our possession; how God's messenger on earth appeared to Hugues de Payens and Saint Omer and demanded the creation of our Templar Order to protect pilgrims travelling to the Holy City; and how the celestial envoy's clothing, torn by our Brother Payens by accident, was preserved in a phial secured at the base of the Cross as an eternal reminder of God's awesome power.

I must entreat you once again to keep its existence a secret and make sure that it is handled by one of us – a pure heart.

Pedro de Montaigu, Grand Master Templar

Paris, 12 October 1307

These are my instructions concerning the safe keeping of our most saintly relic, the Cross of Life. It will be hidden in the fief of a trusted brother and relative of one of our most respected Grand Masters. It will be guarded by the souls of eleven Keepers, all past Masters who will punish with terrible torments whoever dares violate its sanctuary. Should the Cross be removed, it must be returned by a pure heart of the same bloodline as a Master Keeper. Only he can hold the Cross unscathed, be blessed by the visiting angel, and granted the eternal peace he longs for. Pity the unfortunate who attempts to claim the Cross for his own purpose for he condemns his soul to eternal damnation in the pit of Hell.

Jacques de Molay, Grand Master, Temple of Paris

Marie-Ange rolled the documents pensively between her hands. Her fingers played with the dark blue ribbon that kept them together and handed the parchments back to Gustave Karloff. The physician's hand shook as he took hold of them.

'So these are the translations of some of the papers Polycarpe was carrying when he was killed by the Malleval clan,' she remarked. The reference to the pit of Hell had a sinister echo after Malleval's disappearance into the gaping hole in the crypt of Arginy Castle.

Karloff nodded, walked to the window and stared at the rain-swept park and forest. 'I have been thinking about what happened at Arginy, and I fear all is not finished.'

'What do you mean, Monsieur Karloff? We both saw the Templar tomb, Malleval and the Cross thrown into the abyss just before the explosion. How can it not be finished?' Marie-Ange asked, impatience colouring her tone. 'Commandant Picard certainly thinks it is. He said he wasn't going to organise a search party.'

Karloff glanced at her with haunted eyes and turned towards the window and the forest again.

He had arrived an hour before, having been released by Commandant Picard from Beaujeu Prison pending further investigation. He appeared to have aged considerably during his three weeks' incarceration, and there was nothing left in him of the charismatic, sinister man Marie-Ange had once feared.

There didn't seem to be any dark mysteries left at Arginy either.

A civil engineer appointed by Commandant Picard had established that the castle was built on ancient salt mines dating back to Roman times. Several entrances to tunnels had been uncovered, some as far away as half a mile from Arginy. The reports of mysterious balls of orange and blue light and sulphurous smells rising from the ground, of tremors and strange underground noises, which locals had put down to a Templar malediction, had in fact a very scientific explanation. They had their origin in pockets of gas trapped deep beneath the surface, causing explosions in the passages of the abandoned mine. It seemed Hugo had been right … the shadows in the crypt had nothing to do with ghosts of Knights Templar.

Commandant Picard decided it would be pointless and dangerous to call a search party to retrieve the bodies. The terrain around Arginy was too unstable after the explosion, and there could be no doubt that the two men were dead.

Marie-Ange left Karloff to his sombre mood and went down to the library. She sat behind the desk where the accounts ledger she had been working on for the past three weeks lay open, but, instead of studying the fine lines scrawled with figures, she sighed and slammed the book shut. There wasn't any point looking at the accounts now.

Her travel trunk and bag were packed. She would leave for England the following morning with an escort of gendarmes, like a criminal.

It was Commandant Picard who had brought her the news of her exile. Red-faced and apologetic, he stammered so much that she had failed at first to understand what he was trying to say.

'The Emperor … decrees of Lyon of 13th March … recent *émigrés* must leave French soil and abandon all claim to their property … under threat of imprisonment.'

Hermine had reacted with anger. 'The audacity, the nerve of that little man! I don't care if he calls himself an "emperor". The truth is he is nothing more than an upstart. I can't believe he is back at the Tuileries Palace and forced our king to take refuge in Ghent!' She punctuated her outburst with loud taps of her cane on the floor.

'The populace is so fickle,' she carried on after taking a deep breath. 'One year ago they cheered as he was exiled and now they acclaim his return!'

Lyon had given the emperor a rapturous welcome and Napoleon had issued some of his first decrees as France's new ruler there.

Among those was, the decision to expel all the *émigrés* who had returned to France between April 1814 and March 1815 – during the reign of King Louis XVIII.

Marie-Ange was considered one of them.

'I will escort you to Chalons and then to Paris and Le Havre.' Picard looked sorry to be the bearer of such bad news. 'Please be ready by Wednesday morning.'

Hermine might rant against the injustice, the indignity her great-niece was subjected to, but being angry changed nothing. Considered an *émigrée*, Marie-Ange not only had to leave, but she wasn't entitled to claim any revenue from the Beauregard estate either, even if she *was* Malleval's only heir. Her great-aunt had promised to hire a good lawyer to look after her interests.

'We will have you back here soon. In the meantime, I will ensure Beauregard is kept in good order for you.'

Somehow Marie-Ange couldn't share her great-aunt's optimism. If Napoleon had shown mercy towards returning *émigrés* in the past, he seemed to have radically changed his mind now.

Sophie came in with a cup of tea and a plate of sponge cake. The two women smiled at each other.

'I am sure you will soon be allowed to return,' Sophie said, placing the hot drink and the food in front of Marie-Ange.

'After all, you're not even a real *émigré.* You were invited here, by Uxeloup.' She bent her head. Her chest heaved as she tried to suppress a sob.

Marie-Ange stood and walked around the desk to take her in her arms. Sympathy twisted her heart, for Sophie had loved Malleval with all her being. His death left her alone and bereft, but at least she would be able to stay at Beauregard. Marie-Ange had appointed her chatelaine in her absence, under Hermine's guidance.

Sophie wiped her tears, curtsied and left Marie-Ange alone with her thoughts. She stood at the window, looking at the dark clouds in the lead grey sky as her thoughts turned to Hugo. She longed to see him again, but that too was uncertain.

He had written to her the previous week. Napoleon had ordered him to escort the Comte d'Artois, the king's brother, to the port of Sète and ensure he embarked for Italy unharmed. The comte had narrowly escaped an assassination attempt in Lyon and Napoleon didn't wish to start his new reign with an outpouring of Bourbon blood. Hugo was now posted to the southern provinces to quell a royalist uprising.

He also wrote he had been spared the threat of imprisonment for debt and his family was safe in St Genis. Hugo ended his short message with a promise to come to Beauregard as soon as he was discharged.

It would be too late by then, she would be gone.

'Hugo,' Marie-Ange whispered as her fingers traced his name on the window and followed the raindrops gliding down the other side like tears. She summoned the burning memory of his blue eyes and the caress of his lips on her skin. Memories were all she would have of him. She might not see him for many months now that war between France and Great Britain and its allies was, once again, on the cards. In fact, she might not see him ever again.

She gasped for air suddenly, her chest too tight for her to breathe. Wrapping herself in her cloak she went out to walk for a while in the park and around the pond, her heart as heavy as the skies. When her coat and her shoes were completely soaked, she made her way back towards the chateau.

The sound of a horse's galloping hooves made her turn towards the gates. A cavalier was approaching. She froze and waited for the rider to come nearer. He was tall, dressed in a dark grey coat, his face partly hidden by a black hat. She let out a sigh of disappointment. It wasn't Saintclair.

Then she recognised the rider, and panic welled inside her. She ran up the stone stairs of the front porch and pulled frantically at the door.

'Wait!' Christopher called as he jumped down from his horse.

She turned round to confront him.

'What are you doing here?'

Christopher remained at the bottom of the steps. He took off his hat, revealing a gaunt face. Dark circles shadowed his grey eyes, and deep lines cut channels around his mouth.

‘I want you to tell me about my past.’

Marie-Ange opened her eyes wide. ‘Why now?’ She hissed. ‘You weren’t bothered with the truth that night in Lyon, when you stabbed Capitaine Saintclair and tried to …’ The words died on her lips. She looked down at the man standing at the bottom of the steps, feeling like an invisible hand was gripping her throat.

Something was different about him. He looked like he used to, a long time ago. His head was cocked to one side, his grey eyes thoughtful. Although she had resolved to give him up for dead, she couldn’t shut him out, not when he looked so much like the man she had loved.

‘I am sorry. Truly sorry. I didn’t want to believe you. I didn’t want to hear that I might be that man – Norton. There are so many things I want to ask you.’ Christopher smiled tentatively.

Her resolve weakened but she still hesitated. Even if he sounded genuine, she must not forget how dangerous he was. As if he sensed her doubts, he added. ‘Please, Marie-Ange.’

She took a deep breath and opened the front door. ‘Very well. Come in.’ She gave orders for the horse to be stabled, peeled off her cloak and handed it to a maid, then led the way to the drawing room where she invited Christopher to take a place on the sofa opposite her.

‘What do you want to know?’ she asked, her voice guarded, wishing to maintain a distance between them.

He spoke slowly. ‘Since the last time I saw you, in Lyon, I have had flashbacks about that place you told me about … the old manor house.’

‘Norton Place.’

He gazed at the fire. ‘I have been dreaming about England a lot lately. I see people’s faces, but I can’t remember any names.’ He looked at Marie-Ange. ‘And then, I have been dreaming about you … about us.’

She blushed as his eyes skimmed over her body. Remembering how rough he had been with her in Lyon, she clenched her fists until the nails dug hard into the palms. Could she trust him?

Once again, he seemed to sense her doubts. 'I need your help. I want you to tell me about my life – our life together.'

She breathed in sharply. At last tonight he acknowledged she had told the truth. Even though she didn't love him anymore, she owed it to him to help him remember his past.

'I will only help you if you tell me what happened to you after the battle of Coruña and how you became a French agent.'

Christopher stiffened. He gave her a sidelong glance. 'You are aware of that? What else do you know?'

'Only that you go under the name of Nallay.' It was better to plead ignorance of the rest.

Christopher seemed relieved. 'Very well … my earliest memories date from a French field hospital at Lugo. I suffered a serious head injury. When I regained consciousness, I was given what was left of my uniform: a ripped jacket with a few personal possessions; a pouch of tobacco, a clay pipe, a letter from my fiancée – Jacqueline Leblanc – and my requisition orders from the Fifteenth Infantry Regiment. All in the name of Joseph Nallay, from Charenton-sur-Marne. This is who I believed I was … until I met you in Fouché's building on Rue de Condé.'

'Didn't you go back to Charenton to meet your fiancée, your family? They would have realised you weren't Nallay.'

Christopher shrugged. 'Why go back when I didn't remember her, or anyone else? I was made an offer I couldn't refuse by Maréchal Soult's état-major in Spain. And then, I went on to work for … my current employer.'

Fouché, she thought.

'Did you really not know me when you first saw me in Paris, and again at the Palais Saint-Pierre in Lyon?'

'I thought you were one of Talleyrand's spies. He's a devil for hiring beautiful women to ensnare rival agents. But your face haunted me. I started to wonder if maybe you had told the truth.'

He turned to her. 'Tell me about this place in England where I come from and about our life there.'

This time, she obliged. She spoke for a long time about his

earlier life. His parents and his brother, Robert, and about his successful career in the Royal Navy. She recalled their meeting at a county ball, their brief courtship, and short married life before he embarked on the HMS *Amazon* for Northern Spain. Christopher listened without saying a word, his eyes staring right in front of him, his arms crossed on his chest. He was absorbing her every word.

Sophie came into the drawing room to announce supper was ready.

'Sophie, this is my husband, Christopher Norton,' Marie-Ange announced, a little awkwardly.

'Your husband?' Sophie's eyes were wide with surprise.

Marie-Ange had an idea suddenly. 'Is Monsieur Karloff still upstairs?' When Sophie answered in the affirmative she asked her to invite him down.

The physician was a hypnotist. Perhaps he could help Christopher remember the missing weeks between Coruña and the day he woke up in the French military hospital… It was worth a try. She mentioned the possibility to Christopher.

'A hypnotist like this crook Mesmer? Certainly not!'

He flashed eyes of steel at her, cold and heartless, and she felt a shiver of fear snake down her spine. For the second time tonight, she wondered if she could trust the man standing in front of her.

'Monsieur Karloff does have certain abilities which could be helpful to your condition,' she insisted, even if she didn't wish to tell him about her own experience of Karloff's skills.

'At least consider it. This might be your only chance of finding out what happened after Coruña.' Then she added. 'Tomorrow will be too late since I am leaving in the morning under an escort of gendarmes.'

'Yes, I know. As an *émigrée*, you are now *persona non grata* on French soil,' Christopher said. 'Actually, that's partly why I came tonight.'

Curious, she turned to him. 'Really?'

'I have decided to go home with you, back to Norton Place.'

She gaped at him, lost for words.

'You intend to return home?' Her voice was shaky.

He raised his eyebrows. 'That's where I belong, isn't it? And if you will assist me with remembering my former life, I should be able to slip straight back in.'

'How will you explain your years of absence to the Admiralty? Your work as an agent for Fouché?' she objected.

He shrugged. 'Let me worry about that, dear. The Admiralty need not know everything.'

'Will Fouché let you go now he has been reappointed as Napoleon's Minister of Police?'

'You don't sound very enthusiastic about the prospect of my return.' His expression was unreadable. 'And yet I thought all you wanted was to be reunited with me. Your husband.'

Karloff entered the room and regarded Christopher with undisguised curiosity. Marie-Ange introduced her husband and explained what she wanted him to do.

'I have dealt with mental traumas before,' Karloff agreed. 'Battlefield amnesia can be caused not only by physical injuries but also mental scarring. Intense fear, for example, or the witnessing of atrocities.'

'All right. I will try your sorcery.' Christopher stood up. 'I suppose I do need to know what happened to me.'

He put his hand on Marie-Ange's arm. 'But you must give me your word of honour that this man will only ask me about Spain, nothing else!'

'Of course,' she replied, uneasy. 'That's all I wish to know about.'

Was he afraid of revealing any state secrets or any of Fouché's schemes, the plot to assassinate King Louis, maybe?

Karloff needed a dark room to carry out the experiment, so they settled in the library. He instructed Christopher to sit in front of the fireplace, took the place opposite him and asked Marie-Ange to stay at the back. The curtains were drawn against the night. The only light in the library was the golden glow of the fire. The logs crackled in the fireplace, rain pattered against the tall windows, and the clock ticked in a corner of the room.

'Breathe slowly and deeply. Let your shoulders drop and your hands fall into your lap.' Karloff spoke in the quiet, monotonous voice Marie-Ange remembered only too well. He pulled out his golden watch from the pocket of his jacket and dangled it in front of Christopher's face.

'Listen to my voice and the rain outside. Concentrate on your breathing … you are at sea,' Karloff continued. 'What is the name of your ship?'

Christopher's breathing was now deep and slow. 'HMS *Amazon*,' he answered quietly.

'What is your name?'

'Commander Christopher Norton.'

'What is the date, Commander Norton, and where is the *Amazon*?'

'Eighteenth January 1809. We are moored off Coruña.'

'What is happening on board your ship right now?'

'The French are firing their heavy artillery from the hilltops of San Diego. My men are still trying to ferry the wounded from the harbour walls to the ship, but the smoke is becoming too dense. They can't see where they're going. Several rowing boats have sunk already. I can hear men shout as they fall into the freezing cold water, but we can't get to them.'

'Is the *Amazon* safe?'

Christopher shook his head. 'No. We've been hit. The great mast has fallen and the sails are on fire.' Christopher brought his hands to his head as if in pain.

'Are you injured, Commandant Norton?'

'Yes, a blow to the head.' Christopher winced. 'I've jumped into the water now. It's damn cold. I won't last long if I don't get to a boat or some kind of raft.'

Marie-Ange sat on the edge of the sofa, tense and hanging on his every word. At last, he started to remember!

'My second, Wilson, is calling me. He's with Lieutenant Padiham on a raft. They're pulling me up with them. We're drifting. The currents are strong and we have nothing to paddle with. We watch the fire of the cannons on the cliffs and the *Amazon* burn and sink.'

'How long do you drift for?' Karloff asked quietly.

'All night. In the morning, there is a coastline in the distance. We must swim or we'll die at sea. I go first. It's freezing. I must swim quickly. I hear a splash behind me as Wilson and Padiham jump too but I'm not waiting for them. I have to reach the shore.'

'What happens now?'

Christopher shrugged. 'I don't know. I'm alone on the beach. I must have passed out. It's night-time now.' He shivered. 'I have to find food. Find people.'

'Do you meet anyone?'

'No. I'm tired, I lie down behind some rocks and fall asleep. Next thing I know there are gunshots all around. When I look, there are bodies of French soldiers on the beach. I'm wet through, so I strip down to my long johns and undress one of the dead men. I slip his jacket and his breeches on. That's better. There's blood on his jacket but at least it's dry.'

'Do you see any other French soldiers around?'

'Everybody's dead. I walk to a village. An old woman is talking to me in Spanish. God! My head hurts.' He moaned and took his head in his hands again.

'There are French soldiers in the street. They take me to the field hospital.'

'How long do you stay at the hospital?' Karloff asks.

'I don't know. They give me draughts for the pain. Then this man – a lieutenant – comes and speaks to me. He says I can help them with translating English messages. I work from the hospital at first. Then when I'm better I travel with the troops. They feel sorry for me because I don't remember anything of my past. Not even my fiancée in Charenton.'

'Do you stay with the army for long?'

'Several months. I've been promoted, but I'm sick of battlefields, of gore, blood and field rations. So when one of Fouché's men comes to my regiment to recruit new agents for the secret police and asks me to join, I take him up on his offer. I travel to Paris. I have an apartment. More money than I need. The job is easy enough. Fouché and I get along fine.' He snorted. 'We are alike in lots of ways. We don't have any feelings. I can snap someone's neck without …'

Marie-Ange rose hurriedly from the sofa and walked towards the firelight. 'We'll stop now. I gave him my word we would only enquire about what happened in Spain after the battle.'

The clock struck nine, its chiming melodic in the silence.

'Very well,' Karloff said. He turned to Christopher and put his watch back in his pocket.

'When I count down from ten, you will wake up and remember everything you have just told me, Monsieur Norton,' Karloff instructed. He snapped his fingers as he reached one.

Christopher kept his eyes closed for a few seconds and breathed in deeply. Then he looked at the old man in astonishment and shook his head.

'You did it! Your wizardry worked. I remember everything.'

He got up and strode across the library towards Marie-Ange. 'You were right. It was all true,' he said, taking her hands and pulling her towards him.

Marie-Ange frowned. He seemed surprised, as if he had doubts about his past *before* Karloff hypnotised him.

'Now, I am truly ready to go back home. To Norton Place.'

'But are you free to leave? What about Fouché? Your duties?' she asked again, gripped by panic. She needed time to think about what had just happened. The man wanted to pick up his life where he left it six years before, but she couldn't do that. She loved another.

'Don't trouble yourself with that! In fact, everything is turning out quite nicely for me. I shall ride on to Paris tonight to negotiate the terms of my … how shall I phrase it? Release or new assignment?' He laughed as if he had made a joke only he understood. 'Then I will join you at Norton Place.'

Still holding her hands tightly, he bent down to kiss her, but she turned away and his lips only met her cheek.

'I see,' he said, his tone suddenly frosty. He stared at her hand.

'I noticed that you no longer wear your wedding ring.'

She gave a small gasp. The ring. She'd left it behind at Saintclair's quarters in Lyon. She had vowed never to wear it again.

He let go of her and stepped back.

'I suppose we will have all the time in the world to re-establish our acquaintance. Try to find your ring and put it back on. I will see myself out.' He bowed and left the room.

'Christopher!' Marie-Ange ran after him, feeling a mixture of remorse and anger. She didn't know how to behave with him. He expected her to take him back as if six years hadn't passed, as if he was still the same man. But he wasn't. And what was more, she too had changed.

He was already putting his coat and his hat on to leave. He asked a servant to bring his horse to the front of the chateau and turned to meet her gaze with his cool grey eyes.

'We shall be together again soon. Should you get to Norton Place first, do not breathe a word about me. I will do all the explaining.' He touched the rim of his hat and bowed slightly. 'Farewell for now, my dear.'

She followed him onto the front porch, watched him climb on his horse, spur the animal into a trot on the path, and disappear into the night.

'You will return to England with him?' Sophie stood next to her, disbelief obvious on her face and in her voice.

Marie-Ange nodded. Her throat was so tight she couldn't speak.

'I'm not sure you're doing the right thing. He looks a harsh man.'

'Yes, he does but he is my husband,' Marie-Ange managed to

say. 'I have no choice, Sophie.' She bent her head, her heart felt trapped in her chest. 'No choice at all.'

'What of Capitaine Saintclair?' Sophie asked. 'What will you tell him when he comes after you?'

Chapter Twenty-Two

It was still raining the following morning when Commandant Picard and his two gendarmes presented themselves at Beauregard.

'Are you ill, Madame? You look very pale.' Picard gave Marie-Ange a searching look.

'I will be fine, Commandant,' she replied with a tight smile. In reality her head throbbed and she felt drained after a night spent trying to envisage what life at Norton Place would be like, now Christopher was returning. What had once been her dearest dream had become a nightmare.

She didn't think she would ever forgive her husband for stabbing Saintclair in the back or for molesting her. Every time she looked into his grey eyes she would be reminded of his past as an agent for Fouché's secret police. She might never find it in her heart to respect him, let alone love him again.

If only she could stay at Beauregard a while longer, take the time to get to know him again … her husband, this stranger. He had made her uneasy the evening before, oscillating between disarming smiles and ruthless stares. He said he wanted to know all about Norton Place and his past, but never once asked her about herself and her life during his long absence. Instead, he only remarked on the fact she no longer wore his wedding ring. She looked down at her bare finger. She would have to buy another ring somewhere on the way to Devonshire.

Her luggage was loaded onto the roofrack of her carriage.

'It's time, Madame.' Picard bowed in front of her.

She hugged Sophie and climbed into the coach. Numb beyond tears, she turned round for a last look at the chateau. She now understood a little of what her mother might have felt when she left. A grey shadow moved behind a window on the first floor. Karloff was watching. He had promised to leave later today.

The journey to Chalons was uneventful. They reached the small town on the banks of the River Saône in the afternoon. The outskirts of town had been taken over by army bivouacs and the town centre was heaving with soldiers. The coach driver stopped on the main square while Commandant Picard made some enquiries at several inns.

'The soldiers' are going to the eastern border,' he said when he came back. 'Every single room in town is requisitioned for army personnel. We shall carry on. Hopefully we will find an inn nearer Autun.'

Marie-Ange nodded absent-mindedly. She didn't care where or when they stopped. She didn't care if they travelled all the way to Le Havre without interruption. A colourful crowd packed the square. Soldiers in different regimental uniforms, market traders packing up, and townsfolk hurrying to buy food before the market finished. As the coach set off again, a man standing in a corner of the square attracted her attention. He looked familiar and she leant forward to take a better look at him. His dark hair was unkempt. A thick beard partly covered his face. He wore some kind of sheepskin coat and high leather boots, just like one of Malleval's henchmen. A few seconds later, he walked away into the crowd and she lost sight of him.

Should she tell Commandant Picard? It was probably a coincidence. After Malleval's death, his men had fled Beauregard. Some would have gone back to their remote Pilat village, but others might have business to conclude elsewhere.

The next town was Chagny. It was dark when they stopped in front of a large inn on the main square. Picard found rooms for the night, arranged for Marie-Ange's bag to be taken upstairs and for a maid to bring her some supper. She forced herself to eat some soup and drink a glass of wine. Then, feeling weary of the day's travel, she put her nightdress on and took the pins out of her hair. She was just getting into bed when she heard men's voices on the staircase.

'I am sorry, sir, but it's late. I don't think that you should …' It was Picard's voice.

'I need to see Madame Norton now. Get out of my way.'

Hugo! He was here, he had come after her. The overwhelming joy she felt at hearing him was immediately replaced with anguish. She must tell him about Christopher's visit to Beauregard. She had to tell him her husband planned to resume his former life with her in Norton Place.

He already knew.

'Tell me it's not true,' were his first words when she opened the door.

He closed the door behind him and marched straight in. He seemed to take up all the space in the room. She stepped back, alarmed by the thunderous look in his eyes.

'Tell me you're not taking your husband back, after everything you said.' He stopped a few inches from her and she had to tilt her head to look into his eyes. Her heart was beating so fast her chest ached.

'Who told you?'

'So it's true … Sophie was right.' He closed his eyes for a few seconds. When he reopened them, they were cold as ice.

'Why?'

'He came to Beauregard yesterday evening, begging me to tell him about his past life, about Norton Place, his family, and—'

'And you were only too happy to oblige,' he interrupted. 'Sophie said you asked Karloff to hypnotise him to help him remember. So Norton told you all about his vile deeds, the men he knifed or shot in dark alleyways and the women he slept with in exchange for information. And still you found it in your heart to forgive him – even though you said he was dead to you.' He gave a short derisive laugh.

'It isn't like that!' she cried out, putting her hand on his forearm. 'I couldn't deny him the truth about his past, and Karloff didn't pry into his deeds as an agent.'

He raised his eyebrows. 'Why not?'

'Before we started the mesmerising session, Christopher asked for my word that we would only ask him about Spain.'

'How convenient! What a good little wife you are.' He eyed her from top to toe, a sneer appearing on his lips. 'How do you know he's sincere? That he doesn't have an ulterior motive for this sudden need to be reacquainted with his past and return to England? I think it's all very timely.'

'What do you mean?' He didn't reply. 'It would appear you have what you desired. Husband and wife reunited.'

His words cut as badly as his icy glare. She wanted to cry out that he was wrong. It wasn't what she wanted. Not anymore. She loved him and only him. Surely he must understand that if her lawful husband wished to return to Norton Place, there was nothing she could do to prevent him. He owned the place. And in a way, he owned her too. She was bound to leave France under the new *émigrés* law, and there was nowhere else for her to go except Norton Place.

But she didn't know how to start, so she said nothing.

'I was released this morning and rode straight to Beauregard, hoping to see you before you left. I had a proposal for you. Not that it matters anymore.'

'What proposal?'

'I was planning to ask you to marry me … as a way of getting your deportation order cancelled, of course. It would have bought you time to settle your business at Beauregard.'

'Marry you? But it's impossible. I am already married.' A warm feeling spread through her. He wanted her to stay. He had been ready to marry her.

'Only you and I knew that, since Norton denied it was the truth.'

She bowed her head. 'Even if Christopher hadn't come to Beauregard yesterday, I couldn't have committed bigamy. No matter how much I want to stay in France and marry you. It would be wrong.'

'Well, it's not going to happen since he now remembers who he is, so let's forget I ever suggested it.' He stepped forward and put his hands on her shoulders. 'You could still remain in France though. With me. I am owed a few favours. My name and position in the army should guarantee your freedom. I would put you up in an apartment in Lyon.'

Her cheeks flushed with the realisation of what he was implying.

‘You mean, I would live with you as a mistress?’ she interrupted.

He smiled. ‘What else? I’m not asking you to be my stable lad.’

His fingers rubbed her shoulders gently. She breathed in, trying to quell the turmoil raging inside her. She was torn between two men, between love and duty. There was one question she needed to ask Hugo. His answer would determine her decision and her whole future.

‘Why would you help me? I mean, why would you want me for your wife or your mistress?’

Hugo gazed into her eyes. ‘Isn’t that obvious? I told you before. I feel responsible for you – for what happens to you. It’s a damned shame you came all this way only to leave with nothing. If you stay, you will have time to sort out your inheritance, which is far bigger now you are Malleval’s heiress.’

‘You feel responsible? Is that all?’ She felt the blood drain from her face.

He didn’t answer.

‘You don’t have any other feelings for me? You don’t … love me?’ she pressed, hating the pathetic, pleading, sound of her voice.

He dropped his hands by his side, and arched his eyebrows.

‘What are you talking about, Marie-Ange? We have kissed a few times and yes, it was good. Very good even. I would more than gladly take things further.’ His lips curled into a smile. ‘I am sure our arrangement would be to our mutual satisfaction, but please don’t make it any more than it is.’

His voice became harsh. ‘Don’t make *me* anymore than I am. A commoner, a soldier, remember? Not a courtier. I kill, I organise men and I plan battles. I don’t pick flowers or write poems.’ He crossed his arms on his chest and leant back. ‘That doesn’t mean to say we can’t have a good time together.’

He made it sound so coarse, so cheap. She bit her lower lip hard to stop it from trembling. She had her answer. It was plain he didn’t love her. He didn’t even believe in love. They were too different. She would suffer if she stayed with him, so much that with time it would destroy her. Destroy her heart and her soul. It was better to sever her ties with him tonight.

'Thank you for your offer,' she said, trying to keep her voice cool, 'but I will return to England.'

He stared at her a moment in silence.

'It's your decision,' he said at last, before turning to the fire and presenting his back to her.

She squeezed her eyes shut in an attempt to stop the tears. He was so close, and yet so much separated them. Suddenly, she remembered the warmth of his arms and the longing in his eyes as he had held her at Marzac. If they were going to part forever, she wanted a burning memory of him to last her a lifetime. He could be down to earth and ruthless, and so could she. She stepped forward and laid her hand on his back. His muscles tensed. Turning round, he grabbed her wrists and pulled her to him.

'What do you want from me now?'

She was aching for him.

His stare was intense, his breathing fast.

This was probably the only chance she would ever have to make love to him. She stood on tiptoes and kissed his lips. He moaned and pulled her against him, so tightly the metal of his uniform buttons, and the coarse fabric of his jacket bit into her body. He kissed her mouth, her throat, while his hands gripped the curves of her hips.

'Why can't I leave you alone, even now when you have chosen another man?' he growled. 'And why do you let me touch you?'

She didn't reply but put her arms behind his neck and kissed him softly again.

He stroked the outline of her face, her throat, venturing further in the opening of her nightdress to the swell of her breasts. She shivered with the longing for his hands to explore the rest of her body. He bent forward and took her mouth in a hungry kiss, one hand tilting her head backward so he could deepen the kiss. His hands slid down her shoulders and pulled the nightdress aside with such impatience the fabric ripped and the garment fell onto the floor

With feverish haste, he unbuttoned his jacket, loosened his shirt and threw them on the floor before raising a hand and caressing a lock of her hair, which had escaped her braid and was nestling in the curve of her neck.

'I want you, damn it. Why isn't that enough for you?' his voice barely a whisper.

He untied her hair, gave her a slow, smouldering look, hot enough to make her cheeks and her throat burn. He put his hand in the hollow of her waist to pull her against him and his fingers ran along her back. His hands covered the curves of her hips, lingering on their velvety softness, before sliding to the front. She closed her eyes and whispered his name, holding onto his shoulders for fear of falling. His hands, in turn gentle and hard, seemed intent on exploring every inch of her body, on taking possession.

'Are you sure that's what you want?' he asked, his voice low, his gaze burning.

She bit his shoulder lightly. 'Yes.'

He lifted her in his arms and laid her on the bed. He kissed her again, finished undressing and discarded his clothes before joining her. Then he caressed her, in slow, feather-light strokes, his eyes never leaving hers while she arched against his hand and moaned, overwhelmed by waves of pleasure. It was as if he was staking his claim on her body.

He withdrew his hand and kissed her throat, the line of her shoulders, nuzzled her breasts, licked the pale pink skin around her nipples, and then sucked on the hard tiny buds. The harsh stubble on his cheeks rubbing against her skin increased her pleasure tenfold.

She clasped her hands at the back of his neck, ran her fingers through his hair. There was a dull, throbbing need within her that she knew only he could fulfil. He kissed her mouth again, let out a groan before settling on top of her, hard and impatient. She opened herself to him, and he thrust deep inside. He was ruthless, diving deeper and faster, his hands clasping her hips to bring her nearer and higher still.

'Look at me,' he ordered.

She stared into his burning, intense blue eyes as heat exploded inside her. Holding on to his shoulders, she arched her back and cried out, and then it was his turn. He lay on top of her, still looking deep into her eyes as if he owned her body and soul.

Later, he kissed her lips gently and moved to the side.

'Hugo,' she nestled against his body. 'I …'

He put a finger on her mouth. 'There's nothing to say. Are you thirsty?'

She wasn't. He got up and poured himself a glass of wine. She looked at him in the glow of the dying fire. It hurt so much to think that after this night, they would part forever.

He came back to bed and pulled back the sheets to reveal her naked body. Her hair glowed, spread like sunrays on the pillow. He had to look at her, touch and possess her again. He would never have enough of her. He pulled her on top of him and she rested her head on his chest while he toyed with locks of her hair. It used to be so simple, so straightforward. He had never wasted much time thinking about women before. If he saw a woman he wanted, he bedded her. Then he would move on. Sometimes there were tears and recriminations, but they never worried him and they certainly never stopped him. He had never wanted to stay with the same woman for very long … until now. Then again, there had never been a woman he had wanted quite as much as Marie-Ange. His lips curled into a cynical smile. He understood at last what other men had told him over campfires, their eyes dreamy on the eve of a battle they believed would be their last. Some women, they said, a man wanted to hold, make love to, and keep. Forever. Marie-Ange was such a woman. But she didn't want him. Maybe it was justice for all his past sins.

His hands ventured along her back and the fire between them started again, but this time there seemed to be a wildness inside her. She kissed his face, his throat and chest, her lips as light as the wings of a butterfly, her tongue teasing.

He buried his head between her breasts, tracing their outline with his fingers, feeling their soft weight in his hands, taking her nipples in his mouth. Pulsing with need, all he could hear was his own ragged breathing and the blood roaring in his ears.

This was torture. Unbearable pleasure. Surely he wouldn't be able to hold on any longer. He gripped her hips to lift her, she lowered herself onto him and they started moving together, faster and faster. He felt like a soul lost at sea, so intense were the sensations she aroused in him. They both cried out at the same time and she collapsed, shaking on top of him. He held her tight against him, feeling the wild beating of her heart against his own.

They didn't speak. They made love again and were both wide awake when the first light of day filtered through the curtains.

Doors creaked open and shut, footsteps and voices resounded in the corridor and the smells of soup, fried sausages and freshly baked bread wafted in from the kitchens downstairs. It was time to get up. His fingers trailed down the side of Marie-Ange's waist. He pulled her closer, buried his face in her hair and breathed in her scent. She heaved a sigh and pressed her lightly curled fist against his chest, just above his heart, as if she wanted to feel the beats and capture them. He clenched his jaw. Yes, it was time. There was no point in prolonging the inevitable.

He pulled away and got up without a word, then picked up his clothes and got dressed quickly, aware of her gazing at him from the bed, her eyes shiny, her breathing fast and shallow as if she was trying to stop herself from crying. It was as if he was abandoning her when it was she who was leaving him behind. Hell, what did the woman want of him? She had chosen her man, and it wasn't him. With each layer of clothing he put back on he could feel his resolve harden, his anger forming a cold fist in his chest.

'I'll ask a servant to bring you hot water and make the fire,' he said after strapping his sword belt across his hips, his voice harsher than he intended, 'and I'll meet you in the dining room when you are ready.' He left the room without a further glance.

He was having breakfast with Commandant Picard and his two gendarmes when Marie-Ange entered. She was so pale, so fragile with delicate mauve shadows under her eyes, his throat tightened. The men stood up as she approached and he pulled a chair out for her.

'Madame, we will be leaving as soon as the coach driver has harnessed the horses,' Picard announced, his face blushing a deep red. He must be aware Hugo spent the night in her room.

Hugo poured some hot coffee in a cup and handed it to her.

'I'm going back to Lyon this morning. I have been charged with reorganising the Second Cuirassier Regiment in view of forthcoming developments.'

Picard nodded and looked at him admiringly. 'I heard of your promotion. Congratulations, Major Saintclair. Your manoeuvres in the south were decisive in quashing the royalist rebellion. And to receive the Imperial Eagle from Napoleon himself… what a distinction!'

'You were promoted to Major, and Napoleon gave you the Imperial Eagle?' Marie-Ange raised her head, surprised. 'You never said …'

Hugo shrugged; neither seemed that important right now. 'I escorted the king's brother, the Comte d'Artois, to Sète when the mob wanted to lynch him. Apparently, Napoleon was grateful we avoided a blood bath. It wouldn't have looked good for his return to power.'

He paused and added. 'Especially after the foiled assassination attempt on the comte the week before, in Lyon.'

He turned to Picard. 'Commandant, would you please get us some more coffee?'

'Of course, Major.' Picard got up.

Hugo leant over the table.

'This you might need to know,' he started, striving to keep his voice matter-of-fact. 'In the end, the king decided against a visit to Lyon and sent his brother to review the troops in his place. After an evening at the opera, the Comte d'Artois was waiting for his carriage when fireworks were thrown in the street, causing a panic. In the confusion, nobody noticed a man running at d'Artois, firing his pistol. It was sheer luck the king's brother managed to open the carriage door and to jump in. The would-be killer ran off. Witnesses gave a vague description. A tall man. With very pale blond hair.'

Marie-Ange put her hand to her mouth to stifle a cry. 'Do you think it was …?'

She didn't need to say the name. Hugo narrowed his eyes and reclined back on his chair. 'I do.'

He watched as her face drained of all colour and she closed her eyes. Did she understand now how timely Norton's decision to return to her was? The man needed a place to hide until the dust settled both for Fouché and himself, and where better than with his wife back in England? Yet Marie-Ange was so happy to have him back she didn't even question his motives.

'Why the king's brother?' she asked at last.

'What if the purpose of the exercise was not, as we thought before, to clear the way for the emperor? What if whoever gave the order wanted to throw discredit on Napoleon and turn people against him? To make him start his new reign with a cold-blooded execution people were bound to blame him for.'

Marie-Ange shook her head. 'But why would Fouché want to discredit him?'

'The man has a hidden agenda, as usual.'

'He is one of the emperor's closest allies,' she objected.

Hugo laughed bitterly. 'You are very naïve. When it comes to power, allegiances shift. I heard Fouché was plotting for the creation of a Republic with himself as head of state. King Louis was in poor health and the Comte d'Artois was next in line for the throne. His assassination would have killed two birds with one stone. It would have cleared the royalist camp and thrown discredit onto Napoleon.'

'Then Fouché would suggest a completely new regime and become the leader,' Marie-Ange finished.

'The man is nothing if not patient. He may yet have his chance. Napoleon may not have the support he needs to govern for very long. He will soon lose the popular vote when he brings back conscription.'

'Why? Do you think war is inevitable?'

'Unfortunately, yes. Napoleon's emissaries carrying his offers of peace weren't even received by the various governments across Europe. Austria, Prussia, Great Britain, and Russia will soon declare war on France. Napoleon needs to rebuild the army fast.' He didn't add that it couldn't be done and that Napoleon was heading for disaster, along with tens of thousands of men. Including himself.

Picard came back with a jug of coffee. 'There you are, Major,' he said, pouring three cups.

Marie-Ange looked around and dropped her knife and fork on the table.

'That man again!' She pointed to the window. 'I saw him yesterday in Chalons. I think he is one of Malleval's men.'

Hugo turned to the window but whoever Marie-Ange had seen had already left. He turned to Picard. 'Did you notice anyone following you since you left Beauregard?'

Picard shook his head, looking sheepish. 'The roads were busy. I didn't pay attention to the other travellers.'

Hugo stood up. 'Let's go after him, then.' He ordered Marie-Ange to stay in the dining room and gestured to Picard and the two gendarmes to follow him.

As Marie-Ange finished her coffee, a boy dressed in dirty rags ran into the dining room. He pulled her arm and slipped an envelope into her hands.

'What is that?'

The boy ran out without answering.

She ripped open the envelope and something fell on the floor as she pulled out a thin sheet of paper. When she bent down to pick it up she recognised Sophie's ruby ring. Anxious and puzzled now, she read the note.

'If you value the woman's life, come alone now, behind the church. Don't tell anyone or we'll kill her. Hurry.'

Someone had taken Sophie! Marie-Ange looked around her, a helpless feeling gathering in her stomach. Clutching the note and the ring, she rushed out just in time to see Saintclair and the gendarmes riding out of the courtyard. Her shoulders sagged. What should she do? She feared a trap, yet couldn't ignore the ultimatum in the note. She had to go to the rendezvous.

She put the note and the ring back in the envelope, walked back inside and handed the envelope to the innkeeper.

'Please give this to Major Saintclair when he comes back. It's very important.'

The man put the letter in his waistcoat pocket. 'Certainly, Madame.'

She climbed the stairs to her bedroom, grabbed her cloak and her reticule, and ran back down. Chagny was a small place. The streets were almost empty so early in the morning. The bells were ringing for the morning service when she arrived on the church square and half a dozen women crept into the building through a small wooden door.

'*Bonjour, M'ame.*' A gruff male voice spoke behind her. She swirled round and found herself face to face with Rochefort. She stepped back in shock.

'You! We all thought you were dead.'

He chuckled. 'Not so. I fell through a trap and landed in a chamber below the crypt. There were several tunnels branching out and it didn't take me long to gather I was in the disused salt mines.'

'What about Uxeloup?'

'He was in a bad way when he crashed down on top of that stone tomb, but I managed to drag him along a tunnel far enough to avoid getting hurt by the blast of the explosion or hit by the rubble. It did take us a day or so to find our way out, but we made it.'

She gasped. 'He is alive?'

'He sure is.' He came closer, and she smelled the pungent odour emanating from his shagpile coat. 'And you're coming with me now.' He grabbed her elbow.

'Where are you taking me? And where is Sophie?' Marie-Ange tried to gain time. She couldn't believe Malleval was alive. Had he managed to retrieve the Cross of Life too?

Rochefort didn't reply. He walked quickly, pulling her along narrow, deserted alleyways. They soon left the village behind and found themselves near a farm. A black carriage, with four tall horses and two men on the driver's box waited on the road. Her captor opened the door and pushed Marie-Ange inside. He climbed in after her.

'Sit down.' He sat opposite her and the carriage started.

'Where are we going?'

'Back home to Malleval. Now be quiet, or …' He showed her a flask and a handkerchief. She remembered the foul smelling cloth Karloff had put over her face in St Genis to send her to sleep.

'That won't be necessary,' she said. She needed all her wits about her. There might be a chance of escape before they reached their destination.

There wasn't. They travelled all day and part of the night, stopping at isolated inns to feed and rest the horses and use the rest room. Rochefort never let her stray far from his sight. He had bread, cheese and bottles of wine in a basket for himself and his men.

'Do you want some?' he asked her gruffly. She accepted and forced some food down.

Rochefort drank a long gulp of wine and wiped his mouth on his sleeve. 'So the captain and the gendarmes fell for our ruse – what halfwits!' He laughed.

'What do you mean?'

'They walked straight into our trap and followed our decoy. Must be in Autun by now! Saintclair may be able to deal with royalist rebels but he's not so clever when it comes to dealing with the men from the Pilat mountains.' He took another swig of wine.

She ignored him. 'Where is Uxeloup?'

'Waiting for us.'

Although she tried to stay awake, she eventually gave in to the rocking motion of the carriage as night fell. A harsh jolt woke her up. Glancing out of the window, she saw that they had arrived at Malleval.

Rochefort grumbled. 'About time!'

He kicked the door open and jumped down, and Marie-Ange shivered in the cold. Tonight, a snowstorm was blowing in the rugged Pilat mountains.

The wooden doors of the fortress were wide open as they approached and they entered the hall.

'Follow me.' A man holding a torch led the way down a dark corridor.

'I'll tell Monsieur you're here,' he said before leaving Marie-Ange and Rochefort alone in a large room dominated by an enormous stone fireplace bearing the arms of the Mallevals.

A and *M. Ante Mortem.* Before Death. The Death both Edmond and Uxeloup refused.

The fire in the hearth was the only light in the room. Marie-Ange walked to a long table with a marble top on which a silver tray with medical instruments was placed. Long, sharp blades, lancets, curved and twisted implements, a pile of cloth and a white porcelain bowl. A shiver of fear ran down her spine.

'What are these for?' Her voice quivered.

'All in good time.' Rochefort pointed to an armchair positioned in front of the fireplace. 'Take off your coat and sit down.'

She wrapped herself more tightly in her cloak and remained near the table, her heart pounding with dread. Last time she was here, Malleval and Karloff wanted something from her. The words from her mother's song to locate the Cross of Life. What did they seek from her tonight?

'Sit down, I said!'

This time she did as she was told. Rochefort seemed nervous. She looked around the room shrouded in shadows and gasped. In one corner, placed on a high console table, was the Cross of Life standing on the glass phial with the relic inside. So Rochefort and Malleval *had* saved it from Arginy.

'How did you travel back here after the explosion?' she asked.

'I waited near the main road, hidden in the undergrowth, while

Monsieur rested. We were in luck. A couple of peasants drove past in their cart. It was child's play to ambush them and take the cart before riding back here.'

'How is Monsieur Malleval now?' Surely with the advancing ravages of the syphilis and his fall at Arginy, he must be in a very bad shape.

'Not good.'

'Where is Sophie? Why did you take her from Beauregard?'

Rochefort stood up abruptly and came to stand in front of her.

'Will you shut up?' He raised his big hand as if he wanted to strike her but the door flung open. Marie-Ange froze with horror. In front of her stood a man so emaciated he was hardly more than a skeleton. His pale, transparent skin stretched over his bones and was marred with scratches and purplish bruises. His eyes were hollow and feverish.

'Here you are. At last.' He shuffled like an old man across the floor.

'Malleval!' she gasped, putting her hand in front of her mouth and recoiling in her seat.

'Monsieur. Come and sit down.' Rochefort stood up and tried to take Malleval's arm.

The former Hussar shook him off. 'No time for rest. We need to do this now. Before my strength leaves me for good.'

'Do what?' Marie-Ange too stood up.

Malleval ignored her and gestured towards Rochefort. 'Lie her down on the table and tie her up.'

'What do you want with me?' she screamed as the big man grabbed her waist and lifted her up onto the marble tabletop.

Malleval's eyes gave out an evil glare.

'You are going to give me your heart.'

Chapter Twenty-Three

'I should have understood before,' Malleval carried on. 'The answer was there all along, in the parchments from the Knights Templar. A pure heart and the Master Keepers' bloodline were needed to unlock the relic's power.'

He turned his crazed eyes to the Cross of Life. His body was seized by a coughing fit that seemed to drain him of all his strength.

'What exactly do you mean to do?' Marie-Ange's voice quivered as panic welled inside her.

Malleval pointed to the surgical instruments on the table.

'Hold your heart in my hand. Drink your blood so that it runs inside my body, then I'll be able to handle the Cross and gain eternal life at last.'

She shuddered violently as she contemplated the gruesome death Malleval had in store for her.

'Karloff guessed what I meant to do.' He shook his head. 'Old fool ... he told Sophie of my plan yesterday and turned her against me. After that he tried to run away from my men at Beauregard. They had to shoot him down. He should have known better.'

'Where is Sophie?' She had to keep him talking for as long as possible. But then what? Nobody was coming to rescue her this time. Her father and his remaining Turcopilar companion had returned to Sicily, and Hugo was off on a wild-goose chase.

'Upstairs.' Malleval's eyes grew darker. 'She doesn't approve ... She won't even talk to me.'

He coughed again, and then gestured to Rochefort. 'This time I will succeed. I have to, after the fiasco at Arginy and the way I failed my father.'

He pulled a small silver flask from his pocket and showed it to Marie-Ange.

'Don't worry. You won't feel a thing.'

Before she could react, Rochefort lifted her up as if she were just a bundle of rags. She kicked and wrestled against his chest, but he didn't seem to feel anything. Instead he pulled her hair sharply, yanking her head backward, and slapped her in the face. The force of his blow took her breath away. She stopped struggling, her strength ebbed and her mind drifted into unconsciousness. The last thought she had before darkness engulfed her was that Hugo would never know how much she had loved him.

She was floating on the angel's wing. Down below was Malleval's fortress and the village perched on the snow-covered mountains. Nobody could reach her now. She was safe. Muffled voices and the clinking of metal instruments close by intruded on her dream and she fought her way slowly to consciousness. She opened her eyes. Two blurred figures moved against the glow of the fire. Malleval and Rochefort. She wasn't safe at all. Bile rose in her throat. She coughed and tried to turn to her side to be sick but she couldn't move. Her hands were bound tightly on each side to the table legs.

'Please, don't …'

Malleval stood over her. He was holding a sharp, shiny scalpel. Through a haze she saw him lean closer. She mustered all her strength to struggle free, but it was no good. Her bonds were too tight.

'She's awake. She needs more draught,' he said.

He took out his silver flask again and brought it near her lips. As he held her head to force her to drink, a loud explosion outside shook the fortress' walls. It was followed by shouting and the firing of pistols. Startled, he dropped the flask on the floor.

'What's going on out there? Where are the men?'

'A moment, Monsieur. I'll go and have a look,' Rochefort said as he hurried away.

'Damn!' Malleval stepped back.

Marie-Ange breathed a sigh of relief. She heard the door open and light footsteps walk across the floor.

'Sophie, *ma chérie*! Have you changed your mind?' Malleval asked. His voice was soft, full of hope.

‘No, Uxeloup, I have not.’

Marie-Ange heard sounds of a struggle, then a whimper of pain and the thud of a body collapsing onto the floor.

‘I am so sorry, my love. I couldn’t let you do this,’ Sophie cried out.

Marie-Ange felt fingers on her wrists, untying her binds.

‘Quick, there is no time.’ Sophie attempted to lift Marie-Ange’s head off the table. ‘The fortress is under attack. We need to get out through the back door.’

Marie-Ange sat up and something rolled onto her lap. It was the glass phial with the relic inside. Malleval had placed it there, ready for him to handle once he’d cut out her heart … she started shaking.

‘So that’s what it was all about.’ Sophie took the phial and lifted it towards the light of the fire to peer at the piece of fabric inside. ‘It doesn’t look much like an angel wing, does it?’

She helped Marie-Ange stand up and put her dress back in order. Marie-Ange kept hold of the glass phial and, with a last look at Malleval’s crumpled form on the floor, the two women walked out of the study, and hurried along empty corridors through the kitchen and a pantry. Sophie pushed the door open onto the snowstorm outside. The gale had got stronger during the night. Snowflakes swirled madly all around. Gusts of icy cold wind slapped Marie-Ange’s cheeks.

She breathed in deeply, suddenly intoxicated with the realisation she was alive. She had escaped the gruesome death Malleval had planned for her. A familiar voice shouted from outside the fortress walls.

‘Surrender now!’

A warm, elated feeling spread through her. Hugo was there. He hadn’t been fooled by Rochefort’s trick after all. He must have guessed she was being taken to the Pilat and had followed them. It was only a matter of minutes before he and his men stormed into the fortress. All the two women had to do was sneak out into the courtyard and hide in an outbuilding until they were rescued. They crept in the shadows along the wall, hoping Rochefort and the others were too busy defending the place to turn round and look behind them.

The phial was now warm in her hand, and inside the glass the relic glowed, iridescent like an opal catching the moonlight. But there was no moonlight, only the night sky giving way to a murky greyish dawn.

'The stables are just behind there.' Sophie took her elbow to direct her to the stable block.

As they turned around a corner of the building, they came face to face with an armed man.

'Over here! The women are escaping!' he called, before pointing his pistol at them.

Marie-Ange and Sophie stopped dead in their tracks. Half a dozen men appeared and stood menacingly around them.

'Don't shoot!' Rochefort's voice bellowed over the clamour of shouts and gunshots. He came nearer, a fierce expression on his face.

Marie-Ange held the phial up in front of her. 'If you come any nearer I'll drop it.'

Rochefort turned to Sophie. 'Where is Monsieur?' he asked.

'Inside. He fainted,' she lied.

Rochefort gestured to one of his men and ordered. 'Gabet, run to the study and see to Monsieur Malleval.'

Marie-Ange was still holding the phial up in the air. The men looked at it, fascinated by its white glow which was getting brighter and brighter.

'What is she holding? Why is it moving and changing colour? She must be a witch,' one said.

The storm gathered momentum. Ribbons of swirling snowflakes descended from the sky, wrapping themselves around the men, like slippery, ghostly figures.

'Rochefort!' the man named Gabet called. He was carrying Malleval, propping his limp body against him.

Rochefort narrowed his eyes and bared his teeth.

‘What did you do to him? I swear if you hurt him …’ He glared at the two women.

‘He’s still alive,’ Gabet said, ‘but he’s bleeding.’ He looked at the women accusingly. ‘It looks like he’s been stabbed.’

Rochefort pointed to the relic glowing in Marie-Ange’s hands.

‘Let’s see if this really does what it’s supposed to. Hand it over now or I’ll kill you where you stand.’ As he aimed his pistol at Marie-Ange and armed the firing mechanism, there was an explosion at the other end of the courtyard and the large wooden gates blew open. Soldiers came running through, holding their rifles and bayonets in front of them.

Several of Malleval’s men scampered towards the back of the fortress.

‘I said, hand it over!’ Rochefort held his hand out.

The wind suddenly grew stronger. The snow fell in a thick, white curtain. Marie-Ange swayed, stumbled against the wall and dropped the phial. She reached out to retrieve it, but the phial hadn’t fallen on the ground. It swirled in the air in a flurry of snowflakes as if lifted up in ethereal white hands then crashed onto the wall.

‘Where the hell is it?’

Rochefort knelt down and frantically brushed the snow and pieces of shattered glass to retrieve the angel wing. He looked up, crestfallen. His hand was bleeding but he didn’t seem to notice.

‘It’s gone. Blown away.’ He turned to Malleval’s body, lying next to him.

‘Rochefort, we have to go,’ someone urged. Men were running or riding out of the courtyard to escape the soldiers. Rocherfort grunted, lifted Malleval over his shoulder and ran. His bulky figure disappeared in the snowstorm.

‘Marie-Ange.’

Hugo ran to her, a look of sheer relief on his face. She took a few tentative steps. All she wanted was to be safe in his arms but he stopped a few feet from her.

‘I feared I would arrive too late,’ he said.

They looked at each other and for a few moments, they were alone. The sounds of chaos vanished. Marie-Ange no longer felt the whipping wind and snow. All she wanted was to clasp her fingers behind his neck and bury her face against his shoulder. She yearned for the warmth of his arms around her, the sound of his heartbeat against her cheek. Yet she stood immobile and Hugo didn't step any closer either.

'What happened in there? Where is Malleval?' he asked, breaking the silence between them.

'Rocheford took him away…' She heaved a shaky breath.

'He will be dead soon,' Sophie said, gazing towards the hills. She started crying. 'I killed the only man I ever loved, but I couldn't do it … I couldn't let him rip your heart out.'

'What did you say? What did he want to do?' Hugo walked to Sophie and put his hands on her shoulders.

She raised a tear-stricken face towards him. 'He said if he took Marie-Ange's heart and drank her blood, he could hold the relic and become immortal.'

Hugo hissed a breath between his teeth. 'He's gone mad …'

'Will you go after him, bring him back?' Sophie pleaded.

'We'll find him, and the rest of his men,' he promised.

He turned to Marie-Ange. 'Do you still want to return to England?'

She nodded. Nothing had changed. She was still a deported *émigrée*. She was still married to Christopher. And Hugo still didn't love her.

'Then my men will take you both back to Beauregard later this morning, when we've cleared up this den of thieves and murderers,' he said, his eyes and his voice noticeably colder. 'Go inside and wait for me.' He walked away without giving her a second glance.

Marie-Ange was still curious about the phial. Kneeling down where it had broken earlier, she brushed the snow with her finger, careful not to cut her hand on the pieces of shattered glass. Rochefort was right. The piece of fabric, the angel wing, or whatever it was, was gone, blown away by the wind. Or had it been taken by the angel? She may not have believed Karloff's prophecy but she could have sworn she had seen the fluid shape of an arm, the outline of a white hand lifting the phial in the air.

'I'm so cold.' Sophie's broken voice brought her back to reality.

'Let's go in.' Marie-Ange took her hand and led her to a drawing room inside the fortress. 'Try to rest,' she said as the young woman huddled in a corner of the sofa and folded her feet under her body.

Marie-Ange was far too tense to contemplate sitting down. Standing at the window, she watched the soldiers line Malleval's men up in the courtyard. It stopped snowing. A brisk wind blew the clouds away. The sun coloured the sky and the snowy hills in delicate shades of pink and orange.

There had to be something she could do. She went to the kitchens, found a couple of servants hiding, terrified, in the pantry and asked them to prepare some hot food for the soldiers and their prisoners. When the food was ready, they set up tables in the great hall and gathered as many cups and bowls as they could find.

'We are going to serve breakfast to the men,' she decreed.

She organised the soldiers and their prisoners, directed the servants and helped dish out hot porridge, soup, and coffee. It took over an hour to feed everybody. When there was nothing left, she cleared up the dirty bowls, spoons, and cups that cluttered the tables.

He stood watching her tidy up. Her cheeks were rosy and strands of hair escaped her plait and curled at her neck. His fingers remembered the feel of her hair. The feel of her skin. He swallowed hard.

'You would make a fetching tavern girl,' he remarked.

She raised her head and smiled faintly. He took his hat and gloves off and put them on the table.

'I'm afraid there isn't much left to eat but we can have a look in the kitchen if you're hungry.'

'I'm not hungry,' he replied. He closed the distance separating them. 'I'm leaving a small detachment of my men here for the next few days until the gendarmes take over. How are you?'

'Relieved this madness with Malleval is over at last, and glad to be alive, of course.'

He didn't say anything.

'Sophie is resting,' she added, wiping her hands on her dress. 'I will tell her we're ready to leave.'

Hugo grabbed her wrist and pulled her close to him. 'Don't go back to England, Marie-Ange,' he urged. 'I want you with me. I'll sort out the technicalities. As I said before, I can have your deportation order cancelled.'

He bent down and kissed her lips. She remained cold and unresponsive.

'This is the last time I'll ask you.'

Damn it, didn't she know he would look after her? He might not be from the landed gentry like her husband, but she wouldn't want for anything. And she would be his.

Tears filled her eyes. She shook her head. 'You must realise I have no choice. I can't stay with you if you don't lo—'

He didn't wait for her to end her sentence. He let go of her so abruptly she almost fell.

'There is always a choice,' he interrupted. 'Very well. My men will escort you back to Beauregard, where Picard is waiting.' He turned round. 'I almost forgot …' He searched his breast pocket and held out his hand. Inside was Marie-Ange's wedding ring. She took it reluctantly.

'You left it in my room in Lyon. It's just as well I didn't throw it away, isn't it?' He put his gloves and his hat back on. There was only cold anger in his heart now. 'Malleval's men were seen heading for the forest. I'm going after them. I don't think we'll see each other again. I wish you a safe journey back to England, Madame.'

He bowed and walked away. He shouted at a soldier to bring his horse, put his foot in the stirrup, and mounted. He galloped out of the courtyard without looking back.

Chapter Twenty-Four

As promised, a dozen of Hugo's cuirassiers escorted Marie-Ange and Sophie back to Beauregard later that day while the chase after Malleval, Rochefort, and what was left of their men carried on in the mountains.

A cuirassier shook his head and remarked, '*Le Major est enragé!*' Others commented they had never seen Saintclair so angry and reported he had sworn not to give up until he had the fugitives at the tip of his sword, even if it took days.

Before leaving Malleval, Marie-Ange took the Cross of Life from the study and wrapped it carefully in a piece of cloth. Her great-aunt at Marzac could decide what to do with it. As far as she was concerned, the Cross could be locked away in a cupboard or thrown to the bottom of a well. She never wanted to set eyes on it again.

After a silent and uncomfortable journey along bumpy, snowy roads, they arrived at Beauregard late the following morning.

'I don't want to stay here on my own,' Sophie said when she stepped out of the carriage.

Marie-Ange suggested that her cousin the seamstress be invited to stay for a few days and one of Hugo's men was dispatched to fetch her. Another man rode to Beaujeu to inform Commandant Picard that Marie-Ange had arrived safely back at Beauregard.

'What a terrible ordeal, dear Madame,' the gendarme exclaimed when he arrived soon after. He danced from one foot to the other, holding his hat, a blush spreading across his face.

'I am deeply ashamed you should have been abducted while you were in my care. Major Saintclair and I chased after the man for almost an hour before the major realised he was playing a game with us. The scoundrel even slowed down at times, as if making sure we could catch up with him.' Picard coughed. 'The major told me to carry on with the chase whilst he turned back towards Chagny. Thank Heavens he did.'

‘Yes, thank Heavens,’ Marie-Ange agreed, shivering as she recalled how close to death she had come.

She swallowed hard. ‘What about Monsieur Karloff? I heard he was killed.’

Picard shook his head. ‘His body was found in the forest.’ He put his hat back on and informed her they must begin their journey to Le Havre as soon as possible. According to Napoleon’s orders, any *émigrés* still on French soil by the end of the week would be jailed.

‘Can you make sure my great-aunt gets this?’ she asked, handing the Cross over to him.

Picard nodded and promised to send someone to Marzac Manor that very afternoon.

Marie-Ange took her leave of Sophie once again and climbed into yet another carriage. This time she was on the road to exile and there would be no going back.

The rest of the journey was a blur. She looked through the window of the carriage, indifferent to landscapes, villages, and towns they drove through. Each passing hour was taking her away from the man she loved, and towards the stranger who was still her husband.

Picard left her in Paris in the care of a colleague of his. At Le Havre, she boarded a French cutter bound for Portsmouth. This time the crossing was calm and she didn’t suffer as much from seasickness. She spent the journey on deck, staring at the horizon, wrapped in her cloak, her hood covering her head. The sailors called her ‘the widow’ and it brought a sad smile to her face. Now she was no longer a widow, she had never felt more like one.

It was dusk when she arrived at Norton Place, early one rainy evening at the beginning of April. As she climbed down from the carriage, she breathed in the scents of wet earth and fresh grass mixed with the salty breeze blowing from the sea.

‘Welcome back, my lady!’ Rosie, her chambermaid, opened the door and walked out, a smile on her face. Francis followed and muttered a greeting.

‘Is that Marie-Ange? Is she here?’ Robert called from the doorway.

She couldn't help smiling when the young man ran towards her and took her in his arms.

'You've grown taller, Robert.' She kissed his cheeks and ruffled his hair.

'Marie-Ange, I have the most extraordinary, fantastic, incredible news! Guess what?' He jumped up and down like an overexcited puppy.

A cold fist gripped her heart and her smile froze. She knew exactly what he was going to say.

'Christopher is back! Isn't that just wonderful? My brother is alive.' He took her in his arms again and squeezed her against him. Suddenly faint, she swayed against him. She had hoped for more time before facing Christopher. Hugo's revelations about the attempted coup on the Comte d'Artois' life had reignited her doubts that she would ever be able to believe him, let alone love him again.

'I am sorry,' Robert said, frowning. 'It was stupid of me to spring the news on you like that. I should have thought.'

'It's all right, Robert,' she replied, holding onto his arm.

Christopher's silhouette appeared in the doorway. 'Darling, at last! Welcome home.' He descended the steps, approached her casually before stopping a few feet away and opening his arms. He clearly expected her to throw herself against him. Dutifully, and without any of the joy she should have felt, she stepped into his embrace. He kissed her cheeks and whispered in her ear.

'Six long years, my darling, since I held you in my arms. We have such a long time to make up for.'

Her skin prickled with fear. It sounded like a threat rather than a promise of love.

He stepped back and looked down at her. 'You are even more beautiful than the last time I saw you, on the quay at Southampton, that blustery January day when I left for Spain.'

She looked up, surprised. So he didn't want anyone to know about their meeting in France. Why?

'You look different, too,' she remarked, coldly. Then she put a forced smile on her face and a false, joyful note in her voice. She had to pretend to be happy. For Robert's sake.

'You must explain everything, Christopher. What happened to you? Where have you been all these years?'

'Later, my darling.' He kissed her again. She stiffened in his arms and pulled away.

That evening, Marie-Ange played to perfection the part of the quietly overwhelmed but happy wife in front of Robert and the rest of the household. During supper, she asked Christopher again to explain his long absence. With a hushed voice, he talked about undercover missions, state secrets, foreign affairs dossiers. He mentioned recent meetings at Whitehall with Lord Melville – the First Lord of the Admiralty, and Lord Castlereagh, the Foreign Secretary. Leaning towards Robert, he even confided having been entrusted with a very special, highly confidential mission by Lord Liverpool, the Prime Minister, himself.

'I'm afraid my mission will take me away from home again.' He looked up at Marie-Ange. 'As soon as tomorrow in fact.'

'So soon?' Robert protested. 'But you've only just returned.'

The young man was sitting next to Christopher, gazing admiringly at him and drinking in his every word. How different he would look at his elder brother if he knew the truth, Marie-Ange thought bitterly. She was curious though. How had Christopher managed to negotiate his release from Fouché's services and his return to the Royal Navy? There must be some truth in his talk of secret missions.

He smiled and covered her hand with his. She tried very hard not to withdraw it. Looking down at her fingers, he remarked.

'I see that you have misplaced your wedding ring.'

She stared back at him. 'So have you, Christopher. Or was being a bachelor a cover for your very secret missions?' Her tone was biting.

'Marie-Ange, Christopher already said he wasn't at liberty to explain about his work.' Robert flew in his brother's defence.

Christopher reclined on his chair and smiled smugly. 'Not to worry. We shall have new rings made.'

‘That won’t be necessary,’ she replied. ‘My wedding ring is in my travel trunk. You will see it on my finger tomorrow, if that is your wish.’

She excused herself after supper, claiming exhaustion and a headache, and sought the sanctuary of her bedchamber. She prayed Christopher would not join her later and insist on enforcing his rights as husband. The very thought of his hands on her body made her sick with dread. After unpacking some of her clothes, Rosie prepared a bath.

‘It’s good to have you back, my lady,’ the girl said. ‘Sir, too, of course,’ she added, her voice guarded.

It felt so strange to be here. In a way, it was as if she’d never left. Her room was the same. Norton Place was the same. Robert was his usual self, a pleasant and boisterous young man. But she had changed.

She pinned her hair on top of her head and undressed. She asked Rosie to leave her when she slipped into the hot bath. She closed her eyes for a moment.

A noise nearby startled her. She must have fallen asleep. Opening her eyes, she let out a frightened cry. A shadow moved in a corner of the room.

‘You are really beautiful, you know,’ Christopher said, his voice hoarse. As he walked into the light she snatched the towel by the side of the bath and swiftly stood up and covered herself with it.

‘You don’t need to hide from me, wife,’ he sneered. ‘Take it off and come to me.’

She breathed deeply and looked into his mocking grey eyes. He was toying with her. He wanted to upset and frighten her. She would show him no fear.

‘No.’ Her voice may be calm but she was shaking inside.

He strode towards her, seized her arm and dragged her to the bed.

Tipped off balance, she fell backwards onto the counterpane, and he crashed on top of her, driving the breath from her lungs. She tried to wriggle free, but he pinned her down. There was no feeling in his eyes, just the grey coldness of steel. He raised one hand to her throat to stop her from moving.

'Now, my dear, listen very carefully,' he commanded. 'To the eyes of the world, you are my wife. And I will use you as I please. This time, you will not push me away. I have all the power and you have nothing.' He gave a little grunt as his hands slid over her bare skin, still damp from the bath. She gritted her teeth.

'I know you were the French officer's harlot, and I'm going to enjoy making you pay for it.' He chuckled. 'I bet he taught you a trick or two which will make our nights much more interesting.'

Although she felt sick with loathing and her heart beat like a wild bird trapped in a cage, she tried to remain as cold as a statue under his touch. She would have to beat him at his own game.

'If you don't get off me this instant, I swear I will tell everybody how we met in France. I will tell them about Karloff and the mesmerism session,' she said.

His hand stopped moving. He was listening, waiting.

She played her last card. 'I will tell them who is behind the assassination attempt on the king's brother, the Comte d'Artois, in Lyon a few weeks ago. I bet that will change your employer's prospects altogether and yours, too. I gather Fouché is still your employer, am I right? All this talk about missions for the Admiralty and the Foreign Affairs ministry is only half the story, isn't it?'

He withdrew his hand and cursed.

She carried on, pushing her advantage. 'I will go as high as necessary, to Lord Castlereagh … to Lord Liverpool himself.'

He rolled off her and she sat up, covering herself with the towel.

She gave a tight smile. 'If you force me to, that is.'

He stood up and crossed his arms on his chest.

'Well played, darling.' The words hissed between his teeth. 'There are indeed certain facts I would prefer to remain concealed for now. I am amazed at your perspicacity. What do you know about this?'

'About Lyon? And Fouché trying to get the king – or his

brother – murdered to make room for the emperor … or was it to discredit the emperor? Which was it?' She pretended nonchalance, playing with the tassels of her towel. 'Either way, I am sure Fouché would find it tricky to explain himself. Napoleon made it clear he didn't want any member of the royal family harmed.'

He glared at her.

'What do the Sea Lords know about you, then?' she asked. 'Do they know how you really spent the last six years? Do they know you are still Fouché's man?'

He shrugged. 'They know some of it. Other things, like the unfortunate shambles outside the Lyon Opera, I'd rather keep to myself.'

So he was admitting responsibility for the botched attack on the Comte d'Artois.

'Why were you not arrested for treason when you came back to England?'

'My superiors at the Admiralty Board and the Cabinet are aware of my involvement with Fouché. In fact, that's what makes me invaluable to them at the moment. I am their direct line into Napoleon's new Cabinet and with my help – and Fouché's – they have a chance to topple it.'

He walked to the door, but turned towards her, his hand on the doorknob.

So Hugo had been right. Fouché was already scheming to get rid of Napoleon, only a few weeks into his new reign. He had plotted with the British against Napoleon in April the year before, just before the emperor abdicated. This time he had Christopher to liaise secretly with the British.

'Why did Fouché choose you for this particular mission?' she asked, shivering as she recalled the razor-sharp face of the minister of police, his heavily hooded eyes and thin lips. She was reminded of what Christopher had said at Beauregard when he was under Karloff's influence. That he and Fouché were very much alike because they had no feelings. Looking into her husband's cold grey eyes now, it wasn't hard to believe.

Christopher smiled. 'Actually, he chose me because of you. After the opera house incident in Lyon, I had to lie low for a while. He was very displeased with me for failing to carry out my mission. I was about to go into hiding when I remembered you and your fancy story about me being your long-lost English husband. I thought you could provide me with a new start. So I came to Beauregard and pretended I remembered you.'

He sneered. 'And you fell for it. It was all lies, you know. I didn't have any flashbacks of our married life or this place. I didn't remember a thing! Fortunately, you obligingly filled all the gaps for me. I couldn't have asked for a more helpful wife.'

Marie-Ange felt her heart grow colder. 'You mean you didn't remember Norton Place or people from the past. Or even me?'

He gave a short laugh. 'Of course I didn't. When I came to Beauregard, I thought I'd go along with anything you said. Slipping into a dead man's shoes would give me a good cover. It might make me useful to Fouché again, after the Lyon fiasco. If nothing else, it would give me a new identity, a chance to start again.'

He paused for an instant. 'Then you suggested Karloff hypnotise me, and the most incredible thing happened. I found out you had been right all along and that I actually was … myself.'

His voice held a trace of wonder. 'I must say I hadn't expected that. So we can say that whatever happens next in French and European politics will have a lot to do with you, my darling, and with your obstinate belief in me.'

He opened the door and bowed. 'I will travel back and forth to France under my French identity – Joseph Nallay. And I'd rather nobody else but I, the Admiralty Board, and a few carefully chosen people at the Ministry of Police in Place Cambon know about it. So yes, you have won for now.'

His lips stretched into a thin, threatening smile. 'But only because I am letting you win, and only just for now.' He paused. 'Another thing, Marie-Ange, you will remain here at Norton Place until I decide what to do with you. I can see you and my foolish brother are very close, so if you give me any reason to be dissatisfied with you, I promise I'll make him suffer. Trust me, I am very good at inflicting suffering. Goodnight.'

He walked out.

Once alone, Marie-Ange was consumed by uncontrollable tremors. She went to the fireplace, poked the logs to start the fire again, and stood staring at the flames until she stopped trembling. She had an important decision to take. Should she warn Hugo that, as he had suspected, Fouché was plotting against Napoleon? Or should she let Fouché bring down the emperor with the help of the British government? After all, if Napoleon were removed from the throne, there would be no more wars in Europe.

It was late into the night when she reached a decision. She would write to Hugo and warn him about Fouché but she must be very careful. Christopher would be watching her like a hawk. She had made an enemy of her husband tonight. He would never forgive her for blackmailing him and gaining the upper hand over him.

Chapter Twenty-Five

10th August 1815 – Norton Place

'It's all over this time. Napoleon is on board HMS *Northumberland* en route for Sainte Hélène. He won't be coming back to France.' Christopher smiled smugly. 'Not standing, anyway. If he had been sent there in the first place, the carnage at Waterloo would have been avoided.'

He folded his newspaper and looked at Marie-Ange. 'And what carnage it was. The latest figures have now been released. Over twenty-five thousand French soldiers dead – and almost twenty-two thousand of our own coalition forces lost. Thousands still unaccounted for. Mostly infantry, but many cavalry forces, too. Poor souls, they are probably rotting in a ditch under their horses. Do you remember Wellington's account of the battle in the *London Gazette* a few weeks ago, my dear? According to him, the French cuirassiers bore the brunt of the Prussian and Hanoverian artillery. They were decimated.'

He put the paper to one side and tucked into his breakfast of ham and scrambled eggs. Marie-Ange closed her eyes, hearing his voice from a distance. He was now talking about the fall of Paris to the British and Prussian forces three weeks before, about the siege of Lyon by the Austrians and the surrender *en masse* of the French army to the coalition forces. He quoted the names of French casualties from Napoleon's last campaign – the many high-ranking officers who had died or suffered terrible injuries at Waterloo. There was one name she was desperate not to hear.

She finished her cup of tea and looked at Christopher. Cool and perfectly at ease, he talked about the outcome of the war England and its allies had just won as if the past six years had never happened, as if he had never worked for the French side. No, she was wrong, she corrected silently. He worked for Fouché, *not* for France. And now Napoleon was gone, Fouché was leading King Louis' new government with a surprise ally – his old enemy Talleyrand. Both men succeeded in surviving another change of government.

Christopher had good reason to be pleased with the outcome of events. He had helped his master, his 'employer' as he called him, gain a crucial position of power in France once again. He had travelled between England and France incessantly, no doubt delivering important instructions and messages from the British Cabinet to Fouché, and secret information about Napoleon's plans to the British in return.

At least his frequent travels meant that Marie-Ange didn't have to endure his presence at Norton Place too often. Time had not mellowed Christopher and helped him become his old self. He remained a cold and indifferent stranger, so much so that even Robert found it impossible to establish a brotherly relationship with him. After the first few weeks when he had been overjoyed by Christopher's return, the young man had suffered from his brother's sharp tone and constant rebukes.

'I don't know him, Marie-Ange,' the young man confided one evening, his grey eyes tearful and his lips quivering. 'Hell, I don't *like* him!'

Robert had now started his three-year training at the Royal Navy Academy in Portsmouth where Christopher had purchased a commission. Marie-Ange was happy for him. He was at last pursuing his dream. It also meant Christopher had less of a hold on her since he couldn't hurt the young man should she displease him.

Robert and Marie-Ange weren't alone in finding Christopher difficult to live with. She had heard Francis, Mrs Green, the cook, and Elias the gardener comment on their master's nasty temper. 'Don't you dare get on the wrong side of him,' they had urged Rosie one day in the kitchen. 'He's nothing like he was in the old days.'

He had made enemies of Rusty and Splinter too, kicking them out of the way whenever he was at Norton Place. The two dogs had taken to snarl every time he was near, and Marie-Ange had to leave them in the kitchens or the stables for fear they would bite him.

The manor house had changed in the past five months. Christopher paid for extensive repairs to be carried out and Norton Place was now a bright and beautiful home. Marie-Ange did wonder about the source of Christopher's money, though. Was it Fouché's money – in other words, treason money, blood money?

She gestured towards the newspaper, folded on the table next to her husband, and asked him to hand it over.

'Are you sure it's wise? I don't want you having a fainting fit. You already look very pale,' he answered with false concern. Instinctively, she placed a protective hand on the gentle curve of her belly and felt the baby move inside her. It was no more than a flutter but her lips formed a tender, secret smile. She put her hand back on the table straight away. Christopher had no idea she was expecting. The fashion for loose, high-waisted dresses had helped her conceal her pregnancy so far. However, the time had come to tell him. It was the right thing to do. Especially since she also planned to inform him she was leaving him, Norton Place, and England.

Rosie came in with a tray. 'The post, sir.' The maid glanced at Marie-Ange. 'Would you like your correspondence, Madame?'

Christopher clicked his fingers, impatient. 'Bring it all to me.'

Rosie smiled apologetically at Marie-Ange, but did as she was told. As she walked towards Christopher, her foot caught in the rug and she tripped, sending the letters and tray flying off onto the ground.

'Silly girl! Look what you've done!' Christopher raged.

'Christopher, please, this isn't anything to be angry about.' Marie-Ange smiled at Rosie who scrambled to her feet and picked up the letters from the floor.

'I'm sorry, sir,' Rosie said, her cheeks bright red, as she placed the tray in front of Christopher.

He looked through a pile of letters and stopped suddenly, holding a thin envelope adorned with an elaborate red wax seal in front of him.

'This one is for you, dear. How odd … it comes from Catania in Sicily and bears the seal of the Knight Order of St John – the Knights Hospitaller.' He leant over, arching his eyebrows. 'Any idea from whom that might be?'

He toyed with the letter. 'Maybe I should open it myself. You never know, it may be bad news.'

She stood up in protest. At last, news of her father! She had written to Baldassare at the beginning of May and had been waiting anxiously ever since for his reply.

'That is mine, Christopher.'

He held the letter up in the air. She recognised the warning in his eyes.

'I will ask you again, then. Do you have any idea of who this letter might be from?'

She sat down. She hadn't told him about meeting Baldassare in France.

'My father probably, or one of his associates,' she replied with a low voice.

Her husband dropped the letter on the table. 'What on earth are you talking about? Your father died over seven years ago. And his business partners all reside in Plymouth.'

'It's a long story, Christopher.'

He crossed his arms on his chest. 'Go on.'

She coughed to clear her voice. 'During my trip to Beauregard, I learnt my real father was not William Jones but a gentleman from Malta called Baldassare dei Conti. Baldassare belongs to the Order of the Knights Hospitaller.'

She conjured the image of her father's face, of his kind smile, and pure blue eyes. 'I was fortunate enough to meet him. He is indeed an extraordinary man. He said he would write.'

She withheld details about Baldassare being a Turcopilar and the account of their dangerous quest for the Cross of Life.

Christopher whistled between his teeth. 'And you kept this to yourself since our return to England? Why?'

She raised her head defiantly. 'Because it had nothing to do with you.'

'You are my wife. Everything that concerns you is my business.'

She wanted to retort she was his wife in name only. Any feeling and affection had long gone from their marriage, but she held back.

'Will you give me the letter now?'

He didn't answer but tore the envelope open and read it silently, a frown on his forehead.

'This is fascinating. A Maltese family … Knights of St John … well, I'd never …'

He shook his head, folded the letter and put it in his coat pocket before standing up.

'We will talk when I return from London. I must get ready now. Lord Admiral Melville is expecting me in London tomorrow. I shall not be back before the end of the week at the earliest.'

Marie-Ange felt a surge of panic. Black butterflies danced in front of her eyes. She had vowed to tell Christopher about the baby before he left today. She clenched her fists and summoned her courage.

'Actually, there is something I must tell you.'

'Can it not wait?'

She swallowed hard and stood up to face him. 'It's important.'

He crossed his arms, and his lips stretched in a thin grin. 'What is it?'

'I am expecting a child. It will be born in December,' she blurted out, putting her hand on her stomach. Before her courage left her completely, she added, 'And I am leaving you and Norton Place. Now that I am no longer considered an *émigrée*, I will return to Beauregard.'

She expected shouts of anger but only icy silence greeted her words.

Had Christopher heard what she said? His face was frozen in a grin, his eyes hard.

Eventually, he let out a long breath.

'Two, no sorry, three, revelations in the space of half an hour. You are not sparing my feelings today, my dear … Who is the brat's sire?' he asked, but almost immediately raised his hand.

‘Actually, don’t tell me. Let me guess. It’s Saintclair, isn’t it?’

‘Yes,’ she said, breathing out a sigh of relief. She had told him, at last. She dreaded this moment so much that she even contemplated running away to France like a coward while he was in London, leaving only a letter behind to explain herself.

‘Does he know you are with child?’ Christopher’s questions were precise, his tone matter-of-fact.

She shook her head.

‘When was the last time you saw him?’

‘In March, at Malleval,’ she replied weakly, remembering the freezing cold morning, the pink skies after the storm, and Hugo riding off into the snow covered hills.

‘Have you heard from him since?’

She shook her head again.

‘So, for all you know, he may have been killed on the battlefields in June. At Quatre Bras, Waterloo, or somewhere else. Or he may be in some whore’s bed and not give a toss about you.’

Her eyes filled with tears. Christopher gave voice to the very concerns that tormented her in the darkest hours of the night.

‘Surely, Marie-Ange, you know the score with men like Saintclair.’ He laughed. ‘You were stupid to get yourself pregnant, even more stupid if you actually fell in love with him.’ He came closer.

‘I will not allow you to go to Beauregard. You are my wife and you will stay here.’ He put his hands on her shoulders. She tried to shake him off but he pressed down harder.

‘Beauregard is where I want to live. Where I belong,’ she replied, wincing with pain. ‘Don’t you see we cannot carry on the way we are? I believed we might be able to live together, like man and wife again. I was wrong. This is wrong …’

‘How can you say you tried to be my wife when you were carrying another man’s child?’ His voice was cutting. ‘When you blackmailed me to stay away from your bed?’

He let go of her abruptly. ‘We will talk when I return from

London. This child will be raised here as a Norton. I will not have the name of my family dishonoured by a woman who behaved little better than a soldier's trollop.' He clenched his jaws, and a vein throbbed on his temple.

'I won't be here when you come back.' She might sound assertive but inside she was shaking with fear.

'Then I promise I will come for you,' he snarled and shot her a look full of hatred. 'Someday, when you least expect it, I will come for you and your bastard child.'

He turned on his heel and left the dining room. Marie-Ange collapsed into a chair and buried her face into her hands. She needed time to compose herself before facing the servants.

At least she had told Christopher the truth. She was free from him. Her only regret was that she would not see Robert and explain her reasons for going away. The young man would be hurt, shocked, and probably angry, too.

She now had to concentrate on organising her journey to France. She would sell some jewellery in Plymouth to pay for the passage across the Channel to Le Havre and the coach to Lyon. She wouldn't take any money from Christopher. It was ironic she should struggle to pay for her journey considering she was now the undisputed heiress of Beauregard and all of Malleval's fortune.

Hermine had written to say that she was free to return to France and take possession of her estate. Thankfully Christopher had been out the day she received the letter and he hadn't intercepted it like he so often did.

Would she see Hugo in France? As Christopher had pointed out, she didn't even know if he was alive. If he was, would he acknowledge her and the baby? He had never claimed to love her.

She had written to Lucie when she got back to Norton Place at the end of April, adding a line of warning for Hugo. '*Please tell your brother he was right about the fireworks at the opera house and everything else.*' She knew Hugo would understand.

Lucie hadn't replied. She was probably still angry with her, and Marie-Ange had not written again. And of course, in June, there had been Waterloo …

Rosie came in and closed the door. She looked nervous.

'Madame,' she whispered. 'This came for you this morning.' She produced a small envelope from under her white apron and handed it to Marie-Ange. 'The man who gave it to the new kitchen lad insisted it was given to you personally.' She lowered her voice. 'He was foreign. French.'

'What did he look like?' Marie-Ange's throat was so tight she could hardly speak.

'The kitchen lad said that he was tall and dark, with a scar on the cheek.'

Marie-Ange held her breath. Could it be Hugo?

Rosie sighed. 'I'm sorry about the other letter, Madame. I couldn't keep both of them back. When the master told me to bring the tray to him, I only thought about hiding this one, so I pretended to trip. I hope I did the right thing.'

Marie-Ange took the envelope with a shaky hand. 'Thank you, Rosie. You did well,' she said, dismissing the maid with a tight smile.

Her heart thumped and black butterflies danced in front of her eyes. Her fingers shaking badly, she tore the envelope open and unfolded a thin sheet of paper.

'*Chapel on the cliff. Today. Eleven. Come alone. H.*'

He was alive! He was here and he wanted to see her … Her fingers shook as she scrunched up the paper and shoved it in the pocket of her dress.

She looked at the mantel clock. Ten o'clock already. She heard Christopher's voice in the hall and went to him. He was giving Francis instructions with his usual sharp tone of voice. When he saw her, he stopped talking and narrowed his eyes.

She walked towards him, hesitant. This might be the last time they ever saw each other. He seemed calmer now, but she saw the steely glint of anger in his eyes and understood he was putting up a front. She followed him outside.

'Please give me my father's letter back, Christopher. It can be of no use to you.'

His lips stretched into a mean smile. 'On the contrary, my dear … I meant what I said earlier, you know. I *will* come after you, and those you love. Leave me now at your own risk.'

She didn't reply, but he must have seen the resolve on her face. He climbed into the carriage and slammed the door shut. The coachman raised his whip and clicked his tongue and the horses moved off. Marie-Ange heard a whimper and felt something tugging at her dress. She turned round.

'Splinter … good dog.' She knelt down next to the spaniel and stroked its black and brown coat. 'Shall we go for a walk?' The dog wagged its tail enthusiastically. If she walked fast, she would get to St Nectan's Chapel for eleven. She rushed back inside the hall and took her cape from the hook.

A few moments later, she was walking at a steady pace along the path towards the cliffs. Splinter and Rusty were chasing after each other. St Nectan's Chapel stood in the distance.

The sea glittered in the morning sunshine, and as well as the usual fishing boats sailing back to Wellcombe Harbour and a couple of bricks on the distant horizon, a magnificent frigate was moored in the bay. It was flying a white flag – the flag of the Bourbon monarchy. It must be Hugo's ship.

The sun was in her eyes but someone was walking towards her. A tall, heavy-built man. She blinked. Her heart seemed to beat to the same rhythm as the roaring waves crashing onto the rocks below and the shriek of seagulls echoed around her. She waited, her hands twisted underneath her cape for the man to come nearer.

Chapter Twenty-Six

'Madame Norton … Marie-Ange.' Hugo bowed in front of her.

'Major Saintclair.' Her throat was so tight she couldn't manage more than a whisper.

For a few seconds, they stared at each other. His eyes were as bright, as blue as the sea shimmering under the sunlight.

Then he smiled and reached out for her hand.

'You look radiant.' There was a note of wonder in his voice. He hesitated. 'Are you well? Are you happy?'

'As happy as can be expected,' she answered.

She waited, heart pounding, as he squeezed her hand. Why had he come?

'I hope my message didn't alarm you.' He let go of her hand and gestured towards the bay. 'I need to talk to you, preferably on board the *Pénélope*.'

She looked down at the beautiful three-mast warship rocking on the swell.

'Oh. Why is that?'

'We need your help, to rid France of Fouché for good.'

Marie-Ange let out a long sigh. Disappointment churned inside her, so raw, so violent she wanted to be sick. So this had nothing to do with him and her. He hadn't sailed to Devon to take her away. It was all about Fouché.

She adjusted her cape around her slightly rounded body and raised her chin.

'I don't understand how I can help.'

'I will explain when we're on board. It's rather important. Shall we go down to the beach? There's a craft waiting for us.'

She shrugged weakly. 'I suppose so.'

She called her dogs and knelt down next to them, ruffling their coats and scratching behind their ears. 'Go back. Go home,' she ordered, pointing in the direction of Norton Place, but the two spaniels stayed put and wagged their tails.

Hugo found a couple of sticks, which he threw far away into the bushes. With a yelp, Splinter and Rusty sprinted off. He led the way, warning her about loose stones and slippery rocks as they made their way down. When they reached the beach she saw a small craft pushed onto the sand.

Two sailors were waiting. On Hugo's signal, they floated the dinghy and jumped in.

'Please allow me.' She stiffened as he scooped her in his arms and held her against him. He walked into the sea, lifted her into the boat. The small boat rocked precariously when it was his turn to climb in. His breeches and boots dripping wet, he sat on the narrow bench opposite her.

The frigate looked close enough from the beach but it took over half an hour of energetic rowing by the two sailors to reach it. She looked at Hugo but he stared ahead, seemingly lost in thought. The wind blew his dark hair. His face was harder, tauter than she remembered. There were new lines at the corner of his eyes.

She broke the silence. 'I read terrible accounts of Waterloo in the papers. Were you there?'

He nodded. 'Yes.'

'How did your regiment fare?'

'We lost three hundred and seventy-three cuirassiers, and twenty-five still haven't been accounted for.'

'Oh, my God.'

He narrowed his eyes. 'It was a bloodbath.'

There wasn't much she could say after that. They didn't talk until they reached the *Pénélope.*

It was truly awe-inspiring with its two-storey height, double rows of artillery portholes and high rear deck. Marie-Ange wondered how the rowing boat would manage to pull alongside its massive hull without getting crushed. Then she worried about getting on board. One sailor grabbed a thick rope ladder that dangled down the side. Hugo went up first. He climbed quickly, and then it was her turn.

'*A vous*!'

She started to climb, petrified with fear. The ship swayed with the swell, the rope ladder was slippery under her fingers and her dress hampered her movements, but she soldiered on. She tried not to look at the waves frothing below, and after what felt like an eternity, she finally reached the top deck. Looking up she saw Hugo lean over the side.

'Don't be afraid. I'll get you on board.' He put his hands under her arms and lifted her up, keeping her against him long enough for her to breathe in his scent, feel the warmth of his hands on her back. Although all she wanted was to close her eyes and stay in his arms forever, she pulled back. She didn't want him to notice her swollen belly just yet. Now wasn't the time to tell him about the baby. She would wait until they were alone.

The booming voice of Capitaine Martin called from behind them.

'Welcome on board, Madame Norton!'

Hugo let go of her.

'I need to tell you what we expect from you.' His voice sounded official, with no trace of any past intimacy between them. 'Please come with me to Commandant Janvier's cabin. This way.'

He went into the captain's quarters, pushed open a door into a spacious cabin with a large desk covered with maps and papers in the middle. Two men sat behind the desk. They stood and nodded towards her. The tallest one wore a dark navy and white uniform. The other man was dressed in civilian clothes.

'Madame Norton,' Hugo gestured to the smaller man, 'this is Pierre Deval, French consul to the Barbary States.' Deval bowed deeply. 'And this is Commandant Janvier who is taking us to Algiers.'

She started and looked at him, surprised. Did he say they were going to Algiers?

'You are leaving France?' she asked.

He nodded. 'I have been sent to smooth relations between France and the new Dey, Omar Agha.'

Martin laughed out loud. 'Liar! You weren't *sent* there, you volunteered. We have only been at peace for four weeks and you're already bored.'

Saintclair smiled at his friend. 'You may be right … at any rate, it's a worthwhile mission for France.'

'Stuff France! What you want is adventure, treasures to find, and maybe a *belle dame* with dark velvet eyes and silky smooth skin waiting for you in a camel-skin tent near an oasis. Admit it, you scoundrel!' Martin laughed good-humouredly.

Feeling faint, Marie-Ange gripped Hugo's arm to steady herself. So he had volunteered to go to North Africa, he would be there possibly for years to come. There was no point telling him about the baby now.

'Are you not well?' He leant towards her, frowning.

Commandant Janvier offered her his chair and Hugo helped her sit down. He stood behind her and left his hands on her shoulders a few moments, his touch burning her through her layers of clothing. She breathed in deeply and closed her eyes.

'Monsieur Deval and I will leave you for now, Major. Please call for us when you're ready,' Commandant Janvier declared. The two men bowed formally and left the cabin.

Hugo sat behind the capitaine's desk. 'You heard, of course, that Fouché has wormed his way back in government,' he started.

She nodded.

'Together with Talleyrand, they form the backbone of King Louis' new cabinet. The man thinks he is untouchable.' He darted his blue eyes at her. 'However, you know something which will make his position untenable as a royalist minister.'

'Are you talking about the attempt on Comte d'Artois' life last March?'

'Indeed. In your letter to my sister, you wrote something for my attention. Am I right in believing that Norton confirmed what I suspected?'

'Yes. He told me he had been ordered to carry out the assassination by "his employer" as he calls Fouché,' she stated matter-of-factly.

Hugo sat back in his chair, a satisfied expression on his face. 'So we've got him at last!'

'My, my …' Capitaine Martin broke his silence. He looked in turn at Hugo and Marie-Ange, an incredulous expression on his face. 'You've known about that all along?'

Hugo ignored Martin. 'Will you write a statement? An affidavit will give us enough leverage to send him packing.'

She looked at him. What he was asking her could put an end to Fouché's days as a minister. It could also lead to Christopher's arrest, maybe even his execution. Now that France and Britain were at peace, the British government wouldn't hesitate to surrender him to the French authorities, should they ask. Her head was spinning. Could she actually send Christopher to his death? 'Please give me a moment … I need to think about the implications for my husband and—'

Hugo shot her a thunderous look. 'You need to *think*?' he cut in. 'Obviously I was mistaken when I thought you wanted to help. I wasn't taking into account your feelings for your husband.' His tone was scornful.

She straightened in her chair and hissed. 'Don't talk to me about my feelings, Major Saintclair. My feelings are none of your business.'

'Damn it, Marie-Ange!' He put his hands flat on the desk. 'Your husband admitted to the attempted murder of the king's brother – and still you are prepared to cover up for him and save his neck?'

She held his gaze without flinching. Capitaine Martin shifted uncomfortably in his chair.

'Calm down, Saintclair.'

Marie-Ange turned to Martin and forced a smile.

'That's quite all right, Capitaine. I will do what Major Saintclair requests, but on one condition. That you only use my statement as a last resort … Do I have your word, Major Saintclair?'

He sighed, and nodded. 'Yes.'

'Then give me some paper and a quill.'

Her voice might have been cool and composed, but her hand was shaking when she dipped the quill into the inkwell to write what Christopher had told her about his attempted murder of the Comte d'Artois. When she had finished, she put the quill down onto the desk.

'May I?' Hugo took the document from her and read it silently.

'It will be our trump card. There's something else we hope can push Fouché out.'

Marie-Ange raised her head. 'What is that?'

'Fouché is a regicide,' he explained. 'He voted for the execution of Louis XVI and Marie-Antoinette. The king wants to introduce a law banning from government all those who voted in favour of his brother's beheading.'

He stepped outside to ask Monsieur Deval and Commandant Janvier to come back into the cabin and witness and sign the statement, which was then rolled up as a scroll and sealed with molten red wax.

Marie-Ange stood up. She was possessed with a sudden, overwhelming need to be alone and far, far away from the man who gazed at her with such indifference. The man who had forgotten all about the night they shared; the man who had asked her to be his mistress; whose child she was carrying and who would never know it. The man she loved more than ever but who had never loved her.

Now he had proof of Fouché's treason to the royalist camp, Hugo would sail to Algiers. She would try to forget all about him … if that was possible. She fought back her tears.

'I want to go back now,' she said.

Hugo nodded. 'Of course.'

They were soon safely on board the small craft with the two sailors rowing back to shore, Hugo turned to her.

'Did you know that you're now the wealthy heiress of Beauregard and Malleval?'

She nodded. There was no need to tell him she was leaving Christopher, and England, probably later that day or the next. No need to tell him she planned to settle at Beauregard permanently.

'Whatever happened to that Cross you and your father were so concerned about? The one that was supposed to make people immortal, but which almost got us all killed down in the crypt at Arginy.' There was a humorous twinkle in his eyes.

'I sent it to my great-aunt Hermine who gave it to the abbey at Cluny for safekeeping.'

'What about the angel? Do you think he'll ever come?' he asked softly.

'He already came, that snowy morning at Malleval.' She shivered, remembering the white arms lifting the relic … or was it just snowflakes swirling around? 'I believe I saw him.'

'Or her…' He smiled.

'What did you do when you went after Malleval in the mountains? Did you kill him?'

His face became sombre.

'No. The man was already dead when I got to the cave on the hillside where Rochefort and the others were hiding. With his stab wounds and the freezing cold, he didn't stand a chance.'

There was sadness in his voice. 'I killed Rochefort, though, and others, when I could have spared them.' He bent his head. 'I didn't behave the way I should have. I was angry, so angry.'

She resisted the urge to put her hand on his face and caress his cheek. Instead, she folded her hands into her lap. They were getting nearer the cliffs. Soon they would reach the beach.

'Why are you going to the Barbary States?'

'Why not? There's nothing for me in France.'

'What about Lucie? And your parents?'

What about me? she wanted to scream.

'I have provided for them. They will not want for anything. Lucie has a new physician and her health has much improved. My father found a very capable man to manage his workshop and is now spending more time at home with my mother.' He smiled. 'As for me, I long for something else, for freedom and new adventures.'

He shook his head. 'The army has been my whole life. It gave me more than I could ever have hoped for, but I want to carve my own destiny. Algiers looks like a good starting point. And then, who knows, I might very well disappear into the Sahara, like Martin said. There is a place called Bou Saada … they call it the city of happiness. That's where I'd like to go.' He looked towards the cliffs again.

He wanted freedom and adventure. How could she tell him about the baby? She bent her head and put her hands on her stomach, under the cape. Her child would have no father. Well, she would have to love him twice as much.

They remained silent until the craft reached the shore. There was so much he wanted to ask her. She may look more beautiful than ever, but despite the brave face she put on, he felt it had not been easy for her at Norton Place. He clenched his fists. If that bastard so much as laid a finger on her, he would … he tightened his lips. He would do what? He was leaving her behind, along with his old life.

The sailors jumped into the shallow water and pushed the boat towards the beach. He let himself down into the sea and opened his arms.

'I'll carry you to the beach.'

Marie-Ange nestled into his arms and clasped her fingers behind his neck as he strode in the water towards the shore. He put her down gently on the sand, his hands brushing against her back like a caress when he released her.

Pointing to the cliff top, he said, 'I'll see you safely to the top.'

She nodded. 'Thank you. I do feel a little faint suddenly.'

He told the men to wait and took Marie-Ange's hand. She didn't pull away, so together they walked slowly up the cliff path.

Once they reached the top, he said, 'You were here the day I first saw you. There were storm clouds and a mighty strong wind. For a few seconds, you stood in a ray of sunshine, and the sailors said you were an angel.' He turned to her. 'They were right.'

How could he leave her without telling her how he felt? He stepped forward, put his hands on her shoulders and looked deep into her eyes.

'Marie-Ange …' He let out an impatient breath. He may have been decorated several times for bravery on the battlefield but right now he felt shy and awkward. Baring his soul wasn't something he was accustomed to do, and yet there wouldn't be another chance.

'For weeks, months, I tormented myself thinking about you and the time we spent together. Every image of you was imprinted in my mind, in my soul. During the harrowing hell of Waterloo when my companions were falling under enemy artillery fire and I wished for death, it was your smile, your eyes I saw, and your hair curling like a halo around your face. Like an angel. You were my angel …I need to ask, again …' He swallowed hard. 'Is there any chance you would come with me?'

She gasped. 'Come with you? To Algiers?'

He nodded. 'I was proud and stubborn, and so very foolish … I should have told you months ago that you were the only woman I had ever loved.' He took another big breath, and said in a more forceful voice. 'The only woman I will ever love. I want you with me. This new life I am travelling to won't be any good, and Bou Saada won't bring me any happiness without you by my side.'

He took a deep breath. There, he'd said it.

Her eyes were shiny with tears but she smiled – a sweet, loving smile that filled his heart with sunshine. 'Hugo … I love you – so much I thought I would die when I left you and returned to Norton Place. If only you knew how hard it was to remain here, with a man I loathed and despised, and not to know if you were safe.'

He frowned. 'Why didn't you leave?'

'Christopher threatened to harm Robert … but Robert is at the Naval Academy now and can look after himself.' She smiled again.

'Yes, I will come with you, to France, Algiers or the Sahara or anywhere in the world you wish to travel to … but first there is something I must tell you …'

He bent down so quickly she didn't have time to finish and tell him about the baby. His arms encircled her waist and brought her close to him and he kissed her, softly at first, then with more hunger. She put her hands on his chest and he pulled her closer still, tilting her head back to kiss her more deeply. His fingers caressed her neck and roamed through her hair. For a few moments, there was only heat and love, desire and passion between them. And hope, so much hope for the future.

'What a touching scene,' Christopher's sniggering voice said behind her, making them both jump. Marie-Ange swirled round. Christopher stood a short distance away, holding a pistol. Hugo cursed under his breath and quickly pulled her behind him so that his body shielded her, but Christopher let out a harsh laugh and aimed his pistol at him.

'Very brave, Major … Has she told you about the baby yet?' He wasn't smiling any more. 'Shame you won't live to see your brat being born, christened and brought up as a Norton.'

Hugo gave her a searching look over his shoulder. 'The baby? You are …'

She nodded and put her hand on her tummy. 'I was going to tell you.'

His eyes were so full of pride, love and anguish her heart felt like it was breaking. He must realise Christopher was right and he would never know his child …

Christopher cocked his pistol. 'Well, this is all very moving, but I want to finish this quickly. I am after all expected in London.'

'Why did you turn round?' she asked, stepping out from behind Hugo. She had to distract Christopher, and gain time.

'I decided you should come with me so I could keep an eye on you. Rosie said you'd gone out with the dogs but then the two mongrels came back alone and I thought something had happened … But that's enough talk. Marie-Ange, move to the side. I wouldn't want to shoot you by mistake.'

Hugo growled. 'Don't you harm her, you bastard. There are men on the beach – men on that ship over there who will come after you if I don't return. You won't stand a chance. We know about d'Artois' failed assassination attempt, and soon King Louis will know about it too. It's only a matter of time before you're arrested, taken to France and tried for treason along with your master – Fouché.'

'Shut up!' Christopher's features contored with rage and he pointed his pistol at Hugo's chest.

'Please don't shoot him!' Marie-Ange implored.

'You told them, didn't you? Bitch!' Christopher hissed, now pointing the gun at her. He let out a mad cackle. 'And after all, what do I care about that brat of yours? I'll shoot you both, right now.'

Suddenly Rusty and Splinter charged at him from behind, baring their teeth and barking furiously.

'What the devil …?' Christopher yelped in pain as one of the dogs bit his calf, and the other jumped at his throat. He tried to shake them off, but the more he struggled, the more enraged they became. He staggered back until he reached the edge of the cliff and fell backwards just as Rusty and Splinter finally let go of him.

Hugo immediately hurried to the spot where Christopher had disappeared, peered over the cliff then looked her way.

'Is he…?' she asked.

He nodded. 'He's dead.'

She let out a long ragged breath then looked at the two dogs now lying at her feet. They had saved her life, Hugo's and their unborn child's lives.

Hugo was now at her side. He enfolded her in his arms, kissed her forehead, her lips, her hair, pulled her closer. 'Come … I'll take you back to Norton Place then I'll sort everything out,' he said at last.

They were married six weeks later in Beauregard's chapel. It was a small, private affair, with only Marie-Ange's great-aunt Hermine and Sophie on her side, and Hugo's family and Capitaine Martin on Hugo's side. Robert hadn't been granted leave but it was doubtful he would have attended anyway. He was still reeling from the news of his brother's death, and the revelations Marie-Ange had made about Christopher's double identity and his secret agent's life these past six years – not to mention her liaison with Hugo and their plans to live in Algeria. Perhaps one day he would forgive her … For now, he would finish his studies at the Royal Navy Academy, and had asked the family solicitor to appoint an estate manager for Norton Place. The enquiry into Christopher's death had been swift, both Robert and the Sea Lords being eager to avoid unnecessary scandal, and Hugo had remained at Norton Place with Marie-Ange until the coroner had declared Christopher's death an accident and Marie-Ange had been granted permission to leave.

As she now stood in front of the priest, Marie-Ange felt her heart was ready to burst. Throughout the short service, Hugo held her hand, entwined her fingers with his and fixed his gaze on her. All she wanted was to lose herself in his blue eyes. She was slightly breathless when she said her wedding vows, but Hugo's voice was clear and strong in the near-empty chapel.

Afterwards, he smiled and lifted her hand to his heart. 'Forever,' he murmured before bending down to kiss her.

They left the following day for Algiers where they would wait for their baby to be born before travelling south to Bou Saạda. Thanks to his part in exposing Fouché's role in the plot to assassinate the King's brother, Hugo had negotiated an early release from the army. It didn't matter that his family, Sophie and Hermine thought that the couple were mad to travel so far and to such a wild and dangerous land. Marie-Ange and he couldn't wait to start their new life.

'Everything will be just fine,' he said as he held the young woman's hand to his heart again. 'How could it not be when I have my very own angel?'

* The End *

Thank You

Dear Reader,

Thank you so much for reading *Angel of The Lost Treasure.* With this novel, I have gone back to my first love – historical romance. As a teenager growing up in France I couldn't get enough of Regencies, novels by Dellys, Maupassant, Jane Austen and Charlotte Brontë, Juliette Benzoni, and of course the series of 'Angélique' novels, and so many more. Marie-Ange and Hugo's story was much inspired by my hometown Lyon, famous for its mysteries and links to the occult and secret societies, by my fascination for the history of the Knight Templars, and the Beaujolais region North of Lyon. I must say that I was more than a little in love with Hugo Saintclair, and I hope you loved reading about his and Marie-Ange's adventures as much as I loved writing them.

If you did enjoy the story, then I would be very grateful if you could take a few minutes to leave a review. It is a wonderful feeling for an author when readers let you know that they loved your story and your characters. Reviews are invaluable, not only to raise a book's profile, but also to encourage the author to keep writing, especially when self-doubt creeps in.

Please feel free to contact me on Facebook or Twitter. You can find the details on my 'About the Author' page next.

Marie
x

About the Author

Originally from Lyon in France, Marie now lives in Lancashire and writes historical and contemporary romance. Best-selling *Little Pink Taxi* was her debut romantic comedy novel with Choc Lit. *A Paris Fairy Tale* was published in July 2019, *Bluebell's Christmas Magic* in November 2019 and bestselling romantic suspense *Escape to the Little Chateau* in 2020 . She also writes short stories for the bestselling Miss Moonshine anthologies and is a member of the Romantic Novelists' Association and the Society of Authors.

For more information on Marie visit:

www.twitter.com/MarieLaval1

www.facebook.com/marielavalauthor

More Choc Lit
from

Marie Laval

Little Pink Taxi

Take a ride with Love Taxis, the cab company with a Heart …
Rosalie Heart is a well-known face in Irlwick – well, if you drive a bright pink taxi and your signature style is a pink anorak, you're going to draw a bit of attention! But Rosalie's company Love Taxis is more than just a gimmick – for many people in the remote Scottish village, it's a lifeline.

Which is something that Marc Petersen will never understand. Marc's ruthless approach to business doesn't extend to pink taxi companies running at a loss. When he arrives in Irlwick to see to a new acquisition – Raventhorn, a rundown castle – it's apparent he poses a threat to Rosalie's entire existence; not just her business, but her childhood home too.

On the face of it Marc and Rosalie should loathe each other, but what they didn't count on was somebody playing cupid …

Visit www.choc-lit.com for more details.

A Paris Fairy Tale

Is Paris the city of happily ever afters?
Workaholic art historian Aurora Black doesn't have time for fairy tales or Prince Charmings, even in the most romantic city in the world. She has recently been hired by a Parisian auction house for a job that could make or break her career. Unfortunately, daredevil journalist Cédric Castel seems intent on disrupting Aurora's routine.

As Aurora and Cédric embark on a journey across France, they get more than they bargained for as they find themselves battling rogue antiques dealers and personal demons, not to mention a growing attraction to each other.

But with the help of a fairy godmother or two, could they both find their happily ever afters?

Visit www.choc-lit.com for more details.

Bluebell's Christmas Magic

A flick of a feather duster and a sprinkle of Christmas magic …
Cassie Bell is used to mess. Her cleaning business, Bluebell Cleaning, is well known in the Cumbrian village of Red Moss. However, now it's almost Christmas and Cassie has a slightly messier situation to deal with than she's used to.

She's been hired to help Stefan Lambert, an injured army helicopter pilot who's staying at the local Belthorn Manor whilst he recovers. Stefan resents Cassie's interference and is definitely not looking for Christmas cheer. But Cassie prides herself on sparkling surfaces – so, can she bring some festive sparkle to Stefan's life too?

Visit www.choc-lit.com for more details.

Escape to the Little Chateau

Will Amy's dreams of a Provençal escape come true?
There are many reasons Amy Carter is determined to make Bellefontaine, her farmhouse hotel in the French countryside, a success. Of course, there's the time and money she's put in to making it beautiful, but she also has something to prove – particularly to people like Fabien Coste.

Fabien is the owner of the nearby château, and he might just be the most arrogant, patronising man Amy has ever met … unfortunately, he's also the most handsome.

But as rumours circulate in the local community and secrets about the old farmhouse begin to reveal themselves, Amy quickly sees the less idyllic side of life at Bellefontaine. Could Fabien be the man to help prevent her Provençal dream from turning into a nightmare?

Visit www.choc-lit.com for more details.

Introducting Choc Lit

We're an independent publisher creating a delicious selection of fiction.
Where heroes are like chocolate – irresistible!
Quality stories with a romance at the heart.

See our selection here:
www.choc-lit.com
We'd love to hear how you enjoyed *Angel of the Lost Treasure.*
Please leave a review on the eBook store where you purchased this novel or
visit **www.choc-lit.com** and give your feedback.
Choc Lit novels are selected by genuine readers like yourself. We only publish stories our Tasting Panel want to see in print. Our reviews and awards speak for themselves.

Could you be a Star Selector
and join our Tasting Panel?
Would you like to play a role in choosing which novels we decide to publish? Do you enjoy reading women's fiction?
Then you could be perfect for our Tasting Panel.
Visit here for details:
http://www.choc-lit.com/join-the-choc-lit-tasting-panel

Keep in touch:
Sign up for our monthly newsletter Choc Lit Spread for all the latest news and offers:
www.spread.choc-lit.com
Follow us on Twitter: @ChocLitUK and Facebook: ChocLit.

Choc Lit

Where heroes are like chocolate – irresistible!

Printed in Great Britain
by Amazon

63320572R00182